Moveable Assets

E.L. Murray

Dedicated to my late brother Harry

E L Murray is the pseudonym of a writer who prefers the world of anonymity.

The latest book, "The Case of the Overheard Remark", will be published in the Autumn on Kindle and Amazon, featuring Hilary B Lavender, a Librarian, who drives a Library Bus around the Cotswold and…solves murders.

Published by Faraday Publications, Hove, England
First published on Kindle 2014
This paperback edition published 2017

Acknowledgements

The author wishes to thank all the friends who have been a constant source of support throughout the writing of this book.

Special mention for Trevor and Laura together with friends, Ralph A, Laureen R and Mike M, who kept me going in the dark days.

Also, my thanks to Matt at www.dotlabel.co.uk for his fantastic help and Kathy for the original cover.

Copyright E L Murray 2014

This book is copyright under the Berne Convention

No reproduction without permission

All Rights Reserved

This book is a work of fiction. Names, Characters, places and incidents are either a product of the author's imagination or are used fictitiously. Any resemblance to actual people living or dead, events or locales is entirely coincidental.

Prologue

They have a saying in Ireland: 'he has the patience of a saint'.

Michael Boyle, living proof that patience was not exclusively the pursuit of saints, was waiting for his handy work to reap its bloody reward. As one of the youngest-ever recruits to the ranks of the IRA, the training he'd received at the hands of one of the cruellest, toughest and most professional of all the IRA commanders in those lawless streets of 90's Belfast, left no margin for error: neither did the bomb he'd planted which was just about to send six squaddies back to their families in boxes.

It was late evening on Alma Street just off the Falls Road. The date: 6th January 1995. Snow had fallen earlier in the day but only a thin crust of it remained now on this quiet suburban street near the centre of Belfast.

This was their first tour together since returning from Christmas leave, the banter was light. They were having a bit of a wind-up with their corporal; his missus had just told him when he was on home leave that she was 'up the duff'.

Unfortunately, for those squaddies on their way back to barracks in their armoured Land Rover, the luck of the Irish had not rubbed off on any of them that day.

As the driver lifted his night goggles to rub his tired eyes, his brain registered the small bump of snow, out of place in the otherwise flat white surface of the road, a millisecond too late to hit the brakes or swerve away from what was a pressure pad: there were no survivors left to sample chef's chicken curry that night.

A career had begun.

One

Eight years on and the IRA-trained assassin was still putting that patience to good use.

He'd waited eight days this time: the first seven, he'd walked away. Not today. 'So why today?' he wondered. The only answer he could come up with was: 'It felt right'. And in his business, if you couldn't trust your instincts, you were definitely in the wrong line of business.

Today would be the last day that Peter Barrett, the soon-to-be former Euro bond dealer, would taste freedom…or anything else for that matter.

The 135 bus drew up at the stop by Limehouse station, not far from the capital's financial centre, known the world over as The Square Mile.

The assassin, always very precise about blending into the locale of an execution, was today dressed head-to-toe in hoodie uniform: faded light blue hood pulled forward over the face, the jeans mangled and ripped, like they'd been through the wars, the trainers, obvious knock-offs from a shyster stall on the market and the thin multi-creased tee-shirt, so faded and worn, even a charity shop would have refused to take it.

He mounted the step, scanned his one-off Oyster card and sucked his teeth as he did so, making a disrespectful sound. The bus driver looked at the woman behind him, raising his eyes to heaven.

As he reached the top of the stairs to the upper deck, the nondescript scrawny young man, who was often asked for his ID, carefully scanned the faces of the few people sitting there. No-one was looking his way.

Good.

Making sure the hood flopped forward, he ambled slowly to the back seat of the bus where Mr Barrett, probably in a throwback to his school days, was sitting, engrossed in his FT. The bearded eurobond dealer had his gym bag with him. He was probably going training after work. Or so he thought.

The assassin casually swung onto the seat next to him.

'Oi! Watch what you're doing!' yelped the bond dealer rubbing his arm as the scrawny kid jostled him.

'Beg yer pardon, Sir' apologised his nemesis in a mellowed Northern Irish brogue, looking directly into the City dealer's eyes.

The stare from the assassin's cold green eyes brought flashbacks of a safari holiday where the bond dealer had watched a python mesmerise its victim, a wild pig, before pouncing; he shuddered involuntarily.

A couple of people lifted their heads briefly from their papers and then returned them just as quick. 'Best not get involved' was the general consensus; the rest just looked bored. It was only Wednesday; another two days to go.

The muscles in the assassin's neck relaxed. 'Different atmosphere on a Friday. People are happy, it's nearly the weekend: less reading and more chatting on Fridays', he'd found out. No good for him: too many wandering eyes. Less prying eyes meant less risk and in his job, less risk was good. So Wednesday it was.

The bus moved off and everyone settled down.

Satisfied that the rest of the bus were busy with their morning routines, the hoodie leaned over to the bond dealer and whispered in a menacing tone:

'I've just injected you with a poison which will collapse your entire nervous system in less than five minutes.'

For a few seconds, the words didn't connect with the bond dealer's brain; he'd been checking the share price of some company or other he'd been keeping an eye on. Suddenly the meaning of the words broke through the financial gobbledegook. Without warning, he made to stand up, closing the paper with an explosion of newsprint. The assassin jumped at the unexpected loud noise. He could see in the bond dealer's eyes that he was thinking: 'This guy's a junkie and he's tripping!'

The killer knew he had to take control of the situation...and fast.

'Shut up and sit down!' he hissed. 'The more you move the faster it'll act.'

The bond dealer reluctantly sat back down again, the awful realisation that what the hoodie had said could just be true, etched in his face. The killer scanned the heads of the other passengers in front of them: no-one had turned to look in their direction.

'Perfect.'

He continued: 'Your name is Peter Barrett and you're twenty-four. You work for Elliott & Sons as a Euro bond dealer. You live on the Westferry Road in a very expensive duplex. You have a £500,000 mortgage from your company at a very preferential rate, you earn close to £150K and you owe my principal £20,000 for your recreational drugs. That's just so you know why this is happening.'

The killer pulled out a stop watch.

'You now have exactly four minutes and…fifteen seconds to live unless you do exactly as I tell you.'

A very fine film of sweat began to form on Peter Barrett's brow as he nodded his head very slightly.

'Great. Just do as I say and it'll be easier for the two of us.'

With that, the killer pulled out a scrap of paper with numbers on it and handed it to the panic-stricken bond dealer.

'Transfer the money to that account and I give you the antidote. Simple.'

The bond dealer took out his iPhone: no fucking signal.

'Shit.t.t..t!' the bond dealer's brain screamed. He shook the phone and a couple of bars appeared.

He began dialling his bank frantically. He tapped in his account details but had to enter his password twice because his hands were shaking so badly.

'Steady now. Steady! Three minutes and…twenty-eight seconds' announced the hoodie who'd wrapped his arm around the bond dealer's shoulder. Any new passengers coming upstairs would see two mates, like a couple of school kids up the back of the bus, playing a game on their phone. The hoodie's eyes were glued to the screen.

It was then that he noticed the smell; the bond dealer probably wasn't even aware that he was close to shitting himself.

The bank seemed to take forever to process the request.

'Ah, sure now you're doin'' grand' encouraged the killer.

With two minutes and five seconds left on the stop watch, the transfer to the offshore account was completed. 'There, that wasn't hard, was it?' said the hoodie softly as he made to get up.

'Wait! Where are you going?' whispered the bond dealer hoarsely grabbing at the assassin's sleeve. 'Give me the antidote!' he begged.

'Bollocks!' replied the hoodie slapping his forehead with an air of mock surprise 'I knew there was something I forgot to bring out with me this morning. Well, cheerio.'

'Wait! Please!' The words barely came out. The meltdown of his body's functions had begun. It wouldn't be long.

Almost as an afterthought, the killer turned around in the passageway of the bus and said to the bond dealer who, by that time, had slowly begun to slide down the seat:

'That'll teach you to pay your fucking bills.'

He strolled casually down the aisle, rang the bell for the next stop and got off.

As the bus pulled away, he waved to the figure of the bond dealer whose head was lolling against the window, the spittle from his now inanimate lips dribbling down the windowpane, his eyes desperately trying to follow the hooded youth as he walked away from the bus in the opposite direction.

'Another happy customer' declared the hoodie in a loud voice, as much to himself as to his surroundings. He pulled a mobile phone from his pocket and dialled the number he had committed to memory.

'Job done' said the assassin when the phone was picked up.

'I can see that' said the gruff voice on the other end of the phone. '20 grand has just landed in my account. You got your money?' asked the drug dealer.

'Yes. Thank you very much.'

'That should send out a warning to any of those other bastards who are thinking of welching on their debts to me.' declared the man who was one of the Mr Bigs on the London drug scene.

'Whoever me is' said the hoodie laughing.

'You never know, we might get to meet through our mutual friend one day' said the drug baron.

'I don't think so. Anyway, if ever you have need of my services in the future, ring our mutual friend for my number. I only ever use a number once…for all our protection.'

'Hopefully not for a long time. You're good but you're expensive.'

'Not good…the best! Cheerio.'

With that, the young killer hung up, removed the chip and crushed it underfoot. Wiping the phone clean, he tossed it into a nearby bin.

For a moment, he stood there undecided which way to walk. His eyes drifted upwards and tracked the wispy white clouds as they meandered slowly across a sky of Mediterranean blue. He decided the weather was too good to waste, and strolled off to grab a cup of coffee to take into the park. As he walked away, the hood fell to his shoulders, revealing the sort of innocent babyface every mother would want to hug to her breast. With his blond hair in a short ponytail, the 22-year-old was still regularly stopped by the police who thought he was truanting.

He was: the perfect assassin.

Two

Gary Dean's office looked no different to any lawyer's office in London; all smoked glass, chrome and a silence broken only by the occasional clatter of computer keyboards and whispered conversations between colleagues.

It was the man whose name appeared on the company's gold embossed letterhead that made it stand out: the boss was prone to wearing suits which were a little on the sharp side of natty for his chosen profession.

This morning as the 40-year-old stepped out of his room, file in hand, looking for all the world like a Havana pimp, sunbeams streamed through the windows of the office and bounced off the high gloss of the handmade silk pinstriped creation he was wearing.

Add to that, six feet of regularly toned muscle, a smile that any toothpaste manufacturer would pay a fortune to use and the brain of one of the sharpest legal swervers in the business and you have Mr Gary Dean, Owner, Proprietor and main income earner of Gary Dean & partners: emphasis on the small 'p'.

'John,' Gary called over the office to one of the paralegal, '…have you seen Jeannie?'

'Here she comes now' said John, dragging his eyes away from the document he was reading on screen and nodding towards the double glass doors leading to reception.

'Looking for me?' called out Gary's petite redheaded PA.

'Yes, Jeannie. Part of the Raj Singh file is missing and I need it for his appearance this morning.'

'Don't worry, Gary. It's on the top of my pile to do. I'll have it on your desk in fifteen minutes.'

'Good girl, Jeannie. Don't know what I'd do without you' replied her boss smiling, a twinkle in his eye.

As he finished speaking, Gary heard a muffled ringing emanating from his office. Abruptly, without explanation or apology, the smile disappeared as he turned on his heel and re-entered his office, closing and locking the door behind him. He pulled out a key attached to a chain which resided in the left-hand pocket of his trousers and opened the bottom drawer of his desk where the phone was still ringing.

'Yes?' he said into the mouthpiece as he plonked himself down into the hugely expensive Conran-designed executive chair.

'What time's the next Bus?' asked the anonymous voice.

'Call you back in five' said the lawyer tersely.

Gary pulled up a chart on his Blackberry, studied it and then rung the number back.

'Three o'clock at the South Mimms services and this time don't be late! You were nearly spotted leaving last time!'

'Gotcha!' said the anonymous voice and rung off.

Gary hung up and sat for a few moments contemplating the needs of his 'special' clients. 'What would they do without my services?' He thought for a few seconds: 'Probably ten years' he concluded, laughing to himself. Sighing he turned his attention to the Raj Singh file.

'Now then, me old mucker' he said out loud, 'What are we gonna do with you? Looks like Her Majesty's Immigration Service have got Mr Raj Singh by the short and curlies this time!'

Three minutes later, Gary was deeply engrossed in the file when his internal phone rang.

'Yes, what is it? You know I don't like being disturbed when I'm preparing for a hearing.'

Gary listened to 'bird brain' (his description of her at the last partners' meeting) on reception and replied:

'Tell him I can't speak to him now but I'll call him when I get back from Court: should be about two o'clock.'

He waited while she repeated the message back to him and then he said:

'Correct. Now make sure I'm not disturbed again unless it's *really* important.'

The receptionist got the italicised 'really' loud and clear and short of Buckingham Palace calling to offer him a knighthood, Mr Dean would not be disturbed again that morning.

7

A few minutes later, there was a loud bang at the door. Irritated at being disturbed again, he flung the file on the desk. It was then that he heard the loud 'Ouch!' He'd forgotten to unlock his door.

'Sorry, sweetie pie' he called through the door to Jeannie, who was rubbing her head when he unlocked it.

'My fault' said Jeannie. 'I should have knocked. Anyway, here's the rest of the file.'

'Thanks, Jeannie you're a star. Now go and get your head looked at.'

'I should do that anyway, working in a place like this!' joked Jeannie.

'Hmm, whatever else you might've lost, it's not your acid tongue!' replied Gary, laughing.

Jeannie closed the door and left him to it. She knew he hated being interrupted before a hearing.

Gary immersed himself in the file for another half an hour before grabbing his briefcase and ramming the file in.

'What a waste of time reading this load of old rubbish' he thought. 'But better to be prepared just in case the old codger sitting on the bench wants to ask something.'

One of Gary's greatest strengths was his ability to forecast and prepare for most eventualities.

Before he left the office, he pulled open the door of one of the cupboards. Attached to the inside of the door was a full-length mirror.

'Looking good, Gary, my boy!' he thought, studying his appearance as he run his fingers through his immaculate, slightly greying, preppy hairstyle. 'Yes! Definitely still looking good, son' he thought as he slid his arm into the sleeve of the Armani cashmere coat and adjusted it in the mirror. 'It's a shame I couldn't just ring the bloody judge up and tell him: "Look, Your Worship, Raj has done the proverbial runner. You won't be seeing him in this courtroom again, my old love! Sorry!" and leave it at that. Would save us all a lot of time. Still, the law has to run its course and justice must be seen to be done, whatever the cost to society' thought the man who treated the law the same as he treated the society he lived in…with complete and resolute contempt. But hey, at £350 per hour charged out to Legal Aid, Gary reckoned he could afford to.

As he left his room, Jeannie looked up.

'So who looks like they're going to chew the prosecution up and then spit them out again?' teased the PA who knew how to preen the boss' flashy feathers.

'Why thank you, Jeannie. But if this case is like the last three, there won't be any need because the client won't be turning up!' replied Gary who knew that that was exactly what was happening but would never actually say it.

Sometimes he played his cards so close to his chest that not even he could see them.

Three

This particular branch of Lloyds bank was chosen for many reasons; not least being that it was physically the furthest away from any police station in the borough. Also, the fact that it was way behind the times in terms of its security did, it had to be admitted, add to the attractiveness of it.

Both of these factors had been personally checked out by two of the three gentlemen now holding the place up.

While one of the balaclava'd trio waved a sawn-off shotgun around, another was relieving the tellers of their 'loose change'. The air was thick with screamed obscenities as the bank staff and customers froze, stunned. These sorts of things didn't happen at their little branch. Oh yes it fucking did. Right now, it did.

As the first two kept the front office occupied, the third member of the gang practically took the door to the bank manager's office off its hinges and thrust a Glock into the shocked bank manager's face saying that if he as much as looked at the alarm he would get '...his fuckin' head blown clean of his fuckin' little mincing shoulders.'

The bank manager sat stock still. He'd been on training courses for precisely this kind of situation. Stay calm. Don't do anything to spook them. Don't do anything foolish. His staff and customers' welfare was his prime concern. Let Head Office and the police deal with the rest, later. For now, his primary consideration was to get them out the door without loss of life or injury. What good's heroics if you're not around to collect the bloody medal?

But how did they know that he, John Stubbs, was gay? Not even anyone at the branch knew. It was until now, his very personal secret. That was what was worrying him. If they knew that what else did they know? Would they use it against him?

The thought was cut short by robber number three announcing:

'We've got your fancy man, Mr Bowman. Trussed up like an Independence Day turkey, 'e is. One phone call from me and 'is goose'll be cooked. An' I do mean cooked! He's already doused in petrol and just waiting for that call from me. But don't take my word for it; give him a call. Ring 'is mobile…ring it NOW!' screamed the robber.

With sweat dripping from his palms, the bank manager pressed the redial for his partner of twenty-something years mobile. The phone rang and a coarse, uncouth voice answered; nothing like his partner's. In fact, it couldn't be further from the architect's soft undulating tone if it tried.

'Yeah?' the rasping voice said.

'Can I…' the bank manager hesitated and in a moment of absolute clarity realised that these men were in complete control. 'May I please speak with Jeremy?' he asked in a calm, firm tone.

'Certainly. I'll just rip the double-sided tape off 'is gob and let 'im have a word with you.'

'No, no, don't do that!' begged the bank manager. 'Please don't hurt him!'

'Then you do as the nice man says and we'll all be alright and then you and lover boy can have a cosy candlelit supper tonight. Now wouldn't that be nice?'

'How do these people know so much about my life?' thought the bank manager furiously. 'They know more about us than our next door neighbours, for God's sake.'

Every Wednesday, John and Jeffrey pulled out all the stops and had a three-course gourmet dinner prepared by Jeffrey. John would stop off at the wine merchant on the way home and choose a bottle of fine wine to compliment the fare. But they probably knew that as well.

The bank manager replaced the phone back in its cradle.

'What now?' he asked calmly.

'Now you're talkin', pansy boy.'

'Using that kind language is pointless. So, I repeat, just tell me what you want and then go.'

'Well, Mr Stubbs,' said the robber in a mock respectful tone '…I'd like you to open that safe behind you, fairly sharpish, if you would. In fact, you 'ave…' the bank robber consulted his watch, '…two minutes and ten seconds before my boys out there start using your staff for target practice. Now move it!'

John Stubbs knew that these men would not tolerate any delays. Delays would mean fatalities.

The robber held up a mobile for the bank manager to see.

'An' remember! One phone call from me and Jeremy goes up in a poof of smoke!' said the bank robber cackling at his own vile joke.

'Do you believe in Karma?' asked John Stubbs softly as he inserted the key into the safe.

'No, pal, I believe in this' said the bank robber as he pistol-whipped the slightly-built man. 'Now get that bloody safe open.'

John Stubbs had never experienced such pain in his life before but he knew he had to stay focussed. It wasn't easy when your head was throbbing like the engine-room of the QE2.

In less than a minute the robber was forcing bundles of notes into John Stubbs own briefcase, which the robber seemed to know, would be sitting under the desk. John always kept it there, next to his right knee, for easy access.

'How the bloody hell did he know I kept it there?' the bank manager wondered in his confused state.

There was over £500,000 in the safe.

The bank robber checked his watch.

'Good boy!' he said as if he was talking to his dog. 'Do not move from this office until the police arrive. If you do, Jeremy gets it.'

With that, he run into the main banking hall and called out to the other two: 'Right! Leave the rest. Let's go!' Turning to the staff and customers he shouted: 'And the first fuckin' one I see coming out of this door 'he said pointing with the Glock '…will get a bullet in the face. Now get back!' He fired into the ceiling as the three of them rushed out the door of the bank.

As the last robber exited the door, the alarms were set off by someone inside.

'They've asked for it' said the leader of the three when he heard the alarm, '…so we'll give it to them. Bron, do it!'

Bron didn't need telling twice, he pulled something from the inside pocket of his jacket: a grenade. He pulled the pin, held it for a count of three and lobbed it back into the main hall. As it fell on the floor, customers and staff screamed and run for cover behind anything which would give them some protection from the blast.

Outside, the robbers stood to the side of the entrance, waiting for the blast.

Seconds later, the grenade exploded bringing utter carnage. Glass and debris flew everywhere, embedding itself in plaster and flesh and blowing out the windows, showering a passerby with shards of lethal fragments.

Seconds before the blast, a young mum pushing a pram had stopped to look in the window of a nearby charity shop. Whatever it was that caught her attention in the window probably saved her and her child's life.

Weirdly, a cut-out cardboard figure of a financial adviser in the entrance of the bank offering leaflets '…to improve your wealth's health' was still standing…minus its head.

The level of screaming was at an unbelievable pitch but added to that now was the weeping and howling of the injured.

In his office, John Stubbs was torn between rushing to help the injured and the repercussions for disobeying the bank robber's menacing threats if he left his office. He was not a brave man but the agonising cries he could hear outside his door gave him no choice.

He ran out of his office, stopping for a moment to take in the devastation. He dashed for the first aid box, all the time his thoughts jumping from: 'How could anyone do this? Monsters!' to 'Oh God! I hope Jeffrey's safe. Please God, let him be okay'. He managed to keep the rage and fear within him under control as he scrambled from staff member to customer in an effort to help those who were showing signs of life. Those who were silent were either unconscious and beyond his limited ability or…he didn't dwell on the other possibility.

The robbers, meantime, had raced around the corner to the two motorcycles they'd parked there earlier. The first robber pulled a black helmet from the box on the back of his cycle, replacing it with the plastic bag of money collected from the tellers and his gun. The other two did the same but when they tried to stuff the briefcase into the box, it wouldn't fit.

'I can't believe it! All the work we put into this job an' the bloody case don't fit!' screamed the third robber. 'I'll 'ave to carry it. Come on. Move it!' As they mounted the bikes they paused for a second as they heard the sound of police sirens.

The first motorcycle sped off. The second one started to follow but the back wheel spun and driver and passenger almost toppled over.

'Bron! For Christ's sake! The police are gonna be here any minute! Get us out of here, you prat!' screamed the passenger clasping the briefcase to his chest with one hand and the Glock in the other.

'Aaaah!' roared the driver part in frustration, part testosterone-fuelled as he regained control of the bike and chased after the first bike.

'Go, go, go!' shouted the passenger.

Four

Earlier that morning, Jeffrey Bowman left the quintessential Victorian house he had inherited from his grandmother and which he had shared with his partner, John Stubbs, for the past twenty-plus years, at his usual time. Today was no different to any other working day: catch the Tube to South Kensington where he shared an office with his business partner of ten years, Maggie Whitfield. Together they formed the partnership Bowman Whitfield Associates. With a staff of thirty-five and a turnover of twenty million, life was good. Business was even better.

The journey from door to door took on average of one hour: a lot less than it would be if Jeffrey were to drive into town in his vintage Merc. Besides, there was the congestion charge and, of course, the hard-bitten town parkers. He'd already had to have three dents removed from 'Cynthia', his precious 1956 gull-winged baby. No, no. The tube was fine. 'Cynthia' was reserved for high days and holidays.

But the Northern line wasn't called the 'misery line' for nothing. As the train pulled into Highgate station, the platform was pretty full and as the carriages rolled past, Jeffrey could see that it would be a 'standing all the way day' today.

'Still, we've got dinner tonight and before you know it; a weekend of newspapers and walks on Hampstead Heath and double bliss! Copelia at the Opera House on Saturday night. Wonderful.'

That's when it happened.

The pickpocket who dipped Jeffrey's pocket had followed him for a week now, checking for variations in his journey. But there were none. He knew the exact route Jeffrey would take; down to the skinny latte and almond croissant he would order from the café around the corner from his chic office at South Kensington.

And this guy was an expert. He nuzzled up to Jeffrey, letting him get used to the pressure of another body next to him. He waited for the moment when Jeffrey's eyes glazed over telling him that Jeffrey was 'somewhere else'. He knew that was when people were at their most vulnerable.

Jeffrey didn't feel a thing as his thoughts drifted on to work and the meetings he had lined up for that day. His calendar was always blocked out after three o'clock on a Wednesday and by two minutes past that blessed hour; he was out the door, on his way home to prepare for the evening meal. But then this man already knew that.

At Camden Town, the man left the train, keeping up with the speed of the other passengers so as not to attract any attention. He'd got what he'd come for: Jeffrey's mobile phone.

After that, it would be dead-easy to convince John Stubbs that they had kidnapped Jeffrey. And let's face it: it saved having to go through all the mess and bother of doing the real thing.

Five

As Jeffrey Bowman sat in his first meeting of the morning, his mind wandered for a moment: had he left his mobile on the coatstand in the hallway?

'Bother!' He couldn't remember. He turned his attention back to the meeting.

At the same time, the three masked robbers pulled up in a quiet cul-de-sac, three hundred yards away from the bank they had just robbed. The passenger on the second bike alighted. By the time he reached the first bike, the first driver had pulled off his helmet and balaclava as well as the velcroed black leather trousers and jacket and stuffed them into the box next to the loot. Underneath, he was wearing a cheap-looking grey pinstripe suit.

As the passenger mounted the first bike, Mr Pinstripe pulled out a comb and run it through his dark, unkempt locks and began walking back towards the bank.

'See you later boys' he said. 'Leave some for me' he joked.

The two bikes sped off towards their rendezvous.

Two hours and twenty-four minutes after removing the mobile from Mr Bowman's person, the pickpocket was sitting in his black cab, waiting for his 'business associates' to arrive: interesting way to describe some of the most ruthless career criminals that the Metropolitan Police had ever had on their books.

First, the leader and brains of the gang, Dave Cosforth: three lengthy stretches inside, all for robbery with extreme violence. Long after he'd finished his sentence, his victims were still suffering. Unable to stop the recurring nightmares; three of them were still in long-term therapy. Tall with a slight stoop, long greasy grey hair tucked behind his ears and looking like a bag of bones wrapped in leathery old skin, he looked like he couldn't punch his way out of a paper bag. Ask some of his victims what he was capable of: if they'd talk.

Next: Markie Morgan, small-time crook from the valleys of Wales. Thanks to his old schoolpal and third member of the gang, Bron Davies, he was definitely big league now. This was his fifth job with the firm and they were flying. He'd even appeared on Crimewatch, albeit in the uniform of his new profession: the balaclava.

Then: Bron the Bomb as he was called occasionally by the others. Bron was the one who came up with the idea of leaving their calling card behind when they left a job. 'When the boys in blue arrive and see the mess they'll have to stay and help and that gives us that bit of extra time.'

He wasn't wrong. Since they'd started leaving their calling card, they could have stopped and had a full English and still had plenty of time to leg it.

Bron had not long returned from his home-from-home, the Scrubs, after completing his fourth stint at HM's pleasure; aggravated burglary this time.

As the taxi driving fourth member of the gang checked his watch, the boys turned the corner into the quiet side street chosen for its lack of pedestrians and prying eyes.

'Bang on time' thought the relieved taxi driver, known to the others as 'The Delivery Man' and to his wife as 'That Lazy Bastard' but to the rest of the world, he was Mikey Malone; laugh-a minute throwback to the eighties with his curly perm and chubby cheeks. It was his job to pick up and deliver the goods after a job. Someone had to be Mr Clean and as he had no record, as yet, he got the job. Also, there was the added advantage of Mikey's badge. The police give a badge-carrying cabbie a lot of leeway. And he could pick a mean pocket.

As the boys parked up, Mikey got out of the cab and pulled open the boot of the cab to reveal a suitcase with a red and yellow helmet and a can of spray paint inside it.

Bron pulled out the black plastic bag of cash with Markie's leathers and gun out of the lockbox. Mikey grinned and said:

'Nice work, boys. That's another few bricks for me retirement home paid for.'

'An' maybe a bit to spare!' joked Bron as he threw his and Markie's gear into the case and pulled out the yellow helmet and the can of spray paint.

He was giving the can a good shake as he passed Dave with the briefcase and his gun, now with the safety catch on. By the time he'd finished spraying his fuel tank bright red, Dave was ready to do his.

'Give it 'ere, Bron, will you? And then let's get the hell outa here!' said Dave, finishing with a terrible John Wayne impersonation.

Both of them ripped off the false number plates stuck over the real ones, scrunched them up and threw them in the boot of the taxi.

Three minutes later, Mikey took off with the loot and suitcase in the boot with his 'For Hire' sign on. Always better to have a punter in the back of the cab. Good cover.

Before they mounted their bikes, Dave said to Bron:

'Remember to turn yer jacket inside out.'

They both reversed their jackets. Dave's was now white leather and Bron's was light tan. With the new coloured helmets, different number plates and coloured tanks, the police wouldn't have a clue. A complete makeover in six and a half minutes AND no incriminating evidence; easy as you like.

They took off in different direction: Bron to his next sales appointment; he installed coffee machines in offices and Dave to his window cleaning round.

A nice clean job: just like Dave's windows.

Six

Gary arrived at the Courthouse and parked his prize possession: his black Maserati Quattroporte in the carpark of the Court building. As he threw his perfectly creased trouser leg out of the driver's door, he heard police sirens in the distance. He smiled.

'With a bit of luck it's one of my regulars getting up no good. The more skulduggery they get up to, the more business there'll be for me. And more business means MORE MONEY!' he thought as he tried to suppress a smile.

'What're you smirking at?' asked Bernard Davies, one of Gary's competitors, large pile of files held on top of his ample stomach as he kicked his own car door shut. He placed the files on the bonnet while he pulled up his trousers and adjusted his waistcoat to try to cover his bulging frontage.

Gary pressed the remote to lock his car and said:

'Music to my ears, Bernard' as he inclined his head towards the sirens.

They both laughed. That laugh which exists between people who share the same line of business, the same customers and sometimes, the same sense of humour.

'So, how's business, Gary? We're swamped!' he said lifting the files into a more comfortable position.

'I think they'll have to extend the opening hours' Gary replied with a backward nod towards the Courthouse. 'That would please some of those old retirement-home dodgers. Oh, sorry! I meant their Lordships.'

'Be careful how you refer to "Their Royal Beaknesses"' replied Bernard laughing as he bowed respectfully to the Courthouse, '...they might just bite back one of these days. But like you, business is booming.'

A muffled sound like a bomb was heard and they both ducked instinctively.

'Jesus! What the hell was that?' said Gary, half-scared out of his wits.

'Oh, bugger!' said Bernard frustratedly as the files he was carrying cascade on to the ground. Gary helped him pick up the files. Looking towards where the noise had come from, Bernard observed nervously: 'Sounded like a bloody bomb, if you ask me. Which direction did it come from?'

'No idea but I think we should get inside asap. And if it is one of my clients, I wish they'd give us a bit of notice if they're going to blow the bloody place up!'

Gary's extended one-liner helped to relieve the tension as they both mounted the steps of the Courthouse. At the top of the stairs, a policeman's walkie-talkie was spouting info on the incident and they both stopped to listen.

Gary turned to Bernard and asked: 'Did they just say an explosion at a bank?'

'That's what it sounded like to me' replied Bernard hesitantly.

'Thank God for that, I thought it was serious' was the chortled reply.

'What'd you mean?'

'Oh, it's probably only some villain or other trying to earn a dishonest crust. If it was serious, they'd shut the bloody Court. Now that would cause real chaos AND I'd have wasted my morning reading this boring file…for no reason.'

'You're all bloody heart, Gary Dean, do you know that? Some poor sod might have had their bollocks blown off by one of those slimy bastards that you represent and all you can think about is "Poor me! I've just wasted a couple of hours of my very expensive time" You really are the limit, old chum!' replied Bernard furiously.

'Don't take it that way, Bernard. I'm just as shaken as you are' insisted Gary.

'Oh, I don't think so, old darling! Look, I'm still shaking!' Bernard held out his hand which was clearly trembling. 'I think it's time I took my paltry pension and retired to some backwater and did a bit of part-time conveyancing.'

'Steady on, Bernard! You're a bit young to be thinking of retiring from our hallowed profession. How old are you?'

'Old enough to remember the times when villains stuck to killing their own in turf wars with the odd civilian casualty thrown in. Nowadays, it's as if they haven't done their job properly unless there's at least one poor innocent sod that doesn't get to see their children growing up.'

'The only advice I can offer you, my old son is 'pull yourself together' and don't do anything rash. See you later, Bernard. I'm going to have a quick drag before I face the wrath of God's representative on earth.'

Bernard left Gary standing at the top of the steps and entered the Courthouse, still clearly rattled. Gary lit up and listened as people passed up and down the stairs, talking worriedly about what the explosion might have been. For a few moments, he stared dreamily into the distance, sighed and then focused on the buildings around the Courthouse. He saw a bowler-hatted doorman saluting as he opened the door of a top-of-the-range Merc for some high-powered exec. Gary laughed to himself. He did that a lot these days. It was like there was a joke doing the rounds that only Gary Dean knew the punchline to.

A movement at a second-floor window of the building opposite caught his attention: it was a very attractive girl just standing, staring westwards towards Heathrow.

To put off the inevitable a few moments longer, Gary speculated on what thoughts might be going through that beautiful head.

As it turned out, he wasn't that far from the truth.

In her daydream, the girl was on a plane heading out of Heathrow; its destination somewhere hot and exotic. The fluted glass of champagne she was savouring had been poured by her secret lover who just happened to be dark, handsome, very mysterious and of course, filthy rich.

It only lasted a minute or so before reality came calling in the shape of her boss' drony voice calling her name repeatedly. Like a forced landing, it brought her down to earth with a bump: or at least to the second floor of the insurance company she worked for. She sighed and turned away.

Gary checked his watch and decided it was time to face the music. Crushing his cigarette under his highly polished hand-made shoe, he made his way into Courthouse.

He already knew the judge would not be pleased but hey-ho Mr Raj Singh, late of the Punjab's second most populated city, Lahore, was worth a lot more now than the paltry £350 an hour that the Legal Aid Board had been paying Gary to represent him in his Appeal against deportation.

Seven

Gary sat in the waiting area among the losers in life, as he thought of them, clearly irritated and checking his watch every couple of minutes. An onlooker would have assumed that he was waiting for a client who was late, but the truth was he was annoyed that the case hearing hadn't started.

'Bloody old codgers! The trouble is they like the sound of their own pathetic, droning voices too much. Probably the only time they get the chance to speak judging by some of the old battleaxes I've seen hanging on their arms at the Christmas dos. Hang the bastards and move on to the next case…that's what I say.'

About ten minutes later than the case was scheduled to start, the Clerk of the Court walked along the crowds of people calling:

'Case number 13482: Singh v HMG Immigration Service. All parties to Court 5.'

Knowing that it would go straight back to the presiding judge, Gary asked the Clerk:

'Any chance His Lordship could give us a few minutes, Harry? My client seems to be running late.'

'Not a chance, Mr Dean. It's Mr Farquar, Sir. You know what he's like for punctuality. Two hundred years ago, they'd have been sent to the Colonies for being late in HIS court!'

Gary didn't actually give a stuff about being given a few minutes longer. He was merely covering his own tracks but as he laughed at Harry's joke he spotted the Immigration Service's lawyer.

'James! James! Over here' Gary called out.

Slowly, the lawyer ambled over to where Gary was standing.

'Looks like we've got another runner on our hands today, James.'

'Not another one, Gary. The old man will go bonkers!'

'Well,' said Gary expansively, '…you think life's a bitch and then you come up in front of old Farquar and then you realise it can get worse. You ready then?' he sighed. 'Better get it over with.'

With that, Gary linked his arm through James' and they walked along the corridor like an old-time music hall act towards Court No. 5.

On the way, Gary caught the eye of a foreign-looking man. Their acknowledgement of each other was more in their eyes than any outward signal.

Eight

As predicted by James, Gary was on the receiving end of a red-hot roasting from the aforementioned Mr Farquar.

'...this really is not good enough, Mr Dean! That's four of your last five clients have not turned up for their hearings in the past three weeks! If this continues we shall have no alternative but to use our powers to place them on remand until their cases are due for our consideration. This is a sinful waste of the Court's time!'

Throughout this ear bashing, Gary tried, unsuccessfully, to catch James' attention, daring him to make eye contact. James, wisely, refused. He knew that if he did, they'd both probably end up with a spell in the cells for contempt. It happened once before where they'd had a fit of the giggles.

'Did you hear me, Mr Dean?' asked an exasperated Mr Farquar.

'...eh...yes, My Lord. Loud and very clear' replied Gary attempting to stifle a laugh with a fit of coughing.

'Are you all right, Mr Dean?' asked the completely oblivious Mr Farquar.

'I'm fine, thank you, Sir. I'm just sorry that the Court has been put to this inconvenience.'

'The Court accepts your apology, Mr Dean. However, I am issuing a warrant for the arrest of Mr Singh. This case is adjourned until such times as he is found and apprehended. Court dismissed.'

Nine

Markie Morgan ran his finger along the inside of his shirt collar. He was hot. But then he had been wearing his suit under the leathers.

'Phew!' he thought, wiping the sweat from his face with a handkerchief as he walked up the stairs at the NCP car park situated a hundred yards from the bank: he'd parked his company car there the previous night.

He fetched his briefcase and tool box from the boot of the Mondeo but this time, took the lift to the ground floor; the tool box weighed a ton.

Just before turning the corner and facing the mayhem he'd caused less than twenty minutes earlier, he took a deep breath.

'What the...' he cried out for the benefit of the policeman standing nearby on guard. 'What the hell's going on?' he yelled out in fake panic.

'Keep well back there, Sir! There's been an explosion...'

Before he could finish the sentence, the woman with the baby in the pram came rushing towards them screaming:

'There's a man over there, covered in blood! He needs help!'

'I'm a trained first aider' Markie said to the policeman. 'Let me see if I can help him.' Markie didn't bother to mention that his first aid course had been paid for by the taxpayer. You did a lot of courses in nick to relieve the bloody boredom.

The policeman nodded and Markie rushed over to the injured man. He had a serious head wound and would need hospitalisation. There was nothing that Markie could do so he placed the man in the recover position.

He moved closer to the bank. As he did, John Stubbs emerged from the front door of the bank.

'Mr Stubbs, Mr Stubbs!' shouted Markie.

At the sound of his name, John Stubbs shook his head and then for the first time, the chaos outside the bank registered.

'Mr Stubbs, it's me, Markie Morgan. I had an appointment to service the photocopiers. Remember?' asked the crook.

'Er...yes' was all John Stubbs could say. He was numb, totally numb. It was clear that shock was taking hold of him, both in mind and body. He wasn't even aware anymore of the throbbing in his head from the pistol-whipping he'd been on the receiving end of.

'What's happened, Sir?' asked the guy who had caused it all. 'There's been a robbery' was the reply of a man desperately trying to keep it all together.

'I think you'd better sit down, Mr Stubbs. You're a bit unsteady on your feet, Sir' said Markie.

'Thank you. Thank you. But how are the others, are they okay? I tried to help some of the injured inside but some of them aren't moving. God preserve us!' he said and then broke down, sobbing uncontrollably.

But John Stubbs distress wasn't going to get to this crook; he'd seen it all before...in every shade you could think of.

'I'm so sorry...' began Markie as he helped John Stubbs to sit down and rest his back against the wall of the bank.

'...if only I'd...' but the dazed bank manager couldn't verbalise the thought.

'Look, are you okay?' asked Markie. 'I'll have a look and see if I can help any of the others.'

'Go, please, go!' said John Stubbs pulling himself together. 'Go and see what you can do'. He pulled his handkerchief from his pocket and rubbed it over his face.

As Markie straightened up, two ambulances pulled up, sirens wailing.

Markie moved off trying to make it look as if he was comforting the injured; in truth, he was keeping an eye out for anything the police might consider a clue.

'Over here, Sir!' he heard a young constable call out from the entrance to the bank to an Inspector nearby. 'There's an empty shell case.'

'Bag it up, Jones' his boss replied. As he bent down to retrieve it, Markie leant over the unconscious body of the man he'd left in the recovery position earlier and called out:

'Constable, constable! This man's in a really bad way! Can you help?'

For a split second, the policeman hesitated. Should he pick up the spent cartridge case or should he help the injured man? As Markie expected, the policeman hurried over to give the injured man assistance.

While the policeman knelt over the injured man, Markie moved across and surreptitiously pocketed the shell.

'No point in giving them anymore clues than we have to' he thought cheerfully.

He returned to the policeman and said:

'How is he?'

'Lost a lot of blood. Stay here with him while I get the paramedics, will you?'

'Of course' said Markie.

After the policeman had helped the paramedics load the man onto a stretcher, one of his colleagues called him to assist with another of the injured. By the time he'd remembered the spent shell and returned to the spot, it was gone. He assumed that someone else had spotted it and bagged it up. Or, at least, that's what he hoped.

Markie went back to see how John Stubbs was doing: he was still in shock and gave no sign of recognising Markie as one of the robbers but did manage to thank him for his help.

Minutes later, more police began pouring into the area, locking it down.

The most seriously injured were ferried to the nearest hospital; first aid, tea, a number of sympathetic ears were made available to any of the others who were in need of it.

Markie's statement and details were taken by a young probationer. Since he'd arrived after it was all over, no-one took too much notice of his 'I saw nothing' statement.

Yet again, they were in the clear.

Ten

On his way back to the office, Gary found himself stuck in a mile of solid traffic. The police had sealed the place up tighter than a very small crustacean's posterior. No matter which rat-run he tried, and he knew them all, they were either solid or blocked off.

Finally, unable to move, he made a few calls. The first one being to the client who had called as Gary was preparing the Raj Singh brief.

The phone rang at the other end, twice, before it was answered.

'Well, hello' said the voice at the other end of the phone; there was a gentle lilt to it.

'Sham, it's me, Gary Dean. How are you and what can I do for you?'

'Mr Dean, I'm well, sir, and how are you, yourself?' replied the young man who was sitting in the park in his wraparound sunglasses, soaking up the sun. 'Sure isn't it a grand day?' Sham had attended the same private school as Gary's son.

'It might be for you but I'm stuck in a traffic jam going nowhere fast. Now, what is it I can do for you?' he persisted.

'Ah sure, I was wondering when I could catch The Bus?'

'I'll check and call you back in a couple of minutes.'

He hung up and began loading the schedule onto his Blackberry. While he waited for it to come up on to the screen, Gary reflected on the young man who had become a close friend of his son, Harry, and a regular at Gary's house.

It didn't seem so long ago that Sham had saved Harry from a serious kicking by a gang of bullies from the local comprehensive.

Fortunately for Harry, Sham was walking down the road fifty yards behind him when they pounced. One minute, Harry was just ambling along minding his own business; the next, he was set upon by four young toughs looking to beat up 'one of the posh gits' from the local fee-paying school.

Even as Harry related the story to his dad later that day, he couldn't explain exactly what happened. But to the best of his recollection, the first of the thugs had said: 'Your lot's been asking for this, you toffy- nosed git'. The next thing, he pulled a knife and lunged at Harry. Before the knife could make contact, Sham appeared and, double-handed, smashed a wooden stake he'd ripped from a garden fence down on the bully's knife-totting wrist, breaking the stake…and the wrist. Before the others could even blink, he had kicked No. 2 in the balls, making extra sure he would stay down by bringing his knee up to meet the bully's face on the way down; the outcome of which was a loud crunch and a spray of blood from the young bully's broken nose.

The other two didn't hang around to see what he would do to them.

A stunned Harry thanked Sham and they became close friends after that; although Harry never knew about Sham's extracurricular activities. Only Gary knew about that.

When Sham was invited with his parents to a 'Thank You' supper, Gary, who had been around the 'wrong sort of people', as his mother used to call them, for as long as he could remember, knew that there was more to Sham than met the eye. He wasn't wrong.

After successfully defending Sham in Court over the assault and paying for a new garden fence, Gary and Sham had had a little heart-to-heart. Sham became a client and made use of The Bus; Gary's special facilities for a few well-chosen clients.

Sham wasn't his real name; it was Michael, but only his parents called him that now. Sham being short for shamrock.

His parents, both doctors, had been kept busy in the dying years of the Troubles, sewing and patching up the bodies that were found to still have some breath in them; totally unaware that a lot of their work was the result of their IRA-recruited offspring. The Boyos had taught him well.

After a lot of soul-searching, his parents decided to move to the mainland and settled in London. They still missed their close-knit families but there was an upside: they were able to get two things they hadn't had for years…peace of mind and a full night's sleep.

The ping from the Blackberry brought Gary back with a start and for a couple of seconds he stared around the luxury interior of his Maserati.

'This is what it's all about' he thought with sheer out-and-out pleasure.

The schedule was on the screen. The three o'clock slot was already booked out. The next stop would be six-thirty at Clacket Lane services. He pressed redial.

'Six-thirty at Clacket Lane. You know the drill, Sham. I'll let my guy know you're coming. See you soon.'

'Which reminds me' thought Gary '…I forgot to let Freddie know about the three o'clock visitor. Better sort that out now.'

Gary made his next call.

Eleven

The juggernaut with the legend 'James Irvine' emblazoned on the side was passing Junction 15 for Heathrow when the driver, Johnnie Parker looked in his mirror and said to his mate, Freddie Collins:

'Nice and quiet, innit? Just the way I like it, young Freddie.'

'Yeah. No friggin' traffic jams. Oh, shit! Where's a bit of wood?' said Freddie scrabbling in the glove compartment for a pencil. 'Phew, that was close.' he said touching the stem of the pencil three times.

Johnnie smiled and looked over briefly at Freddie.

'I didn't know you were superstitious, you little twat.'

'You won't be saying that if we hit traffic…aaah!' Freddie bawled, throwing his arms up in front of his face automatically, as an old banger pulled in, just feet away from their front bumper, without indicating.

Johnnie hit the brakes, honking his horn and flashing his lights at the car in front.

'Christ!' he yelled out. 'Ya bloody idiot! D'you really want a forty-ton trailer up your arse? Stupid bastard.'

In response, the mature lady gave them the single finger salute in her rear mirror.

'Charmed, I'm sure. What's the world coming to when even pensioners are giving you the finger?' said Johnnie in sheer disbelief.

He would have been even more shocked if he'd heard what the nice little old lady had said about him to her dog sitting in the passenger seat.

Freddie saw his opportunity to wind Johnnie up.

'Come on, Johnnie boy! She's right up your street, just your type. Breathin'. Got 'er own hair. Not sure about the teeth, though!'

'Don't knock it, son, that can be handy' replied Johnnie, laughing.

Johnnie's shoulders visibly relaxed as the younger man's attempt to distract him succeeded. He settled down but kept a wary eye open for mad drivers. 'I can remember in the good old days…' he began.

''Ere we go!'

'…yeah! It was one of the boys told me about 'er'' he continued.

'…one of the boys being…?'

'...in the good old days ...'

'Johnnie get on with the bloody story, will you?' said Freddie, half laughing, half in frustration.

'Don't you rush me' commanded Johnnie. 'As I was saying, she was L.O.V.E.L.Y!' he sighed, recalling one of his favourite landladies. 'Anyway, I was talking to one of the boys who still...or has he retired? Whatever, we was in a little greasy spoon we all used to use when we was up there. Just off the A9 near Perth...in the land of the tartan nutters' he said, doing a terrible Scottish accent. 'Yeah, nice people up there...and obliging. But don't ever upset them.'

'Jesus...is there a point to this story?' asked Freddie, used to Johnnie's ramblings.

'There is a point to this story, actually, sonny Jim. An' that is: 'ave some respect for your elders, you little bastard! Gimme a chance! I'm gettin' there. I'm not as quick as I used to be.'

'You can say that again' said Freddie, laughing.

'That's it, I 'aint telling you nothin'' said Johnnie getting the hump.

'Oh, don't be such an ol' stickin' plaster, you miserable old git! Get on with it.'

Reluctant at first, Johnnie quickly warmed to his subject:

'AS I WAS SAYING...before I was interrupted. Jim used to work for...oh, it doesn't matter! You're right. Anyway, he told me about this landlady who used to run a B&B just outside Perth near the trailer park there and she used to be quite obliging. Yeah, that's the word; obliging! Apparently, 'er old man was away a lot and she used to get lonely and became quite attached to gentlemen of the road like myself.'

Johnnie looked at Freddie, half expecting some sarcastic comment. He waited.

Struggling to keep a straight face, Freddie said: 'Yeah?'

'...one more word out of you, m'lad, an'...'

With an air of false innocence, Freddie replied: 'I only said 'Yeah?''

Johnnie still wasn't sure if Freddie's was taking the mick but continued hesitantly:

'Hmm, anyway, we used to have a bit of rough and tumble in 'er own bed! Then she'd get down to business and remove her...God bless them...' he cleared his throat as he thought about it '...dentures! Oh, yes! Oh, yes!' and fell into a silence with a big grin on his face. 'You see, in the old days...' With a silent sigh, Freddie's eyes looked heavenward as Johnnie continued unaware '...we didn't stay very often in B&B's. We used to kip in the cab and save the money'. Johnnie raises his voice to emphasis the point 'You 'ad to, to make up your money. But once in a blue moon, it was nice to have a bath and with Florrie you got your back scrubbed as well. Well worth the ten bob!' Johnnie lapsed into silence and then changing his tone to one of father to son, said: '...and when you grow up, my lad, and drive a big motor car like this you might get to meet some accommodating ladies of the opposite sex!'

'What?' stuttered Freddie, straining to follow Johnnie's reasoning. Before he could follow it with some barb or other, his mobile rang. He looked at the number, recognised who it was and answered immediately.

'Ello? Oh, 'ello. Yeah. Sure. No probs. Everythin' fine. Sorry, what time did you say again? Sorted. G'bye' and he hung up.

'Who was that?' asked Johnnie. 'Another Pamela Anderson lookalike lustin' after your gorgeous body?'

'Nah!' said Freddie dismissively. 'It was the boss just checkin' up that everythin's okay.'

Johnnie just grunted and continued:

'Anyway, to get back to what we were just talking about. Oh, yeah. You can talk! What about that young lady I caught you with up the pub the other week? She 'ad slapper written all over 'er...'cept you couldn't find it in among all 'er other tattoos!'

Freddie held up his hands in surrender and looked into Johnnie's eyes in the rear-view mirror and said: 'Alright. Truce! Chill!' He stretched and yawned.

'When's our next stop?' asked Johnnie.

Freddie reached for the manifest.

'According to this, we're due to stop at South Mimms at 14.45. Lov-a-lee jub-a-lee!' said Freddie, trying to lighten the mood.

'I don't understand it, Freddie' said Johnnie frowning. 'Why are our rest times so rigid? I can remember the good old days when I would drive eight or ten hours without even stopping to strain my greens, if you know what I mean. Now it's all 'Health and Safety' this and 'Health and Safety' that and 'You must take your proper breaks'. AND it's compulsory to leave the lorry for at least an hour AND sign the timesheet to show when you leave and when you return. Don't you think that's strange?'

'Not really, Johnnie. I suppose they want to cover themselves in case there's an accident. Then they can prove that you took sufficient breaks.'

'Ooooh!' said Johnnie getting back into sarcastic mode. 'Sufficient breaks! Where'd you learn to use big words like that? Oh, I can see it now' said Johnnie in his Bamber Gascoigne-like voice: 'Freddie Collins reading...the Dictionary! Is that our word for today then, young Mister Collins? Sufficient? Ya little tosser!'

Freddie joined in in a high-falutin voice and said:

'Just 'cos hew did not go to h'ay posh school like what I did, doesn't mean hew 'ave to be a complete hignor-hay-mus, you know!'

They both laughed.

Johnnie picked up on the voice and continued:

'H'i went to h'ay very posh finishing school don't you know, my good man! H'it was called St 'ilda's.'

'You mean St 'ilda reformatory school more like!'

'What h'ay cheek!' replied Johnnie in his posh voice. Suddenly he reverted to his normal voice. 'Enough of that, you little prat. 'Ow long before we stop? I could eat a baboon...' back to the posh voice '...from the h'arsehole upwards.'

'Well' said Freddie '...the baboon's arse will 'ave to wait another...' he consulted his watch '...twenty minutes.'

'Jesus wept!' said Johnnie as his stomach let out an enormous rumble.

'So would you with six inch nails through yer hands!' said Freddie, quick as a flash.

They laughed again.

'One of these days, my son, yer Man upstairs is going to get a decent pair of specs and then you'd better watch out for those thunderbolts because 'e'll have you!' howled Johnnie, enjoying the banter.

They both started laughing again as Freddie launched into a chorus of: 'Oh, I do like to be beside the seaside.'

Twelve

Ten minutes before Johnnie and Freddie pulled into South Mimms Services, a London taxi turned off the M25 and took the second turn in the service road for the lorry car park instead the first for cars.

The driver found a quiet spot and waited. There were a several lorries of various sizes parked around the area but no-one was looking in his direction: the muscles in Mikey's neck relaxed. He wouldn't be late this time for the drop off. No. Mr Dean had been quite clear on that score. In and out, fast: that was the rule. No hanging around.

Once he was parked up, Mikey called Dave Cosforth, the leader of the bank-job gang. It wasn't only bank jobs they pulled: they weren't averse to a nice jeweller's, providing they were up to the mark. Nice bit of quality jewellery with the odd Rolex thrown in as a treat for the boys alongside an alarm system which the boys could sort out and they were like little piglets in manure. Things had been going well for the boys lately. Too well, in fact: none of them would get out of bed for a job less than a £250,000. Wasn't worth it with the overheads.

Dave answered on the second ring.

'Hiya, Mikey. Everything alright?' asked Dave who'd stopped squeegeeing the large plate window of 'Good Buys', one of his regulars on the High Street, to answer the call.

'Yeah.' replied Mikey. 'Just waiting for you know what. It's due any minute providing there isn't any holdups on this poxy motorway' Mikey was always cautious about saying too much. Even on the mobile. If MI5 could listen into the Prime Minister's calls, they could listen into any and everybody's. So, mum's the word.

'Got it. Speak to you later, mate' said Dave as he hung up and returned to the by now streaky window.

'Ah, bollocks!' he swore and he squeezed out his chamois and began washing the window again.

Thirteen

Mikey was replying to his missus' text about what he wanted for dinner when Johnnie and Freddie pulled into the service area.

'Sweet as...' thought Mikey as the lorry pulled in bang on time.

He watched Johnnie sign the manifest and then slowly get out and amble across the tarmac towards the main service area.

'Hurry up, you old git' said Mikey out loud. 'I've got a living to make before I retire to sunny Spain.'

Johnnie didn't hear him and even if he had, he had other more pressing matters on his mind.

Mikey gave him three further minutes to make sure he was gone before he made his move. He grabbed the suitcase from the boot and walked briskly over to the lorry.

Freddie had been told that he would have two visitors today. He only knew the visitors by sight; no names allowed. The first one was due anytime now: he just didn't know who it would be.

Freddie saw Mikey approaching, suitcase in hand. There were seven visitors now. There used to be only six but one new one was added to the list recently. As always, Mr Dean had shown Freddie a picture of the new one: he didn't want Freddie turning business away when it arrived. The new one was foreign.

Freddie nodded to Mikey and went around the back of the lorry to open up the door.

They both knew each other by sight but not by name: that's the way things had to be. All of the users of The Bus's facilities knew the score: strictly no talking.

Idle talk cost lives is what they say. In this particular line of business, chit-chat could mean very long prison sentences.

Mikey went in and came out a minute later minus the suitcase.

Nods were exchanged and both went their separate ways: Freddie, to his cab at the front of the lorry and Mikey to his, turning on the 'For Hire' sign as he pulled out onto the motorway.

'Not a lot of chance of finding a fare here' thought Mikey. 'But hey-ho! I'm a few grand closer to retirement. Not long to go now. Life's so hard isn't it?' And he cackled and guffawed all the way for about eight miles up to Junction 20 for Brent Cross when the traffic began to slow to a crawl and then stopped altogether.

'Ah, kiss my ass!' he shouted at the causer of the jam.

As Mikey sat, not moving, in the traffic, he saw the blue flashing lights about half a mile away on the other side of the central reservation, coming towards him.

'Now who could they be looking for, I wonder?' he reflected, but still ducked instinctively as the Five Series BMW went passed, all flashing lights and blaring siren, at about ninety miles an hour.

Fourteen

At the same time as Mikey was hoping that the long arm of the Law couldn't stretch across the central reservation, Johnnie was supposed to be having his lunch; except he wasn't.

Johnnie was in serious trouble.

As if it wasn't bad enough that he was in hock up to his nostrils to a moneylender called Jake Vickers for a lot of money. No. There was something worse, much worse. He had developed an unhealthy habit of scratching. Cards, that is: Lotto scratchcards to be precise. He spent most of his waking life with his guts churning and that false hope that addicts have, namely, that with their next fix, everything was gonna come right. Wrong.

He hadn't had sex with his missus for months: she was convinced that he was playing away from home and he believed that she was too. Trouble was: only she cared.

No sex, no money and all Johnnie could think about was: 'Have I got enough to buy my scratchcards?'

And that's what he was up to right now. His guts rumbling earlier had nothing to do with food. He just couldn't wait to get his next fix.

Sitting in a corner of the cafeteria, his mobile on silent so as not to attract attention to himself, cup of tea in one hand and a pile of scratchcards lying on the table beside him, he was scratching away as if his life depended on it; truth be told, it did.

'Feeling lucky today, Johnnie?' the girl on the counter had asked as he purchased his quota. 'Course, darlin'. Today's the day! So, four £5 and six £1 ones, please, Ida'.

'At least I hope it is' prayed Johnnie silently.

As one by one, the cards revealed another no-win-for-Johnnie-day, he kept his spirits up. 'Come on, you little beauty. I know you can do it' which was usually followed by a 'Bollocks!' and on to the next one. No matter what anyone said to him, Johnnie always believed that it would be the next one or the one after that. The most he had ever won was 200 quid in one scratching session. And that 200 quid had cost him thousands and thousands, but still he believed.

With two left to open, his mobile buzzed on the table top. 'Fuck me!' he thought '…it's 'im!'. The nanosecond between seeing the name and sheer terror registering was just long enough for the brain to send the 'close' command to his sphincter…but only just.

Him, of course, being a certain moneylender looking for his weekly payment. It was a day late. Jake Vickers didn't do late.

'What to do? What to do?' muttered Johnnie to himself nervously drumming his fingers on the table as he looked at the phone and then back at the last two scratchcards.

'Maybe, just maybe' he implored as he ignored the phone and went back to scratching.

A drop of sweat detached itself from his hairline and began to crawl down his neck, past his shirt collar and slowly trickle down his spine. Johnnie felt it slide all the way down and stop at the waistband of his trousers.

'Please God, I'll be a good boy! Honest' whispered Johnnie as he remembered how, as a child, he prayed at the side of his bed. 'Please God, please!'

But God wasn't listening that day. Perhaps his attention was elsewhere.

As he scratched the last of the latex off the very last scratchcard, his heart didn't just sink, it bellyflopped.

'Oh, my God. Now what am I gonna do? How the fuck am I goin' to pay 'im now? This is it. The end.'

As he toted up the two £2 wins and the one £5 win and the 'Oooh! A fifteen pounder! That'll go a long way' he thought cynically, he realised that he'd only have to put a couple of pounds towards his next purchase when they stopped at Clacket Lane Services around six o'clock.

For a few seconds, relief set in with that rose-tinted notion addicts tend to hold on to that their next fix will solve all their problems. That was quickly followed by the thought of facing Mr Vickers and the consequences of not being able to pay him. To date, Johnnie had never missed a payment. But he'd heard of a few who had…and it'd taken a long time for them to recover.

Fifteen

It was a very unhappy Jake Vickers who reluctantly hung up when there was no reply from Johnnie.

'Hmm, what's he up to? He's never missed a payment before! Mmm...' thought the man reflectively who had started his working life as a 'finder' for a moneylender. He would chase around the estates, south of the river, which he knew like the back of his great massively-knuckled mitt, looking for and sniffing out welchers. He was the best. Now he had his own loanshark business and a number of finders working for him. Should he send one of them to look for Johnnie?

It was then the idea came to him. An absolute blinder. But first he had to make a phone call. 'Yeah,' he thought, '...you ARE a fuckin' genius, Jake. If you was running this country we wouldn't be in the mess we're in right now!'

He dialled the number.

'Good afternoon, Gary Dean & partners. Can I help you?' said the switchboard operator, Raquel, known to the owner of the company as 'bird brain'.

'Lemme speak to Gary' growled Jake the Loanshark whose voice had an edge to it that sounded like its owner was about to beat the crap out of you.

Keeping her voice ever so sweet, Raquel replied:

'Certainly, Sir. And may I let him know who's calling?'

'Tell 'im it's Jake' he said gruffly.

'Righto, Sir. Does Mr Dean know you and will he know what the call's about, Sir?'

'Not until I tell 'im' said Jake laughing at his own joke.

Silence.

'Yeah, 'e does know me' he added grumpily when it was obvious that she didn't appreciate Jake's attempt at humour.

'Would you hold the line please, Sir?'

Silence again.

Raquel waited a few moments before concluding that there wasn't going to be a 'Thank you'.

She put the call on hold and turned to her colleague and moaned:

'I've got a right one here, Julie. They ain't half rough some of this lot we have to deal with here. This one sounds coarser than my legs when I haven't shaved for a week!'

'Oooh! Aaah!' said Julie who could only begin to imagine what that must be like.

'Hold the line please, caller. I'm just trying to locate Mr Dean for you' said 'bird brain' in her most professional BBC newsreader's voice.

She received a grunt in response.

'Charmin'! Hmm, hmm, hmm' she hummed as she inspected her nails. It was her way of getting back at what she perceived as rude people. She finally called Gary's extension which was picked up immediately.

'Yes?' asked the boss.

'Mr Dean, I have Jake on the line for you. Shall I put him through?'

'Jake…Jake?' said Gary racking his brains. Then he remembered that there was only one Jake. 'Sure, put him through.'

'It wasn't like this at the last practice I worked at, you know, Julie' remarked Raquel as she put Jake through. 'Nice people. Refined people was what we used to deal with there. Bloody scum of the earth, some of 'em 'ere!'

'Hello, Gary Dean & partners' trilled Raquel with just a touch of the anger still lingering in her voice.

Julie just looked at her, stunned.

Sixteen

'Hello, Jake?' said Gary as he heard the line click through.

'Gary?' asked Jake in return.

'Yes. What can I do for you?' enquired Gary from one of the few villains he couldn't relate to. Jake had not been invited to use the facilities of The Bus, although he probably would have been glad of the opportunity. 'There's just something…' thought Gary as he waited to hear what Jake wanted.

'Need you to do a bit of diggin' for me on a company. Can you do that?' asked Jake straightforwardly.

'No probs' replied Gary cheerfully. 'What's the name?'

'It's James Irvine, the haulier company.'

Gary's stomach practically did a pole vault out of the fifth-floor window but he tried not to let it show in his voice.

'What d'you want to know?'

'I want to know what sort of stuff they carry. Do they do any quality upmarket gear? That sort o' thing.'

The warning bells were ringing very loud and very clear in Mr Dean's head.

'How the fuck did this thick bastard find out?' thought Gary furiously. 'Has someone talked?' but he asked as casually as he could:

'Why d'you want know, Jake?'

'I pay you to work for me, Gary, not to ask fuckin' questions! Alright?' shot back Jake, not happy at the way the conversation was going.

'Sorry, Jake, sorry' said Gary backtracking like fury. 'Force of habit, mate. 'Course I'll look into it. How quickly do you want to know?'

'Asap. I've got an idea about something. Don't want to say too much, if you get my meaning.'

'Absolutely. Mum's the word. I'll get back to you in a couple of days. Will that do? That's fine. Speak to you then. Cheerio'. And Jake hung up. He was well pleased with himself.

Not so, Gary Dean.

'What the hell was that all about?' he thought feverishly.

As thoughts collided in Gary's brain like atoms in a particle accelerator, his internal phone vibrated and made him jump.

'No calls!' he screamed into the receiver before slamming it down back into its cradle.

Not even on his very first Court appearance had Gary's stomach churned so violently.

'What's he up to?' he thought apprehensively. Slowly, the rising panic began to subside. 'All right, Gary. Think!'

He sat for a few minutes forcing himself to calm down. 'You can't think logically without structure. Now then, I need to find out what he's up to. That's for sure. How?'

Gary knew that if you follow a train of thought in a logical way, there can be only one result: a logical conclusion. And he found his.

'I need to get Pete Morris on the job.'

Pete was a private dick whom Gary had used in a number of divorce cases: in fact, he was working on a particularly nasty one at the moment for one of The Bus's users. Maybe he could take 48 hours to follow Mr Vickers, as Jake insisted his borrowers call him, and find out what the fuck he was up to.

'Yeah, that's it!' thought Gary, relieved 'Follow a train of thought, or in this case, Jake Vickers, and he'll lead us to the answer.'

Seventeen

'Hello, Pete?' said Gary into the mouthpiece.

'Yeah. Who's that?' asked the ever-suspicious Pete Morris.

'Pete, it's Gary. Gary Dean.'

'Mr Dean! So sorry, didn't recognise your number. What can I do for you, Sir?' Pete was always respectful to people like Gary who put business his way.

'Need a favour, Pete.'

'Sure, Mr Dean. What can the Morris Detective Agency do for one of its most favoured clients?'

'I need you to follow someone for me. Find what he's up to; who he sees. That sort of thing.'

'Another divorce, Mr Dean?'

'No, Pete. This is for…a friend of mine. Personal like.'

'Hmm' thought Pete. 'Not a very good liar, our Mr Dean' but he said:

'Happy to help a friend of yours, Mr Dean. Who is it and when do you want me to start?' enquired Pete.

'That's the thing, Pete. It's urgent. He wants it, like now' said Gary, knowing that one day that 'You owe me one' scenario would raise its ugly skull. He hated that feeling. But he hated the churning in his stomach, at this moment, even more.

'But what about…' began Pete.

'I know. I know' said Gary frustratedly '…but this'll only take 48 hours, then you could get back on the Fitzsimons case, if that's okay with you' he added.

'No problem, Mr Dean. I'll get on to it straight away. Details please?'

Gary felt the relief surge through him. He was back in control once more.

Eighteen

The Dean residence was located in one of the more prestigious squares in Dulwich.

Gary's wife, Nicki, former model and love of his life, was the archetypal successful lawyer's wife; on the board of a couple of disadvantaged children's charities, now that their only child, Harry, had pretty much cut the umbilical stricture.

To be fair, the gorgeous, long-legged stunner of a brunette that was his wife, didn't have a clue about her husband's business activities; legal or otherwise. Once he stepped outside the door of their well-appointed home in the morning, he did what he did: kosher didn't come into it unless they were entertaining one of Gary's clients.

And so, Gary Dean, scourge of any CPS solicitor who came within a courtroom length of him, was no different to any successful lawyer on the planet with half of his brain cells. When the opportunity arose to squeeze a finger or two into a client's company till, his hand did not waver.

However, a trawl through Companies House records would not have found any mention of his directorship of this particular company; this one was strictly unofficial.

One year earlier Gary had been introduced to the owner of the company, James Irvine, whose name was emblazoned on the side of every one of the company's vehicles. He was considering going into receivership and wanted some good 'unofficial' legal advice. A friend of a friend had recommended Gary as being the man to 'minimise your losses/maximise what you can grab' arrangement.

When Gary checked the company out, however, he saw that what the company required was an injection of cash to update some of the fleet and sort out a few logistical problems.

Generous to a fault, Gary invested and in return received an appropriate percentage of the company, cleaning up some dirty money at the same time. In Gary's world, suitcases of dirty money were often referred to as 'laundry baskets'... and Gary liked nothing better than washing it in the wonderfully cleansing waters of legitimacy. The company flourished and Gary had a good return on his investment... plus a little extra something.

That little extra was an arrangement with James Irvine whereby Gary siphoned off one of the lorries for his own use.

Hence, what euphemistically became known as 'The Bus' was offered to certain of Gary's clients as a foolproof method of hiding ill-gotten gains from prying eyes, usually, but not exclusively, the police...for a small fee, of course.

Gary loved the idea of the police flying all over the place trying to catch his clients with the goods and all the time they were permanently on the move around the M25 corridor. Moveable Assets: Gary still wondered where the idea came from.

Between receiving the call that morning from The Delivery Man about the times of The Bus and reports on the radio of a bank robbery, Gary was pretty sure that it had been pulled off by Dave Cosforth and his crew.

'So, all in all, a very satisfying day's work' concluded Gary as he pulled into the drive of his magnificent detached house.

Twenty minutes earlier, his son and only heir, Harry, had arrived home from a game of tennis with his girlfriend, Amanda, daughter of Jack Clancy, one of London's biggest pimps, big client of Gary's and a regular user of The Bus. Thanks to daddy's immense, immoral earnings, Amanda had been able to attend finishing school in Switzerland. Parent's Day was always a bit of a bummer though: Jack felt that perhaps his knuckle tattoos would not go down well with the minor aristocracy of Europe whose children attended the well-known school. As a result, he was always otherwise engaged and Amanda was left to tag along with one of her friend's parents: not ideal.

As Gary approached the Art Deco stained glass door of the vestibule, the waft of his favourite dish, Fish baked in Salt from Jamie's Cook Book, assaulted his olfactory senses.

'Who loves ya baby?' he yelled in a pathetic attempt at New York Mafioso voice as he walked through the hall, dropping his briefcase by the coatstand before throwing open the door to the kitchen.

'Hmm, hmmm' was all he could manage when he bent over and kissed Nicki on the neck while she gave the vegetables a light stir.

'That smells de-lic-ioso, darling.'

'Thank you, husband of mine.'

An amused Harry and Amanda looked on from the kitchen table, mugs of coffee in front of them.

'Amanda, will you stay and have a bite to eat?'

'Thank you, Mrs Dean but I really have to get on my way.' She took one final sip of coffee before saying:

'See you later Harry. What time you coming over?'

'I'll be there about eight. Okay?'

'Sure. See you then. Bye!' And she kissed him on the cheek.

'Goodbye Mr Dean, Mrs Dean! And thank you for the coffee.'

''Bye Amanda!' they both chorused.

As they heard the front door close, Nicki said:

'Such a polite, sensible girl, Harry. Well chosen!'

Well she was fifty per cent right.

Nineteen

Amanda walked the short distance to her high-tech, high-spec duplex penthouse, courtesy of daddy, with a bit more spring in her step than usual.

But then she couldn't wait to get indoors to try out one of the small packages she'd purchased at the tennis club that afternoon.

Luckily, her dealers at finishing school offered only the very best, so that by the time she left, there wasn't anything she hadn't sampled. Nowadays, though, her tastes were a little more exotic.

The lift seemed to take ages as Amanda hopped from one foot to the other, like she needed a pee, waiting for it to arrive. Exiting directly into the flat, she made her way across the bridge overlooking the huge double-height sitting room and skipped down the stairs, oblivious to all but the high she was about to experience.

The Prada jacket was discarded on the white leather sofa, where Harry had first had his wicked way with her. In that same seductive tone she'd used to bed Harry and as the anticipation caused her to lick her lips, she mumbled: 'Come to mama, you little beauty!' She knelt down by the Ligna Roset glass table carefully unwrapping her treat.

But for Amanda that night, it was to be her last high. 'Wow-eee!' was the last thought to whizz through the neurological pathways of her brain before the fatal cocktail of pure heroin and some other shit that some off-his-tits chemist had cobbled together, caused an explosion like the Hiroshima mushroom in her brain: blood found its way to every orifice...and slowly oozed.

She remained in her kneeing position, head resting on the blood-splattered glass top until she was found.

Twenty

Dinner over, Harry pulled on his tatty-chic Vivienne Westwood jacket and captain's cap to walk the short distance to Amanda's apartment.

As he strolled, his mind turned over something which had been bugging him for a while: what did Amanda's dad do for a living? He had the look of a scaffolder with a hangover on a bad day. The massive bear's paws attached to the ends of his arms were covered in calluses which in turn were covered in tattoos.

Harry knew he was a client of his father's which wasn't necessarily a good thing. But one thing was sure: if he was a client of his father, he had money and plenty of it. He knew how his dad worked: they only got through the door if they had serious amounts of cash in the bank. And Amanda's penthouse must have cost a pretty penny.

'Maybe one of these days I'll find out' he thought as he arrived at the chic minimalist entrance to Amanda's building and buzzed up. He waited a few moments, expecting to hear Amanda's bubbly voice squawking down the intercom: 'Come in! Come in!'

Silence. 'Damn' he thought as he fumbled in his pocket for the key. 'She must be in the bath. Maybe not such a bad idea' he decided as rude images began to drift into his dirty mind. 'Yeah, could be fun.'

Harry let himself into the apartment.

''Manda! Where are you?' he called, starting to strip off as he stepped out of the lift. Silence. It was only when he got no answer the second time then that he started to feel uneasy.

'A…man…da! Stop mucking around. Where are you?' Silence again. Harry zipped up his trousers and tried to hold down the panic that was rising in his chest. 'What's going on?'

He began walking across the bridge towards the staircase when he glanced down into the sitting room below. He froze at the image below.

'Oh, fuck! Oh, no! Oh, my God! What's happened?' He rushed down the stairs but he could see that it was past the time for a 999 call. Call. Who to call? 'Dad' thought Harry. It was always dad in a crisis.

His hands were shaking so badly he could hardly hold the phone let alone dial, so, it was fortunate that the home number was on redial.

'Hello' Harry said as his mum answered the phone. 'Hello, Mum. Is Dad there? Can you put him on, please?'

'Are you all right, dear?' asked Nicki as she heard the quiver in his voice.

'Mum, just put Dad on, please'. Harry was close to losing it. He was desperately trying to hang on.

'Hello, Harry?' Gary's voice, puzzled.

'Dad…dad' was all Harry could say as the tears began to tumble down his cheeks.

'For God's sake, Harry! What is it, son?' said Gary trying to stay calm as Nicki held her head next to the receiver, listening.

'It's Amanda, Dad. She's...gone! She's dead. She's...dead!' he repeated numbly, hardly believing it himself.

'What've you done?' asked his father as calmly as he could although for the second time that day, his stomach was churning like a volcano about to erupt.

'Dad, I've just arrived. She was lying there. There's blood everywhere!'

'Oh, my God, Harry! They might still be there. Get out of there NOW!' commanded Gary.

'No, Dad. No. There's no-one else here' said Harry, calming down as he took in the scene. 'She's taken something. There's a half-empty wrapper on the table! Oh God, Dad! She's taken something.'

'Right!' shouted Gary to get Harry's attention. 'Get out of there now. Right now! Do you hear me, Harry? Out!'

'Yeah. Okay, Dad. It's just….' Harry never got the chance to finish.

'Get out of there now and wipe as much as you can off any surface you've touched. The police would expect to find your prints there but we need time to think, so wipe what you can and go NOW! I'm on my way. I'll meet you 'round the corner in Chalfont Square.'

'Okay, Dad. Okay. I'm leaving now'. He hung up and pulled a packet of paper tissues from his pocket and wiped the areas he thought he'd touched. And that's when he saw it; Amanda's Prada jacket hanging half off the sofa. She was so blasé about things. No comprehension of the meaning of the word 'cost'. And so there it was just lying there like a rag: a 1200 quid rag.

He held it to his face briefly, allowing her Gucci perfume to wafting over him. As he inhaled, he very nearly lost it again, but his father's voice managed to intrude on his grief and bring him back from the brink.

'Better not use the lift' he thought in a moment of clarity.

Before stepping out into the corridor, he ducked his head out to see if anyone was there. All clear.

Walking down the stairs as quickly and quietly as he could, he stopped at each floor, holding his breath and listening. Nothing.

He left the building without being seen by anyone. Well, almost.

As he turned right out of the building, a dark-coloured top-of-the-range Merc turned into the street from the opposite end. Jack Clancy had decided to pay his daughter a surprise visit. He clocked Harry leaving.

'At least I 'aint gonna catch 'em at it' he thought, smiling to himself.

He'd bought Amanda a diamond-studded Rolex from a 'reputable' geezer, if such a person exists, as a pre-birthday surprise. But the surprise would turn out to be his, not hers.

Twenty One

There was nothing he could do. Jack's little princess was gone. He cradled her in his arms and then, when his tears stopped, he laid her back gently on the floor and picked up the wraps that were still lying on the table where she'd left them and put them in his pocket.

'I'll get them, babe. Promise' he whispered.

The 'why' or the 'what' didn't matter: the 'who' did though. And God knows they were gonna pay.

He went to the bathroom to wash his daughter's blood from his hands.

'First of all, I 'ave to get hold of that little toe-rag, 'Arry. He didn't seem the druggie-type. Just goes to show how wrong you can be' he thought as the guilt, recriminations and revenge all lined up in an orderly queue.

Before that though, he called his number two, telling him to 'bring the shooters and some of the boys an' get over 'ere. NOW!'

Within half an hour, half a dozen of London's toughest and meanest were sitting downstairs in two cars, both with blacked out windows, waiting for orders. You don't get to run one of the biggest prostitution rings in London using curates as backup. When you had to show you meant business, you needed the hardest of hard men and there wasn't an unbroken nose among these guys.

Jack slipped into the front passenger seat of the first car beside his number two, Sy the Greek, outside Amanda's block.

'I've been thinkin'...' he began '...get the boys to move a couple of streets away. No need to attract attention. I've just got a couple of things to do and then I'll let you know what's gonna be 'appenin'.'

Sy just nodded to the boss: a man of few words anyway, he knew when to keep his mouth shut.

Twenty Two

At home, just a few streets away, Gary was grilling Harry.

'Have you got anything on you now?' he asked. Harry knew what his father meant.

'Dad, I've never touched the stuff. Not even at school when my friends were smoking pot. I've never, ever taking anything. Honest.'

The phone stopped Gary from pressing him for more information.

'Yes?' said Gary as he grabbed the phone from the cradle.

'Gary' began Jack softly.

Gary swallowed hard before answering.

'Yes, Jack. What can I do for you at this late hour?' he answered, putting on his professional lawyer-to-client tone.

'Gary. Don't mess me around' said Jack in a quiet but clearly threatening tone. 'I need to speak to 'Arry.'

It was on the tip of his tongue to say that Harry wasn't there but Gary knew it would only acerbate an already bad situation.

'I'm not sure I can let you do that, Jack' he replied finally.

'I saw him leaving…Amanda's, Gary. Whichever way you cut it, 'e's... involved' said Jack struggling as he mentioned his little girl's name.

'He's clean, Jack. He doesn't do drugs; I've just asked him.'

'And 'e said "No" did 'e, Gary?' the anger beginning to surface in his voice. 'I need to see 'im, Gary and I need to see 'im now' The emphasis was definitely on the 'now'.

'Can't do that, Jack' said Gary.

'We both know that you don't have a choice, Gary. You also know that if Harry is involved, 'e's dead. I've got some of the boys sitting 'round the corner. They're tooled up. Now do we come and get 'im or are you going to bring 'im round?'

Silence on the line. Gary needed to think. 'Jack, give me five minutes and I'll call you back.'

'Five minutes then' said Jack. The connection was broken.

Nicki, stunned by all of this, was holding Harry, he was cowering in his mother's arms; maybe the umbilical hadn't been completely severed.

'Harry,' said Gary finally, his mind having made some kind of order and sense out of the whole mess '...are you sure you've nothing to do with this? Swear to me!' he said, using the sort of tone he used to intimidate witnesses.

'Dad, I swear!' declared Harry vehemently.

Gary looked deep into his son's eyes; the same way he looked into the eyes of witnesses. He, trying to look into their souls: they, returning that stare, terrified and believing that he could.

'Nicki,' said Gary, he'd made his decision '...would you make us all a cup of tea, please? Thank you, darling' No margin for refusal.

When Nicki had left the room, Gary said to Harry:

'Right. Here's how it is. Jack wants to see you. He wants to talk to you. We're going to see him together but not at Amanda's flat. Definitely not there.'

Gary used his mobile to call Jack, who answered on the first ring.

'Yes, Gary?' That same soft tone that sent shivers down most of the spines of those that heard it.

'You can see Harry but not at the flat. Too sensitive. Too hurtful for Harry and you. So, I want you to come around here, to our house. I'm sure you know the address.'

It made sense to Jack so he just said:

'I'll be there' Gary was left with a dial tone in his ear.

'Nicki' Gary called out '...bring an extra cup, will you? We have a visitor arriving shortly.'

Twenty Three

The doorbell rang, Harry and Nicki nearly jumped out of their designer wear.

Gary went to the door. Jack stood there, leather jacket covered in dark stains, face looking like a thunderstorm about to break.

'Evenin'' offered Jack. Nothing else.

'Come in, Jack. We're in the front room. Harry's there and beside himself, he's still in shock, so go easy on him. I know I can't begin to imagine how you're feeling. All I can say on behalf of Nicki and myself is that we are so, so sorry, Jack. A waste of such a young and beautiful life.'

Jack knew that the only way for him to keep going was to keep his focus on revenge. That and that alone was stopping him from collapsing into a heap on the floor. It was keeping the pain that he knew he would have to face at bay, for the moment. That would have to be dealt with later, much later. But for now, the thought of revenge was the only analgesic.

'Thanks Gary. Now can I see 'Arry?' said Jack, still cold as ice.

'Sure, Jack. Just be gentle with him. I've seen a lot of clients in the state he's in and I know that it wouldn't take much to push him over the edge and then he'd be no use to you or anybody for days, maybe weeks.'

'Got the message, Gary. Now can I see him?' repeated Jack. He too had seen prisoners on remand in that same fragile state where they were just managing to hold it together until something got to them; like someone sitting at their table, on their chair, in the dining room and then all hell broke loose. There would be lock downs followed by internal enquiries where the screws on the floor would always get the blame and they, in turn, would be in a foul mood for days. Anyone with any sense avoided even eye contact with them then.

Gary opened the door of the sitting room and Jack followed.

'Evenin' Mrs Dean' said Jack but his eyes were boring into Harry.

'Would you care for a cup of tea, Mr Clancy? And can I say how very sorry we are about Amanda. She was a darling.'

'Yes she was, Mrs Dean and thank you, I will have that tea'. Turning to Harry, Jack said in that quiet voice of his:

'So 'Arry, tell me what 'appened. And before you say anything, I saw you leave...' Jack was finding it nigh on impossible to keep it together, '...Amanda's.'

As the last word came out of Jack's mouth, a swarm of butterflies hovered in each of the stomachs of the others present.

'Mr Clancy...' began Harry '...I'm so sorry about Amanda. I...we loved each other. I just don't know how it happened.'

'I'll tell you how it 'appened 'Arry: my daughter, my beautiful daughter was given some very dodgy gear. That's how it 'appened. What I need to know, and need to know fast is who...who gave it to her? That's what I came for 'Arry, the name. Nothing else. Just give me that name, please.'

'Mr Clancy...I...I don't know who it was.'

Jack, who'd sat down on the sofa opposite Harry, was up on his feet and just about to jump on Harry when Gary shouted: 'No, Jack! Listen to what he's saying. He really doesn't know. Now calm down or get out. Nicki, could you make a fresh pot of tea, please?'

As Nicki left the room, a feeling of relief swept over her as if she'd just stepped out of a cage with a raging lion in it. But that relief intermingled with her concern: concern on all sorts of different levels. Concern for her son; Nicki had never seen him look so frightened, so vulnerable and for the first time she could see how unfamiliar he was with the ways of the world outside. Perhaps they shouldn't have cocooned him so much. Was there still time or was it too late to show him what living in the real world was really like?

Concern also for the safety of Harry and Gary, the loves of her life. Who was this Jack Clancy really? What did he do? What was he going to do?

Although she had met Jack Clancy on a couple of occasions before, she didn't know him; only that he appeared to be an important client of her husband's. But how far should that allow him to interfere in her family's life?

Yes, it was tragic that his daughter had died but that was nothing to do with her or her family; he should have been keeping a closer eye on her. Now it seemed that he was looking for someone else to lay the blame on. Well he'd better not overstep the mark with her men. Find someone else to blame. That was exactly what Jack Clancy was trying to do.

'Jack, Harry will try to help as much as possible but please do not try to use methods you would normally employ in your business dealings. Do I make myself clear?'

Jack thought about it for a minute. While he was thinking, no-one spoke, no-one moved. Gary and Harry waited. Jack nodded. Gary breathed a sigh of relief inwardly.

'Okay. Let's start again, 'Arry. Where could she have got that gear from? You've been with her a lot recently. Who's she seen? Who has she been getting into little private chit-chats with? Who's she been getting into a huddle with? Who was it, 'Arry? For God's sake, I NEED to know. Please'. Jack begged when the tears could no longer be held back.

For a few minutes, Harry sat, compelling his paralysed brain to function. Who had Amanda been speaking to recently that she wouldn't normally talk to? Who stuck out? Who didn't belong?

Then Harry had an idea.

After Sham had saved Harry from the beating, Harry'd lost his confidence. Nicki arranged for Harry to see a hypnotherapist. The therapist had shown Harry how to use self-hypnosis. It had worked. Later on, Harry found that if there was something he couldn't recall, he could put himself into a light trance, 'rewind' to the situation and re-live it; which is what he did now. He closed his eyes.

A scene from that afternoon crossed the line from Harry's unconscious mind and materialized in his consciousness.

It was in the clubhouse after their game. Amanda didn't like Pete Davidson, said he was 'a creep of the first order' but, she'd approached him. Harry squeezed his eyes shut to bring the scene back into focus, Amanda was leaning over him and whispering. Yes! And when she'd finished speaking, he got up and left the room and...what happened then?

Gary and Jack just sat and waited, knowing glances passing between the two of them. They knew something was going on with Harry but they also knew not to interrupt, not to interfere. 'What happened next?' thought Harry feverishly. The scene shot forward five minutes and Harry saw Pete walking back into the room.

'Five minutes' thought Harry. 'Where had he gone? Could've gone to the loo, I suppose. Hmm, the loo.'

Gary and Jack kept their silent vigil as they watched the emotions appear on Harry's face. They could see that things were shifting, being sifted, in his brain 'But what?' they both wanted to scream.

Harry followed Pete, in his mind's eye, as he returned to the club chair he'd been sitting on. 'Wait a minute!' thought Harry '...Amanda was still sitting on the arm of the chair as if she was waiting. Waiting for what?'

Harry knew then. He totally knew.

Pete leaned over Amanda this time when he returned. Harry's view was partially obscured by Pete's body. Was he whispering to her? No, no, no. He dropped something in her lap. It was meant to be a sleight of hand, but their timing was out. Amanda slipped her hand with whatever that something was straight into her handbag in one smooth movement. As she got up to go, she leaned over Pete. Something she had been holding in her other hand fell into Pete's lap this time. A roll. A tight roll of banknotes.

No. Pete hadn't gone to the loo; he'd gone to the locker room next door. That must be where he kept his stash; in one of the lockers. Perfect place to hide it: respectable tennis club, haunt of respectable middle-class people. The wrong sort of people simply weren't allowed into such establishments. 'Yeah, right' thought Harry.

His eyes sprung open, surprising his dad and Jack with the sureness which now showed in them.

'It was Pete Davidson at the tennis club today' he announced.

'You sure?' asked Jack. 'Just a couple of minutes ago you didn't have a clue. Now you seem positive' said Jack sitting up and paying attention.

'Yes, Harry. Are you absolutely certain?' asked his father.

'Totally is the answer to both your questions' replied Harry confidently.

'What's changed?' pressed Jack.

'You asked me to think about what stuck out: who did she speak to who wasn't 'right'? And that's the answer: Pete Davidson. I saw him pass something to her in the clubhouse this afternoon but it wasn't until I thought about it now that I realised what it all meant. He's the bastard who gave it to her' said Harry, tears welling up.

'Right' said Jack. 'I'm off. Work to do' Now he knew the 'who', he was all business.

At that point, Nicki opened the door and went back to the hall table to pick up the tray with the tea and biscuits.

'Sorry, Mrs Dean. I have to go but thanks anyway'. Turning to Harry, he said:

'Thanks for all your 'elp'. And then to Gary:

'I'll be in touch. Goodnight' and he left.

'God help that guy when Jack finds him' Gary said to Harry.

'There's only one thing that should happen to him: someone should tie him down and give him an armful of his own stuff' said Harry nastily.

'Harry!' called out his shocked mother.

'You might be closer to the truth than you think' replied Gary, who knew the sort of treatment his clients tended to mete out.

Twenty Four

Earlier on in the evening, Johnnie and Freddie were stuck bang in the middle of the rush hour on the M25; nobody's idea of fun.

But surprisingly, they were both happy; it would soon be home time. Or at least, that's what Freddie was thinking about. For Johnnie, though, his focus was on his next fix. The thought of home filled him with dread of the worse sort, whenever it managed to push its way into his consciousness.

'What could I say to Mr Vickers to avoid a warning?' thought Johnnie earlier when he and Freddie had lapsed into companionable silence. Sometimes Johnnie preferred just to keep talking. Talk meant not having to think. Not thinking was good at the moment.

The warning he had been mulling over earlier would probably involve a few stitches in the face and a black eye caused by a knuckleduster tap: that is, if Jake Vickers was in a generous mood. But, for sure, it would be to the face: Jake always liked to make his warnings public, it discouraged late payers.

'But you never know' thought the perennially hopeful Johnnie rubbing his mental hands gleefully, '...maybe tonight's the night! That little fifty grand scratchie or even the million might just be waiting for me to give it a little rub with me magic fifty pence piece': the one which Johnnie had once scratched his £200 winning batch with. It still came as a complete surprise to Johnnie that it hadn't worked its magic on anything of any consequence since.

Freddie was just looking forward to getting the last visitor on and off The Bus asap. It'd been a long tiring day especially dealing with Johnnie's mood swings: '...no wonder the boss didn't want Johnnie to know what was going on.'

'Not sure he could keep his trap shut, Freddie' said Mr Dean. Did Freddie care? Not a jot. He received a handsome bonus every month. In cash. In his hand. What more could a man ask for? So, he just kept his head down, his own trap very tightly shut and made sure that Johnnie didn't have a clue as to what was going on. Besides, it meant he could keep all the money for himself. Nice one.

By the time they got parked up it had just gone six o'clock. Johnnie signed the manifest and went off to the service station; the last one before setting off home.

There were four drivers in all and just two mates, Freddie and Jimmy.

The story that Johnnie and the other driver had been told was that Freddie and Jimmy had to do longer shifts to make up their money. Truth was that Freddie and Jimmy made three times what the drivers did, but kept schtum about it. So, everybody was happy. 'Specially the boss.

The funny thing was: each of the drivers thought that it was the other one who was delivering the non-existent goods in the back of the truck.

In the fading autumnal light, Freddie saw a hooded figure slowly making his way towards the truck.

'It's 'im alright' thought Freddie, recognising the six-thirty visitor, a bit early.

The silence was maintained. Freddie was grateful; there was something about this visitor that made him clench his bum cheeks very tightly; he always felt as if he was going to poo his pants. Freddie recognised 'hard' men when he saw them. He was used to them; he'd grown up in a family full of them. But this one was different. Slightly built, unprepossessing but…he had the look of death about him. Freddie was glad he didn't have to pass the time of day with this one.

He opened the back of the lorry and five minutes later was watching the receding figure of Sham, except he didn't know that was his name, disappear towards the public area of the service station.

Out of the headlighted gloom, Freddie saw another figure approach; it was Jimmy.

''Allo mate! Did I see my favourite visitor just leaving? I haven't seen 'im for a couple of weeks. Here, d'you ever wondered what he does?' said Jimmy who liked to talk; maybe a bit too much for his own good.

'No I don't, Jimmy and if I was you, I wouldn't wonder too long about it, my son, it could cost you.'

'What? Me job?' asked Jimmy, surprised at Freddie's tone.

'Aye and a lot more besides' declared Freddie who still had the shivers whizzing up and down his spine from Sham's visit.

'Maybe you're right' replied Jimmy laughing. 'Wasn't it curiosity that killed the pussy?'

'An' anything else that got in its way' said Freddie grimly. What he really wanted to say to Jimmy was: 'Don't rock the boat, you muppet! It's paying for our little extras in life, so mind your own bloody business.'

In the meantime, Johnnie had cashed his winners and bought his new quota. He was sitting on the throne in the gents' loo, for a bit more privacy, rubbing the latex off this latest batch.

He scratched one of the five pound cards to reveal a fifty-pound win.

'Yes! Oh yes, you little beauty!' he moaned.

A little old pensioner, who was passing at the time, assumed that the gentleman occupying the cubicle was having a wank.

'If only' he thought wistfully and moved on.

For Johnnie, that was as close as he was going to get to the million, just a dream. Unfortunately, with the last card scratched, reality was about to kick him in the teeth, either that or it would be Mr Vickers. But for sure, one of them would.

The thought of going home was beginning to give him the galloping wild shites. So, he stayed where he was a little bit longer, waiting for things to settle down.

Twenty Five

Meanwhile, not long after he received the call from Gary Dean, Pete Morris got on the job.

He found Mr Vickers where Gary Dean had told him he would: in his 'office', the back of a launderette, in one of those little back streets near the Elephant and Castle main drag.

Pete soon located his own office: a greasy spoon opposite the laundry. Pete's strength lay in his ability to get people to open up. He'd start off finding out what 'pulled their chain'. Usually, for the men, it would be football and not surprisingly, Pete just 'happened' to support the same team: rapport established. For the ladies, it was usually the kids or grandkids. Get a woman talking about them and you usually had trouble stopping them, so Pete found. Gradually, conversations would be turned around to local gossip and the rest would follow. But it wasn't necessary on this occasion.

After about half an hour, Mr Vickers, Pete like to keep a bit of mental distance from the people he followed, hence Mr Vickers, left his office and was driven off in a Range Rover with the windows blacked out.

'Subtle' thought Pete. 'They might not be able to see you but the car might be a bit of a giveaway'. Pete left the café and followed the Range Rover at a discreet distance.

'At least it's easy to spot in traffic' thought the private dick.

It wasn't long before he was snapping away with his hugely expensive camera: the one that had proved its worth on many, many occasions. In one recent divorce case, where he'd worked on behalf of the wife, the photos were so clear that you could actually make out the name of the exclusive label on the G-string, which, at the time, was sitting around the ankles of the young lady as her older lover proved that he was still a stallion in the bedroom; although the action was taking place in his car at the time. Interesting reading; that label. The wife's barrister used it to prove that the young lady concerned could not possibly have afforded to buy it for herself and when asked who did, she went all coy. Another happy customer courtesy of Pentax.

As he sat in his ten-year-old Nissan Primera, his disguise for jobs like this, he briefly thought about Gary Dean and what his interest in this clearly violent man could be. But he quickly stopped those thoughts in their tracks. He knew that finding or working things out were not always good for your health. Besides, Gary always paid, no questions asked. 'So, do the job and don't ask yourself stupid questions, Pete' thought the man whose drive-around on his days off was a Porsche Carrera.

Pete stuck to Mr Vickers like chewing gum to a shoe: there was no way Mr Vickers was gonna shake Pete off. Nor did he have the slightest notion that he was being followed: Pete's claim to his clients, and to date it was 100%, was that he had never been spotted by a target yet.

It didn't take long for Pete to work out Mr Vickers's profession. He didn't mind who he gave a clump to: men, women and on one occasion a kid was punched on the back of the head trying to protect his mum, they all got it. And for what? Borrowing a few quid till payday most likely and when they couldn't clear it off plus the exorbitant rate of interest, they were indentured.

'Oh, yes' thought Pete 'Mr Wilberforce thought he got rid of slavery. Well, he should come and have a look around some of the estates in London that I've had to work on. Trust me, Mr W, slavery is alive and still having the shit kicked out of it in London!'

Pete began to dismantle the telescopic lens when one of the henchmen suddenly opened the back passenger door and started walking rapidly towards the hunched figure of a workman, clearly returning from a day's toil and looking exhausted, judging by the way his feet were being dragged, Pete thought.

'Oh, yeah! What's going on here then?' thought Pete. From everything he'd seen, Pete realised that this moneylender preyed on the poorest elements in society: the type that didn't have and never would have, two pennies to rub together.

'Hmm, should I or shouldn't I?' he mused. 'Well, maybe just a few more mugshots for Mr Dean.'

As he began snapping, Pete realised that there was something different about this one. First of all, Mr Vickers had sent one of his henchmen to fetch the guy and bring him to the car. The front passenger window was wound down. Pete couldn't hear what was being said but the guy's shoulders slumped further and Pete could see that he was close to collapse. Then the henchman pushed him into the back of the motor.

'Definitely different!' thought Pete excitedly. 'This one's getting the VIP treatment. With all the others, Vickers would just get out of the car himself, push them against the bonnet, scream at them, land a few punches and then get his henchmen to check their pockets and if she was pretty, her bra as well, to see if they had any money on them. Hmm, I'd better wait to see what happens.'

Ten minutes later, the back door of the car was opened and the guy was roughly shoved out. He grazed his hand as he fell but not a sound came from his lips. He watched silently, rubbing his hand as the black Range Rover speed off with a squeal of tyres.

'What was that all about?' wondered Pete

He watched as the guy sloped off, keeping an eye on him as he climbed the stairs emerging onto a balcony on the third floor. Pete waited as he took out his front door key and went in.

It had been a very long day but that went with the territory. Nevertheless, Pete climbed up to the third floor and clocked the number on the door of the flat: 22.

'Right' he thought as he legged it back to the car 'Quick report into Mr Dean and that's it. Pizza, a couple of Becks, twenty minutes in front of the telly and I'll be well gone!'

He had very simple tastes, Pete.

Twenty Six

Jack Clancy hadn't been gone ten minutes when the phone call came from Pete.

Gary looked at the number calling and knew he had to answer it.

'Hello, Pete' he said without preamble. 'What've you got for me?'

'Not a very nice man, Mr Vickers. I reckon the A & E department at St Thomas' will be busy into the night with just the people he's beat up today.'

'Is that right, Pete?' said Gary still distracted after the episode with Jack.

'Well, I've got quite a few pictures of people he saw today. Nothing special, in my opinion, 'cept one.'

Gary was all ears.

'Yes, Pete? Go on.'

'Well this guy, instead of just lamming him one, he was invited into the car and was let out ten minutes later untouched. Not necessarily unusual unless you'd been following Mr Vickers, like what I have all day. Different, is what I say, Mr Dean. Might be worth a quick squint.'

'If I give you my email address, can you whack it over to me, Pete? I know it's late but this is important…to my friend' he added a little too late.

'Bloody hell!' thought Pete 'It must be important for you to give me your private email address' but he said:

'Sure, Mr Dean. Fire away' and Pete wrote down the email address.

'It'll be with you in five. Let me know what you want me to do, will you?'

'Sure, Pete and thanks again for pulling out all the stops.'

'Not a problem, Mr Dean. My pleasure. Good night.'

'Oh, by the way, Pete, where did this little fracas take place?'

Pete gave him the address. Gary's stomach did a somersault.

'Oh please, let it be someone else! Not him!' thought Gary.

The ball had started to roll. But in which direction? That was the question Gary was to ask himself many times over the coming weeks.

Twenty Seven

As soon as the computer pinged to let him know that Pete's email had arrived, Gary's somersaulting stomach was in his boots.

'I just know it's going to be him'…and it was.

Clear as day, there was Johnnie getting into the Range Rover.

Gary forced himself to sit up straight in the chair, took a deep breath and closed his eyes and began picking up and discarding possible answers to the two questions which were burning a hole in his brain:

'Why did Jake want to know about what was in the lorry and why was he seeing Johnnie? Forget everything else that's gone on tonight, Gary. Get your fucking thinking cap on and don't take it off until you've work this one out.'

He was still distilling the possibilities when there was a knock at the door of the study.

'Hello?' he said wearily.

'Gary, it's getting late. Are you coming to bed?' asked Nicki.

'Not yet, darling. Still trying to make sense of all of this.'

He was her hero. 'All right, darling but don't stay up too long. You're in Court tomorrow.'

'Oh shit!' thought Gary 'Thank you, darling' he said 'Won't be long. Promise. Goodnight.'

'Goodnight' she said but Gary could hear the reluctance in her voice.

'Is Harry still up?' he called through the door.

'No, he's gone up. Probably asleep by now.'

'Lucky bugger!' thought Gary 'Goodnight then, darling' he called.

Gary got back to the problem in hand.

'So, what've we got? Jake asked about what James Irvine lorries carry. Hmm…if he knew what was on The Bus he wouldn't have had to ask. So…that means he doesn't know'. Gary thought about that hypothesis for a minute. It made sense and he relaxed a little.

'So, why does he want to know? And how is it tied up with Johnnie? In fact, is it tied up with Johnnie or is it just a coincidence?'

Another couple of minutes were spent weighing up possibilities and discarding them. 'Johnnie owes Jake money. Obvious.'

That was when Gary struck gold and why his clients paid him a lot of money to represent them in Court.

'Of course! Johnnie owes him money, so Jake's decided that he can get a better return on his money by…hijacking a James Irvine lorry! So, that's why he wants to know what kind of goods they carry. AND now he's putting the screws on Johnnie…because he wants to hijack the one that Johnnie drives! Of all the unlucky coincidences!'

He sat for a moment, smug with himself about having worked it all out.

'Now, that's the who and the why but we don't know the when and that could be soon because Jake wants me to report back to him asap! Okay, Gary, what're you gonna do?'

Gary sat up late drawing diagrams with Jake at the centre and lines connecting him to Johnnie, to The Bus, to James Irvine, to Gary himself.

By three o'clock, he had made his plans.

'You are gonna be so sorry, Jake. But hey, that's business!'

Within three minutes of his head hitting the pillow, Gary was in the deepest of sleeps. He had solved his problem and it didn't matter who got hurt in the fallout…because it wouldn't be him.

Twenty Eight

While Gary was working on his plan, Jack Clancy was working on his.

He got the boys to make a few calls and find out where that 'little shit', Pete Davidson, hung out.

Being the scum that he was, he was hanging out in 'The Rubber Duck', South London's hottest fetish club. Plenty of business there: the fetishists were known to be big users.

'Might 'ave known he'd be somewhere like that' thought Jack.

'We're gonna pay the place a visit, boys' said Jack to his tooled-up gang. 'But I don't want to spoil Baz's business for him. So, softly, softly and drag the little scrot out discreetly. In fact, I might just give Baz a call and tell 'im about the kind of shit that bastard is selling to 'is customers. I don't think Baz will be too pleased with 'im either.'

Baz Foyle was the owner of said establishment and regular client of Jack's. Liked redheads and big tits. Jack obliged, Baz paid top dollar and treated the girls well. So, there'd be no question of upsetting a paying client.

Jack hung up after speaking to Baz.

'How nice is that? Baz is goin' to invite the little fucker up to his office for a chat an' keep 'im there till we arrive.'

As the black-windowed cavalcade pulled up in front of the club, the head bouncer walked up to the front car's passenger side, waited for the window to roll down and said respectfully:

'Mr Foyle thought you might like to park around the back next to his Bentley, Mr Clancy. It's more private there' he said

'Thanks, Frankie' said Jack from the front passenger seat and slipped him a score.

'Thank you very much, Mr Clancy but there's no need, Sir' the stocky bouncer said as he returned the note. 'We heard about your daughter and the boys asked me to pass on their condolences.'

That was the way things worked in the shadowy world of nightclubs and casinos: staff were always respectful to proprietors of other associated businesses. Mostly because they wanted to arrive home at the end of their shift with the same number of fingers they'd had when they left the house that day and because you never knew when you might need a job.

'Appreciate that, Frankie' said Jack choking back the emotion.

So, they drove around the back where it was quiet and parked beside the Bentley Azure in peacock blue.

'It isn't only footballers who can afford them then' thought Jack distractedly.

The back door opened immediately as they approached.

''Evenin' Mr Clancy. Would you and the boys care for a drink, courtesy of Mr Foyle or would you rather I show you straight up to his office?' asked twenty-five stone of muscle.

'Just show us up, will you, Joe?' said Jack.

The boys began fiddling with safety catches but Jack said:

'Leave 'em on, boys, you're not gonna need them tonight.'

Twenty Nine

Baz stood up to greet Jack and the boys as they came through the door of his…bizarre, that was the only word to describe it, office.

It was full of smokey mirrors, which Jack knew were two-way, leopard skin sofas, rubber outfits for males, females and persons of other persuasions as well as assorted instruments hanging on the walls. Bizarre would probably be the word most people would use who had been there and seen it. 'Baz the Bizarre. It rhythms'. Jack had thought on past occasions but not tonight; his mind had other things to occupy it. On a normal night, he might have shared the joke with Baz, who liked a laugh, but not tonight.

As the broken noses looked around, there was a sense of uneasiness. Some even broke into a sweat, nobody asked why: that wasn't why they were there. But it was bizarre.

Harry wouldn't have recognised the shrivelled-up bag of bones sitting in the corner as the Pete Davidson he had seen earlier that day.

'Jack, sorry about your daughter, man. My condolences to you and your family' said the six feet four, shaven headed ex-Barnado's boy who was regularly mistaken for Tee Hee from James Bond's 'Live and Let Die'. Only ever seen in Oswald Boateng suits, he was extremely charming but no-one who met him was fooled as to what lurked below that surface.

'Thank you, Baz. Just one thing: did 'e 'ave any of that shit he's been puntin' on him?'

'Yeah. This is it, I think. At least this is what we found on him' said Baz, handing over a number of wraps. Jack picked up a couple and stuffed them in his jacket pocket.

Turning to the piece of garbage in the corner he said:

'Is this what my daughter took?' What felt like a spider with ice-cold toes run up and down Baz's spine at Jack's tone.

'I am so…oo…ooo glad I am not in his trainers right now' thought Baz gratefully.

'Yes' was the monosyllabic response.

'You do know that she's dead because of it?' asked the grieving father.

For Pete, all the shit in the world just landed on his doorstep.

'Fuck, fuck, fuck, fuck, fuck' Pete thought as the realisation hit him.

'Well then, Mr Davidson, I think we need to 'ave a little chat. Boys would escort Mr Davidson to the car? We're goin' for a ride. Lovely night for it, don't you think?'

It was rhetorical: no-one felt the need to reply.

And that's when thoughts began to career inside Pete's head like billiard balls bouncing off the cushions. 'Do I scream and probably get a mouth full of broken teeth for my trouble or do I go quietly? Are they gonna let me go or not? Oh, shit! How am I gonna get out of this?'

One of the boys held the scrawny kid by the belt of his trousers; that way he couldn't make a run for it. Unless he dropped 'em and legged it in his boxers. Pete knew that was not a good idea. So he went; like the proverbial lamb.

You could've cut the silence in the lead car with a blunt knife. Pete was squashed like a pressed flower between two overgrown gorillas in the back; Jack sat in the front passenger seat. A strange calm had come over him. It was as if now that he had the killer of his daughter within arm's reach, he could let go, but not yet. Jack needed information.

'Okay, son…' said Jack. This was it.

'I need to know who your supplier is. An' I want 'is name now.'

Jack was so calm the way he said it. You could almost delude yourself into thinking that if you gave him that name, he would let you out of the car. Just like that.

Only then did Pete recognise where he was: a place he'd been many times before in his short, harsh life; the old 'lose/lose' scenario.

If he didn't tell Jack the name, he was dead meat and if he did: he would end up as cattle fodder because the nutter who supplied him was the most ruthless of all of the Mr Bigs of the London drug scene, John Pollock. This guy would put a pillow over his own grandmother's face if she spoke one wrong word to him. Just one word: no more because she wouldn't get the chance to utter another one. No question and definitely no qualms.

'So what's he gonna do to me when he finds out I've told Jack Clancy that it was him who supplied me with the dodgy shipment that killed his daughter? My life wouldn't be worth shit. Well, as of now it 'aint worth shit anyway' thought Pete resignedly.

It must have been catching in that car because suddenly Pete felt the same sort of calm which had possessed Jack not a moment before.

He sighed and said:

'I know you're not gonna let me go. I know that it won't count for anything but I am really, really sorry about Amanda: she was a nice girl.'

In one swift, smooth motion, Jack turned from the front passenger seat and punched his daughter's murderer with all the pent-up rage he had held in up until then. Pete's nose disintegrated. The nice smart suits sitting either side of him were splattered with a mixture of snot and blood.

Jack apologised to the boys.

'I'll get you new ones, gents, if that's okay' said Jack as if he'd accidentally spilt coffee on them.

Pete passed out.

'Damn!' said Jack annoyed with himself for losing his self-control too soon. 'Bring 'im round, will you, boys?'

It took a couple of minutes to revive Pete and when they did, he wished they hadn't bothered. He always knew that he had a low pain threshold but at this point in time he was sure that he would prefer the unfeelingness of death to the feeling he was experiencing now. The pain was so bad he hoped they'd get it over with…and soon.

'Now then, son, I just want you to know that on balance, you're probably 10% to blame. So who's responsible for the other 90%?' Jack sighed. 'Let's get this over now.'

Pete look Jack straight in the eye and said through the stream of blood running into his mouth:

'I'll tell you if you make it quick.'

'Promise.'

'It was John Pollock' offered Pete, a strange sense of calm spreading through him now that he'd said the name.

'Right' said Jack emotionlessly. He wasn't a man to shirk what and who had to be done. There would be no half measures.

'Okay boys, I gave my word. Escort Mr Davidson somewhere quiet and be quick. Tony...' he said turning to the driver '...pull over.'

As the front car pulled over the other one followed. Jack got out alone and walked back to the car behind.

'Drive' said Jack '...I need to think.'

Thirty

The following morning at seven o'clock, Gary Dean was sitting at the breakfast table reading the Times.

Amanda's death was described as being a 'suspected drug overdose'. Sitting alongside the article was a brief column about an unidentified body found on wasteland in North London with two bullets to the back of the head.

As a guy who compartmentalised his day, it occupied his mind for only the briefest of moments as he assumed it was Pete Davidson: 'All squared'. Wrong.

He moved on because now he too had a plan.

Within minutes of reaching the office he'd called Pete Morris to move him off the case.

'Pete, its Gary Dean. Listen, Fitzsimmons went ballistic when I told him you might be off his case for a couple of days. So, can you get back on it again, please? And thanks again for your help. I'll speak to my friend and we'll sort something out.'

'Sure, Mr Dean, I'll get back on it straight away and glad to have been of help' said Pete disconnecting the call while thinking: 'I knew I was on to something last night but it's none of my business.'

Gary's next call was to James Irvine, owner of the haulier company. He put on his kid gloves for this phone call.

'Hello, James?' he said when he was put through to the MD's office.

'Yes. Is that Gary?' just a hint of remoteness in the tone. Part of him was grateful to Gary for rescuing the Company but a much bigger part of him resented being held over a barrel and fucked by Mr Dean.

'Yes, James. Listen I've got a bit of bad news, I'm afraid' began Gary.

'God, what now' thought James '...just when there was a glimmer of light on the poxy horizon'. He asked the question he didn't want to know the answer to:

'What is it?'

'I've heard on the grapevine that one of the lorries is going to be hijacked but I don't know when. The worse news is that it's the one I have for my personal use.'

'Then we should call the police' said James straight away.

'Not quite as easy as that, old chum' replied Gary.

'So what are you going to do?'

'Okay. Here's what I suggest and believe me I've thought long and hard about this, James. What we're...' the emphasis which Gary placed on the 'we're' left James in no doubt that 'they' were in this together '...going to do is: lay my lorry up in the yard for the next week or so, because I think that's when it's going to happen and replace it with one of the others. Then, I am going to call the police and tell them anonymously that a James Irvine lorry is going to be hijacked. I'll tell them that the driver's up to his neck in it. I know this for a fact, James: he's in cahoots with the hijackers.'

James spluttered down the phone: 'That's preposterous, Gary! I would vouch for any of my drivers; they've all been with me for years.'

'I know, James, I know. Believe me, I understand what you're saying but I have proof. Trust me. It's Johnnie Parker.'

'Johnnie Parker?' shouted James indignantly 'Now I know you've lost the plot! That guy's as honest as the day's long.'

'He might have been, James but not anymore. He's up to his eyes in debt to the guy who's going to hijack the lorry. This guy's a moneylender. Johnnie owes thousands'. Although he didn't know this for a fact, Gary assumed that Johnnie would have to owe Jake a hellova lot for Jake to be even thinking about doing this.

'Jesus H. Christ!' gasped James as his hand flew up to his forehead and began unconsciously rubbing his temple. James was in serious shock.

'As I was saying, I'm going to call Crimestoppers and give them Johnnie's name. They will contact you. They'll probably want to set up some kind of surveillance and catch them red-handed but DO NOT TELL ANYONE ELSE ABOUT THIS, JAMES. DO YOU UNDERSTAND?'. Gary said it so forcefully that James had to hold the phone away from his ear. 'Once the lorries have been swopped, leave the rest to the police but keep me informed. Have you got that?'

'Er, of course' replied the shocked owner of one of the most respected haulier fleets in the country.

Once Gary was sure that James had got it, he made his next call to the Freephone number for Crimestoppers.

With a handkerchief over the phone and a very bad attempt at a Scouser accent, Gary gave the information across in a way that would make the listener think that the caller was in fear for their life.

Later when the call was discussed and an assessment made, it was decided that the call could be genuine. The National Crime Squad was informed immediately.

So far, that ball which began to roll was moving in the right direction… at least for Gary Dean…and at least for the moment.

Thirty One

As a fine drizzle fell on those inhabitants of the Capital lucky enough to have a job to go to on that miserable Wednesday morning, a slightly dowdy, unremarkable woman pushed her pram through the back streets of the Elephant and Castle pulling up her collar against the shit weather. With her washing stuffed into a black bin liner on the baby seat of the pram, she looked just like any other working-class South London mum whose husband wasn't prepared to get a washing machine on tick. She entered the laundrette. It was seven o'clock and she was the first customer of the day.

DC Annie Oxley had been playing unremarkable women now for almost ten years. Whenever the category 'working-class skivvy' was required, her name always flagged up. With a hairdryer and a bit of lippie she scrubbed up quite well but on the job, she looked the mess she was supposed to.

And it wasn't only her ability to blend in that made her so useful; she had this amazing mental coin she tossed; some people called it intuition, whatever, it would regularly involve split-second life or death decisions of 'do I/don't I?' and with that even-way bet she always came out on top. Lucky girl.

At that time of day on a rainy Wednesday morning, there just wasn't anyone around; not even legitimate users of the laundrette. So, with consummate ease and expertise, Annie found that Mr Vickers' office had been 'left open'...easily done at the end of a hard day's work. Seven minutes later, the whole place was covered from every angle for sound and picture. After she positioned the last camera, she gave a little curtsy for the boys watching and being a conscientious member of the public, made sure the premises were made secure until the owner showed up.

The whole operation was nearly blown with the unexpected arrival of one of Jake's finders as Annie walked out the door.

'Finished already, love?' asked the finder.

'I wish, sweetheart' she replied thinking on her feet '...I was just about to put the old man's boiler suit in the washer when he phones me screamin' that he needs it back. It's filthy! Wait till I show you this'. Annie started rummaging in the black plastic bag.

'Don't bother, love. I can imagine' said the finder wrinkling his nose at the thought of it as his eyes were drawn to the door of the newly locked office.

'Might see you later then?' said Annie with a hint of promise in her voice.

The finder took one look at the ragbag standing in front of him and the stud in him couldn't resist the challenge 'Definitely, princess. Definitely.'

'Right then, lover. I'm off' said Annie who contained her urge to either vomit or leg it out of there like an Olympic sprinter. The finder held the door open for her and gave her bum a slap as she passed.

Annie turned to him as she exited the launderette and said through gritted teeth:

'Ooooh! I'll bet you can be a naughty boy when you want to be!'

'Try me, princess! Try me!' he said leaning against the door frame in that 'I am the man...an' you're gagging for it' pose.

As she walked the three streets to where the observation truck and an unmarked car were parked, Annie fumed.

'I'd rather attend my own funeral, you dirty scumbag!' she thought furiously.

Turning frequently to make sure she wasn't followed, she saw one of her colleagues get out of the unmarked Vauxhall and in one smooth motion, without a word, relieved her of the pram, shoving it in the boot.

Moving on to the truck, she raised her fist to rap on the back door when it was opened and she was beckoned in.

Chief Superintendent Peter Moore, who was running the obo, was sitting in front of a bank of screens, latte and chocolate croissant in hand. Annie looked at the figure appearing on the screen and recognised her pal, the finder, who was closely inspecting the contents of his nose, balanced on the first digit of his right hand, like it was some Page Three bird.

Sitting next to the Chief sipping tea from a takeaway cup, was Sgt Jim Wallis, the Chief's right-hand man.

Peter Moore was just about to take a serious lump out of the croissant when the finder got bored with just observing and decided to… 'Aaaghh!' said the Chief 'In all my thirty years of service I've seen the lot. Woundings, decomposition…death in every shape and form. But that!' he said, pointing to one of the screens '…that…really turns my stomach. Yuk!' and with that he threw the rest of the croissant into the nearby bin.

'An' I nearly pulled 'im!' said Annie in disgust. 'Jesus! Are there no decent pullable men left on the planet?' she asked no-one in particular.

'Well, there's always me' said Jim Wallis.

'That's what I mean…' replied Annie '…no decent men!' and laughed.

All eyes were on the screens as the sound of a new arrival came across on the microphones.

'Mornin' Dave' said the newcomer to the nosepicker.

'Mornin' Gerry. What's happenin' today?'

''Parenently, the boss is getting' the shooters from Frankie Duffin later. So, what d'ye think about this job? I mean, it's nuffin' like anyfink we've ever done before. Friday, innit?'

'Yeah, Friday mornin'' replied the nosepicker. 'I 'ope there's not gonna be any trouble or anyfink like' said Dave the nosepicker. 'I mean, I went to school wif' Johnnie Parker an' he's not a bad bloke…just a bit of a loser. Sad bastard. Still, he owes the boss and when you owes it, you's gotta pay up or be quick on yer tootsies!' They both laughed.

All eyes were now glued to the screen as the Chief made a call on his mobile.

'Hello, Sir, Peter Moore here'. There was a pause as he listened. 'Yes, Sir, we've got contact with them. DC Oxley got a wire in the premises. We have sound and picture' pause again '…the reason I'm calling, Sir, is that we'll need to get SO19 involved' pause '…that's right. I've just heard one of the perps say that they're collecting guns for the job today. At the moment, the job is supposed to be taking place Friday morning' pause '…yes, I appreciate that we haven't got a lot of time but we've only just been passed the information by an anonymous informer within the last 24 hours.' Long pause '...I'll get onto it right away, Sir.'

He hung up and the team could see that he was not a happy man.

'Trouble, Sir?' asked the bravest of them, Jim Wallis.

His thoughts interrupted, the Chief said:

'Er...no, just a lot of organising before the job goes down, Jim'. Hoisting himself up from the chair, he sighed and said:

'I'm going to have to speak to the people at the haulier company. What the boss wants is SO19 in the back of the lorry ready for when they open it up to transfer the goods. In between times, I'm in court this afternoon. Oh, and while we're at it, could you shove that brush a bit further up my arse and I'll sweep the streets of old London town while I'm running around from one job to the other?'

When he finished speaking, no-one said a word. Suddenly, everyone was concentrating on nosepicking Dave and the other toerag who was boiling the kettle. Jim Wallis was really interested that Dave had put two spoonfuls of instant coffee in his mug.

One very pissed off Chief Superintendent finally let out a sigh and said:

'Right, I'd better get started while you lot keep an eye on this lot'. He jerked his thumb towards the monitors as he went to leave. 'Keep me up to date with any new developments will you, Jim?'

'No problem, Sir. You go and get the other stuff sorted out and leave this lot to us.'

'Thanks, Jim' and out the door he went.

'Creep!' said Annie Oxley to Jim Wallis.

'Why are you saying that? You know what the old man's like. He's not so good at taking the pressure anymore. Anyway, you can talk! Fancied the nostril inspector, did you?' and they all laughed.

'Oh, fuck off!' said a very miffed DC Annie Oxley. Even when she was made up she didn't get that many offers and he wasn't that bad looking. Fucking men.

Nothing much happened until Jake Vickers walked in with a holdall... and it wasn't full of dirty laundry.

The listeners heard what they'd been waiting for: confirmation of the date, time and place where the job was going down. It was to be the Cobham Services on Friday morning at 0830. Jake made it clear that Johnnie Parker would roll over.

'Early start, then' thought Jim Wallis impassively.

Calls were made at the highest level of New Scotland Yard. Liaising was left to the lower ranks. When guns were involved, everybody got a bit jumpy; public opinion, bloody Health & Safety and all that.

Thirty Two

Chief Superintendent Peter Moore was put through his paces in Court that afternoon by the defence. The Chief tried, unsuccessfully, to convince the defence brief and the jury that his notes were indeed an accurate account of the events of the night in question.

To make matters worse, it wasn't the first time that Chief Superintendent Moore had crossed swords in the witness box with this quick-witted pain in the derriere of a defence lawyer. Everyone there could sense the tension between the long-serving police officer and Gary Dean. Problem was: Mr Dean had won more than he had lost against the Chief.

'I think you're splitting hairs, Sir' said the police officer frustratedly.

'Oh, I think not, Chief Superintendent' replied the lawyer in a mock resigned tone as he raised his eyes from the file in front of him.

Not long after this verbal duel, the jury acquitted Gary's client and the lawyer left the Court for the day with one definite guilty verdict (couldn't be avoided -- the client had admitted it out of remorse), one deferral for a psychiatric report and the acquittal under his belt.

He turned on his mobile to find that he had several voicemails. Impatiently, he waded through them, mentally placing them in order of importance.

The first one to be returned would be to Jack Clancy. His message was simply: 'Call me.'

Then, a very worried sounding James Irvine would be next.

The rest could wait.

Jack's mobile rang. He picked up before the first ring had finished.

'Hello, Jack?' said Gary, wondering what the bombshell was going to be this time.

'Hi Gary' said Jack, giving nothing away in his tone this time. 'I need a job done. Can you get your man to call me?'

'Sure Jack. Anything I can help with in the meantime?' asked Gary, fishing.

'No thanks. Just need your guy to call asap.'

'Sure. I'll get on to it straight away.'

'Thanks, I'll wait for his call' Jack hung up.

'Hmm, maybe that wasn't Pete Davidson this morning after all but it looks like his number's up now though.'

Gary looked up Sham's latest mobile number on his Blackberry and dialled.

'Sham? It's Gary here. I've got a client who wants to have a word with you.'

Gary passed over Jack Clancy's details and then forgot all about it.

That ball was beginning to gain momentum…but not necessarily in the direction Gary Dean thought it was going.

He made his next call.

'James, hi! Got your message. What can I do for you?'

James told him exactly what Gary had expected. Namely, that the police had had confirmation that the hijack was on and that they were placing SO19 inside the swopped truck.

Gary smiled to himself as he hung up on James. He was back in control. But what really made Gary smile was that he would probably end up getting the job of defending the soon-to-be in custody, Mr Vickers.

While Gary was smiling and giving himself a pat on the back, Chief Superintendent Moore was walking into the CID office at the station in a particularly filthy mood.

'That bastard of a defence lawyer got me again! The most insignificant fuckin' detail and he manages to get an acquittal out of it'. He slammed his briefcase on his desk with a 'Grrr!'

'We'll have him next time, boss. Don't worry' offered his sergeant, Jim Wallis who'd returned to the office and left the others at the obo.

'I wonder if we will, Jim. I really do wonder sometimes' asked his boss, looking him straight in the eye.

The Chief was like this every time they lost a case against a villain that they should have won easily: he always took it personal.

But then again, that's why his clients hired Gary. He would always find that grey area where he could concentrate the jury's attention. For

Gary, the result was what mattered; it was the way you got there that didn't.

Thirty Three

Sham hung up from Gary and rang Jack's number.

'Hello' said Sham in his softened Irish brogue when Jack answered 'Our mutual friend said you needed me.'

'Yeah. But before I say anything: are you sure that this line's safe?' asked Jack.

'Absolutely. I use a new number and phone for each job. Keeps us all safe.'

'Fine' said Jack wanting to get down to business 'I need a job done quickly. It's not going to be easy. So, how quickly can you do it and how much will it cost?'

Sham heard his mentor's voice in his head: 'PPT. Patience. Preparation and Timing.'

'Whoa, there mister! Hold your horses! The honest truth is I don't know. You'll have to give me the details. Then I'll check the lie of the land so to speak and when I'm sure it can be done, I'll come back to you with the cost and the timing.'

'Okay, no name. Here's the deal. I need this done in the next couple of days an' I'll pay you double your normal fee. No questions.'

Sham sucked air through his teeth.

'Sounds like you want this to happen fast and bad' said Sham, who, truth be told, was up for a challenge.

'Spot on' said Jack and let the silence hang for a full minute, waiting for Sham's reply.

'Okay, okay. Tell me who and where they can be reached and I promise I'll come back to you later today with a yes or no.'

'Fair enough' said Jack and he passed over John Pollock's details.

'Jesus! Couldn't ye have found something a bit harder?' joked Sham. 'Isn't he a bit...?'

'An' the rest! Too much for you?' goaded Jack.

'Listen, my friend, you're talking to the best but even I need time to assess a situation. Hmm, leave it with me and I'll call you later.'

'Okay. I'll wait to hear from you.'

'Before you go, just one thing: my fee for this will be thirty thousand, if I decide to do it' said Sham.

'Thirty grand?' repeated a stunned Jack 'Our mutual friend said your normal fee was ten.'

'That's right but you've given me less than two days to set it up and you know the kind of security that there will be surrounding this individual. It's not going to be easy' replied Sham.

'Yer on!' said Jack who would have paid fifty, a hundred grand if necessary to take out the scumbag who had killed his beautiful daughter. 'Do it.'

'Wait! I need to check things out first. But if I can do it, I need paying up front, delivered to our mutual friend before the job.'

'Understood. I'll have it ready. Just one thing…' said Jack.

'Here we go' thought Sham but he said 'What's that?'

'I want it done in a particular way' Jack proceeded to tell him.

'You really want to make a point, don't you?' said Sham.

'Make the point an' shove it up 'is arse wrapped in barbed wire if you get my meaning' said Jack, allowing his toxic, feral rage out of its cage for the briefest of moments.

'I get the message and I've a feeling that he will too. But that shouldn't be a problem. Goodbye' said Sham as he disconnected the call.

Jack hung up to make his next call: to Gary. The number was busy. Gary was speaking to James Irvine. Jack put it on re-dial and a minute later he was speaking to Gary.

'Gary when can I catch The Bus?' Jack asked when Gary answered.

'Call you back in five' said Gary. He knew the deal had been struck.

It appealed to Gary's warped sense of humour that Jack would be collecting the fee from The Bus and delivering it to Gary at the office. Not long after that, Sham would pick up the money and return it The Bus and neither one of them knew that they both used the same facility.

'Perhaps I should offer a broking arrangement, transfer of fees etc' he mused. 'Hmm, but then again, maybe not. Better they don't know about the arrangements I have with each of them.'

In the meantime, Sham put the essay on hold which he was supposed to hand in the following week: 'The World Bank and Its Relevance in Today's Markets'.

'The world needs economists and I need to find a way of stashing my undeclared income. So why not combine the two?' thought the boy who was determined to get a degree to supplement his real job. Or cover for it.

Thirty Four

As Gary was checking out the times of the next Bus stop, a client was mounting the stairs of The Bus. It was none other than John Pollock, purveyor of dodgy designer drugs.

He was, to Freddie's mind, the most frightening guy he had ever come across in his life. Freddie couldn't even bring himself to make eye contact with the geezer. This guy was so tough it was like his tattoos had tattoos.

Pollock, for his part, barely acknowledged Freddie's presence: the only person in the world that mattered to him was him. The rest of humanity was there to serve his needs: men, to do his bidding and women, to service his 'other' needs. Anyone else was surplus to requirements and hence was dispensibly expendable. Except maybe the two Rottweiler sisters, Babe and Frankie, who seemed attached to either side of his thighs by invisible chains. They might have meant something to him; but then again, maybe not. Frankie was named after the woman who brought him into the world; most people would refer to her as mother but the contempt that he felt for her was such that he named a dog after her.

For the last twenty years, he had fought, maimed and killed his way to the top. And no fucker was gonna alter that situation...as in no fucking body.

There were many tales of his ruthlessness in circulation: his latest being the brutal, public execution of Peter Barrett. However, that was nothing compared to the episode where a small-time dealer had tried to stitch him up.

The guy took three days to die: unofficially, that is. For the majority of that time he was unconscious. And in those brief moments where his brain brought him to any sort of level of consciousness, he experienced the worse pain that any human being on this planet could face.

The vat of acid he was hung over ate through his skin and muscle at a rate of two inches every four hours as the timing device Mr Pollock had had set up specially for occasions like this, slowly lowered his body into the corrosive liquid. After seventy-two hours, what was left was unceremoniously dumped into the vat.

The dealer knew things weren't good when he was picked up from his lodgings and taken to one of Mr Pollock's drug warehouses. For hours he was left dangling over the vat. After the first two hours, he began to think it was just a warning, that he'd be let go: which was exactly the way Mr Pollock liked to play it. 'Let them think it's going to be okay'. The cruellest way of all: false hope.

It served to broadcast to the world at large his message, his mantra: 'Do not fuck with me!'

And not very many people did.

This was his regular trip to deposit the week's takings. Business was good. Life was good but there was something else on his mind that day. Something that had been fomenting for a while in the deepest recesses of his brain; something that he had told no other living human being: he was thinking of quitting the business. But there was no way he was going to let ANYONE know until after he had legged it because the internecine war that would follow was one he could do without being involved in.

The long hours of ducking and diving, the beatings, the endless sleepless nights, agonizing about the next one who thought they were hard enough to take him, were getting to him finally. He'd made his pile: now it was time to enjoy it.

The date he had in his head to disappear was only six weeks away. He'd already put a deposit down on a private plane to take him…and four very large suitcases, away. He hadn't decided where yet…he would leave that till the last moment.

Sometimes he'd find himself daydreaming about who would take over and who would kill who and who would… '…what the fuck am I fuckin' thinkin' about? I don't give a monkey's tit who gets it or who fuckin' wins. They can ALL fuck off.'

And when he got to the end of that particular thought, he would smile and his henchmen would look at each other. The most they would venture would be a raised eyebrow, anything else might get the boss' attention…and you didn't do that unless you were either brave or stupid.

Freddie watched the black-windowed 4x4 driven off at speed by the client with his two dogs in the rear as he locked up and returned to the cab of the lorry to eat his sandwich and wait for Johnnie to return.

Johnnie had seemed quiet over the last couple of days.

'Probably 'is missus givin' 'im grief' Freddie chuckled to himself. When he finished eating, he settled down to get a bit of kip. 'Got another twenty minutes before Johnnie boy gets back.'

When Johnnie arrived, Freddie was fast asleep. 'If only,' thought Johnnie ruefully '…it's gonna be a long time before I get a good night's kip again.'

Even winning the hundred quid on the latest bunch of scratchcards hadn't cheered him up. In fact, it had barely registered. But one thing had registered: he'd be driving a different lorry the next day. Mr Irvine said that the other one needed servicing. 'A bit like me, I think' thought Johnnie trying to raise his spirits but not quite getting there.

'Ah well, 'ere we go!' thought the man who had agreed to roll over for Jake Vickers in a couple of days' time. But at least Mr Vickers had agreed to one condition: young Freddie wouldn't get hurt. He didn't mind getting slapped about a bit himself to make it look right '…but leave the kid alone. That's it. An' I'm off the hook. We're all square? Right? I don't owe you anymore. Agreed?' Jake Vickers had spat in his hand and shook on it but only because Gary Dean had come back earlier to tell him the good news that the cargo on a James Irvine truck was usually worth between £100K and £200K.

'I'll be fuckin' quids in!' thought Jake who had already collected five grand on the five hundred quid which Johnnie had originally borrowed. 'There's a mug born every minute and I've been lucky enough to meet most of them in the South London congregation. Hmm, I like that' he thought '…a congregation of mugs!'

''Ere, Freddie! Waken up, you lazy bastard! I don't know…' said Johnnie climbing into the cabin '…young 'uns these days 'aint got no staying power.'

'Don't you believe it, old man' said Freddie, stretching the stiffness out of his joints 'Bring on a bevy of beauties and I'll show you who's got the STAY...ING POW...ER!' jerking his elbow upright to resemble a 'stiffie'.

'Yeah, right' said Johnnie returning, at least temporarily, to his old self '...an' then you woke up.'

They both laughed. Freddie was pleased to see Johnnie back on form. 'Let's hope it lasts' he thought.

Johnnie turned on the engine, got it into gear and released the air brakes.

As he manoeuvred the truck away from the parking lot, Johnnie began to sing: ''Ere we go, 'ere we go, 'ere we go!'

'I wish you fuckin' would an' all!' said Freddie laughing

'Your mother was right, you know' said Johnnie ruffling Freddie's hair with his left hand '...you really are a cheeky little fucker!'

'I know! That's why ya likes me!'

Just another work day, nothing special until Johnnie pulled out onto the motorway. He had barely gone two hundred yards, just beginning to get up a good head of steam when out of nowhere, this old red Ford with foreign number plates doing over a hundred flew across the motorway from the outside lane to the inside one without indicating. Was it racing another car? Was it chasing or being chased? Who knows? But suddenly, brakes were screeching all over the place. Then it happened.

Later, Johnnie would say to Freddie:

'Why is it always the kids who suffer?'

About five cars were involved in the pile-up.

Because the driver of the light blue family saloon in front of Johnnie's lorry couldn't see what was happening in the three outside lanes, he was slow to react. But Johnnie, from his elevated position could, so he started braking...hard. Just as well, otherwise the family saloon would have been history. But it didn't stop the family saloon being hit by the car in the second lane who'd had to swerve into the inside one to avoid the car in front of him that had suddenly slammed on its brakes.

Chaos and mayhem erupted with bumpers and glass and rooftop suitcases flying across bonnets and strewing their contents all over the four lanes of the motorway, bringing it to a complete halt in seconds. It could have been much worse but some of the drivers behind the chaos saw what was going on and had the time and nous to hit their hazard lights, warning other drivers behind them to slow down.

Johnnie managed to pull over on to the hard shoulder and reached over to get the first aid kit from behind the driver's seat.

'Come on, Freddie, there are kids in that car' said Johnnie, pointing to the light blue saloon 'Better see they're all right first.'

Freddie caught Johnnie's arm before he got out the door. 'Johnnie!' he shouted 'You know we're not supposed to stop!'

Johnnie halted in his tracks. He was stunned.

'I can't ignore injured people, Freddie. Kids! For God's sake! Kids! What would you want people to do if it was one of yours? What if we were in a crash? You'd want them to help us, wouldn't you? I can't just drive away!' said Johnnie vehemently.

'I know, I know' agreed Freddie but in his panic, he thought 'But what are we supposed to do? What will the boss say? Jesus!'

Johnnie didn't wait to hear what Freddie had to say; he just rushed over to the saloon.

The car which had swerved into the inside lane was a Toyota Prius; it had caught the saloon sideways on. The front of the Prius was locked into the driver's side door of the saloon. The Prius driver appeared to be in shock but relatively okay.

When Johnnie looked in the saloon, the driver had caught a lot of the impact. He was slumped unconscious over the wheel: his forehead had hit the windscreen; the airbag hadn't inflated properly and blood was pouring from his injury profusely. His smashed glasses were sitting at an awkward angle with one leg hanging off. He was definitely an ambulance case.

What Johnnie presumed was the mother, was in the front passenger seat. The airbag on her side fortunately had worked and absorbed most of the impact. She looked okay but stunned.

It was the kids. The baby's car seat had been on the driver's side at the back where most of the impact had taken place. The baby was quiet, no movement, no screaming, which Johnnie would have preferred; it was as if it was asleep.

The other child, a little girl with a blood-soaked ragdoll still held in her hand was unconscious, blood seeping all over her pink Disney character dress.

In the few seconds it had taken for Johnnie to take all of this in, Freddie was at the other side of the car shouting to Johnnie:

'What should we do?' Freddie had never seen, let alone been in, a multiple car crash before. He was hopping from one foot to the other, clearly distressed. This was not what Johnnie needed. His attention should be concentrated on the injured not the walking lame like Freddie was turning out to be.

'I don't think there's a lot we can do here. Whatever you do, don't move anybody. They'll have to wait for the emergency services. 'In fact,' said Johnnie trying to make Freddie feel less guilty about it '...I don't think there's anything you can do. Why don't you go back to the lorry and wait for me there?'

Before Freddie could answer, the mother came to and started to panic.

'Oh my God! My baby! My baby!' she called. 'Mark, darling!' Nothing. 'Lily...!' she shouted at the little girl with the ragdoll. 'Are you okay, baby?' No answer. 'Lily! Mark!' she shouted at the driver. 'Mark! Oh my God! What's happening? Please, help me' she pleaded as she collapsed into hysteria.

'What's your name, Mrs?' asked Johnnie. 'What's your name?' he repeated to gain her attention.

'Emily' she whispered.

'Well, Emily' said Johnnie gently '...you have to stay with us. So, don't close your eyes, love. You have to stay awake until the ambulance arrives. They'll need to ask you about your husband and the children. Do you understand?'

The noise of traffic was still deafening because the other side of the motorway was still going full pelt. But Emily had heard him and nodded.

'Good' said Johnnie soothingly, 'Now, do you think you've broken anything?'

She shook her head.

'How are you feeling?'

'…er…a bit sore.'

'That's good' said Johnnie sympathetically. 'We're just going to go and check to see if we can help anyone else. It's best if you don't try to move your husband or the children. Okay? Stay in the car. The ambulance will be here soon.'

Emily became hysterical again. 'Please don't leave me! Please…help us! My babies! My husband! Please!' Johnnie reached into the car and put his hand firmly on her shoulder.

'You've got to be strong, Emily. Maybe it would be better if you get out of the car and my friend here, Freddie, will help you over to the verge and sit there quietly until the ambulance arrives. Would that be okay?'

'But I can't leave my...!' She began.

'Trust me' said Johnnie 'I've been driving a lorry around motorways for over twenty years and there's nothing I haven't seen. The best thing you could do now is to sit quietly until the emergency services arrive. Okay?'

Emily nodded and Johnnie signalled to Freddie over the roof of the car to come and help her get out of the car.

When they'd walked away a short distance, Johnnie knelt on the seat she had just vacated and checked for a pulse with the driver. It was there but faint.

'Where the hell are they?' he shouted irritably 'Where're those bloody ambulances?'

Next he leant across and checked Lily. The little girl moaned as he touched her.

'Thank God for that' thought Johnnie even though the sound of her moan pierced him.

The baby was gone.

'Didn't stand a chance, poor little fucker' No marks but no pulse.

'Who's gonna tell the mother? Jesus, I'm glad it's not gonna be me.'

Suddenly, for Johnnie, his financial situation didn't mean a thing. He hung his head; partly in respect, partly in shame.

'It's only when you come across something like this that you realise the stupid situation you've got yourself into is so unimportant' he thought.

Johnnie got out of the car and looked around. All the other cars had people tending to them, so he decided to wait there.

Less than five minutes later a trio of ambulances escorted at the front and back by police vehicles with lights flashing and sirens blaring arrived at the scene via the hard shoulder.

One of the ambulance crew ran over to check out the injured in the saloon. Emily started to get up with Freddie's help to come back to the car.

'Freddie just wait there with Emily a minute while I talk to the ambulance guy, will you?' said Johnnie flapping his hand by his side to indicate to Freddie to keep her away just now.

Emily sat down again completely overwhelmed by what was happening. There was no resistance: she was totally compliant.

'Aw'right mate? It's not good. We've lost the baby, the little girl's badly hurt; I don't know how badly. And the husband's pulse is very faint and he's lost a lot of blood. The mother seems okay, badly shaken from what I could see. Is there anything else I can do?' asked Johnnie.

'Best thing you can do, sir' said the ambulance man '…is give your details to the police and clear your car…'

'Actually, that's my lorry back there' replied Johnnie.

'Even better. When you move, it'll be easier for us to get the worst of the injured to hospital. Looks like we need to call in the air ambulance.'

'Okay, I'll give them my statement and then move out of the way.'

Johnnie gave Freddie a sideways nod to leave Emily, who was out of it anyway, and they made their way over to one of the police cars.

Having given their statements, the policeman said:

'I know you guys have tight schedules to keep…'

Freddie thought: 'If only you knew!'

The policeman continued: '...so there's no need to hang around. Better get back on the road because this stretch is going to be closed for a long time. But thank you for your statements, gentlemen, we'll be in touch.'

As he steered the lorry through the wreckage Johnnie heard a heart-rending shriek. He and Freddie just looked at one another. 'Poor bastard' was all Johnnie could say.

Freddie dialled Gary Dean's number to fill him in.

Thirty Five

Gary was reading through a file relating to his next appearance in Court when the telephone rang in his desk drawer.

His attention was still on the file when he answered.

'Mmm, hello' he said his eyes and attention still on the document.

'Boss, it's Freddie. There's been an accident...'

'An accident?' said Gary sitting bolt upright 'What the hell happened?'

'We weren't involved, guv. There was a pile-up in front of us as we left the service station. We tried to help some of the injured but there wasn't really anything we could do.'

'Freddie, you're not supposed to leave the lorry. Suppose the police arrived and wanted to take a look in the lorry? Oh my God, I suppose the police were there? Jesus!' The thought hung in the air making Gary feel dizzy as he considered the consequences.

'Look, boss, I'm in the cab with Johnnie, so I'm gonna say what I have to say in front of him. We know the procedures and under normal circumstances we would never leave the lorry. But there were kids involved and...and a baby died. It was only a few months old. It was ...' Freddie's voice tailed off.

Gary had two ways of handling this. He could either go ballistic, which he normally would, or let it go this once. He decided on the latter.

'Okay, okay. No harm done this time. But let me tell you, Freddie: Don't ever and I mean EVER do that again! DO YOU HEAR ME?'

'You got it, boss' said a contrite Freddie. 'You're absolutely right an' I'm sorry.'

'Matter's closed, Freddie. But make sure Johnnie knows what he has to do otherwise next time he'll be parking up outside the dole office. Then, YOU won't be getting a 'get out of jail card' and HE won't be collecting nuthin'! Have you got that? Have I make myself clear?'

'Absolutely, boss, sure' was the reply.

'Call me if there's anything else. Oh, did everything go okay today?' Freddie knew what the boss meant.

'We're on schedule, boss' was his coded reply for Johnnie's benefit to let Gary know that there had been no mishaps with the client's visit.

'Right. Speak to you later' and Gary was gone.

'Jesus! Has the man no heart?' exploded Johnnie. 'What if it was his kid? Would he want us to drive on and just wave?'

'Can I make a suggestion, Johnnie? Just leave it. Leave it, mate. I know how you're feelin' but there's no point in gettin' yourself worked up about it. So better just to leave it there'. He patted Johnnie's shoulder, the way mates do to one another, when they're trying to ease their friend's pain.

For the next couple of hours they fell silent, lost in their own thoughts and feelings about what had happened back there.

Thirty Six

Gary sat there motionless after he hung up, the file lying on his desk forgotten, his mind churning over everything that had happened in the last couple of days.

The police had called around to interview Harry about Amanda's death but went away satisfied that he knew nothing. The fact that her father was one of the biggest whoremongers in London had either not popped up on their radar yet or, more likely, they knew, but were playing it low key for the moment.

The phone call from Jake Vickers had set alarm bells a-ringing. But that was under control for the moment.

Within twenty-four hours of Gary's call to Crimestoppers, the police had placed a wire in Jake's launderette. They'd already heard him announce that the job was going down in a couple of days. Or, at least, that's what the police had told James. So, Friday it was.

'Good job that I arranged for them to swap the lorries around at the end of their shift tonight' thought Gary.

He paused as he shuffled the papers scattered in front of him on the desk.

'Hmm. Sham's doing a job for Jack Clancy, so there's the usual commission due there' he thought getting back to business. 'That bank job the boys pulled has been relegated to the inside pages. The heat's off them for now, at least while the police are chasing their tails looking for the loot and clues'. The thought of the police running around in circles still tickled him pink.

'I wonder how much more difficult it would have been for them if I hadn't told them that I had arranged John Stubbs and Jeffrey Bowman's wills? Which reminds me: I must find out how John is and send some flowers. He's going to need me to represent him if the bank doesn't agree to let him take early retirement. Poor bastard's been put through the mill and all they can do is jerk him around. Such is life!' he concluded without any sympathy.

Life, according to the thoughts of Chairman Dean, was full of knocks: you either roll with them or join the losers, you chose.

'Where was I? Oh, yes. Hmm, Mr Pollock's still making his regular deposits on The Bus, so business must be going well for him'. While he was 'in the zone', Gary just let his thoughts flow.

'Could this be the right time to start expanding and offering The Bus' facilities to some of my other clients?' Gary mentally ticked off the names of potential users.

And then the latest two clients to use The Bus came to mind.

He would be in contact with one of them later in the week but from all accounts, business was booming. Certainly, Gary's offshore account was receiving regular payments in, always a good sign from that client.

The last one was the only client he regretted making The Bus' facilities available to.

Gary had heard the many comparisons made between this client and Peter Rachmann of 1950's slum landlord fame. But as far as Gary could see they had only two things in common: ownership of the same first name and their chosen line of business.

No. It wasn't his line of business or working methods that Gary took umbrage at. Not at all. Gary had no objection to anyone charging exorbitant rents or using a bit of muscle to move on undesirables or troublemakers. The moniker 'undesirable' was given to those tenants who fell behind with the rent and had no hope of bringing their account up to date. Troublemakers were those who '…had the fuckin' cheek to ask for a rent book' because they'd popped into their local Citizens' Advice Bureau for a chat, to then inform Mr Fitzsimmons, or 'Tick-Tock' as he was secretly referred to by his tenants because he was 'a walking, talking, fucking time bomb', that what he was doing was 'not strictly legal'.

No. No. It wasn't that. All his working life Gary had dealt with hard nuts but always respected anyone who could make a shilling; dishonest or otherwise. Over the years, his hard nut clients confided in Gary about the kind of tactics they'd used against 'the enemy': be they competitors, grasses or those who thought they were clever enough to get away with stealing from the boss. No. In that line of business 'you throws the dice and you takes your chances' was Gary's motto.

Nor was it the fact that he was hiding his assets on The Bus to protect them from the wife who had finally plucked up the courage to divorce the bastard.

No. Gary's revulsion stemmed from the fact that Mr Fitzsimmons was a good old-fashioned wife-beater. A close number two on Gary's shit list to child molesters. He had always declined to represent paedos and those brave men who took delight in beating the crap out of their missuses. It was an unwritten rule at his law firm that cases of child molestation and domestic violence against women were verboten. In fact, it was one of the few things Gary was keeping up his sleeve for when he got up to those Pearly Gates. 'But Boss, I refused to even look at their cases. Surely that must count for something?'

No. The only reason he was involved with Peter Fitzsimmons at all was because Tick-Tock had already wheedled his way in before confessing to Gary one day that he had a penchant for using the wife as a punchbag. The urge to throw him out of the office, preferably via the window, was overwhelming. It took Gary all his time not to throw up as Tick-Tock gleefully related the latest episode, where his wife ended up having to have both cheekbones re-built; but by then it was too late. Tick-Tock knew the secrets of The Bus. So, all Gary could do was to keep contact with the creep to a bare minimum.

The file Gary had been studying slipped to the floor scattering the loosely inserted pages all over the place.

'Bollocks!' he thundered, coming out of his reverie. As he stooped to pick up the fallen documents, the internal phone rang.

'Anything else?' enquired Gary to the world at large as he lifted the phone. 'Yes?' he said into the mouthpiece.

'It's Chief Superintendent Moore' announced reception.

'What does he want now? I hope they're not gonna be on the phone every five minutes about Amanda' thought Gary as he said: 'Tell him I've left for the day and could he call back tomorrow or if he prefers, I'll call him. Oh, and ask him what it's about.'

Gary held as 'bird brain' went off to ask the question.

'Please could you call him at your earliest convenience, he said and he'll tell you what it's about when you call' was the useless answer from Raquel.

'Thanks' said Gary '...for nothing!' he thought as he replaced the receiver.

He sat for another few minutes scanning the pages in front of him but he knew the outcome of this one before he left the office: another no show. No shows meant a bundle of dough but a load of grief from whichever old codger was sitting on the bench that day.

'Still, everything's got to be paid for' sighed Gary inwardly '...and those regular payments into the offshore account definitely make listening to those old farts droning on, more bearable.'

Thirty Seven

Frustrated, Chief Superintendent Moore hung up on Raquel and put a call into his sergeant, Jim Wallis, the dour, hard-nosed Scotsman with twenty-two years of service, who had returned to the obo. He went straight into one when Jim answered his mobile.

'Why, oh bloody why, do lawyers never take your call? They've always got some excuse or other to avoid speaking to you there and then.'

'Guilt, I expect' replied the Scotsman distractedly as he took a swig from his umpteenth cup of tea of the day.

'Guilt?' said Peter Moore surprised by the response. 'But he doesn't even know what I'm calling about.'

'That's part of the reason why he won't take the call. He feels guilty about representing the scumbags, sorry, the clients that he does. But also, lawyers don't like surprises, whether it's in Court or out. At least that's what a brief told me once an' I've never forgotten it. So, I'm guessin' but that's probably why he wouldn't take your call.'

Sgt Jim Wallis had less than three years to go before he hung up his warrant card to retire to a small island off the West Coast of Scotland, Rothesay, to run a B&B with his unmarried sister, Jeannie. He'd never married himself: couldn't find the girlfriend prepared to put up with his long hours on the job. The daytime job, that is.

And at the day job, there were those who secretly thought that Jim Wallis suffered from OCD. Every single day, his first job when he got to the nick was to draw a line through the previous day on the five-year calendar he had pinned up inside his locker two years previously. He didn't care what any of them thought of it. He couldn't wait to return to the 'Auld' country and to people who spoke proper English.

As he thought of this, he let out a long sigh.

'What was that for?' asked Peter Moore 'And what's going on down there?'

'Nuthin'' was Jim Wallis' reply. He didn't want anyone to know how maudlin he'd become recently. They might think he'd gone soft.

'Jesus!' said Peter warming to his subject 'We've got our hands full, haven't we, Jim? I thought this was supposed to be the villains' holiday time? My old dad used to…'

'Oh God, not a 'my old dad used to say' story, please!' thought Jim resignedly as his eyes began to glaze over.

'…God rest his soul. You know, Jim, he drove a black hack for over thirty years before he retired and the old ones used to call the winter time their 'kipper season'. That was when all the taxi drivers disappeared after New Year. Couldn't get a cab for love nor money' he remembered fondly. 'An' I always think of this time of year as being our 'kipper season': the bastards 'ave got the kids off school an' they usually piss off to the Costa del Crime to mix with their own an' plan next season's heists. Instead, we're run ragged at the moment with this hijack that Jake Vickers is trying to pull off. Now what's he up to? Why doesn't he stick to his own area of expertise? Out of his depth, if you ask me. Then there's Jack Clancy's daughter. Mind you, that looks like it was an overdose: Mr Clancy's not gonna be too pleased. An' the reason I was trying to speak to that brief, what's 'is name?' Jim heard his boss shuffling his paperwork '…oh yeah, Mr Dean! I should know that name by now. He's the one who…' the Chief's tone changed '…will you stop ramblin' on you, Peter Moore?' he said suddenly, annoyed with himself. 'Jim, stop me when I start to ramble, will you? I don't know what's happenin' to me. Tired I suppose'. It was his turn to sigh.

'And what was that for?' enquired Jim, turning the tables on his boss. 'Ye probably need a break, Guv' he continued 'But don't go to the Costa del Crime just yet. It'll be like takin' yer work on holiday with ye.'

They both laughed.

'Thanks for that, Jim' said his boss who was chortling like a schoolboy, letting go of all the crap that had been hitting the fan at a rate of knots recently.

It was just what they both needed; a break from the daily stress of dealing with the less humane side of humanity.

When he had gathered his wits about him again, the Chief continued:

'Anyway, I needed to speak to that brief because eight of his clients have gone AWOL over the last couple of months. So, while its quiet' and they both laughed again '…I thought I'd ask him a few questions.'

'Good idea, boss. But think about what I said. Ye need a rest.'

'You're right. I'll put in for some leave. Not long to go now before I retire. How long have you got? Can't be long for you, Jim.'

There was the briefest of hesitations before Jim answered:

'Two years, nine months and twenty-one days. Of course, that's not including the hours, Guv.'

'Right!' said the Chief 'Er…right' was all he could say. He'd no idea how long he himself had to go but it was quite a bit less than that.

'That's not too long, is it, Jim?'

'Not sure, Guv. I'm getting' a bit tired myself' replied the Scotsman honestly.

'Well don't you be putting in for leave the same time as me otherwise the long arm of the law will be two, or is that 'too', short?' A short laugh from the both of them this time for they knew that they'd had their respite from whatever the day held for them.

'Ah well, Guv. Better get me nose back to the grindstone. I'll let ye know if there's any movement.'

'Cheers, Jim. Speak to you later.'

Chief Superintendent Moore and Sergeant Wallis both hung up and sat quietly for a few minutes deeply engrossed in their own thoughts.

Chief Superintendent Moore was the first to put his thoughts to one side: he couldn't dwell on them for too long: the nick was buzzier than a beehive on a warm summer's night.

Thirty Eight

Little did the two policemen realise as they spoke that neither of them would be going anywhere. In the near future, all police leave would be cancelled for the foreseeable. But then, no-one could have predicted what was about to happen.

Two days. That was all Sham had to put this operation together. Truth was: it excited him.

He had been following the mark for several hours now and, unsurprisingly, his security was as tight as a virgin's and just as difficult to penetrate. So, no different then to most of the hits he'd been called upon to perform in the old country. He loved the challenge; that and the thirty grand.

But everybody as in EVERYBODY has a weak spot; that time when their guard is down and the bodyguards are more than three feet away. This was the hardest part of the job; finding that 'window of opportunity' as the boys in marketing call it. And boy would he need that for this operation; bearing in mind the client's request concerning the 'how'. There was nothing magical about it: just PPT. Patience, Preparation and Timing. And when Sham found that little chink in Mr Pollock's security he would be right in there.

Sham waited close to the Range Rover with the darkened window. From the firm handshakes of the guys emerging from the darkened club, Sham assumed some sort of deal had been struck. He waited until he saw John Pollock get in and held back until the car pulled away from the curb. Only then did he pull on his helmet, tucking his ponytail up at the back and mounted the old 50CC he kept 'specially for jobs like this. 'Totally nondescript' would be most people's recollection of the bike and its rider. 'Just some yobbo on a bike that looked like it didn't have no MOT.'

Sham fell in behind them keeping a discreet distance between himself and the blacked-out car full of black-suited geezers. Nobody took a blind bit of notice of the clapped-out bike and what looked like a scrawny teenager driving it, except the occasional eco warrior tut-tutting at the pollution spewing out of the back of it.

Earlier on, Sham had received a call from Gary to tell him that his fee had arrived at the office.

'He's definitely keen' thought Sham 'Maybe I should have asked for forty. Hmm, but then, you don't want to go pricing yourself out of the market all together now do you? No' he thought '…thirty will be grand. That is, if this bastard opens his legs.'

The thought hit him like the famous 'phantom punch' from Muhammed Ali and nearly sent the bike skidding from under him.

'Of course, that's it! You're a fuckin' genius, Michael! That's how you do it! So, I'll leave him alone for now and check out his routine tonight. That's when it's gonna happen' and Sham hit the indicator and veered off to the left down a side street.

As the car sped towards the next rendezvous, the minders sat in silence, waiting, hoping that the boss would break the silence but Mr Pollock preferred his own thoughts, so silence reigned.

Thirty Nine

Sham made his way to the offices of Gary Dean & partners and collected the package which had been left on reception for him by Gary.

As he left, Raquel checked out the 'rear' view and told Julie that she thought Sham was cute. But there again, Raquel was the sort of girl who thought tigers were cute.

Thirty grand in used readies. How could he turn down a job that offered him more than three times what most people took home in their wage packet in a year?

The client, as he'd discussed with Sham, included the little extra in the package. So, Sham could now do the job and do it exactly as the client wanted. His reputation would be…'Well, let's put it this way,' thought Sham as he carried what he was already thinking of as his thirty grand out to his bike '…when the details of this hit get out, I am gonna be in demand. And how! If I can pull this one off the Universe, let alone the world, is gonna be my Dublin Bay oyster!'

Before he drove off, Sham pressed re-dial on his mobile for Jack Clancy. It was answered on the third ring.

'You were quick' said Jack.

'I said I'd get back to you today and I always keep my word.'

'Well?' was Jack's monosyllabic question.

'You've hired the best so the answer is…yes.'

'Make the bastard suffer and call me when you've done the job' and Jack hung up.

'Jesus' thought Sham as he looked at his mobile. 'An' I thought I was short an' to the point but yer man takes the biscuit.'

He waited for a lull in the traffic and then pulled out to keep his appointment with The Bus. Next stop after that was home and then out for a spot of nightclubbing. It had been a while since he had combined business with pleasure.

Forty

As Gary drove home, the ringing in his ears from the lambasting he'd received from Her Majesty's arsehole on the Bench was beginning to subside. His eyes were watching as commuters jockeyed with each other to get home one car length earlier, but his brain was performing somersaults inside his skull.

He was thinking about ten things at the same time. In particular, there was the conversation he'd had with Mr Huq. The Mr Huq, that is, who was attached to the Visa Section of the Pakistan High Commission. The conversation took place minutes before they'd entered the Courtroom, without the client in tow...again. This guy had qualified from UCL with a First in Light Engineering but his real talent lay not in the forge but in forgery. Or, to be more precise, the manufacture of excellent, almost undetectable, forged passports: a very useful guy to know in certain circumstances.

Gary and he had a very nice working arrangement where Gary would pass the details of his clients from other countries that were close to being deported on to Mr Huq who would then contact the client offering salvation...or at least, that is what they were led to believe initially.

Gary's commission, based on the client's acceptance of Mr Huq's conditions, was paid immediately into Gary's offshore account. Up until today, everything had been hunky-dory and a good time had been had by all. But the conversation earlier today had changed that.

'Turns out our Mr Huq has more twists to his personality than a Uri Geller fork' thought Gary grimly.

They had originally met when Gary represented a Pakistani national who was about to be deported by the Immigration Service. Gary had looked through the paperwork and there wasn't a kitten's chance in Hades that the client would be allowed to stay: not even with the redoubtable skills of Mr Gary Dean. So, Gary was more than a little puzzled when the client came in for a final case review, all bouncy, bubbly and full of smiles.

'You don't seem to be too concerned Mr Sharif. You do realise that the judge will probably make an order of deportation with immediate effect.'

The client nodded his head, still smiling.

'Jesus!' thought Gary. 'What's this guy on? He's been fighting extradition for nine months and now that it's crunch time, he's got a bloody great grin like a Cheshire cat spread all over his face. What's that all about?' but he said:

'Perhaps you don't realise the seriousness of your situation, Mr Sharif?'

The client just smiled then said:

'Am I right, Sir, in thinking that whatever I say to you, my esteemed lawyer, is confidential?'

'Totally, Mr Sharif' said Gary returning the smile while he thought: 'If nothing else, I'll find out why he's got a smile like a MacLeans advert.'

'I won't be going home, Sir. Oh no, no, no.' replied Mr Sharif with an air of smugness as he clasped his hands over his ample stomach.

'I'm sorry, Mr Sharif. Didn't you understand what I said?'

'Oh, very much so, Honourable Sir, but my countryman, Mr Huq of our High Commission has made special arrangements'. The last part was said in a conspiratorial whisper as he leaned closer, nodding his head several times.

'Well that's good to know, Mr Sharif. And am I allowed to know what these special arrangements are?' asked Gary whose antennae were twanging like a Hawaiian guitar.

'Completely confidential?' asked Mr Sharif shifting uneasily in his chair.

'Scout's honour' responded his confidential lawyer.

'Well, Mr Huq has arranged for me to be…the proud owner of a European Union passport which he tells me means that I would be entitled to stay here in your wonderful country indefinitely. Is that not truly sublime, dear Sir?'

'It is, Mr Sharif, but slightly illegal. Perhaps I should have a word with Mr Huq' said Gary but thinking: 'This could turn out to be a nice little earner.'

He wasn't wrong.

Not long after their first conversation, a verbal agreement was reached to both parties mutual satisfaction.

Since its inception, the agreement had worked extremely well for them and soon after, Mr Huq was delighted to be invited to join the elite group who had access to The Bus. And he had taken full advantage of its facilities; making regular, large cash deposits. He was, in fact, The Bus' most frequent visitor.

Secretly, he liked the clandestine rendezvous arrangement with The Bus: he felt like a cold war spy even though he was no James Bond lookalike.

The venture became so successful that Mr Huq didn't make it into the office a lot these days. But suitable remunerations in the right hands kept that problem at bay. So busy was he that he practically had to turn business away: the thought of which nearly made Mr Huq cry. If it wasn't for the large numbers of high denomination notes deposited on The Bus each week, he probably would've.

But just as someone, in the dim and distant past, had to work out that two plus two equalled four, someone else had to be responsible for solving that other important conundrum: what happens when excreta makes contact with a fan? Because that's exactly what was just about to happen to this little arrangement.

'If my offshore account's correct, the little fucker's making a fortune! So now he's decided that he doesn't just want to sell them the passport; he wants them to work it off. Good idea but where's my share? Is that it, I pass the client on to him for a fee and he takes the rest? I do not think so' thought Gary, angry at the unfairness of the situation. 'I should bloody well get a bigger cut'. Gary decided to leave that problem alone for the time being while he considered the more pressing matter of Mr Vickers and his hijack.

'What's gonna happen with that? Jake will go spare when he opens the rear of that lorry and finds SO19 waiting for him! Je...s...us! And he'll probably think Johnnie Parker's grassed him up. Hmm...I'd better clear Friday's diary and tell Nicki I'll be home late for dinner that night. It's gonna be a long one.' For a few minutes Gary enjoyed the juxtaposition of the situation. Not only had he shopped Jake to the police: he'd be the one representing him in Court.

'Nice one, Gary' he laughed to himself. 'If only you could do that with all your business associates, you'd be laughing all the way to the offshore account!'

Forty minutes later, he reversed into the driveway of the house; he always liked to park the car pointing outwards in case he needed to make a quick getaway.

'God I'm whacked with all of this going on. Thank God we're in tonight; it's gonna be a long, long week.'

Twenty minutes later, he was washed, changed and sitting watching Sky News as he sipped a well-filled glass of Rioja which Nicki had thoughtfully opened earlier. It would be a long time before Gary felt so relaxed again. A very long time.

Forty One

As Gary sipped his wine appreciatively, pushing the soft, plush black leather chair into the recline position, Sham was pushing open the gate to the Victorian semi where he lived with his mother and father not far from the Dean residence physically, but about two million quid financially. The motorbike was nowhere to be seen: it was only used for official business and was kept hidden away.

At breakfast that morning, his mother had announced that supper would be served at eight o'clock that night and '…if Michael could fit it into his hectic social calendar, it would be lovely for all three of us to sit down and eat at the same time and place for a change'. In other words, 'be there' was the underlying suggestion.

When he got indoors, Sham made a couple of calls to friends who were party animals and discovered that Mr Pollock used 'The Library', one of the hottest dance clubs in south London, near the Oval, as his local.

His last call was to Harry to persuade him to come out '…for a few jars' but Harry was still in mourning for Amanda and spent his time skulking about the house, hardly stepping beyond the door of his room. It had been only a few days since she'd died. So, Sham let him be and decided to reconnoitre the place without Harry as his camouflage. Camouflage: one of the essentials in his line work.

Mr Pollock, he was informed, attended The Library every night.

But before Sham went out he had to get through supper with the parents; an unusual event at the best of times given the horrendous hours they both put in at the hospital.

After the 'So what have ye been up to?' and 'How are yer studies going?' and then of course, their favourite old chestnut, 'Are ye stepping out with anyone at the moment?', the topic of conversation that evening finally turned to Amanda Clancy.

'Ye knew her, didn't ye, Michael?' asked his father as he carved up the roast beef as though he was at the operating, not dining, table.

'Yeah' was Sham response, hoping that would be an end to it. Some hope.

'I was on duty the night the body came in' said his mother picking up the topic '…thank God, I was dealing with an elderly patient who'd taken a fall. It was Mary Mitchell who dealt with the body. She said she'd never seen anything like it. The body was…'

'Mum, can we leave it there, please?' asked Sham abruptly 'I know you and Dad like to discuss work over supper but I did know the girl and we are eating. Can we talk about something a little cheerier, please?'

Both parents looked at each other. That look which says: 'Not now but we need to discuss this further.'

Torturous though it was, Sham, or as he was referred to that evening, Michael, managed to extricate himself from the family home without any further Gestapo-style interrogation.

Forty Two

As he reached the front door Sham heard the music for the ten o'clock news come on. He quickly closed the door; he didn't want to be delayed by more questions if there were any new developments on the news about Amanda's death. He was off to check the lay of the land at The Library.

The Library was the brainchild of one of the many dropouts from Uni; this particular dropout's name was Frankie Warner. Frankie's hard-working working-class parents would give him a hard time when he told them that he was going out clubbing instead of studying. So, he came up with the idea of The Library. If asked, his clientele could say truthfully that they were going to the library; if the parents thought their offspring were keeping their noses to the grindstone, what right did anyone have to correct their misconception?

By the time Sham got there, the place was already buzzing. He went to the bar and bought a Bud. To anyone seeing him, he was just another cool young guy chilling out; the latest bum-freezing jeans with the Calvin's on show for those who wanted to check the label out, T-shirt which looked like it had been massacred in the washing machine, de rigueur hoodie which could have been H&M's or Versace completed the outfit. The ponytail was down, hair obscuring his features. He needed anonymity tonight; he was not on the pull.

Taking his time, he discreetly checked the place out, keeping in mind his old instructor's motto, PPT: Patience, Preparation and Timing.

Each time that acronym surfaced in his consciousness, Sham was transported back to that first meeting in the staunchly Republican bar, Feeney's, on Winter Street with Sean Lennon, the IRA commander who taught him everything he knew about the art of assassination. 'Those three little letters will save your scrawny little fuckin' neck one day' he had told Sham. Sean didn't know the word 'acronym' let alone how to spell the fucking thing. 'PPT' became Sham's mantra and so far, Sean had been spot on.

But for this job the mantra had been discarded like last night's takeaway: '…thirty grand is thirty grand and that's a fucking lot of money' replacing the mantra.

He looked like he was chilling out but his mind was charging around like a Formula One racing car: calculating the odds, anticipating the pitfalls, building in contingencies. Should he carry a weapon or not? If he did, it might just give him those crucial few seconds needed to make a getaway. But, if he got caught with it, he would surely be a dead man. In the end, he decided against it. That decision having been taken, he put it out of his head and concentrated on the next logistical hurdle.

He did three dry runs, timing them from start to finish. There was a variation of eleven seconds: he could live with that.

The next part of the plan involved the first part of the mantra he'd temporarily discarded for the sake of thirty grand: patience.

He found himself a vantage point on the mezzanine level overlooking the target area. Leaning on the polished chrome rail, Sham looked like any number of guys, checking out the talent down below.

Forty-five minutes he waited. A couple of girls and guys tried hitting on him, but tonight was business, not pleasure, so he passed politely and resumed his watch. Except for the one guy who was on something so didn't quite hear the edge in Sham's voice when he said 'No, thank you'. That is, not until Sham motioned him to come a little nearer. Looking into those cold, piercing green eyes, he did manage to hear the 'No' this time…and knew that Sham meant it. He decided to finish his trip elsewhere.

Finally, the patience paid off: Mr Pollock arrived. Six muscleheads cleared a passageway to the bar. Strolling behind them in his violently shiny blue Versace suit complemented by a white open-necked starched shirt was the shaven-headed boss with two massive unleashed Rottweilers in tow. Casually ignoring the mass of sweating bodies around him, Mr Pollock reached the bar just as the bodyguards 'politely' moved on some of the patrons.

'Usual, Mr Pollock?' asked the unfazed barman. There were some pretty scary people came into the club, mostly friends of the owner, Frankie Warner. The barman was used to them and their funny ways.

An upwardly dismissive jerk of the head was the reply as Mr Pollock spread his eyes around the place, checking out...whatever it was he might be looking for on that particular evening. Sometimes he would be making sure that the pushers were doing their job, others, he would be deciding whose luck would be in that night. Thirty seconds later, a large Glenlivet with a small jug of water were placed on a clean bar mat in front of him.

'So you're the John Pollock' thought Sham to himself from his vantage point on the mezzanine. Unbeknown to Sham, this was the man who had ordered and paid for the hit on Peter Barrett. Sham had killed upwards of forty people since his apprenticeship with Sean Lennon, so, John Pollock didn't frighten Sham. But from the looks of him, Sham could see why Pollock deserved his reputation.

'A seriously hard nut...' thought Sham grimly '...but not for very much longer. We all have to die, Mr P, but the how and the when we do, doesn't always necessarily tally with how we would want the most momentous occasion of our lives to take place. So, my friend...' he said, toasting John Pollock with his Bud '...savour your favourite tipple and...the last forty-odd hours of your sad life.'

'Sad' definitely was not what John Pollock was feeling. His thoughts as he looked around the dance floor at the gyrating bodies were of sheer anticipation:

'...I cannot bloody wait. Only six more days and I'm off!" He'd decided that he couldn't last another week, let alone five, and had brought forward his 'last day of work'.

'I'll grab the final bit of dough and then I'm free of shitholes like this forever'. His face, though, remained completely impassive: no-one could or would ever be able to read John Pollock.

His henchmen, in the meantime, continually scanned the club looking for undercover police and nutters. Sometimes it was difficult to tell them apart but whichever they were, it was their job and their lives on the line if they got it wrong.

'PPT' was still in play…for another thirty minutes. It was then that the situation which had nearly knocked the motorcycle from under Sham earlier on in the day, occurred.

Mr Pollock went to the john. Sham noted, as he had hoped, that John Pollock left his henchmen and his dogs outside when he went for a piss. 'Good so far' thought Sham. And then, the piece de resistance: the bodyguards stopped anyone from entering the toilet. 'Gets better all the time.'

Sham started the timer on his watch. He needed to know how long he had. Five minutes and eighteen seconds. Plenty of time…if…and Sham knew it was a big fat IF…that was how it happened every time.

Straightening up and stretching, in that way which says: 'I've had enough. I'm going home', he made his way down to ground level. But in what would've appeared to an onlooker as someone who had just taking a reading on his bladder only to decide that he wasn't going to make it home; he pushed his way through to the loos.

He went into the 'sit-me-down', as his granny in Ireland used to call it, put the lid down and sat there listening carefully to the comings and goings of the club clientele. Not a lot of chat, mostly guys doing what they had to do and then going: very few washing their hands. 'Dirty bastards' thought Sham.

So, it wasn't that busy but…and again that big fucker of an IF…that's what it was like the rest of the time, it was definitely do-able.

He'd find out in less than two days' time.

Forty Three

With Friday fast approaching, Chief Superintendent Peter Moore was like a bull in a ring with a couple of bandarillas stuck between its shoulders.

He was not best pleased at the drain on his resources and budget when very little was now being gleaned from Jake Vickers office.

'If I see him pick his nose once more I'm going to puke in your mug!' declared DC Annie Oxley disgustedly.

'Ye wonder where it all comes from. I mean, look at that: his finger must be inside his brain!' said Sergeant Jim Wallis, grimacing at the sight on the monitor in front of him as he took another sip of tea from his mug. Nothing put Jim off his tea.

'Yuk, Jim! Do you have to be so graphic? Anyway, why are we still here? We know when the job's going down. So, why don't we just up sticks and get on with something else?' asked Annie.

'Word from on high apparently. Because shooters are on the cards, they don't want anything unexpected to happen and then for the papers to get hold of it. They do not want any more flak from the tabloids.'

A knock at the door halted the conversation. Jim looked out the spy hole and saw his boss waiting there. 'Hmm, still no sign of a smile' thought Jim sarcastically as he opened the door of the van.

'Mornin' Sir! Everything alright?' asked the Scotsman as he let him in.

'No it's bloody well not, Jim. This damn obo is costing me a fortune. My budget for the year is practically blown already. Anything happening in there?' he said nodding towards the monitor.

'Nuthin'' replied the Scotsman '...except I think Annie's lookin' to do a degree in nosepicking. He...' said Jim pointing at the figure on the monitor '...has not had his fist out of his nostrils since I got here' he looked at his watch'...and that's nearly two hours ago. Isn't that so, Annie?'

'Jim, please!' begged Annie 'No more! I will vomit in your cup, I will!' she threatened.

'Alright, you two. Alright' said the Chief testily 'I know it's boring but the powers that be have insisted. Right' he continued wearily, 'I'd better get back to the station and see if there are any new developments there. Cheers! See you soon. If there's any developments, give's a shout, will you, Jim?' and he was out of the door mid-blink for Annie.

'He's a quick mover for his size, isn't he?' said Annie, surprised by the Chief's speed.

'Faster than ye'd think' agreed Jim Wallis. 'Right then, let's get back to studying for yer degree' he joked.

'I'm warning you, Jim! One more word…!'

Forty Four

It's late Thursday night and Dave Cosforth, the leader of the bank robbers had called a meeting at his house. The missus was sent packing to bingo. Their next job was on for the following morning.

'Now, you're all sure you know what you're supposed to be doing in the morning?' asked Dave, scanning the faces seated around the kitchen table.

'I'm at the lockup at six o'clock, Dave, checking the bikes and the shooters' offered Markie Morgan.

'Check' said Dave.

'And I'll be parked at the far end of Denton Road by the waste ground at nine forty-five, Dave' said Mikey Malone the taxi-driving pickpocket. 'I'll have the helmets, suitcase and paints all ready for when you guys get there.'

'Check' replied Dave as he turned to the final member of the gang. 'Are you with us, Bron? You look like you're somewhere else.'

'Er, sorry, Dave. Yeah! I'll…yeah, I'll be at the lockup by seven an' stop off on the way to pick up a grenade from my gran's house.'

'Fuckin' 'ell, Bron, how could you do that to your own gran! 'Aint you got nowhere else you could stash 'em, mate?' said Mikey in disgust.

'Shut it!' ordered Dave. He did not want a debate about morality, tonight of all nights.

Mikey looked peeved but did as he was told.

'It's the best place in the world, Mikey' continued Bron trying to justify himself. 'She's ninety-two, deaf as a doorpost an' I'm the only one that ever visits her.'

'Yeah, an' if she ever finds the fuckin' things she could blow herself an' the rest of the neighbourhood to kingdom come.'

'But…' began Bron.

'I said SHUT IT!' screamed Dave. 'We've got more important things to worry about. Now let's go through this once more an' then get ourselves to fuckin' sleep because we're gonna need it.'

When Dave was sure that they all knew what they were supposed to be doing, he pulled a bottle of scotch and four glasses from the cupboard above the sink, pouring them all a generous tot and made a toast.

'Here's to a nice clean job tomorrow, boys!' toasted Dave.

'An' showing the cops a nice clean pair of heels...' laughed Mikey.

'...an' of course, a nice clean crime scene...with no dabs' finished off Bron.

'I'll drink to that!' the others chorused 'Cheers!' and they all downed their drinks in a oner and slammed the glasses down on the table.

Meanwhile, in another part of the Borough not twenty minutes from Dave's house, another Dave, Dave the nosepicker, was sitting fidgeting in Jake's office. He'd been elected to ask the question on everybody's mind.

'Boss?' began nosepicking Dave nervously. No-one questioned Jake's judgement.

'Yeah?'

'If this job's all sewn up, why're we carrying shooters?'

'Because I cover all angles, Dave. Yeah, Johnnie Parker isn't gonna put up a fight but you don't know about his sidekick. An' you don't know if some stupid fuckin' member of the public might decide to 'ave-a-go. So, we go in tooled up. Anybody else got any questions?'

Silence.

'Then that's it. Andy, you an' Jimmy'll be at the warehouse. I'll call you two minutes before we arrive. Do not open the doors until I call. Yes?'

'Yes, boss' they replied.

Jake had many friends who would loan each other, for a price, whatever was needed: muscle, guns, explosives, places where goods could be stored discreetly. Questions were never asked: answers wouldn't be given anyway. 'Right, I'll see the rest of you here at six o'clock an' DON'T BE LATE!' yelled Jake, like he needed to. 'Oh, an' Pete, did you get that stuff I asked you to get?'

'Yeah, boss. Here it is' and handed over a tightly-wrapped plastic bag which Jake instantly shoved into the inside pocket of his jacket.

It was on the tip of Dave's tongue to say: 'What've ya got there, boss?' but managed to stop himself in time: a smack in the mouth did not appeal.

'An' Pete?'

'Yeah, boss?'

'Make sure the van's got petrol in it? I don't want to have to stop off to fill up. You know all them petrol stations have got CCTVs an' I do not want to be appearin' on Crimewatch next week. Capiche?'

'Got it, boss!'

'Good' replied Jake. 'See you in the morning an' let's make ourselves some serious wonga.'

For the first time that night, the other five members of the gang broke into grins and shouted: 'Yeah, let's do it!'

The police caught it all on tape.

At the same time, another tape, the CCTV tape at The Library, caught Sham as he walked in that Thursday night. But then again it recorded close to a thousand other people who walked through the door that night.

And Sham wasn't stupid. He faked a sneeze and blew his nose as he entered the CCTV's viewing area: there was no chance of identifying him from that image. Camouflage: the name of the game.

From the previous night, he knew the layout and hopefully the routine. He casually ambled over to the bar and bought a beer.

'Well, this is it' he thought. 'If I've got it right, Mr Pollock should be here...' he checked his watch, '...very soon.'

In less than five minutes, the said Mr Pollock strolled in like he was King of the Castle.

'Yer a feckin' genius, Michael' he thought as he took a slug of beer.

After Mr Pollock's grand entrance, Sham made his way to the 'sit-me-down' in the loo where he kept a watch through the crack in the door. The boys came and went; still didn't wash their hands. Finally, in walked 'Mr Thirty Grand' as Sham was beginning to think of him, John Pollock, to take his nightly piss. Sham watched, timed and smiled.

'Yeah, yeah, yeah!' thought Sham as Pollock left the loo. 'This is doable. Thirty grand in my hand. Ye...e...s!' he whispered to himself as he made a fist and punched the deodorised air.

Before he left the cubicle, he turned the reversible hooded jacket he was wearing outside in. Now the CCTV camera would show some kid with his black hoodie up instead of the kid who came in wearing a white one with it down. Camouflage, which in turn leads to confusion: the assassin's friend. As Sham was sitting on the throne waiting for John Pollock to point Percy at the Porcelain, Gary Dean was brooding in his study. It was no good. He had to speak to the man; otherwise, it was just going to fester. He checked his watch, ten o'clock: he dialled the number.

'He...llo?' said the voice at the other end of the phone hesitantly.

'Good evening Mr Huq. Sorry to bother you so late. It's Gary Dean. Is it convenient to speak?' asked Gary in his best professional voice.

'Er...er, yes, Mr Dean. What can I do for you?'

There was no way Gary would speak about it directly over the phone.

'I was wondering if you could spare me half an hour tomorrow for a chat?' said Gary.

'Certainly, Mr Dean. May I ask what it is about?' enquired a nervous Mr Huq.

'I think it would be better if we talk about it when we meet, Mr Huq' said Gary, the need for discretion clearly coming across in his tone. 'It's about the arrangements we have.'

'I see, I see' said the hesitant diplomat. Gary could almost hear Mr Huq's brain whirling around at the other end of the phone.

'Half an hour should cover it' said Gary as casually as he could: the fear was trickling down the line and oozing out of Gary's earpiece.

Finally, the voice at the other end of the phone said: 'What sort of time did you have in mind, Mr Dean?'

'About ten o'clock? Would that be convenient?' Gary had decided to have the meeting on Friday morning because he'd previously cleared his diary and he didn't want Jake or the police thinking that he was sitting around waiting for their call.

'That will be most convenient, Mr Dean. So, your office at ten o'clock tomorrow. Yes?'

'Yes, thank you Mr Huq. Goodnight and again apologies for calling so late.'

'No problem. Goodnight to you, Mr Dean.'

So ended a normal Thursday evening south of the River Thames.

Forty Five

Friday morning four o'clock. The briefing room was packed.

Chief Superintendent Moore surveyed the room. There were fifteen of his own men in civvies as well as twenty SO19 in full riot gear for 'Operation Shylock', so named in honour of Mr Vickers' line of work. The top brass were taking no chances.

The Chief stood on the rostrum with the man in charge of the SO19 team, Inspector Paul Morrison. The Inspector was a man of few words, forty years old and well-known as a rock-solid leader and supporter of his men: he didn't take kindly to people who tried to fuck with his team. And when twenty–two stone of muscle on a six-feet four frame didn't take kindly, people had a tendency to do as he 'requested'...unless they had spent many, many years cultivating their stupidity or were so off their tits on drugs or booze that living was no longer at the top of their priority list.

As he surveyed the room, the noise, a mixture of testosterone and bravado, was deafening. Before he spoke, a brief thought passed through the Chief Super's consciousness: 'Bloody years I've waited to nab this bastard and now he's handed to me on a plate. What a swansong!' smiling to himself, he cleared his throat and called out:

'Listen up you lot! You all know what we've got to do. And remember: they're armed, so, no heroics, please. Our lords and masters do not want to be attending any funerals. Especially yours! They're busy enough, bless their little cotton socks'. Laughs all round. Chief Superintendent Moore turned to his fellow officer on the rostrum and asked:

'Inspector Morrison, any last words of wisdom for the troops?'

'Thank you, Chief Superintendent' responded the quietly spoken policeman '...just to say, please wait until they've opened the doors of the lorry and we've got the situation under control. Then, they're all yours, gentlemen. At the moment, we have an ETA on the lorry of 0830 hours. Good luck!'

A cheer went up. There were a lot in that room who'd waited a long time to see Jake Vickers in a prison uniform: most would've given up their overtime pay and done it for free just for the privilege of being there when he got nicked.

'Right!' said the Chief 'Anyone who's entitled to carry, sign your weapons out: the rest of you, get yourselves down to the yard, saddle up and let's get nicking!'

SO19 travelled in convey to the James Irvine yard: they were let into the yard by the nervous owner of the company, James Irvine himself.

Unnoticed by Inspector Morrison as he checked and re-checked that his team were safely tucked up in the rear of the lorry, James' gaze kept returning to a lorry parked up not twenty yards away from where the Inspector stood.

James didn't know, and indeed did not want to know, what the lorry, or as the cognoscenti called it, The Bus, contained. For him ignorance was not bliss but a way of mentally blocking out what Gary Dean was up to with the name 'James Irvine' emblazoned on the side of it.

When Inspector Morrison was satisfied, James closed the back doors of the lorry plunging the members of the SO19 team into total darkness and silence. He left the latch off the lock on the doors so that they could be opened from the inside and returned to his office to await the arrival of Johnnie and Freddie who would be clocking in soon.

As far as Johnnie and Freddie were concerned, the lorry was carrying a normal load. Only Johnnie, or so he thought, knew that it would never reach its intended destination.

In the meantime, the Chief and his lads made their way to the Cobham Services and parked their five unmarked cars in the public area. The time was five o'clock.

According to the videotape, the hijackers were due to arrive at the service station at seven o'clock in one single van. Johnnie and Freddie were scheduled to arrive at the services at eight thirty.

A number of unmarked police cars were in position along the route to take over surveillance of the van and keep everyone informed of the villains' progress.

The team in civvies spread themselves out in the various all-night restaurants at the services, mingling with the early starters who'd already begun to arrive looking for some sustenance to kick start their day.

At eight minutes to seven, the call went out: 'Shylock now approaching destination'. The hijackers' van was turning into the lorry park. For a few seconds, the van stopped just inside the entrance. The lack of movement made the Chief Superintendent jittery.

'Come on. Bloody move! What're you up to?' asked the Chief from the top of the service building where he'd decided to oversee the operation. 'D'you think they're on to us, Jim?' he asked his Scottish sergeant, who was standing next to him, anxiously.

With his eyes glued to the night vision binoculars, Jim spoke without turning to his boss:

'Patience, boss: they're just gettin' their bearings, that's all. Relax.'

Jake Vickers could be seen sitting in the passenger seat looking at a piece of paper which, Jim assumed, was a map of the area where Johnnie Parker would be parking the lorry. Jake's hand jerked to the left and the van began to move towards the far left-hand corner of the service area. Once there, the lights and engine were cut.

With his own night vision binoculars pressed so hard against his eye sockets that it hurt, the Chief eyed the figure of Jake Vickers when he turned to speak to the guys in the back of the van. Without any warning, Jake pulled what looked like a sawn-off shotgun out of a holdall.

'Shit!' uttered the Chief who'd assumed it would be hand guns only: the whole team heard it through their earpieces. Spooked, he spoke directly into his walkie-talkie:

'Get someone up here with a directional microphone now! I want to know what's being said in that van.'

Five minutes later, the mike was pointing at the van and the familiar voice of Dave the nosepicker was being transmitted over the noise of the increasing early morning traffic to the entire squad's earpieces.

'...so Charlie, me and Stan'll go an' have a sniff around in there an' see what's 'appenin. Yeah?'' he said flicking his thumb towards the restaurant area of the services.

'Yeah. An' if there's anythin' suspicious AT ALL, let me know. Got it? AT...FUCKIN'...ALL! If not, see you back here in fifteen minutes' said Jake roughly. 'An' another thing...' the boys looked at each other nervously, '...there's only one thing worse than looking like one...an' that's smelling like one. I don't know which one of you it is but when you get your share of the dosh today, treat yourself to a bar of carbolic an' some clean clothes. Now fuck off and get on with it'. As the boys started to get out he turned to the others still in the van and shouted: 'An' will someone open a window? It smells like fuckin' Billingsgate on a bad day in 'ere.'

As the three villains walked towards the services, each of the boys in the van surreptitiously tried to sniff their armpits. It was Friday: bath night. You were bound to get a little whiffy towards the end of the week. What was the boss' problem?

The night vision binoculars couldn't pick out the sweat cascading down Jake's back but from the edgy sound of his voice, it was clear that the adrenalin was starting to overload his system and that, in the Chief's experience was when things could go wrong.

The next voice the squad heard was the Chief Superintendent's.

'Okay, gentlemen, you've got about two minutes to do one. These guys know what they're looking for. Skedaddle!'

An orderly scramble was made with the team flashing their badges to sleep-deprived cleaners, cooks and shop staff, who were all preparing for the day's breakfast traffic.

They all made it with seconds to spare except one: PC Frank Hare known in the squad as Bunny. For those first few precious seconds after the order went out, he decided to gulp down the cup of scalding hot coffee he had just purchased. Bad move. Very bad move.

As he sped through the atrium, he could see the gang through the giant plate glass windows walking towards the main entrance. Bunny panicked and dived under the shutters of a newsagent's which were just rising.

'Police!' he whispered urgently to the young shop assistant, showing her his badge. In a flash of inspiration, he pulled off his jacket and said to her:

'Let me stand at the till.'

By this time, the three gang members had entered the building and were looking around casually; the way people do when they're looking for the loo.

'You check upstairs, Charlie, an' me and Stan will give down here the once over' said Dave.

As Charlie made his way up the stairs, Dave and Stan began eyeing everybody up, looking for anything out of the ordinary: they'd had their fair share of dealings with the police. They knew what to look for: the shoes, the body language but always, always, the eyes. Most ordinary people look at you and then look away…but coppers eyes lingered just that fraction longer; just enough for them to clock that little bit extra something about you. That was the giveaway. That's how you spot a copper: that's what they were looking for now.

Dave clocked the newsagent's shutters going up and decided to buy some chewing gum. He wasn't able to indulge the first finger of his right hand, not in front of the boys, so he thought he'd buy some chewing gum to take his mind off the burning itch up his hooter.

As he walked in, the first thing his beady eyes noticed was the mini-skirted bum of the pretty, young female assistant leaning over cutting the plastic string on the piles of today's newspapers. For a split second, the temptation was there to use one of his famous chat-up lines and then he remembered what he was supposed to be doing. If Jake ever found out…he shuddered and moved over to the counter, picking up a packet of spearmint-flavoured gum.

'How much, Chief?' he asked Bunny. The young female assistant, whose name badge carried the legend 'Happy to help – Just ask!' and the name Jo, straightened up and looked at Bunny in alarm.

As it happened, Bunny didn't have a fucking clue but he'd scanned the wife's shopping often enough at the supermarket, so he said to Dave:

'Give it here will you, Sir, and I'll find out.'

Like a true pro, he scanned the chewing gum and mercifully, it beeped and a price of 55p came up.

'Bit steep' said Dave.

'Oh I know, Sir, but just think of all the shoe soles that you'll be able to stick with it.'

'Never thought of that!' laughed Dave and pulled out a pound coin.

'Oh, shit!' thought Bunny 'What do I do now?' 'Em...em...' he stuttered.

'Oh, Pete...' Jo called out to Bunny 'I haven't had the time to put the change in the till yet. How much is the gentleman's purchase?'

'55p' replied Bunny/Pete.

Jo put her hand in the pocket of her miniskirt and withdrew a fifty pence piece.

'There you are, Sir' said Jo in a voice that screamed 'I'm definitely up for it!' All doe-eyed, she pressed the coin into Dave's hand. 'You've had a result. You've saved 5p already and it's still only seven o'clock.'

Dave pulled at his collar as if the heat in the service station had suddenly been turned up ten degrees and dropped the pound on the counter. Jo was given one of his most seductive smiles before he legged it. Stan was waiting outside for him.

'What was that all about?' asked Stan.

'I just got pulled' said Dave, still not believing his luck. He should have remembered his old mum's motto: 'If it's too good to be true then it's too good to be true.'

'Never mind getting' fuckin' pulled, son! We're supposed to be checkin' this place out! If Jake ever 'ears...'

'Yeah, awright, awright. Let's get on with it' replied Dave who was well pissed off that he'd had to pass up such a gorgeous arse. Reluctantly, he followed Stan as he moved off to continue the search.

Meanwhile, in the newsagents, Bunny was declaring his eternal gratitude to Jo. 'You are a life saver, young Jo.'

'No problem. Although, if he does try to take me up on my offer, I want to be entered in the witness protection programme. What a sleazeball!'

'…and I will personally see to it that you do!' and they both laughed.

Five minutes later, Dave and Stan returned to find Charlie waiting for them at the bottom of the stairs.

'All clear up there' said Charlie.

'Likewise' said Stan. He didn't bother to mention Dave's luck to Charlie. A few hours later he wished he had.

Forty Six

With the three villains making their way back to the van, the all-clear was given and bodies started emerging from all sorts of places; walk-in freezers, staff-only cloakrooms, storage cupboards. One of the sergeants on the squad even got a cleaner to lock him in a broom cupboard. The important thing was that they'd gotten away with it: Mr Vickers was none the wiser.

The time was 7.15 just over an hour to go before all hell would break loose in the lorry car park.

'This is a message for those of you who are in the building' began the Chief. 'I want you to stagger your exits and get into your cars and drive to the next junction and come back.'

Some of the younger members of the squad looked around at their colleagues, thinking: '...the old man's lost the plot' But when they heard what he had to say next, it all made sense.

'Now that we know where it's going to happen, I want you to return and park near...listen to what I'm saying, gentlemen, near Shylock, in such a way that we'll have him surrounded. Any questions?'

The only sound was the static on the radio frequency.

'On your way then, gentlemen' he said calmly.

At a steady pace, the teams left the building, making sure not to bring attention to themselves.

Forty Seven

Johnnie had just punched his card when Freddie walked in. It was quarter to six.

'Mornin', boss' said the ever-upbeat Freddie as he clocked on. The Company still used the old-fashioned card and stamp machines. 'Not everything has to be twenty-first century' was just one of the many Luddite thoughts of James Irvine.

'Mornin', son. Awright?' enquired Johnnie: he did not sound good.

'Come on, Johnnie boy, it's not that bad. Look, it's nearly the weekend!' said Freddie doing a little jig. 'Jus' think. All that lovely beer and…birds galore! An' who knows, even you might meet a nice young lady on our travels today who is prepared to remove her teeth for old geezers like you!'

Even Johnnie couldn't help smiling at that.

'That's better' said Freddie, giving Johnnie a playful punch on the arm 'Come on, we'll have a laugh today'. And he began to sing and wave his arms as if he was conducting:

'Pack up your troubles in your old kit bag and smile, smile…' he looked at Johnnie's face and continued '…fuck's sake…SMILE, Johnnie!' he sung. The thought of being stuck in the cabin for the whole day with Johnnie in one of his moods did not appeal.

Johnnie forced a laugh but Freddie knew him too well: it was gonna be a long day. The only thing was, he just didn't know how long.

A shadowy movement on the window of the offices above caught Freddie's eye.

''Ere!' said Freddie suddenly 'Is that the boss up there, Johnnie? What the fuck's he doin' in 'ere at this time? 'Ere, you don't think the missus' boyfriend kicked 'im out of bed early, do you?'

'I wouldn't let Mr Irvine hear you talk like that, Freddie. He doesn't appreciate jokes about his wife' said Johnnie sombrely.

'Aaah, only joking, Johnnie! Come on, lighten up, me old mate. Otherwise it's gonna be a hellova day!'

'If only you knew, you stupid little sod!' thought Johnnie with a heavy heart. As he'd dragged himself from the marital bed earlier, several possible scenarios for avoiding today's proceedings had occurred to him as he performed his ablutions: he could throw a sickie, take a different route, even avoid the Cobham Services altogether but the outcome would be the same: him in hospital, dead or barely alive. Johnnie was well aware of Mr Vickers' methods of dealing with welchers. No, he'd have to go through with it.

'Awright,' said Johnnie with clearly no enthusiasm at all 'let's get this show on the road.'

Freddie checked the manifest while Johnnie walked around lorry pulling at straps and checking that everything was as it should be. Two minutes later he announced 'Okay, we're ready to roll.'

'It's gonna be one of those days' thought the cheerier half of the partnership.

As they pulled out of the yard, the SO19 team in the rear of the lorry turned on their lamps: they'd had to wait until they were on their way just in case Johnnie or Freddie spotted any light escaping from their hiding place in the back. Also, there was no way they could arrive for their meeting with Shylock having sat in total darkness for over two hours: they'd be blinded by the light when the lorry doors were opened.

Now, it was just a question of time and timing.

Forty Eight

At roughly the same time as the James Irvine lorry laden with SO19 and the two unsuspecting employees left the depot, Dave Cosforth was sitting at the breakfast table, crunching on the burnt offering his long-suffering wife, Doris, referred to as toast. Still in pink fluffy dressing gown and mules with her immaculately dyed blonde bobbed hair as yet uncombed, Doris sat at the opposite end of the kitchen table, sucking on a fag. She eyed up her husband's craggy face while he spread marmalade over the last half slice of toast.

As far as Doris was concerned, her husband was doing what he always did on a Friday morning: getting ready to hit the High St, which indeed was his intention…but with a gun in one hand and a bin liner stuffed full of goodies in the other as opposed to his normal Friday morning: a bucket and squeegee.

As was her habit, Doris prattled on.

'…just two numbers short I was' she droned '…just two numbers an' I'd 'ave had a share of the twenty-five grand top prize.'

Silence.

'Did you 'ear me, Dave? I said twenty-five grand!'

'I 'eard you, Doris, but me mind's on other things'. In an attempt to take her mind off his lack of interest in her near win at the bingo the previous night, Dave asked:

'What's for tea tonight?'

'What'd' ya mean "What's for tea tonight?"'. Same as we always 'ave on Friday nights: takeaway fish and chips! 'Ere, are you starting to lose your marbles or sommit? Your head's been in the clouds this past three weeks.'

With that distraction not working, Dave tried another tack.

'Listen, how do you fancy a bit of an 'oliday?'

'Where to?' asked Doris, sitting up like she'd just sat on a nail.

'Majorca.'

'When?' was her next question.

'Next week.'

'That's a bit sudden. 'Ow long for?' asked Doris, surprised by the unexpected turn of the conversation.

'Couple of months, maybe three.'

'Wh...at!' said Doris stuttering with surprise. 'Ere! You 'aven't gone and won the bleedin' lottery and not told me, 'ave you?' 'Just need a rest, that's all. I'm getting' bloody sick of washin' those pissin' windows all day long. It's doin' my 'ead in.'

'What about the dog?' They had an eight-year-old greyhound, Charlie '...what'll we do with 'im? An' what about your round?' said Doris, referring to his window cleaning business.

'We'll put 'im in the kennels. He loves it there. Reminds him of his days when he was a champion racer' he continued '...an' I've arranged for Bob to do my round while we're away. He's already rubbin' his 'ands with glee at the thought of makin' a bit on the side to top up 'is benefits.'

'But for two months? That'll cost a fortune!'

'I need an 'oliday. So, I don't care what it costs' said Dave finally.

'Oooh, if that's the case, Mr Moneybags, can I 'ave some money then for a new outfit? All the stuff I wore last year is gettin' past its sell-by date.'

'Yeah, alright. How much d'ya need?' said the guy who was planning on making this his last job.

While she was on a roll, Doris decided to try and push her luck.

'A monkey would do' she said casually, patting down her dressing gown, but her eyes gave her away, they were darting all over the kitchen, nervous like.

'What? Five 'undred notes? You must be jokin'! We're goin' to Majorca not fuckin' Buckin'ham Palace to collect me knight'ood!'

Dave went into his back pocket and pulled out his wallet. Doris' eyes lit up: he had a big wad of fifties. 'Where'd you get all that?' she asked as she took another drag on her fag, and then regretted it. Dave didn't like her asking questions like that.

He glared at her.

'Never you mind. 'Ere!' he said angrily as he pushed three hundred across the kitchen table towards her. 'That's yer lot.'

'Ta very much' said Doris, the small bundle of notes disappearing into the pocket of her dressing gown quickly before Dave could say: 'Give's it back', which he might easily have done.

'Right, that's it, I'm off' said Dave yawning and stretching and swiping the crumbs off his dungarees as he got up from the breakfast table 'I'll see you later an' don't go spendin' all o' that at once. I 'aint made o' money.'

'Don't worry, honey!' said Doris, all sugar and spice. She couldn't wait to call her friend, Betty, to go out 'shoppin' till she was droppin'.

Dave collected all his window-washing gear from the hallway and he was out the door.

He checked his watch as he got into the van: 7.20am. Turning the ignition on, he drove off in the direction of the lock-up. The side of his van bore the legend: 'Winner of the Cleanest Windows South of the Thames 2005'

He smiled every time he looked at it. No-one had ever asked who the award was from: just as well, there was no such bloody award.

Forty Nine

Avoiding the main roads where he could, Dave ducked and dived around the local rat runs towards the lock-up. He saw the woman walking the dog too late. She was already reaching for the button on the pedestrian crossing and before he could fire up the engine to race through, the lights had turned to red. He stopped; there was no way he was gonna risk getting caught running a light today. Waiting for the lights to change, his mind roamed.

'One more job an' that's me out of it. Finito. I'll sell the cleanin' round and between that an' the proceeds from this last job, we'll 'ave a nice retirement, me an' Doris. I'll 'ave to wait till she's 'ad a few bevvies down 'er neck in Majorca an' then I'll spring it on 'er: surprise 'er with the brochures for the 'ouses I've been lookin' at. In fact...' thought Dave excitedly '...if we find one when we're out there, we'd only need to come back to pack up and sell my round and we'd be off. Just think we could be livin' there in about three...'

The lights began to flash amber and Dave moved off. Suddenly, a young mum pushing a pram rushed onto the crossing and brought Dave's daydream to a halt as he slammed on his brakes.

'Fuckin' 'ell!' he screamed as he wound down the window 'What you bleedin' playin' at, Mrs? You trying to get yerself and the little 'un killed?'

By way of apology, the young lady shouted back 'An' you can fuck off an' all, old man! Pedestrians 'ave got right of way. So, FUCK YOU!' she screamed as she gave Dave the V sign.

On a normal day, Dave would have been out of the car and given the gobby little mare a right gobful back, but not today: he had things to do.

Shifting into gear, he moved off and ten minutes later arrived at the lock-up to find the boys there: everything had been checked and re-checked.

'Nice one, boys' said Dave. 'But if you don't mind I'll just run through me own check list.'

For the next five minutes, Bron and Markie sat in silence, watching Dave as he checked everything was in order.

'Right then everything seems to be okay. But why 'ave you got two grenades today, Bron? Expecting trouble, are we?' Dave's attention to detail had saved them on more than one occasion.

'To be honest, Dave, there's a cop shop not far from the jewellers today an' I just thought it might be better to carry some extra gear. "Better safe than sorry" as a cat burglar I shared a cell with used to say when he was explaining the finer points of housebreaking.'

'Good thinkin', son' said Dave. 'That's what keeps us ahead of the game.'

Their ETA at Franks the Jewellers on the High St was 8.50am: twenty minutes after the fun at the Cobham Services would begin. It was gonna be a busier than normal day for the police in South London, that was for sure.

From their day jobs, Dave and Bron both knew that the only person on the premises at that time on a Friday morning was the owner, an old Yiddisher guy called Manny: he was seventy-two, crippled with arthritis; just the sort of stiff opposition the boys liked.

'Now don't go too hard on the old geezer, Markie, he's not a bad guy and 'is health 'aint too good. Havin' said that, if he don't come up with the goods…you do what you 'ave to do.'

'Gotcha, boss!' replied Markie, who was not averse to giving someone a good pistol whippin': he found it gave him a little tingle in his nether regions.

'What time d'you make it, Bron?'

''Bout ten to eight' said Bron, pressing the dial on his watch which lit up at his touch.

'Nice bit o' shmutter' said Dave admiring Bron's flashy watch.

'Latest thing on the market. It was designed for cavers. Not a lot of light down those big fuckin' holes in the ground, 'parently. Sometimes I wear it in bed and hide under the covers just to turn it on and see it light up.'

'Yeah, I know what you mean...' said Markie laughing '...'cept I hide under the covers to do somethin' else!'

'You are one sick bastard!' Bron replied when it dawned on him what Markie meant.

Quick as a flash, Markie came back with: 'It takes one to know one!'

Dave joined in the banter: it helped to relieve the tension. Let's face it; if those tossers in the City can have their yoga classes at lunchtime to relieve their stress, why can't a couple of bank robbers have a laugh about a wank which has the same effect? To each of them, it's a job. How they get relief from the pressure is up to them.

'Just one thing, Bron, ditch the fancy wristware. Someone like Manny might just remember it'. Attention to detail. With any luck, Dave's eye for it might keep them all from breakfasting at one of Her Majesty's dining halls.

The next forty minutes passed quickly. At 8.30am, Dave told the boys that they were moving out in five.

'Let it go smoothly, please' Dave prayed to whoever/whatever was up there that might be listening. Not one for organised religion, Dave. 'If you don't ask, you don't get' was his motto.

Exactly five minutes later, the guns had been checked and the safety catches on. The three of them donned their woollen face masks and pulled on their helmets. Markie and Bron mounted the motorbikes while Dave walked out into the deserted lock-up area to make sure there were no prying eyes. When he was sure, he gave the boys the thumbs up and they took off down the road towards number 237 The High Street, Manny Franks jewellers: Dave's last job.

Fifty

As Dave and the boys were pulling out onto the Old Kent Road, the silence in the back of the James Irvine lorry was broken by static in Inspector Morrison ear, telling him that the ETA of the lorry was three minutes. Word was passed along: this was it.

Weapons were checked and safety catches removed.

In the cabin, Freddie was jabbering on, desperately trying to lighten the mood, but Johnnie wasn't biting: it was taking him all his time not to roll down the window and puked up the bile that was sitting at the back of his throat. He could taste its bitterness but knew that he had to hold it together. A couple more minutes and then...he tried not to think beyond parking the sodding lorry at the spot where he knew Jake would be waiting.

Johnnie wasn't the only one getting jumpy. In the car park, Jake took one last look at his watch as the thumping got louder and louder. Was it his heart or was it in his head? He didn't know but he was sure the others could hear it. But it would take more than that to stop Jake Vickers: he had one more trick up his sleeve before it all began to kick off.

On top of the service building, Chief Superintendent Moore saw movement in the van and swore.

'What's that bastard up to now?'

Jim Wallis didn't answer immediately as he grasped the full meaning of what he was seeing through his night vision binoculars.

'Ah, shit' was all he said in his broad Scottish accent.

'What's happening, Jim?' asked his boss.

'If it's what I think it is, Sir, we're in deep dodo.'

Unlike Jake, a calmness came over the Chief in situations like this one; that's why he'd made it to Chief Superintendent. In his capacity as a copper, crisis was the order of the day.

'Go on, Jim, what is it?' asked the Chief, the already deep lines on his brow creasing even further.

'He just handed each of them a wrap, Sir. My guess is: it's coke.'

'Oh, for fucks sake!' said the Chief as the implications hit him. 'Patch me through to Inspector Morrison. Quick!' he said into his walkie talkie.

'Hello, Paul' he said as the voice of Inspector Morrison came on the line with the drone of the juggernaut's engine in the background. '...we have an unexpected development' he continued.

'Go ahead, Sir, I'm listening' came the resigned response from a man used to last minute flaps.

'We've ust seen Shylock pass what we think is cocaine around to the others.'

'Friggin' Nora!' was Paul Morrison's initial thought as his pulse rate quickened. However, a deep breath later everything was back under control and he began to mentally adjust the plan which thirty seconds earlier was to have been put into action in less than two minutes. His restrained reply to the Chief gave nothing away: 'Thanks for that, Sir.'

He stood up: his men immediately knew that it must be a change to the original plan as he clung onto the side of the lorry to counter the sway of the lorry.

'Listen up, men' he began, raising his normally quiet voice so that the whole team could hear him over the whine of the engine 'The hijackers have been seen taking something; we think it's cocaine. So, you don't need me to tell you that they're gonna be unpredictable and unstable in the extreme. Gentlemen, you know what we have to do and that is: go in even faster and harder. We will have less than a minute to take control of the situation. Otherwise, we've got trouble.'

In his usual understated way, he did not expand on the 'otherwise we've got trouble' scenario; he didn't need to. The picture of four coked-up guys with guns potentially running around loose in a public area did not bear thinking about.

The mike in his ear informed the Inspector that the lorry was approaching the slip road to the services, but he already knew that; he could feel the gears crunching as Johnnie slowed to take the curve in the road and then again as he turned into the lorry park.

No more time to think. Time for action.

Fifty One

Chief Superintendent Moore had earlier stationed two plain-clothed police officers at the exit to the car park to stop people going back to their vehicles.

Likewise, once the lorry had turned onto the slip road, entries and exits on both sides of the motorway had been blocked off. No-one would be going in or coming out for the foreseeable.

'That's all I'd need: some bloody member of the public getting it. The papers would have a field day!' he thought as he descended to ground level to join his men. Checking his own weapon, he said to the assembled group:

'Right, gentlemen! This is it. No heroics. Do not take any chances! Let SO19 do what they have to do and then we go in. Any questions?'

As he spoke, Bunny was having problems with the zip on his body armour: it wouldn't budge.

'Sarge, can you help me here? This bloody thing won't move' he said frustratedly.

The sergeant tried to pull it up: the zip was stuck.

'Sorry, Bunny, you'll have to stay here. Can't risk you going out there.'

'Come on, come on!' shouted the Chief impatiently. 'Let's go!'

Bunny stood and watched, disgust and disappointment clearly etched on his face. He wanted to be part of it; to share the locker room banter in the weeks to come. It wouldn't be the same if he wasn't out there at the kill.

'Oh, fucking bollocks!' he thought as he watched his colleagues fan out. 'Just my poxy luck!'

Fifty Two

By this time, Jake and the boys were so high they could have flown to the moon and back and still been back in time to pull the job off.

Chief Superintendent Moore watched them from behind a removals van, he gave the order for the other plain clothes policemen in the cars to 'Get into position. Now!'

Every pair of eyes in the lorry park turned as the huge lorry with the James Irvine name on the side slowed down and steered towards where Jake was parked. Johnnie knew from long experience that this particular part of the lorry park was never busy because of the long walk to the service area. Lorry drivers were no different to members of the public: they were all lazy bastards and wanted to park up the arse of a place.

Jake's eyes were glued to Johnnie's face as the lorry got closer. It was ghostly pale.

'Here comes our little piggy bank, boys. Bang on time!' said Jake getting higher by the minute.

'I bet he's shittin' 'imself' he thought, savouring the power he had to instil such utter fear in people. 'Come on then, you wanka!' he said impatiently in a hoarse whisper as he stared at the back of the lorry, waiting for the engine to be cut. The others now looked at Jake in total silence, sensing the pent-up rage that was about to erupt...and not wanting to be the one that it was aimed at. Especially the way he was jiggling that sawn-off shotgun from one hand to the other.

Johnnie sat there for a moment, letting the engine idle and knowing, dreading, what was about to happen. His right hand hovered around the ignition key. For those few moments, he stared out the window of the cab.

'Release the brake, put your foot down and get the fuck out of here!' his brain screamed and for those few moments he was close, so close to doing it.

For he knew, knew for sure, that Jake's promise not to hurt the boy meant nothing. People like Jake were no respecters of promises; promises were words, airy fairy things. Fists, baseball bats, guns, bullets, they all made things happen. People did what they were told when they had those things hanging over them. Words? At the end of the day they mean nothing. You only had to listen to politicians on the telly: they'd say anything, tell you anything, ANYTHING, to get your vote. Then when they get in...it's another story. Funnily enough, stories are made up of words. And then you're back where you started.

'Come on, Johnnie, I'm starvin'. I'm so hungry I could eat a scabby pussy with a bit of ketchup on it' declared Freddie, trying once more to lift Johnnie's spirits. Normally, Johnnie would have made some disparaging remark about his friend's lack of breeding, but not today. He just looked over at Freddie and smiled, sadness in his tired eyes.

'Come on, then. Let's get on with it' said Johnnie more reluctantly than he'd ever said anything in his entire life before. He switched off the engine.

Every pair of ears in the lorry park heard the lack of sound from that engine and froze; breathes were held.

Dave the nosepicker simply whispered in a tiny voice: 'Jesus.'

In that brief moment before the cab doors opened, there was a hush where, for the first time that morning, a lot of those in the lorry park noticed the chirping of the birds in the trees surrounding the parking area.

In the back of the lorry, the SO19 team shuffled towards the back doors of the lorry. In the practised silence, there was a calm; a calm like the one before a hurricane hits landfall.

The cab doors opened both side of the lorry. What happened next made Dante's Inferno look like a picnic for privileged children.

Fifty Three

'Masks!' was all Jake said. Screamed actually.

In what seemed like one single movement, the six hijackers pulled down their ski masks, threw open the van doors and were charging towards the lorry like a pack of hounds descending on a cornered stag. The coke scooting around their bloodstreams helped them find their voices as they split up. Jake, nosepicking Dave and Charlie veered towards the passenger side of the cabin. The others went after Johnnie. Freddie's foot was midway between the footplate and the ground when he heard the screaming. It was a sound Freddie had heard many times before; on a Saturday afternoon on the terraces at Millwall. Feral. Bloodthirsty. Terrifying.

Before he could turn to see who was responsible, a massive hand grabbed the collar of his jacket and slammed his head against the open door.

'What the fuc…' was all Freddie managed to say before Jake shoved him to the ground. 'Get down and fuckin' stay down, you little bastard or I'll blow your fuckin' bollocks all over this car park!' and to prove it he kicked Freddie viciously in the balls, followed by an even more vicious one to the face. One of Freddie teeth flew in what seemed like slow motion from his bloodied mouth. The coke was doing its job.

On the other side of the cab, Johnnie was pushed roughly to the ground and told 'Don't move!' but that was it. These guys lived on the same estate as Johnnie. They'd still see him and have to face him when this was all over. He was in on it; he didn't put up a struggle. So why take things further?

But that's why Jake was top dog and why they worked for him.

Top dog was still giving Freddie a good kicking when Johnnie shouted: 'Stop, leave the kid alone! 'Ere's the keys, take 'em!' he screamed throwing them on the ground close to where Jake was to get him away from Freddie. But, old habits die hard and Jake, as always, was enjoying this opportunity to humiliate and beat another human being to a pulp; someone he considered his inferior. After a few more gratifying body blows, Jake picked up the keys.

Chief Superintendent Moore watched the whole thing in horror from his position behind the removals van. 'Where the fuck is SO19? They should be out there by now!' he shouted to no one in particular.

His walkie-talkie crackled.

'This is Paul Morrison. The doors are locked and we can't get out. Repeat. We cannot exit the lorry.'

When Johnnie had walked around the lorry checking it before they left the yard, he'd spotted the lock not fully secured and closed it.

SO19 were now stuck in the back of the lorry going nowhere.

'Oh, fuck!' screamed the Chief. Then he shouted into the walkie-talkie 'We have a "Go, go, go!"'

The sergeant, who'd tried to help Bunny, switched on the megaphone he was carrying.

'Armed police! Put down your weapons! You are surrounded! Put down your weapons!' he screamed.

In the mayhem that followed, it was fortunate that the police cameraman on the roof was getting everything on videotape.

Jake let out a blood-curdling roar as his brain shifted into 'fight or flight' mode. But there's only one way for the Jakes of this world: fight. He began waving the sawn-off shotgun around, looking for a target. And he was going to use it. No fuckin' cop was gonna take him.

Unfortunately for Jake, he was on his own. Dave the nosepicker pissed his pants and nearly fainted while the others hesitated for a tense sphincter-clenching moment before laying down their weapons: beating up grannies whose pensions didn't quite cover the interest on their never-ending loans was about the extent of their hardness.

The sergeant with the megaphone shouted more instructions; it focussed their attention away from other possibilities.

'Lie face down on the ground and put your hands behind your head! Do it NOW! Do it!' he said with all the force he could muster.

But Chief Superintendent Moore could see that Jake wasn't having any of it.

'Move in!' he shouted into his walkie-talkie. Jim, who was crouched beside him said: 'What're we going to do about Vickers, Sir? He's as high as a kite! Do we shoot?'

The Chief thought about it and spoke into the walkie-talkie, addressing the sergeant with the megaphone:

'Sergeant Ellis...I want you to repeat this, word for word.'

The sergeant did as he was told.

'Jake Vickers! Lay down your gun now! You have five seconds! Lay it down NOW!' he commanded.

Instead of the use of his name throwing him off balance, it had the opposite effect on Jake. It lit a fuse; a very short fuse. Jake decided he could take them all on and win.

'Come and get me...if you're brave enough, copper!' he screamed.

He looked down at the crumpled body of young Freddie and realised how he was going to get himself out of this mess. And when he did, whoever had set him up was gonna get it. But that was for later.

He pressed the barrel of the shotgun to Freddie's temple. Freddie was his Get Out Of Jail card.

'If anybody moves, he gets it!' he bellowed.

Jake was in control now. And they all knew it.

The sergeant tried one more time. 'Put the gun down! Put it down now!' he persisted.

'Back off or the kid gets it!' he screamed and then turned to nosepicking Dave and Charlie and said:

'Right, you two! Pick the kid up and put him in the passenger seat. Hurry up...do it!'

The two men picked up the half-dead body of young Freddie whose only crime was occasionally dipping his wick in the wrong hole. They shoved the body into the passenger seat and stood back.

Keeping the gun pressed into Freddie's face, Jake climbed over him into the driver's seat, all the time keep his eyes on the police; watching for any sudden movement. Nothing. Jake smiled to himself. He knew then they were flapping around like chickens in a coup with a visiting fox.

'What now, boss?' asked a dazed Charlie. Nosepicking Dave was just standing beside him; the drugs had left his body via the urine soaking into his trousers. He was too drained and shocked to speak. But the drugs in Jake's veins were having the opposite effect: he was in orbit somewhere now.

'Shut the door and wait here!' yelled Jake. 'I'll be back for you in a minute!' he laughed as he pushed the key into the ignition and started the engine.

In the back of the lorry, the SO19 squad could only stand in silence and listen: for the hijackers to become aware of their presence now could only make a bad situation worse.

The engine roared into life and Jake moved the gear stick into reverse with his right hand while his left held the gun firmly against the unconscious face of Freddie.

In the back, Inspector Morrison and his team put their safety catches back on and braced themselves.

Johnnie Parker was still lying there by the driver's side door where he'd hit the ground at the start of this debacle. He was completely inert...in mind as well as body.

But there was someone who was not.

The whole of these goings-on had been observed from the service station area by Bunny and he was already ahead of the game. He'd already worked out that Jake was going to try to make a run for it in the lorry. A dozen alternatives whizzed through his brain until he was left with only one.

He began running towards the curve in the road where the lorry would have to slow down to take the corner before joining the motorway.

In the cab, Jake was still laughing, pleased with himself: he'd beaten the police. He watched them through his drug-induced haze as he drove passed; guns dangling uselessly by their sides, resignation written all over their faces: he'd won. Jake Vickers was still king. He wished he had a third hand to give them the 'wanker!' wave.

'Load of tossers, the whole fuckin' lot of you! Nobody beats Jake Vickers!' he screamed.

As he left the parking area, Jake dropped the gun on the seat between him and Freddie while he changed gears to slow down on the approach to the bend in the road.

'Better get rid of the surplus stock' Jake thought, looking at the inert body of Freddie. As the truck slowed, he leant over and opened the passenger door, shoving Freddie's motionless body out. The young man's body hit the tarmac with a thud rolling over several times.

'That's better. Just Jakey to look after now.'

Crouching in the bushes close to the spot on the bend where the lorry would be moving at its slowest was Bunny, watching and ready to pounce as the lorry passed his hiding place.

Bunny saw Freddie's body fall and his mind was made up.

Had Jake bothered to look in his side view mirror at that point, he'd have seen Bunny running for all he was worth alongside the driver's door. But he didn't.

Suddenly, the door of the cab was wrenched open and Bunny, who'd got a toehold on the footplate, was making a grab for the wheel before Jake could take in what was happening.

Instinctively, Jake slammed on the brakes. In the back, the SO19 team went flying. If Bunny hadn't grabbed the wheel, he'd have gone too.

Jake's left hand scrabbled for the shotgun as Bunny wrestled with his other hand, trying to prise it off the wheel.

The struggle lasted no more than a few seconds.

Jake brought the gun around and rested it on the arm Bunny had been struggling with, pointing it straight at Bunny's face. He just held it there, looking into Bunny's eyes. For his part, Bunny believed that Jake wasn't going to use it. Jake gave Bunny a crooked little enigmatic smile, savouring the moment. Then, he gave Bunny both barrels in the face. Bunny's head exploded. Blood and brains sprayed all over Jake.

Later, Bunny's widow would have to formally identify him from the crooked nail on the big toe of his right foot, the result of a childhood accident and their kids' names tattooed on his left forearm: he'd had them done on the day each of them were born.

So, Bunny had been there after all for the kill: he just wasn't expecting it to be his own.

Fifty Four

The sound of the gun going off made everyone jump and freeze at the same time. Everyone, that is except Manny Franks, the arthritic seventy-two-year-old owner of the jewellery store, who had never missed a day's work in the thirty-five years he'd had the pleasure of owning his emporium of 'sparkling opportunities' as the sign over the window announced.

Mr Franks was well-known and liked in this local community; he would always rustle up a deal that would suit his clients' pockets. 'Pay a little here, a little there and before you know it, you are the proud owner of one of the finest jewels this side of Buckingham Palace's gates!' That would always get a laugh from his customers; ladies and the gentlemen. More importantly; they'd buy.

But today, these customers were not looking to pay on the 'never never'; they were not looking to pay at all. No, these schmucks were the reason his lovely wife, Miriam, wanted him to give up the business and retire. Retire! Him, Manny Franks? What would he all day? Eat matzos and play kalooki?

Besides, he liked the banter with his clients, the cut and thrust of making a deal, the pleasure of seeing his customers walk out of his little shop with a smile on their faces and he, a modest profit in his pocket.

There wasn't going to be much profit made today. But he was not going to give it away either. Not without a struggle. He'd had visits from the likes of these ferkukte gunaves before. Four times in thirty-five years to be precise. And he knew their method of working. And so far, they'd stuck to the script.

He had just opened up. His usual time: quarter to nine, fifteen minutes earlier than it said on the door.

'Ah! You never know who might be looking for a little something special and if I open a little earlier than the competition...who knows?' was Manny's philosophy in life. He wasn't doing anybody any harm.

Unlike the masked men who came crashing through his door screaming and shooting their guns into his ceiling.

'Please let the flat be empty' was Manny's first thought as the bullets penetrated his ceiling, causing bits of the false ceiling to land on Manny's head. The O'Malleys had live above his shop for the last twenty-odd years. Mr O'Malley left each morning at four o'clock; he worked in Covent Garden Flower market. Mrs O'Malley cleaned in some of the big houses around the area but he was never sure what time she left. They were nice, hard-working people; like his own mother and father. Aveh shalom.

'But damn these mumzas to Hell' was his next thought as one of the raiders tried to jump over the counter.

But short, slightly rotund Manny wasn't as slow as he looked; although most of the time it suited him for people to think this. No, he could still kick a ball around the garden with his grandchildren. Alright, maybe only for five minutes before his lungs and joints begged for mercy and maybe he shouldn't have a second helping of Miriam's delicious chicken soup but it would never occur to anyone looking at him that he was capable of such energy. That was the robbers' first mistake: they only saw what Manny wanted them to see.

The next one was that window-cleaning Dave had been careless. Unusual for Dave who prided himself in his attention to detail, but their success had made him sloppy. He should have spotted it: the long thin bladed knife, the kind used by butchers to slice through the meat to the bone before using a hacksaw, by the side of the counter. Ostensibly, Manny kept it to open parcels; but it had a secondary purpose; situations like this.

By the time Bron was half way over the counter, Manny had grabbed the knife and, with a strength born out of his sense of fairness or maybe unfairness, hit out blindly at the robber. The knife tore through Bron's leather jacket and kept going, lodging in his shoulder. Bron fell to the floor screaming, dropping his gun as he went. This was not the 'like taking sweets off a kid' scenario they'd been expecting.

In the next few moments of ensuing chaos, Manny pressed the panic button which sent a signal to the police control centre and set off the alarm which could be heard up and down the High Street. Quite a number of the other shop owners reached for their 'ostensible' parcel openers: crowbars, brooms, baseball bats and came running along the street towards the shop.

Manny was a popular shop owner: he would look after the other shopkeepers when they needed that special present.

In the shop, Manny was scrabbling on the floor behind the counter with Bron, out of sight of the other robbers, both of them trying to grab hold of the gun. The others wavered, unsure what to do: grab the jewellery and run or help Bron? Those few seconds of uncertainty were their undoing.

Manny got hold of the gun and at the same time had the satisfaction of ramming the knife deeper into Bron's shoulder. To say he squealed like a stuck pig would be a fair statement; except it would be disrespectful to the owner of this kosher establishment to make such a comparison.

Dave took the lead on the other side of the counter. He risked a quick look to see what was going on behind the counter. Bron was rolling from side to side, clearly in a lot of pain. Manny was half sitting with his back against wall, deep in shock, the gun held in both hands which were shaking badly. He pulled the trigger as Dave's head appeared over the counter. Fortunately for Dave, the combination of the recoil and Manny's unsteady hands meant the shot went wide but it brought them to their senses.

'Get the fuck out of here!' screamed Dave.

Bron managed to scramble to his feet, pulling the knife from his shoulder as he did so. He looked at the old man, half-lying half-sitting there.

At the end of the day, he was seventy-two. So, here endeth the story of Manny's bravery. Bron could see that shock was setting in. Grudgingly, he admired the old geezer because his own father could never have done that; his old man had died from cirrhosis of the liver when he was in his fifties. Bron prised the gun from Manny's fingers; there was no reaction from him.

Outside, Bron could hear a lot shouting and screaming going on.

'What the fuck...?' he thought as he made for the door. As he came out into the insipid sunshine that was beginning to break through the clouds, he saw Dave and Markie, surrounded by an angry mob of Manny's would-be rescuers who were just about to clobber the pair of them.

Bron didn't fuck around; he let off a couple of rounds into the air.

'Get back!' he screamed, swinging the gun around in an arc, pointing it at faces in the crowd. They backed off...but only just, for there were a couple of 'have-a-goes' among them.

Bron knew what had to be done. He reached for his inside pocket.

'No time to piss around' he thought 'We've only got one chance to get out of here in one piece.'

But the unbearable pain in his shoulder stopped him. He couldn't reach the grenade. The pain was excruciating. There was only one thing for it. If he couldn't get the fucking thing out and use it... he'd have to blag it. So, he shouted:

'I've got a grenade in here! You've got five seconds before I pull the pin!'

Nearly everyone there had seen the headlines in the newspapers about 'The Hand-Grenade Mob' who'd blown up a bank and killed and maimed dozens of bystanders.

Suddenly, the dynamics of the crowd changed. Bron now saw fear on the faces; he could almost taste it. This was their only chance. Dave and Markie had managed to get to the bikes and were revving up the engines, waiting for Bron: maybe there is such a thing as honour among thieves.

'Five...' screamed Bron reaching towards his inside pocket. 'Four...'

That was it. The crowd fled; they would have climbed over their invalid grannies to get out of there.

'Come on, Bron! Quick! Quick!' shouted Markie.

Bron jumped on the back of Markie's bike.

'Go...ooo! Get us the fuck out of here!' he screamed as he clutched his injured shoulder.

Fifty Five

In the back of the truck, the SO19 team were checking themselves for injuries. The team were a bit shaken but okay. They turned to their Inspector, waiting in silence anticipation for their orders while their torch lights bouncing off the walls of what had become their very own giant prison cell.

There was no question in the Inspector's mind, no hesitation.

'Get those doors open. Now!'

His number two, Sergeant John McBride, the exact antithesis of the tall, muscular, reflective introvert who was their Inspector, moved towards the back of the truck and shouted:

'Everybody move back! I'm going to shoot the lock out.'

The muffled sound was heard by Jake whose brain couldn't work out what it meant or where it was coming from. Did the sound come from the back of the truck?

Whatever it was, he wasn't stopping. He shifted the gearstick and was about to release the handbrake when the doors at the back of the lorry flew open and he heard those bloody words again:

'Armed police! Throw down your weapon!' as the SO19 team poured out of the back. Jake could see them in both of his side view mirrors.

By then, between Jake and the SO19 team, there was enough adrenalin pumping to win a dozen gold medals at the Olympics. 'Oh, for fuck's sake! Not again! I've been proper stitched up 'ere'' he realised. That realisation and the dead body now lying by the verge caused the blood to pump around Jake's body even faster now: the only difference was that it wasn't chemicals doing the pushing this time. Oh no, this was something much more powerful, it didn't cost a penny and was one hundred per cent natural: fear.

Police don't like cop killers.

Jake released the handbrake.

'Stop that lorry. Now!' commanded Inspector Morrison.

One of the team shot out the back tyres. Seconds later, Jake could feel the loss of control but continued on until he turned the final bend where he saw the police cars blocking the exit. He knew then he was going to have to ditch the lorry. With the loss of control, he didn't feel he'd have enough time to build up the speed he would need to smash his way through them. Or so his addled brain told him.

'Jesus fuckin' Christ! Gimme a break, will you?' he screamed. But Jake wasn't beaten yet. Like the cornered animal he was, he picked up the shotgun and got ready to jump from the cabin, leaving the massive lorry rolling towards the police blockade.

'That'll keep them busy for a while' he thought as he leapt into the bushes by the verge.

The SO19 team came around the bend in the search and find formation. Inspector Morrison's walkie talkie crackled.

'Paul' shouted Chief Superintendent Moore 'What's going on? We heard gunshots! We've got the other muppets but Shylock got away.'

'We know, Sir. We're in pursuit. We have someone down' The Inspector stared at the markings on the jacket. 'It's one of ours, Sir, but we don't know who. I'll keep you posted' replied the Inspector in calm measured tones. His main priority was to find and neutralise the perp.

He left one of his team to stand guard over the body at what had now become a crime scene and moved on.

He was in control now. This was what he did best: nicking villains.

Fifty Six

Jake was disorientated. The drugs had left his system; he was completely on his own now. No help from anyone or anything. It was up to the latter part of his 'fight or flight' mode to save him.

He was blundering through the scrubby bushes and trees which surround most services stations. The sort you see as you drive in and then as you drive out again but not the sort you'd ever dream of going for a stroll in.

And Jake certainly wasn't taking a stroll now. He knew that if they got the chance, the police would blow him away under their favourite mitigating circumstances heading: resisting arrest.

If only one of the SO19 guy hadn't turned the corner just in time to see him diving into the bushes, Jake might have stood a better chance. The policeman spoke into his walkie talkie:

'The suspect has left the vehicle and is now on foot in scrubland to our right.'

It was then that there was the almightiest of bangs.

Jake laughed out loud when he heard it.

'I knew that would keep them busy while Uncle Jake legged it!'

Wrong.

The Inspector spoke into his walkie talkie and simply said:

'Stay focussed, gentlemen. Others will deal with that. We have our job to do.'

There was going to be a lot to deal with.

Fifty Seven

Jake had left the lorry careering towards the blockade as it reached the downward slope. Gaining momentum, it smashed its way through the first two police cars in its path like they were cardboard cut-outs and kept on going. The sound of metal and glass being crushed under forty tons of unstoppable wrecking machine was horrendous. Fragmented shards of glass flew in every direction as those close by fled from its path.

The next two police vehicles nearly stopped it but it took one more, a paddy wagon which had been parked fifteen feet behind them to finally bring it crashing to a halt.

If that had been the end of it, the final count would have been: four police patrol cars and one paddy wagon out of action. So far: mess, yes, carnage, no.

But then there was a spark: one single, tiny, electrical flash that altered everything.

The quick succession 'boom-boom-boom' of three fractured petrol tanks was heard three miles away, the plume of smoke could be seen for ten.

Fuel from the ruptured tanks cascaded down the slope in rivulets and where the fuel went, the flames followed.

Still the Inspector kept himself and his men focussed. He pulled out a map of the service area that he'd spent time pouring over before the team meeting at the station and began issuing orders to the team.

'Everybody fan out. We know the general direction he's headed in. Make sure you can see your colleague to the right and left of you. That way he won't slip through and you can cover each other' he said into his walkie-talkie.

In these circumstances, a helicopter was not only perfect but essential. But no-one had expected things to turn out the way they did, so that wasn't an option.

Under the Inspector's direction, the team moved out. It didn't take a native tracker to work out which direction Jake was heading: the crashing noise he was making as he scrambled desperately through the bushes could have been followed by a boy scout on his outdoor challenge badge.

'Gentlemen,' said the Inspector into his mouthpiece as they closed in on Jake 'he's already killed a colleague, so he won't think twice about doing it again. May I remind you: no heroics but take him alive if you can. Finally, when we do meet Shylock, please keep your emotions under control because this is one nasty piece of shit that needs to be swept off our streets.'

The thought occurred to a number of them '...you're not managing to do that very well, at the moment, yourself, Sir.'

But those thoughts would never be verbalised; not to each other or anybody else.

They'd never heard their boss talk in such emotive terms before and they had seen him in some tight spots. They assumed, rightly, that the killing of one of their colleagues back there was the reason. Cop-killing aroused strong emotions in all the ranks; even in those who were long in the tooth.

They had practically caught up with the noise when suddenly it stopped. Silence. Where was he? Why had he stopped?

The team froze to a man, waiting for instructions. Inspector Morrison made hand gestures for some of his men to circle around the area where they'd last heard the noise coming from to cut Jake off. This was one evil bastard who was not going to escape, '...not if I've got anything to do with it' thought the Inspector grimly.

When the team were in position, the Inspector spoke quietly and calmly into his walkie-talkie:

'Move in.'

Fifty Eight

The last fuel tank to erupt was the lorry's. More and more flames soared higher and higher into the sky as pieces of red-hot twisted metal flew in every direction. The bonnet of the lorry was flung high into the air landing at the feet of a young, rookie female PC who had been standing more than forty feet away. She was badly shaken...but managed to dine out on it for months.

The danger from flying glass and metal, mixed with the acrid smoke of melting tyres, made up the mind of the senior officer in charge of the patrol cars: he pulled all his officers away from the immediate area to wait for the arrival of the Fire Service. All they could do was watch and wait.

And wait they did.

The long queues at the height of a morning rush hour on the M25 are not a pretty sight and this was a Friday morning; only marginally better than a Monday. What made it worse was the dickheads: those really clever people who think it's smart to pull in behind an emergency vehicle to bypass all the queuing traffic; sometimes, they even wave to the other motorists to show them how clever they are. However, when, and if, they ever looked in their rear mirror and see more flashing blue lights behind them, they try to pull in...with the usual outcome: the other motorists won't let them. That kind of behaviour could delay an emergency vehicle by several minutes...often the difference between life and death.

But on that morning, the dickheads must have had a lie-in because it took less than twenty-three minutes from when the call was received for the first fire engine to arrive at the chaotic scene and begin to get it under control. For them, situations like these were the equivalent of a spillage on aisle nine in Asda's: no-one had been injured so it was nothing to get your knickers in a twist about.

But it would be several hours before they would bring it completely under control.

In the meantime, the ambulances arrived. Apart from one dead body, they weren't needed. So far.

Fifty Nine

For the SO19 team the explosions were like background music as every one of their senses was concentrated on the job of locating Shylock, otherwise known as Jake Vickers.

The team started to move slowly and quietly towards the centre of the circle they had formed; to where the sound had last been heard.

But where was he?

The signs of where he had been were clearly there but then suddenly, like the noise he'd been making, they stopped.

'No sign, Sir' reported Sergeant McBride.

'Nothing here either, Sir' said another member of the team.

'Same here, Sir.'

'Where the fuck has he disappeared to?' thought the Inspector trying not to let his frustration blur his normally detached, logical way of solving even the toughest problems: like the Times cryptic yesterday, it was a bugger but he'd got there in the end.

'Gentlemen, stay in your positions. Stay where you are. There's something not right here.'

And if something doesn't seem right then it isn't. Not the 'then it usually isn't' like some people say. It just isn't.

As he looked up to the sky for inspiration, a light breeze blew allowing the faint rays of the sun to break through the solid mass of leaves and branches. The light bounced off something: it was metal. And there he was; Jake, sitting on one of the sturdier branches of the tree, pointing his gun at the nearest member of the team standing immediately beneath his dangling feet.

'Got you, you bastard' thought the Inspector. The situation was extremely dangerous but he knew what to do.

'Jackson, continue to move forward and keep going. Do not look to the right or left. Just keep moving.'

There was no hesitation from the most recent recruit to the team, as soon as the instruction came through his earpiece, he began to move, unbeknown to him, out of the danger zone, out of Jake's line of fire. In

SO19, you learn not question orders. If you were lucky you'd be told the reason why it was issued, later.

Once Jackson was out of immediate danger, the Inspector, whose eyes never left Jake, said the words the team had been waiting to hear:

'He's here and he's ours, gentlemen. He's in the tree which Jackson has just passed under, sitting in the branches. His gun is clearly loaded, judging by the way he was pointing it at Jackson. So, gentlemen; slowly, slowly catchee monkey.'

In other circumstances, he might have laughed at his unintentional humour; although in Jake's case, gorilla might have been more apt.

'Jake Vickers, this is the police. You are surrounded. Remove the bullets from your gun and throw them on the ground. Then throw your gun down. Do it! Now!' the Inspector called out forcefully. They would deal with getting Jake down afterwards once he had parted company with the shotgun.

The whole team were well aware that the situation still posed significant risk. There were three possible scenarios. First, Jake might decide that there was nothing to lose and take a pop at them. His chances of hitting anyone at this point were remote: all of the team were positioned behind trees, so difficult, but not impossible, targets. Next, he wouldn't be the first cornered rat to turn the gun on himself. And there were more than a few on the team who would have rejoiced at that outcome: an eye for an eye, no expensive protracted trial and the saving of a small fortune to keep the bastard locked up for twenty years. All in all, a very satisfactory outcome but from what the Inspector had read on his file, highly unlikely. Jake was a typical bully: only brave when the odds were well in his favour. And finally, the third, and potentially worst, scenario of all: a siege.

And there is a point where, if nothing happens, the siege develops. This was what the Inspector desperately wanted to avoid. But how to get that bloody gun away from Jake?

For what seemed like ages, nothing happened. The silence broken only by the distant popping of windscreens and shouted warnings from colleagues dealing with Jake's improvised escape plan.

Not a sound from Jake. The time was fast approaching for stalemate to set in.

Inspector Morrison needed a distraction: something which would dislodge Jake and his bloody shotgun from his perch.

Desperate situations invariably produce a desperate solution; for sure, this one wouldn't be found in any police manuals.

'But it might just do the trick' he thought as he weighed up the pros and cons.

One of the main prerequisites of his job was the ability to think outside the box, big time. There were very few black and white situations that SO19 were called on to deal with: mostly they were every shade of grey under the rainbow. So, although desperate, this was almost a daily occurrence for the Inspector.

He issued the order to the team:

'Gentlemen, we need to distract Mr Vickers. So, I want you to collect half a dozen stones each and on my command, I want you to begin pelting the tree above and around him. But do not aim for him. We don't want accusations of his human rights being infringed!' he added with just a hint of sarcasm.

Less than a minute later, the Inspector said: 'Everybody ready?'

A chorus of 'Yes, sir' came back.

'Then on my count. Three...two...one...begin!'

Seconds later, the already frazzled brain of Jake was trying to work out what the fuck all the noise was and why the tree was suddenly shedding branches that were falling all around him.

It did the trick.

Momentarily, Jake lost his grip. He fell backwards with the gun exploding harmlessly into the air before he and his empty shotgun landed with a crash at the base of the tree.

All the air and bravado had been sucked out of the would-be hijacker.

He just lay there in a daze as the team rushed through the bushes towards him screaming a chorus of:

'Armed police! Do not move! Do NOT move!'

Within seconds, in a well-rehearsed move, they had Jake lying on his face, cuffed and pulled to his feet. There was no resistance from Jake as Inspector Morrison read him his rights.

Not a hair of his head had been touched by the team at that point, each of whom would have liked five minutes on their own in a locked room with him. He thought he was tough; they fucking knew they were.

Inspector Morrison could now relax and respond to the crackling in his earpiece: it was a frantic Chief Superintendent Moore.

'Speak to me, Paul! We heard another gunshot! Is anybody hurt? Paul! Are you there? Over!'

'We have Shylock, Sir. No further casualties. Where do you want us?' The job was done. The Inspector's blood pressure was back to normal.

A very relieved Chief Super replied:

'Bring him back to the service area, will you Paul? We're all finished here. It's down to the Fire Brigade and Forensics now'. There was a second's hesitation before he said: 'Did you know Bunny Hare? It was him that Vickers shot. Nice guy: two young kids and a wife who's now a widow. A damn shame. Initial reports suggest that Bunny tackled Vickers. It was probably him who stopped the bastard.'

Inspector Morrison refrained from informing the Chief that what had probably stopped Jake was his team shooting out the lorry's rear tyres. No need. If they wanted to make Bunny's last act an heroic one, who was he to disabuse them? Better his family and colleagues remembered him as a hero.

The Chief Superintendent paused again and then blurted out 'Stupid! Stupid! Stupid! Such a waste of a good copper. Oh, God' and his end of the communication went quiet. It was the closest the Chief ever came to breaking down. He cared for his men: they were his family.

'I understand, Sir' said Inspector Morrison who empathised. 'I'll let the boys know.'

He turned to the team who were clearly enjoying that moment of a successful nick. But in their relief, they'd temporarily forgotten the body lying back there in the police vest.

'Any of you boys know Bunny Hare?'

The team stopped what they were doing: the euphoria instantly disappeared. Silence hung over them as they waited for their boss to continue.

'It was him back there' was all he said, jerking his thumb back towards where the dead body lay. Nothing more.

A couple of the team could be heard whispering in shock 'No, no'. No-one else said a word. For some, there was sadness at the death of a colleague. For others, anger. But in that numbing silence they were united. All eyes turned to Jake.

The name Bunny Hare didn't mean anything to Jake but he quickly picked up on the mood change.

'What's the matter, boys? Cat got your tongues?' he mocked. He knew they'd be throwing the key away for what he'd done. He just hoped he'd be around when they did it.

One of the team, John Riley, had done his training at Hendon with Bunny. They'd spent many a good night sharing a few pints and a bit of banter. They weren't bosom buddies or anything like that but John knew Bunny was a decent bloke.

So, Jake's words hit John like a taser. The eighteen stone ex-rugby league player from Hull let out a cry of pure venomous hatred that came from the Neanderthal buried deep in his being, and he charged at Jake.

Before any of the others could, or maybe wanted to, stop him, John hit Jake with that satisfying crunch he used to feel on the pitch when he'd tackled an opponent and put him down; knowing he wasn't going to get back up again in a hurry.

It took five of them to pull him off.

They say what goes around comes around; this was just the beginning of Jake's turn.

In normal circumstances, the Inspector would have had John Riley up on a charge...but not this time. Jake deserved more than just a decking for what he had done.

'The bastard' thought the Inspector as his emotions tussled with one another. But with Inspector Paul Morrison, as always, reason won.

'Right!' he said, clearing his throat and bringing himself back to the here and now as the rest of the team picked up the garbage from where John Riley had put him.

'And you, Riley, be careful where you're going next time: you could've injured someone running like that!' For discipline's sake, he hoped he didn't sound too flippant. Turning to the others, he said 'Gentlemen, escort the prisoner back to the Service Area. They're waiting for him there.'

At those words, Jake shot the Inspector a look. It was the way he'd said the word 'waiting' that had sent a shiver shooting down Jake's spine, ending in his bladder. He knew he'd be getting a kicking: probably several. In fact, they were probably forming an orderly queue right now. So, this was just the start.

For just a couple of seconds, that feeling, combined with the pressure on his bladder, took Jake straight back to when he was a kid when his drunken stepmother would scream at him: 'Wait till your father gets 'ome! Then you'll get yours, you little bastard!' He still bore the scars all over his body from the heavy metal buckle. He took his beatings in silence then...he'd do the same now.

But Jake did have feelings of regret.

Regret that he hadn't escaped, that he'd been caught, that the job hadn't worked out the way he wanted, that he'd be banged up. Loads of regrets. But Jake's regrets were reserved for him and only him. The cop that got it? Nosepicking Dave and the rest of the crew? 'Goes with the job, dunnit?' thought Jake without a single shred of pity.

As the rest of the team dragged Jake away towards the service area, John Riley stood there watching them, hands on hips, dragging air into his heaving lungs in between spitting out the gobfuls of saliva that keep forming in your mouth when you know you've done something really satisfying...even though it was wrong.

It took a lot to surprise Jake Vickers these days. Over the years, his reputation as a hard bastard meant that he just didn't show any kind of reaction in front of others, no matter how much blood and guts were spilt. But, for once, Jake's jaw fell. Sitting there as he was frogmarched into the service area, were not only Dave, Stan and Charlie...but that little shit, Johnnie Parker...in cuffs!

'What the hell is going on?' thought the leader of the failed hijack.

Sixty

By the time Jake and his crew were on their way to the police cells at the Walworth Road nick, Gary was sitting in his regular traffic jam on his way to the office.

Was it Gary's imagination or was it worse than normal? And whoever it was that came up with the expression 'rush hour' definitely had a warped sense of humour. 'Rush'? You could hardly move let alone rush!

The sheer boredom and predictability of the journey meant that at least half of Gary's brain was always somewhere else as the Quattroporte inched its way closer to the office.

On the radio, the Capital One DJ was blabbing on in the background about the party he'd been to the night before where every star on the planet had been in attendance when suddenly there was a 'we interrupt this programme' bulletin.

It instantly got Gary's full attention and he turned up the volume.

Was this it? Was this the news he'd been waiting for?

There was a dramatic few seconds of silence before the announcer began:

'The M25 between junctions 6 and 5, both ways, have been closed causing massive disruption. The whole of the surrounding areas are gridlocked. You are advised to avoid the area if possible. It is apparently due to a huge explosion and fire at the Cobham Services on the M25. Thick black smoke can be seen billowing into the air for miles around. According to unconfirmed reports, a lorry was leaving the services when it crashed.'

Gary was so intent on listening that he failed to notice that the car in front of him had moved ten feet. The driver of the car behind Gary sat on his horn.

'Is it any wonder that so many London motorists suffer from high blood pressure?' thought Gary, glancing in his rear mirror at the face in the car behind as he released the handbrake and allowed the car to roll forward.

He listened intently as the announcer carried on:

'...according to one unconfirmed report, shots were heard and the police are in attendance at the scene. No other information is available at this time.'

Gary reached for the volume control but stopped as the announcer continued:

'There have also been reports of an armed robbery at a jeweller's store on the High Street near the Oval cricket ground. Again, reports indicate that shots have been fired. Hold on. I think we're going live to our reporter at the scene, Allan Davey. Yes...yes. Allan. Are you there?'

There was a delay of a couple of seconds before the reporter spoke, a cacophony in the background: horns were sounding, people could be heard calling out, some panicking, some frustrated and the reporter's mic picked up a policeman's voice calling out '...come on, move along now, please. We have to clear this area.'

'Thank you, John. Yes, there has been an attempted robbery at a local jewellery store here in the High Street just around the corner from the famous Oval cricket grounds where, according to locals, the owner, a Mr Emmanuel Franks, seventy-two, fought the robbers off single-handedly, despite a number of shots being fired by the raiders. Mr Franks has been taken to hospital but initial reports suggest that he is uninjured. I have Mr Raj Patel, a local shop owner here with me. Mr Patel, you arrived at the scene shortly after the shooting began. Can you tell us what happened?'

'You know, we have been saying for months that we need more police patrols here. Three of our local shopkeepers have been attacked in the last six months. It is not good enough! And now poor Mr Franks. These guys meant business. They had guns!' Mr Patel nearly spat out the last word; it was clear that he was getting more and more agitated as he began to relive the scene. 'When we heard the alarm go off, we have a very supportive community here, you know, we all came running. I picked up the nearest thing I could find, it was a brush but what use is this against guns? One of the robbers said he had a hand grenade he was going to set off.'

'Did you say a hand grenade, Mr Patel?' interrupted the reporter.

'Yes! He reached into his pocket for it and that's when we all panicked and they escaped on their bloody motorbikes! I, myself, come from Kashmir and we lived with this kind of fear every…'

At that point the reporter realised that Mr Patel was in full flow and wasn't going to stop, so he had to do it for him.

'Thank you, Mr Patel. That's all we have time for now. Back to you in the studio.'

'Thank you, Allan Davey at the Oval.'

The DJ then voiced what most of his listeners were probably thinking:

'Two gun related incidents on our streets at the same time. What's the world coming to? What's happening, Londoners? It's beginning to look like we don't own the streets of our Capital anymore. We should write to our MPs and demand an explanation!' he declared vehemently. In the next instant, the 'Outraged of Tonbridge Wells' voice had disappeared and the DJ had reverted back to his usual undulating airheaded voice, announcing: 'And appropriately, our next song is Mr John Paul Young singing 'Love is in the Air''.

Most of London's seventy-plus MPs missed his call to action on air but they found out about it the following day when the letters came pouring through their constituency office letterboxes. He certainly wasn't going to be on their Christmas card list that year.

Gary couldn't wait to get to the office to find out more. Surely the first incident was Jake. But what about the other one? Who was that? Was it Dave Cosforth and his crew? The mention of the hand grenade was the clue. The Hand-Grenade Gang had been all over the papers recently and Dave seemed to be getting bolder.

'He'd better watch out' thought Gary, concerned about a fee-paying client 'He's getting sloppy! The Delivery Man was nearly seen leaving The Bus when he dumped the stuff from their last job. But it sounds like he got more than he bargained for on this latest job. A seventy-two-year-old? What went wrong there? How much of a fight can an old man put up, for God's sake?' And then it dawned on him. 'That's why the bloody traffic's so bad!'

Sixty One

One hour and twelve mind-numbing minutes of inching later, Gary finally steered the Maserati into his reserved space at the office. By the time he got to the office some days, he felt as if he'd done a day's work already. London driving was the pits.

Jeannie had seen the car pull in from the window of her office and clicked 'save' on the file she'd been working on before making her way to the kitchen to prepare the two sugar, double espresso Gary liked to start his day. She'd already taken the call Gary was expecting; except she didn't know that he was expecting it.

When Gary walked through the main doors into the open plan area, all eyes turned to him. And in those eyes could be seen a variety of reactions.

Some of them crinkled as their owners' faces broke into a smile: they were pleased to see the man who paid their wages and wasn't at all a bad employer. In fact, he was one of the more decent and respectful ones who also happened to paid a very generous bonus every Christmas. Enough? It was for them.

Then there were the eyes which checked out his appearance every day: noting the sharpness of the suit, the immaculately polished handmade shoes, the diamond-encrusted Rolex Oyster wristwatch that screamed their favourite mantra: 'I've got fucking money...and loads of it!'

Finally, there were the ones who were a little in awe of the man who, not only could get away with wearing suits which would not look out of place at a mafia convention, but who could find the smallest chink in a prosecutor's argument and charge through it in a Sherman tank. A man then to be admired? That was enough for them.

'Morning, everyone. It's Friday! Nearly there! Ye...s!' declared Gary, flashing his perfect set of gnashers as his fist shot into the air.

'Morning, Gary' was the cheerful reply from one and all.

As Gary strode past their desks he offered a word of encouragement here, a smile there, a pat on the back for the boys. He knew how to work a crowd; especially a jury. They all returned to what they were working on with fresh energy.

'Gary. Can I have a word?' asked Jeannie as she made her way across the office to meet him, the steam rising from the cup of espresso in her hand.

'You can have two words as long as I can have that coffee' he begged.

Gary knew what she was about to tell him but acted the innocent; a bit like most of his clients. It was an unwritten rule in the mornings that Jeannie leave him alone for about fifteen minutes to digest his coffee and catch up with the day's 'to do's' before hitting him with any problems. So, he frowned as if he was surprised. He'd been told on more than one occasion that he'd make a good actor.

'Yes, Jeannie?'

'Did you hear on the news about the incident on the M25?'

'Yeah, something about a fire at the Cobham Services. Terrible. It'll be pandemonium all day on that stretch of the motorway. Glad I'm not using it today. It's bad enough on a good day on there but...' Gary wittered on deliberately; a picture of pure innocence.

'Sorry to interrupt, Gary, but I've had a call about it.'

'Oh, yeah?' enquired the lawyer/actor.

'Mr Vickers, Jake that is, not Frankie who looks after our IT, has been arrested in connection with the incident.'

'What for? He hasn't added pyromania to his list of skills, has he?' joked Gary.

'No, it's much worse than that' replied Jeannie with that tone in her voice she reserved for only the most serious of situations. 'He tried to hijack a lorry and in the process, he, allegedly, killed a policeman.'

Gary gasped. Now that did catch him off-guard. He knew about the first part but what the hell was Jake thinking about killing a cop? That was serious shit.

'Jes...us!' was all he could think to say as he stood rooted to the spot. Jeannie stood and waited, knowing that it would take all of thirty seconds before Gary marshalled his thoughts and started issuing instructions. She was out by three seconds. Twenty-seven seconds later Gary had made his list.

'Right. Who called...and from where?' The momentary shock brushed aside, it was business as usual for the sharp legal brain which had built up one of the most lucrative criminal practices in the City.

'It was Jake himself who called. They're holding him at Walworth Road station. He sounded in a bit of a state.'

'Jeannie,' observed Gary '...he's a cop-killer: he's lucky he's still alive.'

'Oh and one other thing: he says he's innocent and he's been stitched up. I'm using his words, of course' she finished.

'What the hell has he gotten himself into, Jeannie?' said Gary sounding concerned for a client but in his head he was thinking:

'You stupid, stupid man! Why couldn't you leave well alone? Now you're really for the high jump. And it's up to me to persuade a jury that you're innocent. How in Hell am I supposed to do that?'

The truth was that for the amount that Jake would be paying him, Gary would do his best, his very best. Even though Jake wasn't Gary's favourite villain at the moment and despite the fact that he'd tried to turn Gary over by hijacking his lorry, he would still get a first-class service. But in his heart Gary knew that his best would still be at least ten years...on a good day.

'What about the rest of his gang?' asked Gary, thinking aloud as he prepared for the battle he was about to join.

'Pardon?' replied Jeannie, taken aback by the unexpected question. 'I never mentioned a gang.'

Gary instantly knew that he'd slipped up. Jeannie hadn't mentioned 'a gang'. But Gary knew they were there.

'Oh...what I meant was, he wasn't be trying to hijack a lorry on his own, was he? So, what's happening with them? Are we representing them?' he said recovering quickly as he thought on his mental tootsies.

'He...never mentioned them' she replied hesitantly, still frowning, still trying to work out how Gary knew that there was a gang.

'That's typical Jake: looking after Numero Uno!' he said, trying to laugh off his error. 'Ah well, I'll find out when I get to the station after my meeting. Which one did you say again, Jeannie?'

Gary was watching her very carefully, watching for any sign that would indicate she wasn't convinced by his explanation; just like he did with juries. He spent a huge amount of his time in court watching jurors' faces. Were they convinced by his argument? Did a point the prosecution made hit home? Most jurors tried not to show any reaction but when you were as long in the tooth as Gary Dean, you got to know the signs. Usually, it was the eyes. When Gary or the prosecutor made a point, sometimes, one or two of them would turn to look at the defendant. 'Now, was that a look of support or antagonism? Were they with him or against him on that one?' Gary would regularly ask himself. Then there were the ones whose seats would suddenly become uncomfortable as something disagreeable was mentioned. For a few minutes, they would become restless as the thought stayed with them until the next thing caught their attention. 'Now what did that mean?' he would ask himself, constantly raking them over, weighing them up. With others, it was a little cough; that nervous clearing of the throat, as if something was stuck in it. Was it something he or the prosecution had said? Did it tip the balance more in the defence's favour or the prosecution's? If it was for the prosecution, how did he redress the balance? If it was for the defence, how did he keep it and build on it? Which jurors, did he think, were for and which against? Was there any chance of turning any of the antis to pros? Interpreting these signs would leave Gary exhausted at the end of a Court day. But that's what made him so successful. Yes, the argument had to be convincing but no matter how powerful the argument, if the jury didn't want to believe it, if they took a dislike to your client or you then you had to try another tact and have it ready, just in case.

That is, unless a defendant takes it upon themselves to wreck their own defence. Like the pimp Gary was defending who turned up for the first day of the Court hearing, wearing a suit not dissimilar to the sort that Mr Dean himself would have chosen. The first day, Gary let it go. But the next day, he turned up in a different suit but of a similar ilk.

There was no time for beating around the bush. Gary told it like it was.

'Get yourself home now and get changed. If the jury see you in another flash suit, they're gonna wonder how a man who claims to earn his living as a pizza delivery man for his best friend's business is able to buy such expensive gear and so much of it. So, you've made your first appearance in your Sunday best. Fine. From now on, I want you to come to Court wearing what most of the male members of this jury would wear on a day to day basis and what they would expect you to be wearing, if you're not living off immoral earnings, and that is plain and ordinary. Most of the people on juries have very mundane, uninteresting lives. They struggle to make ends meet. I want them to think that you're one of them: one of their own. That way we get them on our side. And what that will mean is every time the prosecution opens his mouth, he has to work ten times harder to get his point across. So, we're talking: sports jacket, plain trousers, not too perfectly pressed shirt, drab tie and rubber, yes, I did say rubber...' Gary repeated when he saw the look of disbelief in his client's eyes '...soled shoes...and not too shiny! Remember, you're a pizza delivery man not the CEO of a plc. Now get movin' and get back here fast. His Lordship does not take kindly to be kept waiting. You got it?'

He got it and he got off. Lesson learned.

It wouldn't be quite that simple in the case of Regina v Jacob Tindell Vickers aka Jake the moneylending cop murderer. No Siree.

Sixty Two

At ten o'clock precisely, a nervous Mr Huq pushed open the swing door leading to the offices of Gary Dean and partners.

Raquel gave him her most engaging smile and directed him to one the plush leather sofas in reception. The offer of coffee gratefully accepted, Raquel phoned through to Gary to let him know his client had arrived.

It was a pleasant day outside, not warm but certainly not cold. Nevertheless, a fine film of sweat was visible along the diplomat's receding hairline. From time to time, he dabbled at it with his spotless, oversized white handkerchief which he retrieved from his breast pocket as he mulled over the purpose of this meeting.

For reasons of security, communication between Gary and him were restricted pretty much to the occasions Mr Huq called to enquire about the available times of The Bus. The only other communications being the transfer of monies to Gary's offshore account following successful negotiations with the clients whose names had been forwarded, in code, to Mr Huq's secure Embassy email address, by Gary.

'So what can the problem be now?' he fretted. 'Are the facilities of The Bus being withdrawn? Have I overstepped the marks?' he wondered in his imperfect English 'Where else could I place such large amounts of cash without raising the suspicions of the British Establishment or indeed my own people? Oh, dearee, dearee me.'

So deep in his own thoughts was he that he didn't hear Jeannie call his name. After failing to get a response a second time, Jeannie walked over and touched him on the shoulder.

Had he been holding the coffee cup at the time, its contents would probably have ended up on the ceiling.

'Oh, I'm sorry Mr Huq, I didn't mean to startle you. Are you alright?'

'I'm fine, dear lady, I must have been dreaming' he explained, pulling himself together.

'Mr Dean is ready to see you now. If you'll follow me, please.'

'Yes, indeed, please.'

Gary rose from his desk, his best smile plastered across his face for the overwrought, overweight minor diplomat as Jeannie ushered him in.

Oddly, she hadn't heard of or seen this client before but Gary and he seemed to be acquainted. 'Probably knows him from one of those 'power breakfasts' they have for businesspeople in the City' she thought.

'Mr Huq, thank you for coming! Please, take a seat. Can I offer you a coffee?'

'No thank you, Mr Dean, I was very kindly offered one when I arrived.'

'Then shall we get down to business?' asked Gary, conscious that he needed to keep this meeting short: Jake was waiting for him.

'Ye...s indeed' replied Mr Huq hesitantly.

'Thank you, Jeannie. I'll buzz you if I need you' Jeannie closed the door behind her and left.

Gary's desk was clear except for one item lying in the centre of it; a calculator.

'What is the problem, please Mr Dean?'

'There is no problem whatsoever, Mr Huq' began Gary disarmingly.

Mr Huq's shoulders relaxed visibly.

'We just have a bit of renegotiation to sort out' Gary offered with another quick flash of the pearlies.

Mr Huq's shoulders returned to their previous position.

'You see, I reckon...' began Gary as he reached for the calculator.

Twenty-five minutes later, Jeannie was showing a very subdued Mr Huq out while her boss collected everything he needed for his next meeting at Walworth Road nick with Jake.

'20% of the extra he's making seems very reasonable to me' thought Gary gleefully. 'I think if I'd asked for 25% he would've cried. Ah well! That's the way to do it!' he said to himself in his best Mr Punch voice.

'Onwards and upwards!' he declared as he prepared for his next battle.

Sixty Three

The reprisals would come later: the 'why didn't you do this?' and 'you could've done that' tit for tat sort of scenarios. It wouldn't be pretty and would get nasty. When a job goes wrong, fingers are pointed all over the place but the reality was they failed. Didn't matter whose fault it was.

But for the moment, they were all pulling together, the shock keeping them focussed on survival.

Once they were out of immediate danger, Dave and the boys slowed down to the law-abiding speed limit.

Bron managed to stem the flow of blood by keeping pressure on the area surrounding the wound, even though it hurt like hell but held on until they got to the lock-up: he didn't have a choice. End of.

Once inside, Markie removed Bron's leather and ripped his blood-sodden shirt open to check out the damage. It was not the most hygienic of surroundings, lock-up garages very seldom are, but the alternative of walking into A&E didn't come into the equation.

'Good job I did my St John's Ambulance First Aid while I was in nick, eh, Bron?' said Markie trying to lighten the mood.

'Just fuckin' do it, will you, boyo?' shouted Bron, the pain broadening his Welsh accent.

Dave, in the meantime, was on his mobile to Mikey.

'...yeah, yeah, it was us. Look, we'll talk about it later, Mikey. No, later! Okay? It's a complete fuck-up! The old geezer stuck Bron; Markie's sortin' 'im out now. You just empty the boot and I'll catch you later' said Dave referring to the incriminating evidence Mikey was carrying. He hung up and rubbed the heel of his hand into his suddenly tired eyes, slowly emptying the air out of his lungs in a hissing sound. He held it there for a few seconds before slowly sucking air back in again, feeling the oxygen feed into his brain; they were far from being out of the woods yet. He needed to think and think fast but now that they were out of immediate danger, the adrenalin that had kept him going was gone and he just wanted to curl up and sleep. However, he also had customers' windows that would not wash themselves. He had to get back on his round so as not to raise suspicion.

'Here...' said Markie handing over two strong painkillers to Bron '...take these. They'll take about fifteen minutes to kick in. You know, it's not that bad...considering' said Markie interrupting Dave's thoughts as he wiped the dried blood away from the puncture hole with a wet wipe from a packet which Dave had just handed to him. 'Another few centimetres and we'd 'ave been havin' a wake for you, Bron boy. It's gonna be painful for a good few weeks to come. There'll be no bank jobs for you for the next couple of months.'

'There'll be none for any of us' growled Dave ominously '...for a long time to come. We're all gonna have to lay low for a long time. An' by the way, Mikey heard about us on the radio. It's probably on the telly by now. Shit!'

When Dave was in that sort of mood, it was best to let him be. He needed thinking space. So, Markie and Bron spoke in hushed tones as Markie continued to clean up the wound.

Dave moved over to the bike Bron and Markie had used and began checking it for bloodstains; no point in handing evidence to the police on the proverbial silver platter. But had they left anything at Manny's? Dave tried to take himself back to the shop and 'see' the chaotic scene they left behind. Was there anything that would lead the police to them? Because if it led to one of them, they'd all get their collars felt. And Dave did not fancy standing in the dock in front of twelve just men/women. The thought of watching their faces as Bron's grenade-tossing escapades were relived in minute detail by a prosecutor who would relish passing photos of the devastation left behind by the gang to a jury who would be thinking 'Christ! That could have been me or the wife or me mum' or for that matter, the cat, did not appeal. By that stage, they're really beginning to hate you because they're projecting into the future, convinced that if you hadn't been caught, someone they knew would've got it.

'I cannot believe it' thought Dave. 'One lousy fuckin' job an' I was out of it, clean as a whistle. Should've been like takin' candy from a kid! An' here was me feelin' sorry for 'poor old Manny'. Tellin' the boys to go easy on 'im. The old bastard! I should be headin' to the Costa, sippin' cocktails by the pool! Now what am I gonna do? Shit!'

The mood stayed with him for a while as he inspected both bikes for any telltale signs.

'By the way, Bron, where's the knife? You did bring it with you, didn't you?' asked Dave.

'It's in my inside pocket' Bron replied. Dave gingerly picked up Bron's jacket trying to avoid getting blood on himself. As he was about to put his hand inside, Bron called out 'Wait!'

'What the fuck's the matter now?' yelled Dave, clearly on a very short fuse.

'The grenades are in one of the pockets and the blade's in the other, so be careful!'

'Christ! A right pocket full of posies you've got!' said Dave using two fingers to extract the knife.

Grabbing hold of it in his right hand with the blade pointing upwards, he turned it slowly, fascinated as a beam of light from the overhead neon bounced lazily off the blood-encrusted weapon.

'So this is it? This is all we've got to show for this morning's work?' The more he turned it, the darker his mood seemed to become. 'That pathetic old bastard managed to fight off three of us, who, by the way, just happened to be tooled up an' this is all we have to show for all those months of casin' the bloody joint.' His tone got nastier and nastier with each turn. 'This is fuckin' it, is it? This? Bollocks!' With one sudden motion, he threw the blade at the breezeblock wall of the garage with such force that it shattered, falling to the floor in bits.

With his back still to the boys, he said: 'Between the police and the newspapers there's gonna be a lot of heat, boys. So, we stay away from one another; we all go back to our jobs an' act normal? Right?' He turned to look directly at them and finished off with 'An' we don't panic. Understood?'

He missed off 'Or else' at the end; he didn't have to. The boys got the message loud and clear. They knew what he really meant was: 'Don't do anything stupid that would get us caught, 'cause if you do...'

'Okay we can't stand around all day chattin', I've got work to get on with. Bron, you'd better ring in sick for a couple of days an' dose yerself up on painkillers. Is he gonna be alright, Markie?'

'Just needs to rest, Dave. It's gonna take a while to heal but as long as he keeps it clean and doesn't try to mug old ladies for a few weeks, he should be fine.'

'Very fuckin' funny, Markie!' said Bron through gritted teeth.

'Right, well let's go then. I've got windows to wash' said Dave slipping into his work overalls. 'An' remember: stay low! D'you 'ear?'

'I don't think any of us fancy a long stay at one of Her Majesty's B&Bs, Dave' said Markie, speaking for the two of them.

Dave's response was a low 'Hmm' as he stared at them for a couple of seconds in silence. Looking from one to the other, into each of their eyes, he was looking for something which could...worry him. But when he saw that his message had gotten through, he nodded slightly, turned and walked over to the up and over garage door and threw it up. As he walked towards his van, he said:' You boys go first. I'll wait a couple of minutes and then lock up. An' only make contact if there's an emergency. Otherwise, schtum.'

Markie had helped Bron into his work suit; he looked reasonably presentable. At least the bleeding had stopped and the painkillers were beginning to kick in although, for Bron, the shoulder still felt like it was on fire. Markie also put Bron's leather jacket into a couple of black binliner bags.

'Remember the grenades are in there, Bron. What're you going to do with them?'

'Now that you've reminded me, Markie, I might drop them off at my Nan's before I go home. She'll probably try to feed me up, like she always does, an' that should keep me going for the rest of the day; save me havin' to go out again.'

'What about meetin' for a pint, maybe tomorrow?' Markie asked as they walked out of the lockups.

'Are you mad?' replied Bron, not believing what he'd just heard.

'If Dave heard what you just said he'd shoot us 'imself, you twat!'

'I'll take that as a 'No' then, shall I?' said a disappointed Markie.

'Too fuckin' right!'

He and Bron regularly met for a few jars after work but Dave had said they should stay low. Wouldn't it look strange if they didn't meet?

By then, they'd reached the end of the lockups and they split up without another word, going in opposite directions.

Two minutes later, Dave drove past Bron without a second glance; just another workman off to join the rest of the world trying to scratch a living. Within twenty minutes, Dave was back on the High Street again...only this time he was armed with a bucket and a squeegee.

Sixty Four

Gary was kept waiting a long time at the custody desk; the usual friendly banter, missing. But then he was there to defend a cop killer. The regular custody sergeant, Ken Morris, on duty today, barely acknowledged Gary even though he was a frequent visitor to the cells there; Gary's clients kept both sides of the legal fence in regular employment.

On one particular occasion at that station, Gary had been kept waiting a long time to see a client and, as you do, his thoughts drifted. He would regularly return to that thought, it amused him: what would happen if one day scientists invented a pill which was to be taken at night, like one of those constipation tablets that guaranteed you had a good clearout the following morning, and the criminal woke up the following morning to find he was a law-abiding citizen? 'Cleared out', so to speak, of all criminal tendencies. 'And why not?' he thought 'They're discovering all sorts of cures all the time. So, why not something which could cure old lags?'

He smiled at the thought, following it through.

'So what would clients like Jake Vickers do then? Hmm, he owns a Laundromat, I suppose he could do service washes' He got a fit of the giggles which drew strange looks from those around him; custody suites were not normally places of jollity.

He went through the list of his 'not entirely straight' clients, people like Jack Clancy, the biggest pimp, by the sheer number of girls he controlled, in the Capital.

'Now what could he become after he swallowed his 'night before' pill?' At his play on the 'morning after' pill, he laughed out loud.

'You alright, Sir?' enquired the custody sergeant, looking over the shoulder of a drunken teenager whose details he was patiently trying to extricate.

'Yes, thank you. I just remembered an inappropriate joke one of my clients told me' he lied.

The custody sergeant's eyebrows flipped quizzically as his eyes widened. 'Oh, really, Sir?'

No. Amusement was not on the menu in custody suites; at least, not in the ones Gary Dean frequented. Anyway, he decided that as Jack Clancy was so good at 'hiring' young ladies then maybe he could get a job as a talent scout: they're good at spotting young ladies' attributes.

'Your client's ready for you, Mr Dean' said Sergeant Jim Wallis, appearing from the area of the interview rooms and interrupting Gary's train of thought. According to Sergeant Wallis, Chief Superintendent Moore and he, had just concluded an initial interview with Jake.

Apart from confirming his name and address, Jake's replies to their questions was an unsurprising 'No Comment' But the policemen weren't too bothered; they had enough evidence this time to ensure that Jake ate at the table of one of Her Majesty's Category A's for a very long time to come. In fact, Jim Wallis hoped that when his turn came to join his fellow masons in heaven's lodge that Jake would still be dining at the said Category A. For him, to die knowing that the bastard was still inside would be what most people call job satisfaction.

Gary was shocked when he entered the interview room: Jake's face was a mess.

He waited until Sergeant Wallis had left the room before saying 'My God, Jake! What happened?'

'I fell' replied Jake gruffly through puffy lips. Both of his eyelids were beginning to close.

'What? On to someone's fists? You can't let this go, Jake. You...'

'Thanks for your concern, Gary, but can we get on with this? I really just want to get a kip' replied the man who had fully come down to earth. Would he have killed the cop if he hadn't been high? This question didn't even enter Jake's consciousness: he dealt only in 'what happeneds' not 'what ifs'.

'Well, have you seen a doctor? D'you want me to get one before we start?'

'Just leave it. I'll be fine' said the guy who knew how the system worked: he had a lot more of that to come. 'So better get used to it' he thought resignedly.

Gary paused for a moment: the realisation that it was all down to him, hit home.

'You're sure there's nothing I can do for you, Jake?' he asked again.

'I'm sure, Gary. Listen, I've been stitched up: the police were waiting for us'. There was a pause. 'But I know who did it' continued Jake, looking directly into Gary's eyes. Jake stopped speaking and the silence of the room became unbelievably oppressive. Gary desperately wanted to run out of that room and not come back: but he knew he couldn't. He held Jake's stare; he had to. If Jake caught any hint, any indication that Gary was involved or knew anything, Gary would be in serious danger: it wasn't only the law that had a long arm.

'I'll deal with him when the time's right. For the moment, he can just sweat it out...an' wait for me to come an' get 'im.'

All the time, Jake kept staring into Gary's eyes through the puffy slits surrounding his own.

Gary felt like an ice cube had just slid down his spine.

'Jesus, Jake...' said Gary '...you're beginning to frighten me.'

'Then can you imagine how he must feel? God, Gary, you've just made me feel a whole lot better. The satisfaction of knowin' that 'e knows and 'im just waitin' for it. Oooh yes, I do feel a lot better' said Jake sitting up in the uncomfortable bucket chair that is a stalwart of interview rooms the world over.

'Okay. We'd better get started. We've got a lot to do to convince a jury that you're innocent. And when we're finished here, I'm going to make sure they take photos of your face; I want to show this police brutality to the jurors.'

'Whatever, Gary' said Jake smiling first and then grimacing at the pain any movement of his facial muscles caused.

'Oh, just before we start, who's looking after your boys? Have they got their own briefs?' said Gary, not meaning to be funny.

'Well, they won't be getting into my knickers!' replied Jake, trying not to laugh.

'You know what I mean.' Even Gary smiled at his unintentional humour.

'You got someone in your place that could deal with 'em? Not you though, I need you to concentrate on my problems and besides, you're way too fuckin' expensive to deal with those useless wankers, Gary.'

'Let me just make a quick call to the office and see who's free.'

A couple of minutes later Gary had sorted it: Jeannie was organising things at that end. Within the hour, three of his staff would present themselves at the station to consult with their new clients.

'So, tell me, Jake, what happened?' That phrase which Gary had used a thousand times to clients, allowing the floodgates to open with the usual mixture of fiction and a little bit of fact thrown in. Back to normality; or at least, the sort Gary was used to dealing with.

Of course, Jake admitted shooting the policeman...but only in self-defence: in the seconds before he pulled the trigger, poor Jake was in fear of his life. Music to Gary's ears: he was already constructing the defence argument. He would give a jury a run for...his client's money.

Two hours and fifteen minutes of relating his version of events coupled with the spin Gary put on it and suddenly Jake began to think he could actually beat the rap.

There was no chance of that but Gary failed mention it: his job was to give the client hope. Hope meant the client would continue to pay for his services and add to the bottom line profit of the case. Gary Dean was a pedlar of hope...and hope was a good paymaster.

As he left the police station, Gary realised that people like Jake were an argument against his 'night before' pill idea.

'Let's be honest,' he thought as he got into his car 'just think how much employment is created by the Jakes of this world. There were probably thirty or forty police at the stake out. Then there's the detectives who'll be following this case through, the prosecution team, the defence team, of course! Now then, who else?' he thought as the engine, unlike a Ferrari or a Lamborghini, gave a muted roared, hinting at the beast beneath the bonnet, when he turned on the ignition. 'Ah yes! And what about the chasers, the enforcers, and the banks he probably keeps in business with his excellent cash flow. Never goes into overdraft. There's probably a lot more and Jake's just one very small minnow in this world of low finance. No, it would be a sorry day for the economy if the Jakes of this world ever got hold of the 'night before' pill' he concluded.

Sixty Five

There was a fifty-foot cordon around Manny's by the time Dave worked his way down the High Street to the small emporium. All the time, listening to the comments, the gossip, listening for any small thing which might give him a clue as to whether the police had anything: he would not be caught out twice. Success had made him sloppy. Not spotting the knife at Manny's had been careless and his fault alone. It wouldn't happen again; this time, Dave's ears were on high alert.

'Hey, Dave!' called out one of his regulars, Mr Patel from Pat's Supermart as he approached the window cleaner 'Good job you weren't here earlier...' he continued at a lower pitch when he reached him '...otherwise you might have got your bollocks blown off!' and he laughed.

Dave joined in saying 'You can't believe it, can you, Mr P? You just don't expect it to 'appen 'ere.'

'It's not good you know, Dave. Five times this month I've had to chase people out of my shop who were pinching stuff. Five times!'

'What's the world's coming to, eh, Mr P?'

'Well, at least this time the police have something to go on' announced Mr Patel importantly.

'Oh, yeah? What's that then?' replied Dave as casually as he could, hoping that Mr Patel wouldn't notice the slight tremor which had just begun in the hand holding the squeegee.

'I did my public duty, Dave. I told the police something very significant about the robbers.'

'Come on then, Mr Patel, quit teasin'. What're you talkin' about?'

Unable to resist the sense of importance it gave him; Mr Patel came closer to Dave and spoke in a voice just loud enough for Dave to hear above the noise of the passing traffic:

'I'm not supposed to say anything to anybody about it, Dave. The policeman I told said not to say anything. But...' Dave was beside himself. Apart from grabbing the small rotund Asian shopkeeper in the Prince of Wales check suit by the lapels and shaking it out of him, he didn't know what to do. Looking back on it later, he didn't know how he stopped himself. 'You know I won't say anything to anyone, Mr P. Mum's the word'. Dave offered like a father confessor. He needed to know and fast.

'Well...' Mr Patel hesitated again. Dave could see the regret in his eyes that he'd begun this conversation at all.

'Look, Mr P, if you think it's goin' to get you into trouble, then keep it to yourself' said Dave trying some reverse psychology. Apart from throttling the little bastard on the spot, in public, and choking it out of him, Dave was running out of options.

But in the end, Mr Patel's need to share his knowledge and show how clever he was, got the better of him.

'Well, it is only a little bit of information' he began by way of preparing Dave in case Dave wasn't going to be too impressed.

'Come on, you twat!' screamed Dave's brain but his mouth managed to keep it together as he calmly said:

'I'm sure it must be important if the policeman told you not to say anything about it, Mr P'. Dave's blood pressure was rising faster than a high-speed lift: the difference being though that a lift eventually stops.

Mr Patel had literally opened his mouth to say 'it' when out of the shop sauntered the fragrant Mrs Patel. If ever there was a time when Dave wanted someone to self-immolate, this was it.

'Ranjit!' she called angrily 'It's Friday morning, we have a queue almost out the door and all you can do is stand on the street corner gossiping like an old woman? Come on, we have work to do.'

Mr Patel looked at Dave apologetically and said 'Don't mind the wife, Dave, she gets a bit agitated sometimes. Better go.'

Dave thought he was going to throw up. He gave it one last shot.

'Don't leave me in suspense, Mr P!' Dave called out to the departing shop owner's back 'What's the clue?'

Mr Patel stopped in his tracks and turned reluctantly, mixed emotions clearly etched in his face. Finally, he said 'One of them called out a name. I heard it. It was...' he paused, Dave's head was swimming '... he said

'Ron'. That's what I heard 'Ron'' He turned away from Dave and continued on his way towards the entrance to his shop.

'Well spotted, Mr P' replied the robber whose blood pressure dropped so quickly his legs nearly gave way. 'That should help the police a lot, I'll bet. Mum's the word, eh?' he said tapping the side of his nose.

'Mum's the fuckin' word, pal' he whispered to the retreating back.

''Ello, Dave' said a deep bass voice from behind. Dave spun around so fast that he kicked his bucket and some water sloshed onto the pavement. He was desperately hoping that whoever the voice belonged to, hadn't heard the last thing he'd said...or the menacing way in which it'd been said.

'Here, careful young man' said the voice of the local beat cop, PC Walker. 'I might have to nick you for littering Her Majesty's highways' as he dodged the flow of water which trickled down towards the gutter.

John Walker had been pounding this beat for over twenty years and was months away from retirement. There was nothing he didn't know about the locals. Well, nothing, that is, apart from the fact that the window cleaner he was talking to now was wanted for some of the most brutal and spectacular robberies in the Capital over the last couple of years, including this one; he wasn't to know that Dave had already decided that this job would not be appearing on his CV.

'Oh, 'ello, John. You startled me! I was a million miles away' while he thought to himself 'I wish I fuckin' was!'

'Might as well be, Dave. It's the end of the road for you today, my lad.'

The blood pressure that was on its way down after Mr P's revelation, took to the stratosphere again and Dave put his hand against the window he'd just washed to steady himself.

''Er Dave, are you alright, mate?' a concerned PC Walker asked.

Dave had come out in a cold sweat, the blood draining from his face as he replied hoarsely:

'You got the wrong guy, gov.'

Many years ago, when Dave started out on his criminal career, one old lag had given Dave a bit of advice which he'd never forgotten: 'When they nick you, son, the arresting officer 'as to read out in court what the suspect said when they were arrested an' it always gets a laugh from the jury when they consult their notes and read out: 'You got the wrong guy, guv.'

It was finally going to be Dave's turn to see if it worked.

''Ere you need to sit down, son. I'll get you a chair' and the policeman rushed into the supermarket to find something for Dave to sit on.

He came back with a stool, followed by Mrs Patel carrying a glass of water.

'You did take a turn there, Dave. Sorry, mate, I didn't mean to make you jump. I thought you'd be pleased.'

'Pleased?' repeated Dave, confused.

'Yeah! I thought you'd be pleased to 'ave an early finish 'cause you can't go any further. It's a crime scene down there an' so you'll have to knock off early. I thought you'd think it was your lucky day.'

'Aw...yeah. Yeah, my lucky day' a relieved Dave replied, colour returning to his cheeks.

'That's a bit better.'

'God, I think I've been overdoing it lately' said Dave, pulling out his handkerchief and wiping his face. 'Doris 'an me, we're off to Costa del Sol tomorrow an' I've been puttin' in some extra hours 'cause we need the money, like.'

'You want to be around to spend it, Dave' offered the policeman. 'Now you get yerself 'ome. That'll be okay, Mrs Patel, won't it?'

'No problem, Dave. You take it easy today and have a nice holiday. And come back nice and fresh.'

Dave stood up and made sure his legs had stopped shaking enough to get on his way: he desperately wanted to be out of there.

'Right then, boys and girls. That's it. I'll be off then!' said Dave pulling himself together and making his way through the crowded pavement to the kerb where he emptied his bucket and squeezed his sponge out.

After the encounter with Manny, Dave could've done without Mr P's near-miss revelation, followed by PC Walker's attempt at gallows humour. His old nerve ends didn't just feel shattered; they felt like they'd completely disintegrated.

'Maybe I am gettin' too old for this game' he thought to himself as he strolled along among the Friday morning shoppers. 'Maybe it is time to retire the old swag bag gracefully and hang it over the fireplace for my Christmas presents'. At least, the thought of it made Dave laugh.

As his back disappeared into the Friday morning crush, PC Walker and Mrs Patel stood together watching him. Mrs Patel's face wore a worried frown as she turned to the policeman and said:

'I sometimes worry that my husband works too hard, you know. And then this morning when poor Mr Franks' shop was robbed, he grabbed this broom and went charging off down there! It's not good for him at his age.'

'Especially when there's guns involved, Mrs Patel. Next time, please tell Mr Patel to leave it to us; we don't want anybody getting hurt. These guys meant business and it could have been a lot worse. But you've got to hand it to old Manny...' he said smiling at the thought '...he sent them packin'! He wasn't goin' to let them get their 'ands on 'is stuff! Boy, did they pick the wrong geezer! More power to his elbow, that's what I say.'

'He was a brave but foolish man, I think, Mr Franks...' replied Mrs Patel, reflecting on it '...especially at his age. They could have killed him! And if it was that damn 'Hand-Grenade Gang' that they've been talking about in the newspapers, I'm surprised that there wasn't anybody killed. What's the world coming to, Constable Walker? What is happening to our world?'

'That, Mrs Patel, is a mystery beyond me. Every day I see and hear things which, to be honest, make me want to go and live on an uninhabited island.'

'But surely if you lived there it wouldn't be uninhabited anymore, Constable Walker?' she laughed.

'Hmm, you have a point there, Mrs Patel! An' I could stand here all day debatin' it with you but I've got 'tea leaves' to catch an' truanting kids to return to school. Friday. It seems to bring out the delinquents!'

'And the children, Constable Walker?' came back Mrs Patel with a twinkle in her eye.

They both laughed. Friday morning was returning to normal on the High Street. As the hours marched on, preparations for the weekend were becoming more hectic.

Party time...for some.

Sixty Six

Gary stood on the steps of the police station lighting a badly-needed cigarette, the interview with Jake over, he was reflecting on the train of events which had led him there when his mobile blasted him out of his reverie with its strident American ringtone.

'I must change that one of these days' he decided, irritated at being interrupted mid-thought.

It was home.

Nicki rarely called unless it was urgent: she knew that most of the time, Gary was either in Court, where it would be turned off or in conference with clients, where it would be on silent. So, whatever it was, it must be important.

'Yes, darling?' he answered, concern clearly in his voice.

'Sorry to bother you, Gary, but it's Harry. I just passed his bedroom and the poor lamb was sobbing his heart out. He's really taken Amanda's death pretty badly. I didn't knock, I just don't know what to do'. Nicki wasn't one of the 'wrap them in cotton wool' brigade by any means but she still worried about her only child.

Gary immediately put Jake and his problems onto a mental shelf to be dealt with later: his family crisis took precedence.

'What do we do, Nicki?' asked Gary.

'I don't know, Gary. I really don't know.'

The silence which hung between the two of them lingered on as both of them racked their brains trying to find the solution which would heal their child's heartache.

'What about a holiday? Or maybe go to visit your mum? He loves his Nana Gertie' said Gary clutching at a few feeble straws.

'No, no. He can't. I don't want to interrupt his studies. They're too important.'

'I think we all need a break. This last week or so has been horrendous. I haven't even had the chance to ask you how you are, Nicki. How are you coping, my love?'

She might not belong to the 'cotton wool' brigade but she was definitely a fully paid up member of the rigid upper lip mob: one tough cookie was Mrs Gary Dean.

'Oh, I'll be fine' she said with conviction. Then back to the silence.

'Listen...' said Gary, the germ of an idea pushing its way past all the others '...what about us all going down to Brighton for the day on Sunday? We'll go to The Grand for lunch and have a walk along the beach, skim a few pebbles over the waves and give the cobwebs a good blow. And maybe for good measure, we'll go on the pier and try a couple of rides. Fancy that, babe?' He only called her that in times of stress.

'I'd love to but I'm not sure Harry will go for it.'

'He will. Trust me. I'll talk to him when I get home tonight. I won't be late, darling. Listen, better go. See you later.'

'Thanks, Gary. You're like my little personal sticking plaster: you always ease my pain. Bye, my darling.'

'Poor bastard' thought Gary as he hung up. Taking a few moments to himself, he watched the world and his mother go by. 'At Harry's age, I remember, the worst thing that could happen was for a girl to dump you. The embarrassment, the pain! But for him to have found her like that. Will he ever get over it?' Gary took one long last drag on his cigarette, dropped it and squashed it under one of his immaculate brown crocodile shoes. 'He will, if I have anything to do with it.' he concluded fiercely.

Chief Superintendent Moore and Sergeant Wallis came out of the front door of the station, noticed Gary and stopped mid-conversation but not before Gary had heard the dour Scotsman say something about '...I've just heard that the body's been identified as Peter Dav...'

Gary could see from the drawn look on both faces that the death of their colleague still hung over them. They nodded curtly, and continued on their way.

There was no question about it: Gary knew he was regarded as a pariah by the local fuzz: he was the enemy. It went with the territory. Weighed against the remuneration he received, however, it was a small price to pay and worth it. Unlike his clients, who took on the system and tried to beat it illegally, Gary got a real buzz from using the system's own antiquated, pedantic rules to knock it flat on its back... and while he was at it; kick it in the teeth and rub its nose in it, and all at the same time, if he could.

He wanted to shout out to the two police officers: 'You're not the only ones, you know. My son's just lost someone very precious to him and he's devastated too.'

But he didn't. Instead, he took Jake and his problems off the shelf and began to think about what rabbits he could pull out of his legal hat to tip the jury's opinion in Jake's favour. It wasn't going to be easy. 'But if it was easy, every two-bit solicitor would be getting in on the act. No,' he concluded, '...there aren't too many Gary Deans in this town to assist the sick Mr Vickers' of this sick world.'

Sixty Seven

He wasn't the only one deep in thought. Anyone looking in on him in his bedroom that afternoon would have thought that Sham was in the middle of some Transcendental Meditation exercise. He was sitting in the classic Lotus position on his bed, for all the world looking like he was on another plane. They would, of course, have been completely wrong. He was, in fact, running over every single detail for tonight's job: every twist, every turn, of every corridor. Location of light switches. Doors: which ones opened inwards and which, outwards, where each door led to, which ones belonged to store cupboards, which were locked. Everything. He left nothing to chance normally and it applied doubly for this one. This was the big one: entry to the big league. But then it wasn't some snivelling little bond dealer on a London bus who'd welched on his debts. No. This was John Pollock, the John Pollock, his two nasty pooches and his henchmen that Sham would be dealing with.

Even though the dummy run was only in his head, Sham could feel the adrenalin rush coursing through his whole body. But what he was looking for was the bit which separated him from your average hitman. The bit which most of them not only got wrong, they weren't even aware of its existence: balance. And that balance was between fear and excitement. That's what Sham was checking out right now. Was the excitement chasing the fear or was it vice-versa? Did it look like one was overshadowing the other?

Allow fear to overtake the excitement and a job would never get done; flight would become the overall consideration. If excitement took over, gung-ho became the order of the day and that's why the Charge of the Light Brigade became legend: but a legend littered with a lot of dead ex-gung-hoers.

So, for Sham, neither of these scenarios could be allowed. Balancing them was the all-important factor. That's what set him apart. That's why he was the best.

Having gone through all of the potential 'what if?' situations like 'what if someone walks in?' or 'what if this door or that window is locked tonight?' and all the others his mind conjured up, Sham came to the point where he felt confident that he could deal with all the eventualities tonight would throw at him.

'Okay, Mr Pollock, I respect who and what you are but the old "what goes around comes around" is just about to knock at your door...and it's fallen to me to make sure you get yours and at the special request of my client, it's gonna have barbed wire wrapped around it. So, there you have it' thought Sham, grimacing at the image of it.

He opened his eyes and reached over to the top of his bedside cabinet and picked up his iPod. Scrolling through the choices, he went to classical and selected the Bach's Double Violin Concerto, his favourite piece of chill music and pressed play as he slowly stretched out on the bed. He loved his garage and eighties' classics like Barry White to dance to but nothing came close to the complete feeling of serenity induced by the likes of Smetana's Vltava or Renee Fleming singing Schubert's Ave Maria.

And for a job like this he needed to find that calm before the storm.

Just how big a storm he was about to unleash on the London drug scene, no-one could have foreseen but South London would begin to resemble Alfred, Lord Tennyson's 'Valley of Death' before this weekend was over.

Sixty Eight

As the last notes of the Violin Concerto died away in Sham's ears, he sighed. It was just what he needed: total immersion in something other than the job at hand.

During the performance, his mind had drifted back to the first time he'd heard the piece at The Grand Opera House in Belfast with the Ulster Orchestra. The names of the two world-renowned artistes escaped him mainly because, at the time, his attention had been fully occupied by a dark-haired second violinist whose ample cleavage seemed to bounce to the music: his fourteen-year-old eyes locked on them like a couple of Exocet missiles. Was the memory of the dancing boobies, which the music always brought to mind, the reason for it to be his all-time favourite piece? He wondered sometimes.

At a loose end for the next few hours, Sham decided it'd been a while since he'd chewed the fat with Winston of 'Winston's Vinyls' on the High Street. Winston, a Jamaican, whose encyclopaedic knowledge of 'everyting musical' drew people from all over the Capital for his advice and company, had broken through the normally impenetrable barriers Sham had erected, with his gentle humour.

'Yip' he decided. 'Winston's here I come.'

With a last reluctant sigh, Sham pushed himself up off the bed and smoothed out the creases in the bed cover. There were only a few items on display in his room and each was in its place; anything ever moved was put back in its proper position. His room was a perfect reflection of his life; like a ghost passing through the ether of its own existence with only a trace left behind in its wake.

A minimalist's Nirvana perhaps but a copper's Hades: so few clues as to the identity of the occupier. Did traits of Sham's other occupation spill over into his private life or was it vice-versa? He often wondered about that. Which came first, the personal or the professional habit?

For now, the rest of today was about not thinking too far ahead: tonight would come soon enough.

With one last look around, he left his tidy cocoon and set off towards the High Street.

Sixty Nine

Sham was as relaxed as you like strolling along among the high-spirited Friday afternoon shoppers on the High Street when he saw a pale-faced man throw an empty bucket angrily into the back of a van. Glancing fleetingly at the name on the side of it, Sham noticed that its owner had won an award for the cleanest windows in South London. Briefly, he wondered if the traumatised-looking man getting into the driver's seat was the winner of the accolade.

Suddenly, there was a screech of tyres and an angry exchange of horns. When Sham looked back, the window cleaner's van had pulled out, probably without indicating, and caused a white van to slam on its brakes.

'Makes a change' thought Sham sarcastically 'But that window washing malarkey must be a pretty stressful job.'

'Why don't you fuck off!' screamed Dave Cosforth as he floored the accelerator. He knew he was in the wrong but the exchange between him and PC Walker had left him badly shaken. 'God I need this 'oliday!'

Behind the white van, the driver of an ambulance had had to brake too. He turned and apologised to his colleague and the patient in the back: Manny Franks. They'd wanted to keep him in overnight but Manny had insisted on getting home in time for Shabbat. Why should he let those schmucks interrupt his life anymore?

The traffic on the other side of the road, meanwhile, was at a standstill and among its many frustrated drivers was Gary Dean, who sat quietly fuming.

'Bloody Friday afternoon traffic; should be banned.'

He didn't notice Sham ambling along on the other side of the road among the crowds but he did catch a glimpse the badly driven van and its driver as it shot passed him.

'Wasn't that Dave Cosforth?' he wondered, turning in his seat to catch another glimpse of the receding van. 'I presumed, from the description on the radio, that it was his mob who fucked up that raid on the jewellers this morning. So, what's he doing here now? I'd have thought he'd be keeping a very low profile.'

The traffic began to move and his mobile rang interrupting his train of thought: it was Jeannie. Where was he?

Gary was tempted to say: 'Where do you think I am? Sipping tea at the Ritz?' But he curbed his frustration. It wasn't fair to take it out on Jeannie, not that she'd have let him anyway. She could hold her own and then some. He'd heard her on the phone to some of his CPS colleagues.

'Be there as soon as I can, Jeannie, but it looks like I'll be another half hour at least'. He hung up. Everybody on the planet wanted to clear their desks and get the weekend started.

Before Dave Cosforth's sudden attack of bad driving, he, Sham, Manny and Gary were actually within fifty yards of each other while another hundred yards away on a side street just off the High Street was a club called 'Judy's', where a certain Mr John Pollock was having a business meeting.

So, just another normal Friday afternoon get-together of neighbours in any South London High Street.

Seventy

It might have been the beginning of the weekend for some but that wasn't what was on Jake Vickers' mind as the slop which passed for food was slid under the door of his cell by the custody sergeant.

No. By now, Jake had had a couple of hours of the silent treatment. He knew the game: the hope that when he was interviewed next time he would sing like a canary. Yeah, right!

Were the silent, staring eyes glaring at him through the peephole every fifteen minutes supposed to unnerve him?

'Think again, coppers. This is Jake Vickers you've got here. Jake Vickers, the cop-killer'. Jake knew that if he was going to go down for it that his crime would give him a certain amount of kudos in the slammer and that appealed to him. He'd be able to 'big' it up among his own.

But that wasn't what was going on in his head at this precise moment. No. Jake was trying to work out who had gone to the police.

He'd already worked out that the original prime suspect, Johnnie Parker, was not the one who'd stitched him up. Why would he? Why should he? Where was the advantage to him? The job was going to wipe Johnnie Parker's slate clean with Jake. So, why go to the police? Cold feet?

'Naa!' decided Jake finally. 'There's something else I'm missing here. What is it?'

Jake came to the conclusion that the only way the police knew was that someone else had snitched. Could it have been one of his boys? Again, the 'where's the advantage to them?' rule applied. But Jake came to the conclusion that '...they're all stuck inside like me. So, it doesn't look like it was one of them. However, if one of them were to get a 'Not Guilty' at the trial then that might change things. Especially if it's Johnnie Parker.'

The more he thought about it, the more it didn't make sense.

He'd sat there with them in that van, waiting. Sure, there'd been a bit of 'pre-match nerves' but nothing out of the ordinary. He'd have felt it. Some people call it their sixth sense, others, premonition, but whatever its name was, his 'sense' had pulled him back from the edge, made him stop short many times when the police were trying to get something on him. No. The guys were definitely all up for it. Besides, they'd all been with him for years. One word to the police and they could have had him put away for a long time with what they knew. So, why now? No. It just didn't stack up.

He dismissed them from the equation.

So, who does it leave? Who knew about the job? Did Johnnie Parker tell his missus? Did one of the boys let it slip?

All of these thoughts were swirling around in Jake's brain but none of them felt right. These guys had never spoken out of turn before. If they had, Jake would have known about it...and dealt with it. And Johnnie Parker's wife didn't even know about Johnnie's loan; one of the reasons why Johnnie had never made a late payment.

'I think he'd rather take a kickin' from me rather than let her know' thought Jake as he smiled at the thought of her reaction.

'No. There's still something I'm missing. What is it?'

Two hours later, the door was thrown open and Jake was led off to his next waste-of-everybody's-time session: he was still no closer to working out the identity of the bastard who'd blown the whistle on him.

But he would.

Seventy One

Gary had hardly gotten through the swing doors of the main office when he was assailed from all sides. Questions were thrown at him from every angle. Jeannie walked out of her room, held up her hand and shouted:

'Me first! Me first!' half laughing, half serious.

Then Gary heard it: his special phone was ringing.

'Guys! Guys!' pleaded Gary, holding the palms of his hands in a 'back off' motion 'You'll all get a chance but give me five minutes to catch my breath, please. And Jeannie, I could murder...sorry I mean I could kill...sorry' Gary stopped mid-sentence trying to formulate an appropriate expression and settled for '...could I have a cup of coffee, please, sweetie pie?'

'Sure. Okay. But me first. Agreed?'

Gary was too knackered to answer and just nodded as he made his way quickly into his office. Opening the drawer with the softly persistent ringtone, he picked up the phone and said into the mouthpiece without finding out who was on the other end:

'Just hold a minute' and proceeded to throw his ridiculously overpriced hand-made cashmere coat into a ball onto his visitor's chair before locking the door.

'Now then,' he began as he picked up the receiver and flopped into his chair '...what can I do for you?'

Gary could tell from the tone of Dave Cosforth's voice that he was still rattled...probably from this morning's debacle but Gary certainly was not going to mention that, not on this or any other phone. Calls on this line were kept to a minimum and as per the rules: anything said was always in code.

'I need to know when the next Bus is?' said the terse voice.

'I'll call you back in a couple of minutes. Just a quick question though: did I see you in the High Street this afternoon?'

'Was I driving like I was at Le Mans?' asked the harsh voice, laughing.

'It was you then' Gary concluded.

'Yep. Let me know, will you? Thanks' and the connection was broken.

Gary pulled out his Blackberry before he remembered that The Bus was laid up in the yard at Irvine's.

'Damn!' he swore as he slapped the top of his desk with the palm of his hand.

'Ouch!' yelped Jeannie from the other side of Gary's office door 'Gary, could you please open the door?'

'Sorry, sweetie pie: force of habit' he called as he dashed to open the door.

'I've got more bumps on my head since I started working for you than a phrenologist's bust.'

'But much prettier' observed Gary.

'No wonder you win so many cases. I bet you schmooze the lady members of the jury into submission' laughed Jeannie as she put the tray of coffee and biscuits on his desk and rubbed her head.

'Guilty as charged!' replied Gary joining in the laughter.

'I need another few minutes, Jeannie and then I promise...' Jeannie threw him one of her looks '...scout's honour!' and held up his three fingers in salute '...I'm all yours.'

'I'll believe you...hundreds of millions wouldn't' teased Jeannie.

She left, closing the door behind her.

Why did Gary always lock his door when that phone in his desk drawer rang? A mistress, perhaps? Or, someone passing on inside information on shares? That was the extent of Jeannie's curiosity. Then it was all forgotten about. The very generous amount which landed in her bank account each month, which some people called salary, convinced her that things which were none of her business should stay that way. Whatever it was, clearly, Gary wanted to keep it private. So, private it would stay.

Gary picked up the phone and dialled Dave Cosforth's number: this was not going to be an easy call. Clients paid a lot for this service and Dave would not be pleased.

'Ah well, here goes' thought Gary taking a deep breath. The phone was picked up on the first ring.

'The Bus is out of service for a couple of days, sorry, I forgot' declared Gary before the voice at the other end spoke.

He had no intention explaining why: nobody's business but his. He'd already arranged for Freddie and a new driver to get back on the road on Monday. As usual, the new driver would know nothing about the goods the lorry would be carrying. Freddie would see to that.

Besides, the other lorry had been totally destroyed in the blaze at the Cobham Services: he'd leave it to James and the insurance company to sort that one out.

'Today is going from bad to fuckin' worse' moaned Dave Cosforth.

Gary could almost hear the cogs clicking away in Dave's head but he kept schtum.

Eventually, a sigh came from the other end of the phone.

'Maybe it's just as well. It was probably a knee-jerk reaction. I'm off on holiday for a few weeks...it was going to be a couple of months but things didn't work out today.'

'I know what you mean' said Gary emphasising the 'know'.

'I'll call when I get back. G'bye.'

'Have a nice holiday' and they hung up simultaneously.

In the solitude of the lock-up, Dave had decided to call it a day, pick up the dosh from The Bus and split it with the team. The boys probably wouldn't be happy but they'd had a good run. Maybe it was time to call last orders before their luck ran out and they were run in. He'd think again when he got back from the Costa.

'Phew!' thought Gary as he sipped his large double espresso and savoured the quietude of the next couple of minutes. He knew that after Jeannie, the members of his team who'd presented themselves at the police station to represent Jake's guys would be champing at the bit to have a meeting about co-ordinating the defence.

'Great. Nearly three gruelling hours of Mr Vickers' cheery face followed by a rerun of a traffic jam like a Bank Holiday Monday. I could do with going home and crashing out with a very, very large glass of red'.

However, he quickly put that thought out of his head, rubbed his eyes, gulped down the last of the bitter scalding coffee, walked to the door and called out:

'Jeannie!'

Fifteen minutes later, Jeannie had gone through the calls, the urgent and the mundane, and run through what was in the diary for the following week: it was going to be a beaut.

Gary thanked her for all her help, as he did at the end of every week, and told her to wrap things up and get herself home.

For the next two hours, Gary was on high alert; listening carefully as the various versions of the story, as related by Nosepicking Dave et al through Gary's team, unfolded. Fortunately, the coffee had done its trick and he was able to focus on the defence situation which was not looking good or put another way; there was no defence...at the moment. As the meeting drew to a close and the 'Good nights' and the 'Have a good one' floated through the office, Gary sat with his own door open and let his mind wander. He was truly shattered but there were still things to be done. Or at least thought about.

What did Jake mean when he said: 'I know who did it' and it wasn't Gary's imagination that Jake stared and stared hard through those slits. Unconsciously, Gary shifted uneasily in his chair at the thought of that stare.

The question was: did Jake really know? Was he trying to put the frighteners on Gary?

But it didn't take one of the sharpest legal brains in the country to work out that the answer was a big resounding 'No'. Jake was tough and smart but in a streetwise sort of way. He was no Machiavelli. If he'd known that Gary was involved, he would have reacted the way he did with any of his recalcitrant customers; he'd have used his fists.

No. He came to the conclusion that Jake didn't have a clue.

Anyway, how could he? Gary had done it anonymously through Crimestoppers.

Gary was safe.

With that sorted, some of the tension went out of him. He yawned. 'God I'm whacked' he thought as he threw his arms in the air and slowly stretched to ease the tension in his aching body.

'That's it. I've had enough and done enough to earn my crust this week. Time to concentrate on Harry.'

But as he left the office, calling his 'Good nights' to the late stragglers and the cleaners who had arrived by then, there was something niggling at the back of his mind.

What was it? Something...something he'd read that morning; something which bugged him all the way home. What the fuck was it?

Seventy Two

By the time Gary reversed into the driveway, a knot had formed in his stomach, a knot which was churning up his guts like the time in Florida that he eaten some bad sea food.

He still couldn't think what it was and that was making matters worse because for it to have this effect on him, it must be damned important.

'Hi, Nicki, I'm home' he called out trying to keep the timbre of his voice nonchalant.

'And about time too, Gary Dean' replied his wife as she came out of the kitchen wiping her hands on her apron. She held his head, kissed him and then surveyed his face, looking for clues as to how the day had gone.

'Bad one? Or, really bad one?' she enquired solicitously.

'How about the two of them together?' replied Gary laughing, attempting to keep it light.

Nicki could feel the tension in his body but said nothing, just looked deeper into his eyes trying to read more.

'I'm doing your favourite' she announced suddenly.

'Which one?'

'Eggs, beans and chips.'

'What? Two slices of bread and butter and a cup of tea?' said Gary excitedly, forgetting the unknown problem for the moment.

'Well, maybe one' teased Nicki.

'I only asked you to marry me on the basis that it was two slices! If you're going to break the contract then the deal's off and I've only one thing to say to you.'

'Oh no, please Gary, not that!' she replied in mock panic.

But he ignored her pleas and began to sing the most tuneless version of Dolly Parton's song ever heard:

'D..I..V..O..R..C..E.'

'Oh God, Gary, okay, I give in! Two slices, promise!' and the two of them fell about like a couple of school kids.

This was a ritual they'd gone through since they'd first moved in together all those years ago. Forget all the fancy meals in those hugely expensive restaurants which he took Nicki to, the food of his childhood was still his favourite.

For a few moments, the two of them held each other in silence, Nicki hugging herself close to him.

An embarrassed cough behind them brought them back.

'Mum, Dad. What're you doing?' It was Harry.

'Er...nothing, son' replied Nicki as she run her hands down her apron, smoothing out the creases.

'Your mum was just telling me what we were having for tea' said Gary.

'Supper!' reproached Nicki.

'Of course, supper!' repeated Gary. 'You know, you can take the boy out of Balham...'

'We know...' chorused Nicki and Harry '...but you can't take Balham out of the boy.'

For those few moments, the world and all its problems were left outside the front door: they were a happy family.

'Right, well I'd better get the chips on' said Nicki.

'Don't you mean 'pommes frites', darling'?' said Gary taking the mick.

'Oh, do piss off...darling!' said Nicki gaily in a la-di-dah voice.

'Mum!' said Harry aghast at his mother using such language.

'Now run along, you two, and wash your hands! Chop! Chop! Dinner will be ready in twenty minutes.'

'Yum! Yum!' said Gary. Harry missed it but Nicki didn't. The double entendre. She knew that Gary was admiring her rear as she pushed open the door into the kitchen. She turned around, looked him straight in the eye with that 'come to bed' look but then declared:

'In your dreams, Gary Dean.'

Gary went upstairs to have a wash, as did Harry, while Nicki returned to the kitchen to prepare her man's favourite meal. After recent events, moments like those were precious to Nicki.

'Thank God Harry's never gotten involved in drugs. Otherwise...' and she thought about Amanda and what could've happened to Harry. Her heart went out to Amanda's father. 'Such a nice girl. What a waste! He must be missing her terribly'. For the next couple of hours, they sat and chattered away, like the good old days. Those days that seemed a lifetime ago but, in fact, had been a regular part of their lives only a couple of weeks previously.

Gary chose his moment well; Harry was definitely not in that dark place.

'Harry' began Gary '...your mum and I fancy going down to Brighton on Sunday for the day, give the cobwebs a bit of a blow. Fancy joining us? I've promised mum that I'll take her on that big arm thingamajig that cranks you up slowly over the sea and then suddenly drops you...but only after we've had lunch at the Grand. Then you get your money's worth...and so do the spectators below 'specially if they're standing too close.'

'Gary!' protested Nicki 'Please don't talk like that. I've just eaten and I'm beginning to feel queasy already.'

'Hmm...' began Harry hesitantly '...I'm not sure, dad.'

Gary and Nicki could see the demons begin to return.

'Oh, go on!' said his mum light-heartedly. 'It'll be a laugh.'

Gary didn't say a word: for a minute, he was back in the courtroom: watching, waiting, checking the eyes, the body movements, ready to jump in when he thought things could take a wrong turn.

Just as Harry was about to say 'No', Gary instinctively sensed it coming, so he said:

'And if the weather's okay and we get down early enough, we could have a game of volleyball.'

The killer punch. Just like with his juries: Gary knew what to say and just when to say it.

Harry loved any kind of contact sport. He and his dad had passed many an enjoyable hour on their jaunts to Brighton, on the beach, playing in the spontaneous six-a-side teams with Nicki acting as unofficial cheerleader on the sidelines.

Tears welled up in Harry's eyes and Nicki moved as if to comfort him but an almost imperceptible shake of the head from Gary stopped her.

'That would be great, dad' was all Harry managed to say.

'Great! Nicki, would you book the Grand for us? I am so looking forward to this.'

'Me too!' replied Nicki with gusto 'Let's have a blast!'

'A blast, mum?' said Harry, wiping the tears away and laughing at the same time. 'You are so Eighties, mum.'

'You better believe it, son'. Throwing her arms in the air, Nicki began to wave them around slowly, gyrating the upper part of her body as she put on a deep sexy voice and began singing one of Barry White's slow, sensual songs.

Gary's eyes dilated: it was definitely working for him but Harry, all embarrassed shouted: 'Mum!'

'Oh, get over it!' countered his mum. 'Now that's what I call music.'

'More like pornography' replied the prude.

'Well, I'm not complaining' laughed Gary.

A little later, Harry returned to his bedroom and Nicki started to clear the table and stack the dishwasher.

'That went well' said Nicki.

'Yeah' answered Gary whose thoughts kept returning to the niggle in the back of his mind.

'Listen love,' began Gary 'I've got to check out a couple of things. Won't be long.'

'Promise?' asked Nicki. She knew that once Gary got into something that was it. He could be gone for hours.

'Sure. You check what's on the telly and I'll join you shortly.'

Nicki watched his receding back. He worked too hard. She wasn't keen on the kind of work that he did and the sort of clients he had to deal with but '...someone has to do it, I suppose'. That was as far as Nicki probed. She loved her man and he brought home the bacon. Life was good.

Seventy Three

On his way to his study, Gary stopped and listened at Harry's door. Silence. The door was opened a crack and Gary quickly scanned the room through its limited field of vision.

Harry was sitting upright on the bed with his Bose headphones on. Gary could see the pain on his face; he was probably listening to something that reminded him of Amanda.

'You're going to have to get over her, Harry' thought Gary. 'She's gone. Life has to go on. Life will go on and you have to grab it with both hands. But we can't do it for you, son'. Painful though it was to do, Gary pulled himself away from the door and walked across the landing to his study. When it came to his family, Gary was a caring, loving father but when it came to the rest of the world? Well, it was dog-eat-dog and Gary Dean was up there with hungriest of them: there were no qualms, no scruples in Gary Dean's world, only money and he wanted all of it for himself.

He opened the door of his study. Gary loved this room. The huge picture window looked onto the garden at the back of the house with its perfectly manicured lawn and his desk, neatly stacked with his papers, faced directly on to it. Often, just sitting watching as the branches of the lush evergreens swayed in the wind would be enough to clear his head and help him break a problem down into bite-size chunks.

He flopped into the Conran chair; it was identical to the one he had in the office; mentally, it put him into work mode. He let out a long, low sigh. Between Harry and the Jake Vickers episode, this had been a hellova week, but he'd gotten through it. This should be playtime now. So, why were his antennae still twanging? Something had happened. And somewhere in the back of his mind he knew it was important. But what the fuck was it?

Gary sat up and began flicking through the last couple of day's copies of The Times which Nicki carefully folded and placed on his desk after he'd finished with them at breakfast. At the end of the week she would bin them.

He had long ago mastered the art of speed reading: you had to with Court documents. It wasn't only the old farts on the bench who liked to spout their wisdom; some of his own colleagues would produce page after page of defence/prosecution documents that would say absolutely nothing. He was never quite sure if it was for their ego or to justify the fees they charged to clients. Whatever. The name of the game was to skim and mentally highlight the important bits.

A couple of minutes of skimming and he found it.

'Right, that was it. Now what is it that's bugging me about it?'

He read the article again...and again.

He muttered parts of the article out loud as he read it.

'Two bullets...white male...early twenties.'

'Okay' thought Gary rubbing his hand over his stubbly chin, he was really tired. 'Okay. I remember thinking it could have been Pete Davidson. Right. So? Wait a minute. Hold on.'

Gary had a flashback to standing outside the police station when the Chief Superintendent and his sergeant came out.

'He said it; said the body had been identified! It was Pete Davidson. But I knew that this morning. What's wrong with that? Where's the problem?'

He sat there running over the events of the last couple of days.

And then the veil lifted from his tired eyes.

'Jack Clancy's job for Sham. I assumed it was to sort Pete Davidson out. But the timing's wrong. It couldn't have been him. So...' Gary ground his fists into his eyes '...so who does Jack want done in? Who's Sham's target? Oh shit! I do not like the look of this. It's beginning to have a bad smell to it.'

Then he remembered Sham's parcel.

'It was huge: much bigger than usual. What does that mean?'

'Bigger parcel. Bigger parcel. Bigger parcel means there was more money in there. Yes. More money means someone much more important than Pete Davidson. But who? Who?'

Now he really was worried. He reached for the phone as he looked at his watch.

'Ten o'clock. A bit late. But it's got to be done.'

If there was one thing about Gary Dean it was that he didn't mess around once a decision had been taken. He dialled Sham's home number. As he waited for it to be picked up, he concocted his story.

'Sorry, Harry. Hate to do this but you're my cover' he thought.

'Hello?' It was Sham's mum.

'Hello. Is that Dr Boyle?'

'Yes. Who is this, please?'

'Dr Boyle, it's Gary, Gary Dean. I'm sorry to disturb you so late but is Sham around? I just need a quick word. Nicki and I are worried sick about Harry and I wanted to ask Sham if Harry's said anything to him about how he's feeling.'

'Sure, aren't they a worry?' was her reply. She didn't expand on the subject of Amanda Clancy: client confidentiality. 'Anyway, I'm sorry to hear that. Look, he's in the shower and then he's off out. Shall get him to call you?'

'That would be kind, Dr Boyle.'

'Not at all. Goodnight.'

'Goodnight and once again my apologies.'

Gary hung up and waited...and kept waiting.

Seventy Four

Sham was standing under the powerful jets of water allowing them to rinse off the foaming shower gel. It was as if he was purifying himself for battle like the warriors of a past age. He was calm. Everything was prepared. He was prepared. The weapon was primed.

Within ten minutes he was dressed and closing the front door.

On the way out, he heard his mother call out as she stepped into the hallway after him but he was already in the zone; it would have to wait. It was then that she noticed his mobile sitting on the hallway table, switched off, where he'd put it before going out the door. When questioned by his mother about it, his excuse was: '...you know what it's like when you've had a few jars, ma'. The truth was he only did it when he was on a job: the last thing he needed was one of his friends phoning up for a chat when he was in the middle of 'something'. 'Oh, hello, so-and-so, could I call you back? I'm just in the middle of finishing off my assignment'. But he always carried his one-off pay-as-you-go phone...but then she didn't know about that one.

'That boy's like a shadow' said his mother in frustration to her husband. 'He moves so fast; he's disappeared before you can take breath.'

'Sure aren't they all like that? I remember when I was young...'

'Oh, for Christ's sake, let's not get on to that subject, Anthony Boyle' and she laughed. 'I was supposed to get him to call Harry Dean's father back. His parents are concerned about him. Amanda Clancy, that girl who overdosed, was his girlfriend.'

'Was she?' replied her husband vaguely, one ear listening to her and the other, the BBC news weather report.

'D'you ever listen to a word I say, Dr Boyle? Sure didn't I tell you about the girl who...oh never mind!' she said exasperatedly.

'Darlin'...I work in a hospital' he began matter-of-factly dragging his eyes away from the TV. 'I hear about these sorts of things twenty times a day. I'll be honest with you, I switch off; otherwise I'd be round the twist myself.'

'You mean even more around the feckin' twist than you already are, don't you?' and they laughed and settled down as Anthony flicked over in time to see the titles for Newsnight begin to roll.

Fifty minutes later as the programme was about to finish, the telephone rang.

'Oh please, let us have just one night of peace' begged Sham's dad who had already put in a fourteen-hour day.

'Hello' he said into the receiver resignedly.

'I'm really, really sorry to disturb you again, Anthony' It was Gary Dean.

'Sure an' what can I do for you, Gary.'

'Is Sham around?' asked Gary, trying to sound casual, knowing already that the answer would be 'No'. As he'd waited for his call to be returned, his unease grew. There was something he was missing and until he spoke to Sham, it wasn't going to go away.

'Sorry, Gary, no. He'd gone before Mary could give him your message. Can it wait until the morning?'

'Course. No problem' said Gary nonchalantly, desperately struggling to keep the conversation light 'So where's he off to tonight, then?'

'Oh, he was telling us over dinner that he's been checking out this place called the Library for the last couple of days. Apparently, it's the latest "in place"' replied Anthony who sounded like he'd heard that before, many times.

'Yeah. I think I've heard Harry mention it' Gary lied. 'Oh, to be young again, eh, Anthony?'

'I'm not so sure about that, Gary.'

They both laughed.

'Sorry I couldn't be much help.'

'And I'm sorry to disturb you again. Goodnight.'

Gary sat twirling a pencil between his fingers like a drum majorette. 'What to do. What to do.'

He grabbed the phone again and dialled Sham's mobile: it was turned off. Sham's phone was never turned off unless...

'Oh Jesus, he's already on the job!' thought Gary, the knot in his gut tightening even more. So, what did it matter to him who Jack Clancy wanted topped? But for some reason this one did bother him.

He googled the address of the club and sat for a minute trying to deal with it in a logical fashion, but getting nowhere.

'I don't know the 'who' but I know the 'where'. Hmm. What to do' he thought as he tapped the pencil absentmindedly on the desk pad.

Finally, he made up his mind: he was going to have to go there.

He left the study and grabbed his old anorak from the hallstand. Then he went into the den, where Nicki was sitting, fast asleep in front of the TV.

'Darling' he whispered softly into her ear. No response. 'Nicki' he said a little louder.

'Hmm?' muttered Nicki as she moved to put her arms around his neck.

'I have to go out, darling. A client's been taken into custody; drunk and disorderly. Insisted on me. Just what I need on a Friday night! Sorry, lovely.'

'Why can't these people take up yoga or something to relieve their bloody stress instead of getting pissed all the time?' she complained, yawning.

'...because we need them to pay our bills. Don't worry, my love, I'll make sure he pays for disturbing our weekend.'

'Be careful out there, Gary. You know what Friday nights can be like' cautioned Nicki sleepily.

'I will, my love. I will.'

Gary gave Nicki a quick peck and watched her rear, with regret, as she mounted the stairs to bed. Only then did he step out into the damp, chilly night.

'The things I do for my clients'...only this time, he wasn't smiling.

The engine gave its usual subdued roar when he turned the key in the ignition and drove through the dimly lit streets towards the club.

Friday nights in South London. For some reason, it seemed like the entire population of under 25s, south of the river, had a need to cruise the streets. It was like King's Road Chelsea on a Saturday afternoon back in the Seventies; there was every colour of suped-up racer with shiny chrome wheels through to the usual motley collection of old bangers. They were Kings of the Road and from the sounds blasting out of them, Black Sabbath through to Abba, they were having a good time.

At least three young guys wound down their windows to let Gary know that his wheels were, in the words of one of them, 'supa dupa, man'. Traffic was bloody slow, so slow, in fact, that Gary almost did a U-turn twice. It took nearly thirty minutes to do a journey he could have made on foot in fifteen.

Finally, he swung past the entrance to the club.

The Friday night crowd was out in force and a queue was already forming, kept in order by some nasty looking individuals or as Gary liked to think of them: future clients.

This was not going to be easy. For a start, Gary wasn't dressed for it. Also, judging from what he saw of the crowd, he could have fathered most of them and so, would have stuck out like a sore thumb at a thumbless convention.

He parked the car around the corner and sat in the warmth of the plush interior, running through his list of options.

After considering and discarding most of them, he concluded that if things were going to go off, as he suspected, it was crucial that he wasn't connected with it in any way.

'So do I stay or do I go?'

'I'll give it half an hour' he decided finally and checked his watch.

That's all it would take.

Seventy Five

'Miriam, please!' said Manny exasperatedly. 'I'm okay! Honestly, darling!'

If she plumped his pillows once, she'd done it twenty times since he had gotten back from the hospital.

But fuss him she would continue to do; after fifty years of marriage, she had the right.

She had been preparing the Shabbas supper when the phone call came and she'd had to rush to the hospital.

'Maybe now you'll listen to me' she said sitting on the edge of the bed taking his hand in hers.

Manny let out a long sigh. He'd seen himself in the dressing table mirror when the ambulance crew had helped him onto the bed. Pretty, he wasn't. Between the memory of that image and the aching he was still feeling in his bones, Manny knew that Miriam was right. Sometimes the hint you get is like a little whisper in your ear and sometimes it's like the old Harold Lloyd silent films where the falling bank safe just misses you; this was one of those times. Hint? More like the ten plagues of Egypt joining hands and hitting you all at the same time.

'So maybe I should think about it' conceded Manny finally.

'So maybe you should' replied Miriam tenderly, knowing that that was Manny's way of admitting she was right without losing face. 'Rest now' she whispered as she helped him settle into a comfortable position. Manny's eyes fluttered then closed as he fell into a light slumber.

Miriam kissed his forehead and wiped away a tear. She could so easily have lost him. It wasn't just South London where this sort of thing was happening; it was the world over. She had seen the changes coming in the sort of calls she'd taken over the past twenty-odd years or so in the Crypt of St Stephens, Walbrook, in the City of London, as a Samaritan: Miriam 2663.

'And what about the children, their innocence lost so young these days?' she pondered and sighed. 'Maybe now this silly old goat will be around a bit longer to drive me meshuggah'. But she was content.

Manny's emporium was sold to an East European and opened as a pawnbroker. He joined a kalooki club. Life was still good.

Seventy Six

It was about the same time as Manny was falling asleep that Sham was settling himself down in the sit-me-down of the men's toilets in the Library.

Twenty minutes earlier, he'd clocked the arrival of Mr Pollock and his crew; all on schedule.

He removed what looked like a pen from the pocket of his Vivienne Westwood shirt. However, a writing implement it wasn't. It was a syringe, a syringe which Sham had earlier filled with the little 'extra' which Jack Clancy had left in the parcel along with thirty grand at Gary's office. Jack had picked it up from Amanda's coffee table on the night he'd found her: it was the remnants of what she'd been using.

Whatever it was, Sham handled it with extreme caution. Being the son of two doctors did have its advantages. When it came to sourcing or administering the best drug for a 'hit', Sham was your man. The only question he ever asked was 'Do you want it to be slow or quick?'. But this unknown little beauty was something else.

He picked up the syringe and stared at it. This substance had killed Amanda Clancy instantly and, in a very short time, it would do the same to John Pollock.

His thoughts were interrupted by the squeak of a door; someone was coming in. Sham squinted through the crack in the sit-me-down door. It was still early but bladders can work in mysterious ways. He knew. Sometimes he could have a skin full and sleep all the way through the night like a baby. Other times, he would have one bottle of beer and at three o'clock in the morning it would feel like there was seven pints of lager demanding immediate evacuation.

False alarm: just some young guy unburdening himself. Within a minute or so, he'd zipped up and was gone.

'I wouldn't like to share a beer with you, mate' thought Sham as the young man left without washing his hands. The thought of coming into contact with something the guy might touch, made Sham shiver: it was just so repugnant. 'Were they not taught the meaning of cleanliness or hygiene by their parents?' he thought. He'd been appalled at the lack of hygiene in the young men who used the club's toilet facilities. However, Mr Pollock always washed his hands very thoroughly. 'This club must be saving a fortune in soap; forget about the cost of running the hand dryers.'

For all his outward show of normality, Sham had an interesting take on life.

The door squeaked. Same again, only this time it was two twenty-something 'camp as a row of tents', as his mother would say, gay guys talking about a new member of their group who was bi-curious. One of two had the hots for him and would like to introduce him to the joys of gay sex. That wasn't exactly how they said it but Sham managed to filter out the more graphic stuff.

As they were leaving, another guy came in, pushing passed them. The two gays just drew him a stinking look but said nothing. He was drunk.

'Here we go' thought Sham as he watched through the crack.

The young guy shook the handle of Sham's cubicle. 'Oh shit!' he roared as he made a dive for the sink. He made it but it was one of those dry retches; nothing came out. After hanging over the sink for a couple of minutes, he splashed cold water on his face, checked out his appearance in the mirror and with a lopsided grin said to his own reflection: 'It's Showtime, folks!' and left to rejoin the party outside.

'That was close' thought Sham 'If he'd messed the place up, they'd have closed this loo and made everyone use the one upstairs. Then Mr Pollock would have been given a stay of execution but not tonight. No, tonight is your time, Mr P.'

Sham waited.

Seventy Seven

John Pollock stood at the bar, sipping his single malt with Babe and Frankie, his Rottweilers, sitting either side of him, looking up adoringly at their master. He was definitely the leader of their pack. Pity the poor sod that they thought was trespassing in their master's space; they'd get a low growl warning and if they didn't take the hint then, they were either stupid or had a death wish.

In the meantime, his minders were doing a good job at keeping the riff-raff at bay, but, of course, he'd never tell them that: they might want a rise. The atmosphere was happy, happy, happy as it always was on a Friday night; his dealers would be making a killing.

John Pollock looked around him at the faces milling around. 'Thank you one and all for your contribution to my retirement fund! It's not long to go an' I cannot bloody wait!' thought the brain of the man with the poker face. Anyone, including his minders, looking at the impassive expression present on his face at that moment could easily have believed that he wasn't actually thinking of anything at all. He just looked so totally blank. But inside was a different matter. His brain and his stomach were competing to see which could do the biggest somersault.

Mr Pollock was tired, so tired, in fact, that two days earlier he'd decided to bring his retirement forward. He'd called the jet hire company and changed the date; it was to be following week.

'Six more days and...YOU'LL BE FREE!' his brain screamed inside but the poker face remained.

He had deliberately not planned beyond take off. But once the wheels of that plane lifted off the tarmac, his life was going to change forever. No more looking over his shoulder. No more paranoia when he meets a new face. Are they undercover police? Are they working for rivals? Is someone trying to nick my business?

'Well, they're bloody welcome to it now, mate' he thought. The very slight movement of his lips in an upward direction as a direct result of this thought was immediately picked up by his minders, causing mild panic. 'What's the problem? Have I/we missed something? Done something wrong?' they communicated to each other with their eyes. He was, in fact, only smiling; a situation so rare that the minders' 24-hours deodorant stood no chance. The sweat positively dripped. Meanwhile, the fantasy, which had occupied a lot of their boss' waking hours recently, surfaced again. The one where he was strapped in on the plane and the captain's voice announced over the tannoy '...we've just been cleared for take-off. Would cabin crew please take their seats' and he's just sitting there looking out the window with a large single malt in front of him and thinking...

'Stop, no more!' he commanded. He'd been slipping recently; his brain wouldn't let it go; it'd been teasing him with thoughts of the endless pleasures ahead.

Yeah, right.

Seventy Eight

Sham sat there, totally focussed. He knew it wouldn't be long now. His pulse was as normal as if he was sitting at the breakfast table having his cereal not waiting to murder someone in cold blood. He had no need for deodorant: he was cooler than a cucumber in a supermarket fridge.

He checked his watch; ten thirty. If Mr Pollock's bladder was sticking to its schedule, he should be pushing open the door within the next five minutes, he reckoned.

Six and a half minutes later, Sham heard someone open the door and quickly checked through the crack in the door: it was one of the minders giving the place the once over. Sham lifted his feet. The minder didn't even bother to check to see if there was someone in the lockup.

Thirty seconds later the door swung open again. John Pollock casually strolled over to the urinal and slowly unzipped his flies, letting out a sigh of pure contentment.

Sham picked up the syringe and waited till he heard a steady flow.

He silently opened the loo door, took the two paces needed to stand directly behind the stooped figure of John Pollock. Sham was so close he could smell the whisky off his breath. Pollock was so engrossed in emptying his bladder that he hadn't hear a thing until Sham whispered in his ear 'This is for Amanda' and plunged the needle deep into the drug baron's neck, pushing down until the syringe was empty. There was no time for John Pollock to react except to utter his last words on this earth: 'Ah, shit!' Sham grabbed him and held him by the neck of his suit jacket, keeping him faced forward to avoid the fountain of blood that was spewing out from each orifice in his body.

John Pollock was used to pain; he'd been brought up on it. But this wasn't pain. It was a kind of ultimate high followed by instant death with nothing in between.

Shame he didn't bring his 'retirement' forward by one more week. Still, it was his turn.

It was only when the forensics came back from Amanda and John Pollock that the police began to piece together what had happened. A person or persons unknown had introduced a powerful new, violent strain of Ebola into one of the packets within the consignment John Pollock had taken delivery of just before Amanda had purchased her deadly dose. A competitor? A disgruntled employee? Whoever it was, was one nasty piece of work. The police never caught the culprit. Once it hit the news channels, there were a lot of hungry dealers signing on at the job centre. Drug-taking, for a short while anyway, lost its attraction. Only the hardened addicts took no notice.

By now, piss was mingling with blood on the floor, Sham let go the lifeless body.

'Job done. Time to go.'

He stepped over the body, stuffed the syringe, carefully, into his jacket and calmly washed his hands. The whole thing had taken less than a minute, so the minders wouldn't even be concerned.

Now came the tricky part. Sham always knew it. But he'd put together the best plan he could in the short time he had.

He opened the door, rushed out and shouted 'There's a man fallen over in there! There's blood everywhere! I think he must have hit his head or something! Someone call an ambulance!'

The minders were there in an instant, pushing each other out of the way to get in.

In the confusion, Sham moved over to the blind spot on the CCTV camera and reversed his jacket from white to dark grey. Pulling up his hood, he made his way towards the exit through the heaving mass of people having a good time, totally unaware of what had happened. Even those who'd heard what Sham had shouted weren't bothered. So what? Someone's hit their head and needs to go to hospital. Big deal. It happens all the time. This is Friday night, party night. Someone else can deal with it.

Sham's idea of reversing his jacket worked perfectly. No-one would be able to identify him or pick him out on the CCTV. There was however one major flaw in his plan and it was just about to raise its ugly mug.

The minder who'd checked the loos came out and was looking around for the kid who'd found the boss. He scanned the faces but what did he look like? They'd only seen him for less than five seconds before they went one way and he went the other. He was sure there was more to that kid than met the eye. And whatever it was that happened to the boss, he hadn't bumped his fucking head. What a fucking mess. He began to panic. He knew if someone had 'done' the boss, he'd be the one carrying the can so he'd better do something about it...and quick. The minder made for the exit. He knew that if the kid was involved he'd try to get away as soon as possible. He shoved the party-goers roughly out of the way.

'Hey, take a chill pill, man!' shouted one guy out of his head on John Pollock's shit. Or, to be precise, the late John Pollock's shit.

To which, the minder, whose name was Spiv roared 'Fuck off you piece of shit!' and tried to head butt him out of the way.

Sham never knew it but he probably owed his life to that young guy, whose friends closed around the minder and tried to hold onto him, delaying him for only a few, but precious, seconds. If they hadn't, the minder would have caught up with the only person he could see who was making their way out of the place. What that person was wearing was irrelevant to him. He just wanted to get hold of the little bastard.

Sham didn't turn around. He didn't have to; he sensed that something was not right. Even now, his pulse barely rose as he quickened his pace.

Head down as he approached the glass doors of the entrance, Sham amended his original plan of turning right out of the club to head up towards the High Street, losing himself among the late-night revellers. He realised that he had to put some distance between him and the club, fast. The danger of his original plan was that if there were too many people on the High Street it could slow him down.

In one smooth, seamless move, he turned left out of the club, heading towards the maze of small streets which surround all High Streets: he could probably outrun anyone who might be following him and besides, he knew these streets like the back of his hand, it was his home turf.

He hadn't gone ten yards when he heard: 'Oi you, come 'ere!' The scream from the minder was not only pure aggression; it was also one of desperation. Without someone, namely Sham, he would be shouldering the blame on his own. Not an attractive prospect.

Sham turned, making sure his face was concealed by his hood. He needed to know what the opposition was only then could he take whatever steps were necessary.

In the two or three seconds it took, Sham calculated that the minder was about thirty years old, six feet two and about two hundred and sixty pounds and judging from the muscular frame bulging out of the black suit, a serial abuser of steroids. 'There's a surprise' thought Sham still in calm mode. The time for flight was just about to kick in.

'Come 'ere you little bastard!' he shouted again and started to run towards Sham.

'Hmm. Surprisingly quick for someone so bulky' thought Sham as he took to his heels.

As Sham approached the corner he had to make a split-second decision. Left or straight on? Fortunately, the luck of the Irish was with him that night.

He turned left.

Seventy Nine

Gary had the radio on low, it was Classic FM. Whenever he had a problem he needed to work out, he found that classical music allowed his mind to drift and with a normal turn of events, a solution came. But not this time.

For sure he knew that Jack Clancy had hired Sham to hit whoever he thought was responsible for Amanda's death. But who? Judging by the size of the package that was left for Sham at his office, Sham had charged a pretty penny for the job. No-one, not even Jack Clancy would pay that kind of money to have a nobody whacked. Who the fuck could it be?

Gary was convinced that whoever it was, was inside the Library, probably getting it right now. Who would go to a nightclub, albeit cheap glitzy, that was important enough for Jack Clancy to pay that kind of money?

Gary sighed. Maybe he should go. If he was right about the hit happening tonight, it wouldn't be good for him to be anywhere near the place when it went down.

He switched on the engine, turned on his headlights and was about to pull out when he glanced in his rear mirror and all of his theories and questions flew out of the window with the sight of Sham running for his life and some massive geezer not far behind.

Gary quickly leaned over and opened the passenger door and shouted 'Get in!'

Sham saw the car door flung open and immediately recognised the car and the voice, although he had no idea what Gary was doing there. He jumped in and Gary floored the pedal: it was as good a time as any to check out the manufacturer's claim of 0-60 in 5.1 seconds.

The minder became a blur of pure frustration in black, kicking the side of a parked car in the dimly-lit street, as Gary sped away, watching him in his rear mirror.

He 'tsk, tsk'd and said: 'Naughty, naughty!'

'What's the matter?' asked Sham, the adrenalin still pounding through his veins.

'That naughty man who was chasing you has just committed criminal damage...he'll need a solicitor'. They both chuckled which went some way to relieving the tension.

Gary drove on for another minute, thinking how he could broach the subject and then said:

'Look Sham, you know I don't get involved in your business but what the fuck happened back there? That guy looked like he would've ripped you limb from limb if he'd caught you.'

Sham was still out of breath and took a couple of seconds to answer.

'It was John Pollock' was all he said. He didn't need to say anymore. Gary would know what he meant.

'What?' yelled Gary, clearly shocked as he spun around to look at Sham and then back again, narrowly missing a parked Merc.

'Apparently, Jack Clancy found out that it was him who supplied the shit that Amanda used' Sham paused. 'Mr Pollock is no longer with us' he stated in his calm, detached way.

'Oh, fuck' said Gary as the implications hit him and the lawyer in him took over. 'Right. First thing, we ditch the car. That guy back there would have clocked it; one of the disadvantages of having such a distinctive motor. Then, I'll report it to the police...no, better...I'll wait for them to contact me. Honestly, you can't even leave your car outside your front door at night and expect it to be there the next morning these days.'

They both laughed and the tension went down a further notch.

'I suggest you get home and get a good night's sleep and leave the rest to me, Sham. Hmm. I don't think Jack Clancy thought about the consequences. Still...' continued Gary, 'I don't suppose I would have done any different myself if something had happened to Harry.'

'Sure, an' I'd have given you a friends and family discount, Mr Dean; It's the least I could do!'

'I should bloody well hope so!'

Five minutes later, Gary found a quiet spot and cut the engine. They waited for a minute to see that the coast was clear.

'Speak to you soon, Sham.'

'Gary, thank a lot. I really mean that' said Sham with genuine feeling.

'The things I do for clients. Now, I'm a taxi service. Get outa here!'

Again, they laughed and Sham got out of the car.

The experts claim that laughter helps with a multitude of ailments and problems. Well, here's another one they can add to the list: getting over murdering someone.

'Goodnight, Gary.'

''Night, Sham. Now piss off and let me prepare the car for the police to find it. I'll ring you tomorrow.'

Sham strode off into the night, he'd be home in seven or eight minutes, while Gary started wiping all the surfaces, especially where Sham had been sitting and removed all the little things which a thief would take: loose change, CDs, Versace sunglasses, the Mont Blanc pencil which he used to write notes when he was called in the car. When he'd finished, he got out of the car and tried not to hang around but it was difficult because it was his baby, his pride and joy, and to leave it hurt, if he was being honest.

'But it's got to be done' he thought finally. Reluctantly, he closed the car door and just let the catch hold without closing it fully. Sighing and with one last look full of regret, he began to walk away.

'Bye' he whispered. 'See you soon' like he was leaving a baby who had finally drifted off to sleep.

Fifteen minutes later, he pulled out his front door keys and let himself in.

He crept up the stairs; Nicki was in bed fast asleep and Harry's light was out. A two-minute wash and he slipping between the sheets himself.

As he lay there drifting off, he reflected that he wasn't used to being personally involved in his clients' work; he was usually the one cleaning up the mess after the event. But he had to admit it: secretly, he got a bit of a thrill.

So much for a quiet weekend.

While Gary was creeping into bed, Sham still had one more thing to do before he could crash out himself. He retrieved the pay-as-you-go mobile from his jacket, careful to avoid the syringe which he'd dispose of in the morning, and made the final call on it before it too was disposed of.

Jack Clancy had obviously been waiting; he answered on the first ring.

'Well?'

'Sorted' was Sham's succinct reply.

'Good' was the cool response but Sham could tell that he was pleased. After a few moments of silence, Jack Clancy said:

'Don't ever contact me again' and the connection was broken.

'My pleasure' replied Sham sarcastically to the airwaves.

Job done. Satisfied client. Sham joined in the only activity, to date, where the human race could not get itself involved in conflict: sleep.

Eighty

It was about six o'clock when the banging started: the banging that is on Mr Gary Dean's front door.

Nicki sat upright with a start as did Gary but at least he knew what it was going to be about. Gary switched on the bedside light.

'Nicki, listen to me' began Gary urgently '...I haven't got time to explain just now but I didn't leave the house last night. Got it? We were here together all night. You fell asleep, which you did, and I watched the snooker. Trust me. There's a lot of shit about to hit the fan and it's going to get very messy.'

Gary took Nicki by the shoulders and looked straight into her eyes 'What I promise you, babe, is that I was a completely innocent bystander and wasn't involved in any way. So, it'll be easier if we stick to the story that I was here all night. That's all I need you to say. Okay?'

Nicki didn't understand but after a second's hesitation, she nodded her head. She trusted Gary. She knew he'd tell her later what she needed to know with the emphasis on the needed.

As he walked out onto the landing, tying the cord of his dressing gown, Harry appeared at his bedroom door.

'What's going on, dad?' he asked, yawning and running his fingers through his hair.

'I've no idea, son, but whoever it is, it'd better be good or I'll have their guts for garters.'

Harry smiled in that sleepy half-awake sort of way. He knew his dad, complete trusted in him. It was like having a big woolly blanket permanently wrapped around you when he was there. You felt totally safe. Dad always knew what to do, just like when Harry'd found Amanda.

As Gary approached the stained-glass door to the porch, he counted at least four uniforms and one plain clothes policeman.

'Must be something important' he thought, smiling to himself.

A very tired looking Chief Superintendent Moore, who'd been dragged from the bed he'd finally managed to get into after one very long day, stood there.

'Good morning, Sir. Mr Gary Dean?'

Gary nodded.

'Chief Superintendent Moore and this is Sergeant Wallis. Sorry to disturb you at such an early hour, Sir, but do you own a black Maserati with the licence plate GD55VKZ?'

Again, Gary nodded.

'Where were you, Sir, between the hours of ten thirty and midnight last night?'

'Look what's this all about, officer?' demanded Gary.

'A car with that registration, colour and make were seen driving away from the scene of a serious crime last night.'

'I was here with my wife all evening and my car hasn't left the drive, officer. As you can see.'

'Where exactly is your car, Sir?'

'You passed it on the way in. You know, the big black shiny thing with four wheels parked in the driveway' said Gary sarcastically.

'There's no need to take that tone, Sir, and for your information, there is no 'big black shiny thing with four wheels parked in your driveway...Sir' There was just the slightest of pauses before the 'Sir' was added.

'Wha...t?' exclaimed Gary with just the right amount of indignation as he pushed past the police to view the empty space where his cherished possession had been parked not eight hours before.

'Believe me now, Sir?' asked the Chief Super, returning the sarcasm.

'I don't understand it' declared Gary 'I arrived home from the office at around seven last night. It had been a long day. Previously I'd visited my client, Mr Vickers at...'

'Yes, Sir' interrupted the Chief impatiently 'We do know where you were, Sir. I saw you myself outside the station, remember?'

'Yes, of course' replied Gary. 'Anyway, what is this 'serious crime' that's been committed? And you say my car was involved? Was it a hit-and-run?'

'No, Sir. I didn't say it was involved. I said it was seen driving away from the scene of the crime not long after a crime had been committed.'

'Well, was my car damaged?' Gary asked, playing the self-centred little rich boy to perfection.

'Your concern for the victim is touching, Sir; I'll pass on your condolences to the victim's relatives. To answer your question: no, your car wasn't damaged but the person against whom the crime was perpetrated very much was. His name is or should I say, was, Mr John Pollock and he's very much dead. Cause of death...murder...by person or persons unknown.'

'John Pollock?' gasped Gary, staggering. 'He's...was...a client of mine!'

'We are aware of that, Sir. Not a good time at the moment to be one of your clients, is it?'

'What do you mean?' said Gary indignantly, keeping up the charade.

'Well, one way or another, we're dealing with three of your clients at present. Mr Vickers, Mr Pollock and sadly, Mr Clancy whose daughter died from an overdose.'

'I knew Amanda. She was a nice girl. She was going out with my son. Tragic.'

'We are aware that they were stepping out together, Sir. Anyway, I take it that your wife can confirm your alibi?' asked the Chief Superintendent.

'Of course, I can, officer' stated Nicki in a firm voice as she wafted up behind Gary in a pale blue silk kimono. 'We were here all evening.'

'Then I won't detain you anymore for the present. Obviously, we'll be keeping your car for forensics and it'll be returned as soon as we've finished with it. Again, my apologies for disturbing you.'

As Gary closed the front door he heard one of the constables say to his colleague: 'What sort of guy represents scumbags like that? Three of the lowest of the low. Still, someone did the world a favour last night...'

'PC Davis, would you keep your voice down and your opinions to yourself, please!' said the Chief irritably. 'I don't need an official complaint about police bias added to my workload! Now let's get back to the station, fill out the forms and get some kip.'

Gary smiled to himself at the young constable's words. "What sort of guy represents scumbags like that?" he repeated to himself in a sarcastic, namby-pamby voice in his head. 'I'll tell you, you pathetic little oik!' thought Gary with utter contempt. 'A fuckin' rich one! The more the merrier, I say. Bring 'em on!'

As he turned back into the hallway, Nicki noticed the look of contempt on his face and wondered what it meant.

'You alright, darling?' she asked, concerned.

'Oh fine, thanks Nicks. I was just thinking about what that uniformed twat just said. You put them in a uniform and suddenly they're the judge and jury of what's right and wrong! All black and white for them, no grey! Let me tell you, a lot of the police I come across are only in it for the early retirement and pension. All they're interested in is clearing up their bloody crime rates. So, they get kids who've committed some petty crime to confess to others they didn't commit just to make their clear up rates look good and get themselves promoted...and it's my clients who're the scumbags!' Gary's eyes were blazing by the end of what sounded like a closing speech to the jury.

'Ever regretted asking somebody something?' joked Nicki.

'Sorry, darling. Was I getting on my high horse?' laughed Gary.

'...white charger actually and you were half way down the High Street, that's all!'

'Sorry! Let's have a cup of coffee.'

'Kettle's boiled. Come on' and Nicki slipped her arm through her husband's and walked through to the kitchen.

Gary told Nicki the truth without the frills; that he'd been near the club when it all kicked off; that he'd panicked and sped off; that he'd abandoned the car because someone might have seen him driving off at speed and think he was involved. End of.

Nicki accepted what Gary said: he might represent some dodgy characters...but he was not one of them.

Eighty One

It had been a while since Jake Vickers had spent time at one of Her Majesty's hostelries. The accommodation hadn't improved nor had the smell. The walls in those places seemed to ooze fetid boiled cabbage into the air of the permanently overheated shitholes that they all were.

The thin mattress he'd spent the night tossing and turning on was still as lumpy as he remembered. In fact, it could have been the same one he'd been issued with the last time he'd done some bird and that was about seven years earlier if his calculations were correct.

The ME had given him some painkillers the day before but they'd worn off hours ago and so each small movement was causing him excruciating pain, pain which kept him awake for most of the night.

Apart from the odd ten-minute doze, sleep had eluded Jake and that left him with a lot of thinking time. No matter which way he looked at it, he just couldn't see that it was Johnnie Parker or one of his boys who had blown the whistle. But how was he gonna to find out who did snitch on him? Because he wasn't gonna stop until he did.

Maybe he could ask the police.

''Scuse me, officer, but if I ask very politely, like, do you think you could just whisper the name of the nonce who stitched me up? I'll make it worth your while.'

After what he'd done the day before, Jake assumed that there'd be a queue of volunteers around the block to pull the lever on the scaffold; except they'd done away with capital punishment in 1969. No, he didn't think they'd be very receptive to that request. Although in the good old days…

So how was he gonna find out? Who did he know that could do a bit of discreet sniffing around? He'd have to think about that one carefully, he decided. 'Anyway, no need to rush. I've got about twenty years or thereabouts to sort out the bastard or bastards who did this' he thought grimly. Jake sat up with a start.

What if there was more than one of them?

For the rest of his first night back behind bars, conspiracy theories went through Jake's mind at the speed of an express train. Each one ending with the tag line 'Is he/she the one?' By the time the slimy egg, greasy bacon and burnt sausage which passed as breakfast was shoved through the sliding hatch in his cell door Jake was all conspiracy-theoried out.

It was then that he knew he had to find out soon, forget about twenty years; it was doin' his nut in and that was in less than twenty-four hours.

At 0930, the key turned in the lock of Jake's cell and the door swung open to reveal his brief, the Mr Gary Dean, decked out in one of his many Cuban pimp outfits; this one, black, double-breasted, shiny silk with a silver pinstripe running through it, a plain, pale cream shirt with its double cuffs held together by gold cufflinks with the 'G' insert made up of tiny diamonds. But it was the top and tail which got you. The multi-coloured Versace tie was so bright that you almost had to wear sunglasses just to look at it. And finally, the shoes: black, handsome, handmade slip-on crocs. You almost didn't notice the gold Rolex on his wrist in among that lot.

As the custody sergeant moved out of the way to let Gary in, a waft of cologne assaulted Jake's nostrils which, for a few seconds, managed to overwhelm the reek of stale cabbage and Jake was transported back to church; the powerful smell of incense in Gary's cologne was so overpowering. The memory, however, was stirred not from attending services; it was based on a time when Jake had been casing the joint.

'Morning, Jake. How are you feeling today?'

'Great' was Jake's sarcastic monosyllabic reply. 'You smell good' he said as an afterthought.

Gary shot him a look as he sat down on the edge of Jake's bed. What was that supposed to mean? He decided to duck it: there were more important things on the agenda today.

'Okay, Jake' said Gary passing smoothly over the comment '…they've convened the court 'specially today…'

Jake interrupted. 'What? 'Specially for me? 'Aint that nice of them?'

Gary stopped and stared at Jake.

'Come on, Gary. Laugh!' he barked. 'It was supposed to be funny.'

Gary wasn't sure if Jake's mood swings were a result of coming down from the drugs he'd pumped into himself the day earlier or what. But whatever it was, Gary was going to have to treat him with kid gloves for the time being. 'Jake, listen, if we're going to beat this, you've got to help me, so concentrate'. Gary waited a couple of seconds to let what he'd said sink in before he continued. 'As I was saying, all we'll be doing today is confirming your name, address and date of birth: we won't be entering a plea at this stage. We'll ask for bail, but I'll tell you now, we haven't a cat's chance in hell of getting it. I just want to warn you.'

Gary had this very clever way of making it appear as if it was the two of them fighting the system by using 'we' not 'you' when he spoke about the case.

Jake unconsciously picked up on it and settled down.

'How long before it goes trial?'

'Attaboy!' thought Gary, relieved. 'Settle down now, Jake, and let's get this over and done with asap so as I can go back to enjoying my weekend.'

'How long's a piece of string? It all depends on the CPS but I've got a feeling that they'll want to get this in front of the Courts quite quickly. So, two...maybe three months?'

'What are my chances, Gary?'

'Look, we're going to have to do some pretty fancy footwork, Jake. I won't mislead you. But we'll have a bloody good shot at it!'

Gary stopped: he couldn't believe what he'd just said.

'Oh...' he stuttered.

But Jake just laughed.

'Nice one, Gary. I like it' he chuckled.

For once Gary was sort of stuck for words.

'I...suppose so' said Gary reluctantly smiling. 'Before we go, do you need anything?'

'Nah' said Jake who was getting used to the pain. In early childhood, most kids had comfort blanket; for Jake, it was pain. If his old man missed giving him his regular beating, he got twitchy because he knew that next time the old man would more than make up for it.

Ninety minutes later, they were back at the police station with the cameras of thirty or forty paparazzi popping fifty to the dozen as they fought to get the first photo of the cop killer.

When they arrived inside, Chief Superintendent Moore and Sergeant Wallis were standing by the desk, waiting.

'We're ready to interview Mr Vickers now, Mr Dean.'

'Oh, fucking bollocks' thought Gary, fuming internally. 'I want to go home.'

'Certainly, gentlemen. Can I have a few minutes with my client?' said Gary through his forced smile.

'We're in Interview Room Two. Will twenty minutes be sufficient?' asked the Chief.

'That should be adequate' replied Gary, while seething internally, 'Shit, bollocks, tits and fannies!'

Eighty Two

In the interview room, their bums had bare touched the seats before Jake dropped his bombshell.

'Gary, I need you to do me a favour' he began.

'Sure, sure, Jake. What is it?' said Gary with an uneasy feeling in the pit of his stomach.

'I want you to do a bit of sniffing around this James Irvine mob'. All the time, Jake was looking at Gary intently or so Gary thought. A worm of sweat wriggled down his spine.

'Er...yeah, Jake, what for?' replied Gary whose bladder had begun filling rapidly.

'There's something that ain't right about it. Look, someone's stitched me up and I'm not gonna stop until I find out who. There's more to that place than meets the eye, I just know it' declared Jake vehemently.

'What kind of information are you looking for?' asked the man whose bladder was by now feeling like Old Faithful, the Yellowstone Park geyser, about to erupt.

'I dunno. Something don't seem kosher. Know what I mean, Gary?'

'I'm not sure, Jake, but I'll do my best. I'll start on Monday.'

'Sure. Sure. Now then what about this interview? I assume I say 'no comment' to everything?'

'That's about it, Jake. And if you get the urge to say something, check with me first.'

'Gotcha.'

'I think I'd better go to the toilet before this thing gets started. D'you need to go, Jake?'

'Nah, I'm okay.'

Gary knocked on the door and one of the two policemen standing guard opened it.

Gary fled to the loo. He opened the door to find the custody sergeant standing at the urinals. Normally, they would have shared a few pleasantries. Not now. A brief contemptuous look was all Gary got as the sergeant shook it and left.

Gary stood there until he'd squeezed every last drop out, but his body had not finished with him yet: the stress had not drained away with the mere emptying of his bladder. As Gary rinsed his hands he suddenly bent over and dry-retched into the wash basin.

Splashing cold water on his face and looked at his reflection in the mirror, he thought 'What the fuck do I do now?'

Conflicting thoughts were bumping into one another like dodgem cars at the fair. Jake really had caught Gary off balance.

Grabbing a handful of paper towels, Gary dried his face and hands, straightened his tie and put on his professional face.

As he entered the room, Jake took one look and said:

'What happened to you? Somebody goose you in the bog?'

'No. It's nothing really' replied Gary shaking his head. 'I had the police knocking at my door in the middle of the night, I'm just tired. Some little scumbag nicked my motor and used it in a getaway.'

'Cheeky little fuckers!' laughed Jake. 'I 'ope they don't ask you to defend them. They'll probably end up with a longer sentence than me.'

'At least you still have your sense of humour, Jake' smiled Gary.

A knock at the door interrupted them.

Sergeant Wallis' head popped around the door. 'Chief Superintendent Moore would like to know if you're ready to begin?' he asked.

Gary looked at Jake who nodded.

'When you're ready' replied Gary.

The formalities of those presence in the room for the tape over with, the interview began.

Jake enjoyed the look on the two policemen's faces as his replies of 'No comment' wound them up.

After about five minutes of 'No comments', Sergeant Wallis asked:

'Where were you yesterday at 8am?'

'No comment' was Jake's reply accompanied by a sly smirk to Gary.

'Are you not capable of even remembering where you were yesterday morning, laddie?' goaded the increasingly frustrated Scotsman.

Jake's eyes narrowed as he pointed a threatening finger at the sergeant. 'Are you trying to take the piss?' he said, rising to the jibe.

'Nah, sonny, I'm succeeding!'

Gary knew his client, knew the kind of response a comment like that would evoke and he wasn't wrong. Before Gary could reach out a restraining hand, Jake was over the table and lunging at the Scotsman.

The Chief Superintendent did a bit of lunging himself, for the panic button, before trying to pull Jake off his sergeant. Within seconds of the alarm going off in the corridor, the room filled with uniforms of every rank.

What occurred to Gary later, when he'd had time to reflect on it, was the speed and number of policemen who suddenly became available. It was almost as if they'd been waiting around for it to happen. Was it prearranged? Did Sergeant Wallis deliberately provoke Jake?

For sure, there were a lot of punches thrown in Jake's direction but Jake took them all and looked for more because by now he'd completely lost it. He wanted to kill the world and his mother and as they weren't available, a room full of coppers would have to do.

Pain or no pain, Jake was still a big lump of a guy and by now, he was feeding on the pain, of which there was plenty.

In the end, the police managed to pin him down, cuff him, and get the leg restraints on him but, even then, he was still lashing out. One of the older policemen, who should have known better, was trying to keep Jake's head still when his hand slipped and his wrist got too close to Jake's face. Big mistake; even after the stitched were removed, the teeth marks were still clearly visible.

Gary was no shrinking violet; you didn't grow up on one of the roughest estates in Balham without being able to look after yourself, but in these situations and wearing one of your favourite suits, he stood back and let them get on with it; he'd be there to pick through the legal pieces later. Besides, he'd gotten what he wanted anyway; there would be no more interviews today. Alleluia.

Jake was manhandled back to his cell and probably opened a few doors on the way with his head. 'Nothing new there, then' reflected Gary as he waited for the ME to check Jake out.

He sat in the public area swigging watery coffee from the vending machine.

'Hurry bloody up, will you?' urged Gary silently, checking the time on his watch: he wanted to get out of his work gear, pull on a pair of jeans and polo neck, read his weekend newspaper, the Independent, cover to cover, and take a stroll down the High Street with Nicki. No Sloane Square today; it would be too busy by now.

In the time it took to empty the contents of the polystyrene cup, the ME had checked Jake out and arrived to inform Gary that apart from a few new bruises on top of the existing ones there was nothing broken; he'd sedated Jake and doubted he'd make much sense for the rest of the day.

Music to Gary's ears; he was out the door faster than a greyhound out of the trap at Wimbledon.

Five minutes later, on the way home in a taxi, he called Sham on his mobile to be greeted by a sleepy 'Hello'.

'You alright?' asked Gary without preamble.

'Yeah, fine thanks' replied Sham stretching the stiffness out of his joints as he lay there. 'What time is it?' he asked through a yawn.

Gary checked his watch. 'It's about 1130, you lazy little sod' said Gary laughing. 'I've had the police at my door at six o'clock this morning, watched while a client tried to take on the entire Metropolitan Police Force and nearly beat them and you're still in your kip.'

'Isn't life one motherfuckin' bitch, Mr D?' drawled the laid-back hitman.

'I'll speak to you later' said Gary in between bursts of laughter.

Gary laughed so loud that the taxi driver looked worried, convinced that Gary had taken some illegal substance in the back of his cab; wouldn't be the first time.

'You never know what you're gonna pick up in London these days. This geezer looks respectable but, oh, he's probably on something' thought the cabbie resignedly. 'I hope he 'aint gonna cause any problems when it comes to puttin' 'is hand in 'is pocket.' As the cabbie had thought, Mr Dean turned out to be the nicest, most polite fare he'd picked up in a fortnight. Not that he was unduly influenced, in anyway, by the fiver tip Gary dropped him when he got out of his cab.

Eighty Three

Ten minutes later, Sham, having slept the sleep of the innocent, poked his head around the kitchen door, where his mother was sitting at the breakfast table browsing through The Guardian.

'Mornin', Ma' he said as he waltzed in, in his pyjamas. 'Any chance of a cup of tea? I'm parched.'

'And good afternoon to ye, Michael' replied his mother without looking up from the newspaper 'And what time did ye get in last night?'

'It wasn't late, Ma. I just fancied a long lie this morning.'

'Alright for some' muttered his mother under her breathe. 'What will ye have for yer breakfast?'

'I'm not hungry, Ma, but tanks anyways' His accent thickened up and the vernacular of the old country always surfaced when he spoke with his mother or father; memories of childhood were never far away when they were around.

'Sure ye've got to eat something, Michael Boyle, if only to soak up some of that booze ye were chucking down yer neck last night' declared his mother firmly.

'I didn't realise ye had such a high opinion of me, Ma, but if ye insist, I'll have a well-done piece of toast with marmalade.'

'Ye'll have two an' there's an end to it.'

'Awright, Ma, whatever ye say.'

As she bustled around the kitchen, waiting for the toast to set the smoke alarm off, 'Him and his bloody well-done toast'. She decided to put a washing on.

Living with two men had taught Mary Boyle a thing or two. One of them was that when men throw their dirty washing into the washing machine, they throw it...and it's usually all bundled up. So, she pulled out the clothes that were in there to separate them.

'Oh, my God, Michael! Where did that come from?' she asked in alarm, holding up Sham's bloodstained tee shirt from the previous night. 'I didn't want to upset you, Ma, but last night this guy collapsed at the club and I caught him as he fell to the floor; he was in a terrible mess, sure he was. That's how the blood got there.'

Not a word of a lie had passed Sham's lips.

'Was he okay?'

'To be honest, I didn't hang around.' The truth. 'Other people rushed to help him and I didn't fancy staying around after that so I left.' The whole truth and nothing but the truth. 'Sorry about the blood, Ma. I just put it in there and thought ye wouldn't see it. I didn't want ye getting yerself upset.'

'Upset, was it? If ye hadn't been here when I saw it, I'd have gone mad with worry, tinkin' the worst! Ye're sure ye're okay?' asked his mother as her expert eye gave him the once over.

'Honestly, Ma, that's exactly what happened an' I'm fine. Feckin' starvin' waitin' for my toast but apart from that...!' he grinned.

'Yer grandmother always said ye could charm the birds out of the trees, Michael Boyle, an' she was right. I do love ye, ye wee scallywag' and she grabbed him and hugged him tightly.

'Aw, ma!' he shouted in false protest.

'Caught ye in the arms of another man, have I, Mary Boyle?' declared her husband, Anthony, chuckling away as he walked into the kitchen. 'An' put that boy down. Ye' don't know where he's been.'

If only they knew. But Sham would never allow that to happen; he was very possessive and protective of his parents and their love.

'Ah sure, Anthony, an' look at this!' and she waved the bloodied tee shirt at him.

'Jesus! What the feck...!' began her husband as he automatically checked out Michael himself.

'Are ye okay?' asked his dad.

'Fine, Da. But ye should see the other guy.' The truth again.

The smoke alarm going off not only let them know that Sham's toast was ready but saved Sham from giving the explanation again as his mother waved a tea towel underneath the alarm attached to the ceiling to stop it.

'He's alright, Anthony...'

'...apart from the fact that he's starvin' to death because his cruel mother wouldn't give the poor wee lad a scrap of food' interjected Sham/Michael. 'I'm fine, Da, honest! This guy collapsed at the club last night an' I caught him. Nothing else.'

Having had two sets of expert eyes agree that he was indeed okay, the conversation turned to the rugby which Michael and his dad were looking forward to watching later; it was the Scotland v England game at Murrayfield.

'I think it'll be a good game' began his dad. 'Scotland have been playin' well the season.'

'Are ye havin' a laugh, Da?' goaded Sham.

'What d'ye mean?' asked his dad feigning surprise.

'England'll tank the boys from across the border; they always do.'

'Ten quid says they don't.'

'Ye're on! An' no IOU's this time!' said Michael biting into his crunchy toast.

'Would ye listen to the noise he's makin' with that toast' said his mother.

'Ah, ye're only jealous, Ma, 'cause ye're watchin' yer figure and would love to have some yerself.'

'An' isn't that the truth?' declared his dad as he grabbed his wife from behind, giving her a big cuddle. 'There's hardly anythin' left to grab hold of.'

'Too much information, Da!' declared Michael in between mouthfuls of toast.

'An' how d'ye think ye were made, ye little fecker?' continued his dad.

'Aaah! I can't eat anymore, I'll be sick!'

'What time is it?' asked his mother matter-of-flactly.

'Twelve o'clock' answered Michael. 'Why?'

Mary Boyle turned to her husband and said in that little girl's voice:

'D'ye think we've got time to make another little one before the rugby starts?'

Sham fled shouting 'Aaaaaaaah!' all the way up the stairs to his room.

'Got 'im!' declared his mother as the both of them fell about laughing.

Eighty Four

As Gary walked through the front door of the house, he slung his briefcase beside the coatstand and began to peel off his work clothes. Before he got to the foot of the stairs, the tie was off. As he mounted them the jacket was slipped off and he started fidgeting with the cufflinks. By the time he arrived at the bedroom door, his shirt was undone and he was pulling it out of his trousers. Opening the door, he slipped his shoes half off and kicked them in the air towards the side of the bed, undoing the zip of his trousers as he did so.

Standing there in his brilliant white Calvin's, he gave himself the once-over in the wardrobe mirror.

Regularly-toned had become 'irregularly' recently, due to his work load. As he scrutinised his body, he noticed something: was that the beginning of middle-aged paunch? He'd felt it this morning when he slipped on the trousers of his suit; they weren't tight yet, but in another couple of months...

'Now then, do I watch the rugby this afternoon or do I get myself down to the gym and a sauna? Hmm...'

He was still undecided as the bedroom door opened and Nicki walked in.

'Oh, you gave me a scare, darling!' she said startled. 'I didn't hear you come in. Is everything alright?'

'Yeah, everything's fine, babe'. For Nicki, everything would always be alright; even if the bank was coming around in an hour to repossess the house. Everything would be alright because Gary would somehow make it alright for her. He was an unusual combination: half eternal optimist with an equal dollop of pragmatist. It made for an interesting mix. 'Jake Vickers kicked off in the interview and that, as they say, was the end of that! There were about twenty police all trying to...'

Before he could finish, Nicki cried out: 'Stop, I don't want to hear! God, what is it with these men? Can't they control themselves?' She stopped for a moment, thinking about she'd said and continued 'Of course, I don't include you in that statement, darling.'

'What? You don't think I'm a man?' joked Gary pumping up his muscles and doing his Charles Atlas pose.

'Hmm, you are joking aren't you, you gorgeous hunk? Come 'ere, my lovely!' she purred in her best slutty voice.

Gary found another way to burn off a few calories over the next hour and all thought of the gym receded.

As they lay on top of the bedcovers afterwards, half-dozing, Nicki snuggled up to Gary and said:

'Oh, the insurance company called back to say that some company or other would be delivering your courtesy car this afternoon.'

'Did they say what it would be?' asked Gary from semi-conscious land.

'Yeah, it would either be a Merc or a Discovery.'

'What?' said Gary sitting upright, suddenly awake 'A Discovery? Euch! What am I paying these huge premiums for, for them to send me such a shit car? What a bloody cheek. Wait till I speak to them. A bloody Discovery! It'd better be the Merc.'

The thought of driving a Discovery, albeit for a very short period, wounded Gary's sense of style, mortally: worse, it could ruin his street-cred forever.

The doorbell rang and they both jumped.

Fortunately, they heard Harry's door open and footsteps running down the stairs.

As they dressed quickly, they could hear a mumbled conversation going on downstairs.

'Dad!' Harry called. 'Dad, are you there?'

Gary opened the bedroom door and called out: 'What is it Harry?'

'There's a man here with your courtesy car. Can you come down and sign for it?'

There was a mumbled interruption.

'...and bring your driving licence, please?'

'I'll be down in a minute' Gary called out. 'Just ask him to wait, will you, Harry?'

One minute later, Gary was kitted out in Armani jeans, Versace polo shirt and top of the range Nikes. As he sauntered down the stairs, still glowing in the aftermath of the previous hour's exercise, he felt quite chilled. Whatever the bloody car was sitting outside, the messenger would not be shot today, he decided...but come Monday...

'Hi! What have you got for me then?' asked Gary in his 'we're all mates together' voice.

The guy delivering the car must have been sixty-five, if he was a day. Gary instantly felt sorry for him.

'Probably needs the job to supplement his pension' he thought in a rare moment of compassion.

'Got a TdV6 for you, sir. Top of the range. Got everything: leather, air-con, all electric seats, sun roof, automatic, everything really. Lovely car, lovely drive, I have to say' replied the man with genuine enthusiasm.

Gary popped his head around the door to look at the metallic silver grey monstrosity sitting in his driveway.

'Yes, well we'll see. And automatic diesel, did I hear you say?' he enquired politely but thinking to himself 'Can it get any worse?'

'Yes, sir' replied the delivery man, thinking that the client was interested. 'You'll get great mileage from it.'

Gary had done the polite thing long enough.

'Hmmm' was the answer from the face with scepticism written all over it.

'May I see your driver's licence, sir?' asked the old fella, who was beginning to get the feeling that maybe the client wasn't as pleased as he'd anticipated.

'Better get going while the going's good' thought the guy who was grateful he didn't have to stack shelves at one of the big supermarkets like some of his friends; it would've killed his knees which were bad enough at the best of times.

All the formalities covered, the man showed Gary the workings of the car and was sent off with a tenner for his troubles.

Harry had waited patiently as his dad filled in the forms and checked the paintwork for scratches.

'It's not that bad' began Harry.

'Do not try to mollify me, son. It's vile, middle-class shit' said Gary slowly emphasising each word. It wasn't very often that Gary's working class resentment about the privileged kids who'd swanned their way through university, surfaced. But he could still remember the MacDonald's smell as he stood under the shower after he'd finished his shifts. The worse bit was when the cascading water hit his hair: he'd had to hold his breath to stop gagging and shampoo his hair twice to get rid of it.

'So you do like it then, dad.'

Gary nearly pissed in his Nikes, laughing.

'Yeah, right.'

'Look, dad, it's only for a few days. It might be alright. Let's see what it's like tomorrow. We are still going to Brighton, aren't we?'

'Abso...bloody...lutely, darling!' came the reply from behind, it was Nicki.

'Did you see my lips move?' Gary asked his son, chortling.

Even Harry had to laugh. It was good for Gary and Nicki to see.

'As my unmoving lips said Harry: "Abso...bloody...lutely, dahling!"' repeated his dad in his best imitation of Nicki's lah-di-dah voice.

'I don't talk like that!' said Nicki bashing him on the arm.

Her two men laughed even more.

'I don't!' she protested to no avail.

'Come on, son...' said Gary sensing that he was on to a winner '...let's go and watch the rugby. Should be a good game. D'you think?'

'The Scots are unpredictable, dad. One minute they play a blinder, the next they're all over the shop.'

Gary had put his arm around his son's shoulders and gently guided him towards the lounge.

'I'll make us some bacon sarnies' offered the mother of the household.

'Are you up for it, boys?'

'Actually, mum, I'm starving' replied Harry.

A look of hope passed between husband and wife.

'Me too!' replied Gary with gusto.
'Then bacon butties it is then.'

Eighty Five

Someone had brought a small telly in so that the boys who were on duty could keep an eye on the Scotland v England game.

'Revenge! Revenge!' cried out Sergeant Wallis as he walked up and grabbed a seat close to the TV. He began to wail the song which brings a tear to the collective eye of Scots the world over: 'Flower of Scotland'.

'Give it a rest will you, Sarge?' pleaded one of the on-duty uniforms who was filling out a report on a seventy-five-year-old woman who'd been caught nicking food for her cat because she couldn't afford it.

'You wait and see, laddie. We shall have our revenge!' he continued '... proud Edward's army...'

'Jim, keep it down, will you?' put in the Chief 'People are still upset about Bunny. And besides, Bannockburn was probably the last time your lot beat us.'

'You can mock, but we shall overcome!'

If there's one thing that galvanises the various factions in Scotland, it's the thought of tanking the English.

After the rush of the previous day, the station had returned to its daily routine of quiet chaos. So, just the usual assortment of scrots, muggers, pickpockets, thieves, domestics and assorted missing pussies and people: it was almost comforting.

The warm up had just begun on the telly when the Chief leaned over to Jim Wallis and said: 'I'm gonna nail that bastard this time, Jim. Got to, for Bunny's sake. It's never easy, at the best of times, knocking on someone's door to tell them the news but when I got to Bunny's house yesterday, I just stood there for ages. Three times I lifted my hand to knock but I couldn't bring myself to do it. And finally when I did and Jean opened the door...it was awful. She knew. They always do, don't they? The wives. They seem to have this sixth sense. Or, are they're waiting, waiting for the knock that finally comes? Terrible it was. Nothing I could do.'

Like he'd been doing for thirty-odd years, Jim Wallis just let his boss talk.

'Get it out' he thought 'You'll feel better once you've got it off your chest. The murderers, rapists, wife abusers; they all feel that sense of relief when they've shared. So, you just let it out.'

When he sensed that his boss had finished he waited a few moments out of respect and said 'Don't worry, Sir. We'll get him. An' I hope they throw the fuckin' key away an' he gets raped...every...fuckin'...day of his incarceration.'

The funny thing is that people think it's just the pretty boys who get it in prison. Wrong. It's not only about relieving themselves; it's about control and reminding those on the receiving end who's in charge.

'Comforting, that thought, isn't it Jim?' replied the Super with feeling.

'It is that, Sir.'

On the TV, the Scots kicked off and so did the crowd.

For the next fifteen minutes, every pair of eyes in the room was glued to the screen; all of them waiting to see who would draw blood first. And it was the Scots. Jim Wallis went mad. He stood up and did his version of a Highland Fling accompanied by an 'Oh yes! Oh yes!' That is until two minutes later when the English side replied and the rest of the room erupted.

'Luck. That's what it was. Pure luck. If that stupid full back had caught the ball instead of fluffing it...' said the sullen, dour, bitter Scotsman.

'An' if my auntie had had bollocks she wouldn't have gotten into the chorus! If, if, if!' cried out one of the uniforms to gusts of laughter from the crowd around the TV.

'Come on Scotland' thought Jim Wallis defiantly 'Can ye no whip the pants off these bastards just once? Please?'

Eighty Six

Jake lay in his cell with two things to keep him company; the pain and his thoughts. One he could live with, the other was driving him around the bend.

He could take his mind off the pain; he'd lived with that all his life, even though there wasn't a part of his body which he could move without it starting a chain reaction to most other parts of his battered and mangled body. No, the secret was not to move at all, to lie absolutely still and breathe as shallowly as possible unless there was no other choice.

And the 'no other choice' scenario finally came home to roost when he realised that he was definitely going to piss his pants unless he moved.

The pain of turning over onto his side took his breath away; he nearly passed out. He jiggled his feet towards the edge off the bed and slowly let them drop down towards the floor. As he tried to push himself up into a sitting position, nausea swept over him and his head spun. There was only one way, he decided, that he was going make it; he'd have to crawl. Slowly easing his tortured body onto the tiled floor and using his elbows, he dragged his sorry body towards the stinking stainless steel latrine.

When he finally reached the toilet bowl, he pulled himself up into a sitting position against the wall as he unzipped his trousers and tried to pull the trousers and underpants down together. Some bastard had kicked him in the nuts during the fracas in the interview room so there was no way he'd be able to stand to do it, the pain would be too great; he'd have to sit like a girl.

After several painful attempts, he finally lowered himself carefully onto the bog and was able to release the contents of his bladder...but the pain was excruciating; it was like pissing through barbed wire with shards of broken glass attached. The relief of emptying himself was soon forgotten as he looked between his legs and saw that he had pissed blood; they'd done a good job on him. He'd mention it to the ME next time he saw him. No point in asking these bastards now to see a doctor, they'd just laugh and he was not about to give them that satisfaction.

Dragging himself back towards the bed, he stopped several times to catch his breath. Covering that short distance from the latrine to the bed sapped most of his willpower and all but drained him of his ability to self-anesthetise. After several attempts to pull himself up onto the bed he succeeded and fell onto it with a groan of rage; someone was going to pay...and how.

He lay there drifting in and out of consciousness. In his conscious moments, the thoughts swirled around in his head. They were all lining up, queuing up, one after the other, with one recurring theme; who was the bastard who'd shopped him?

In the end, his exhausted brain gave into the body's plea for oblivion but not before he came to the only conclusion possible: the leak had come from Johnnie Parker's side.

'No other explanation makes sense' was his last thought before the darkness enveloped him.

Twenty minutes later, the spy hole cover was silently pushed to one side and an eye peered through, observing Jake for a full minute. The eye could see no movement, no apparent rise and fall of the chest to suggest that breathing was taking place. By the time this information had transferred from the eye of the custody sergeant to his brain, it had become a question: 'Is he dead?'

'There's only one way to find out' he concluded and he gave the door such a whack with his truncheon that prisoners two cell doors away jumped at the unexpected explosion of sound.

The reaction behind the door he'd banged on was entirely different: Jake's brain, in sleep mode, awoke, convinced that it was under attack and instructed the body to 'flee'. It took just a couple of milliseconds for the brain to regret that decision; the body regretted it more.

As Jake instinctively jumped up, every part of him from his bruised balls to his lacerated face objected in the strongest possible terms.

The pain could not have been any worse if the sergeant had placed Jake's cock on a table and belt it with that fucking truncheon.

But what made it a thousand times worse? Jake could hear hysterical laughter from the other side of the door.

Eighty Seven

It was only later, looking back on Friday night's events that it should have occurred to someone in the pay of Her Majesty's Constabulary that the death of such a major player as John Pollock might create a power vacuum. It would, of course, be filled...but not before a lot of blood-letting and old score-settling took place.

The bad boys of South London saved that up as a surprise until Saturday night.

So, while the police were taking it easy watching the Scotland v England game that afternoon, their opposite numbers were flying around the estates on their patch forging new alliances, planning assaults on the competition and generally making sure that the police forces of South London would not be having a quiet weekend. In fact, there would be no let up for the foreseeable. And so, as the Gary Deans of this world relaxed in their cocoons of wealth and the prisoner, Jake Vickers, lay in agony but safety in a police cell, the rest of the population of South London were soon going to wish that they could join them instead of ducking bullets that weren't even meant for them.

And so, it began.

The first to get it was Georgie Smith known to one and all as 'Creepy' because of his place of birth: Crawley.

As John Pollock's No.2, he was the target of several factions; it was just a question of who would get to him first. The police found him hanging half out of his black Porsche with the blacked-out windows and two bullet holes to the skull with assorted others to the body after one of his elderly neighbours complained about a disturbance; he'd thought it was kids letting off fireworks and it'd frightened his cat. In his death throes, Creepy had floored the accelerator and that's how they found him: the car leasing company would not be pleased when it was handed back.

For Creepy it was a bit of 'what goes around comes around' scenario. He'd disposed of an unknown number of individuals himself in exactly the same manner; it was simply his turn.

Still nobody twigged. It was only after the second body was found in a wheelie bin that alarm bells began to sound at a number of police stations around the South London patch.

The second body had belonged to Mr Pollock's accountant. He was the guy who collected the dough from the dealers who had an account with the late Mr Pollock. And Sammy Lesner was one tough cookie; a former boxer who was banned from the sport for biting the tip of an opponent's nose off. The balaclava'd guys who did him, knew the man and his history. So, there was no fucking around; they emptied two semi-automatic Russian-made Baikal IZH-79's into him. He didn't give them any trouble after that.

Later, when the police made enquiries, it turned out that his neighbours on the estate had heard and seen nothing; but kept their kids in and their doors locked anyway.

One brave soul called it in after the body had been shoved in the bin and after the two unidentified assailants had been given sufficient time to get clear of the area. Phone it in too soon and it could be you next.

Next to get it were two of Mr Pollock's regular dealers, who between them owned six pit bulls. They'd had tentative talks about making a joint takeover bid for their former distributor's empire. The first one was found at the base of the building where he kept a twentieth-floor council flat he used as his office: it appeared that he'd committed suicide and the dogs, unable to face life without their master, had followed him.

The second one was at home when the doorbell rang. As he opened the peephole to see who was there, the silenced gun pressed against the other side of it blew away most of his eye socket but left a very neat hole in the door; the gunman had had his ear pressed to the door listening for the sound of the peephole cover being slid back. The dogs went mad. The unknown killer pushed the gun through the letterbox and shut the noisy little fuckers up.

This was the start of a turf war which was not going to be decided in one night of scum-letting: alliances and allegiances would change over the coming weeks in less time than it takes to load a bullet into a chamber with the inevitable consequence of the police having to invest heavily in extra body bags.

Eighty Eight

By the time the first body was found, Dave and Doris were well settled into their small semi-detached villa in Puerto Ventura. It came with a forty-foot swimming pool attached to it. Dave had taken it on a two-week renewable lease.

Doris was deeply impressed. It was seriously posh compared to their previous holidays which consisted of two weeks in three star hotels with a million screaming kids running up and down the corridors at all hours of the day and night...and when it wasn't the kids, it was the parents. Spain and sangria have a funny effect on the British. Or it could be sangria and Spain.

'I could get used to this' said Doris slightly tipsy after draining the last of her second Malibu on ice, purchased at the duty-free. She was lying by the pool, smothered in suntan oil in her new polka-dotted bikini, courtesy of her old man's generosity. She liked a bit of colour did Doris, so, suitcases were left unpacked until it got dark as she got down to the serious job of topping up her tanning shop colour.

'Oh, could you now?' asked Dave slipping on his sunglasses as he lay down on the padded recliner after swimming a couple of lengths of the pool; it was nice not to have to fight over the recliners with the Germans.

'Yeah, I really could. 'Ere Dave, you couldn't get your old Doris a top up, could you? Please?' she asked, lifting her sunglasses and fluttering her eyelashes at him as she held out the long-stemmed glass in his direction.

Dave picked up the bottle of Malibu from the ice bucket and poured a generous measure.

'Oo, ta, love' replied Doris taking a long slow sip of her favourite tipple, feeling it spread all over her insides. 'Hmm, that just hit the spot.'

'This is the life, innit Doris? I could get used to this myself' Dave looked over at Doris. He was going to save it as a surprise and tell her over dinner but the urge was too great.

'Doll....' he began which made Doris suddenly sit up: he only called her that when he had something really important to say. '...what would you say to us maybe moving out here permanently? I could sell the business and we could sublet the 'ouse and buy a little place out here.'

'I'd think I'd died an' gone to 'eaven! Either that or I'd waken up from the bloody dream' Doris thought excitedly. 'Permanent sunshine? Unlimited cheap booze? A South London girl's dream come true!'

'Oh, go on then, twist me arm!' replied his peroxide wife, laughing so much she almost spilt her drink. In her late fifties, Doris was often puzzled by the reaction of complete strangers in the street, especially men. Unbeknown to her, they would check out the rear and walk faster to get in front to have a look at the face. Fortunately, Doris couldn't read their minds but mental comments such as 'body of an angel, face of an 'orse!' and such like, were not uncommon. Years of tanning machines and long hours of lying in the sun had taken their toll. From the back, they'd think they were admiring the rear of someone in her mid-thirties; full frontal was seventy plus on a bad day. But her old man still loved her and that's what mattered.

'Good. Then I'll tell you what I'm gonna do. In two weeks time, I'm goin' back to sort things out an' you can stay here till I get back.'

Doris went to interrupt but Dave held his hand up.

'Let me finish, Doris. I'll leave enough to keep you goin' till I get back an' when I do; we can start lookin' for a place. Now what'd you think?'

'I could get used to this' she repeated and laughed. Life was good and getting better by the minute: and the Malibu was definitely helping.

'That's settled then. So, let's lie back and let Capstan take the strain' said Dave laughing at the old advertising slogan of the fags he used to smoke in his youth.

'Cheers, Dave!' called out his wife a little too loudly but who cared? The nearest neighbours were a hundred yards away. 'We deserve it, don't we, Dave? Especially you, you old so-and-so. You've grafted all your life and now you're gonna reap your reward. Cheers everybody!' and Doris held up her glass and toasted the whole of the coastal resort; her new best friends.

Eighty Nine

California had its gold rush: the South East has its coast rush. A bit of blue sky and it seems like half the population of London heads off to one of the coastal resorts and as Brighton is the nearest and easiest to get to, it gets hit the hardest.

The forecast on the news on Saturday night was good. And sure enough the following morning, the skies were the colour of Paul Newman's eyes. The wisps of white cloud didn't stop sunbeams from reaching into the darkest corners all over London. On days like that, every road leading to the coast would be chocablock; everybody and their granny would be making their way to Brighton.

Gary, Nicki and Harry set off early. The three of them climbed into the Discovery and slammed the doors closed. For a few seconds everything went quiet, nobody moved. Nicki and Harry held their breath: how would Gary react?

'Ah well,' said Gary sighing as he inserted the key into the ignition 'here goes' adjusting his electric seat to a comfortable driving position when the engine turned over.

The first thing he noticed was that the engine was surprisingly quiet for a diesel.

'Hmm' was Gary's only response. Like his Maserati, it was automatic. In London, you really didn't want gears; all that changing up and down malarkey when all you wanted to do was to get from A to B as quickly and effortlessly as possible. No, automatics were the answer to London driving.

The traffic and the banter as they drove along the South Circular was light and easy until Gary caught sight of a James Irvine lorry when they were joining the M23 to Brighton. It reminded Gary that there was still some unpleasant, unfinished business to be taken care of. It took all of his willpower for him to shove it to the back of his mind; it was not going to spoil today.

The drive to their favourite parking spot on the seafront was uneventful and although Gary didn't admit it out loud, surprisingly smooth. The 'vile middle-class shit' had actually turned out to be a very relaxing drive indeed. He'd checked out the acceleration a couple of times and although not as responsive as his Maserati, it still had a bit of poke, which pleased Gary and he liked the fact that you could see for miles from the raised sitting position.

'I'll be honest with you; that wasn't as bad as I thought it was going to be' he shared with Nicki and Harry as they strolled along the quirky little streets of the seaside town. All three of them loved the relaxed atmosphere of the place: it was the complete antithesis of London where it was all 'Go, go, go!' In Brighton, the atmosphere was more 'Whatever' It was like the entire population of the town had shared a very large joint; everyone seemed so relaxed and accommodating.

Gary noticed it especially in cafes and restaurants. In London, everybody wanted their food 'Now!' and no excuses. Here in Brighton, the Londoners seemed to have caught the 'Whatever' bug and would smile and chill even if their food took a while to arrive.

Strolling along, hand in hand with Nicki and Harry trailing behind, Gary wondered if it was being so close to the sea or maybe the sea air that had this effect.

'Perhaps the Courts should send criminals to seaside resorts instead of prison to get rid of the anger inside of them that seems to fuel a lot of their crimes' he thought.

In his mind Gary heard that old fart, Farquar, pronouncing sentence as he dragged on a joint '...I hereby sentence you to three months in Brighton...blah, blah, blah' Gary burst out laughing at the thought.

'Alright!' said Nicki 'What's so funny? Come on out with it' and she poked him in the ribs which made him laugh even more. 'Come on, tell!' she commanded.

Giggling away like a schoolboy, Gary told her that if he did tell her, she'd think he'd lost the plot entirely.

'I've been thinking that for years' she declared. 'Well, if you won't tell us then you have to buy Harry and me an ice cream.'

'So suddenly I'm made of money?'

The whole day was filled of laughter and shared jokes. Before lunch, they strolled down to the beach volley ball area but it was so crowded that they knew they'd have no chance of getting a game, so they let it pass. "Next time!" declared Harry merrily.

Every so often, Gary or Nicki would give Harry a furtive glance, just checking to see how he was, and seeing the old Harry begin to rise to the surface; the cheeky easy-going young man that was their son. It would take a long time for the pain of Amanda to recede but the healing had begun. When the time came to make their way back home, it was Harry who was said 'Oh, not yet, dad. Please!'

'What d'you want to do then?' asked Gary who was happy to put off the inevitable; facing Jake Vickers.

'Anybody fancy a run along the coast?' asked Nicki.

'Why not?' agreed Gary. 'You up for it, Harry?'

'Yeah! Good idea, mum. It's nice just to look out to sea and watch the waves; it's sort of peaceful.'

'You see, Gary Dean, I'm not just a pretty face and a nice pair of legs.' joked Nicki.

'Or did you mean 'Not even?' shot back Gary.

'Oi, you!' came back Nicki 'I'll have you know that my legs have often been admired.'

'Yeah, mum. At Crufts!' said Harry joining in.

'And you can...' Nicki left it trailing in the air but the boys got the gist.

Ninety

They set off in the direction of Rottingdean, the pretty little village situated just fifteen minutes from the centre of Brighton.

On the way, they passed Roedean, the independent private girls school which had produced the likes of Phyllis Pearson, creator of one of the most thumbed books on the planet, the London A-Z, that is, until the invention of its nemesis, the sat-nav.

As Gary stole a glance at it, the sight immediately brought back memories of when he was a kid of no more than ten, when his parents took him and his sister on their summer holidays: a day out to Brighton pier. It was all they could afford. The Bus took them passed the imposing cream-coloured building with the red slate roof sitting high on the hill, for all the world, looking like some Austrian schloss. On the top of the double-decker bus, his dad had ranted about the privileged middle-classes and the down-trodden working class. Gary was never able to erase the memory of the anger etched on his normally placid dad's face and the sight of the building brought it all back.

'Arabella went there, you know' offered Gary as they drove past. Arabella Smythson-King had worked at Gary's firm for over two years.

'I know' sighed Nicki 'You tell us every time we pass. Where are you taking us?'

'Oh, I don't know. I thought I'd just put this jalopy through its paces... see how it does.'

'Oh...my...God!' exclaimed Nicki, amazed. 'You actually like it. Don't you? Go on. Be a man, Gary Dean. Admit it!'

It stuck in Gary's throat; he couldn't bring himself to say it.

Finally, he managed to blurt out: 'S'alright.'

'You little liar, Gary Dean. You like it!' exclaimed Nicki not missing out on the chance to get Gary to admit that all things middle-class are not necessarily evil.

'I wouldn't go as far as to say that' he replied but the smile on his face said different.

'Well I never' said his wife who'd gone to private school herself. 'Harry...' said Nicki turning in her seat to face her son in the back '...you do realise that we have just witnessed St Gary's Road to Damascus? It's nothing short of a miracle...but don't go blind on us, Gary! Not while you're driving.'

Harry shrugged; he couldn't see what the big deal was. Occasionally his dad would get on his high horse about class; given the stories of the poverty his dad had had to endure when he was young, he could understand it.

His gaze returned to the sea and the graceful sailboats gliding smoothly through water while the speedboats and cruisers zigzagged their way across the waves, causing the boats moored at the jetties to rock quite violently.

'It fascinates me how they manage to construct things like that' said Harry pointing to a partly-constructed pier jutting out into the cold waters of the Channel. Entry was barred by two flimsy wire gates; obviously nothing worth stealing there then.

Gary and Nicki briefly glanced at the half-built structure: just another point of interest along the coast.

On their second spin around the picturesque village square, Gary could see that there wasn't enough space to park a Dinky car let alone a hulking great brute of a Land Rover. It was always going to be like that on sunny days on the coast, be it summer or winter, so they decided to call it a day and make their way home.

Fortunately for them, they managed to miss most of the traffic on the way back; the sun was still shining and the world, its mother, granny and all the kids were trying to squeeze the last few hours of pleasure out the weekend before returning to another five days of misery on the treadmill of industry.

It was only when they got past Croydon that they joined the bumper to bumper brigade. It took them nearly as long to do the last five miles to home as it did to do the forty-odd miles from Brighton: the madness that is London.

But the trip was worth it: Harry seemed to be coming around to his old self and they'd had a brilliant family day out. And to top it all, although he hadn't told Nicki yet, Gary had decided that he was getting a Discovery...but only as a second car. Nothing would or could take the place of his beloved Maserati. So, fuck the middle-class image; the Discovery was a bloody good car.

The moral of the episode for Gary? Don't judge a car by its owner.

Ninety One

As Gary sat in the usual traffic jam which every city the length and breadth of the planet has on Monday mornings, he had time to reflect on, as he now mentally referred to it as, 'the situation'. He would give it no more sinister title because to do so would confer more importance on it than Gary wanted.

'Young Mr Vickers,' Gary's train of thought began as he waited his turn to get through a particularly nasty set of lights 'what do I tell you about James Irvine that would satisfy you and stop you looking any further, hmm?'

The answer was not forthcoming; usually solutions sashayed into Gary's brain with ease, but not this time.

'Come on, Gary. Get your fucking brain into gear' he thought savagely as he jumped a red light to a fanfare of car horns.

'And you lot can all fuck off as well!' he shouted to the owners of the blaring horns but really it was to the world in general this morning.

'How do I get Mr Vickers to let it go?' he asked his formidable brain again.

Nothing. Not a fucking sausage.

Gary sat fuming all the way to the office car park. The angrier he got, the less his brain produced in the way of answers.

As he waited for the lift, his only option came to him: '...tell him that you've looked into the company and that there's nothing to see. They're a transport company and nothing else. And 99.9 per cent of that is true. Only one of the lorries isn't kosher and not even the police have been able to work that one out! But what a perfect solution, if I may say so myself! Instead of keeping the gear in a lock-up or stuck in some static safety security box that the police probably keep tabs on anyway; a lorry constantly on the move. The police would never find the gear. And if they don't find the loot, my clients stay out of chokey and are allowed to keep their ill-gotten gains...oh, and pay me for the privilege. It's like their own portable investment fund. Moveable assets. I like that!'

The thought of his own genius cheered Gary up and by the time he passed through the glass doors into reception, he was his normal self; smiling and in control.

'Good morning, ladies' he said to 'bird brain' known to the rest of the office as Raquel and her colleague, Julie, who together made up the first line of defence of Gary Dean & partners against the outside world.

''Morning, Mr Dean' the girls chorused as their nostrils detected a delectable whiff of very expensive, masculine cologne; they both came over all peculiar.

'Oooh, I'd do anything for that man!' cooed Julie all doe-eyed as they both watched the receding shapely, sharply-dressed figure bestowing 'Good Mornings' to one and all in the office.

'Me too' said Raquel huskily '...and more!'

'Raquel!' retorted Julie shocked at the sexual inference in her co-worker's response. 'What? More than anything?'

'I'd rip me G-string down an' let 'im do me over the custard creams! Right now!'

The 'Right now!' was so loud that heads turned in the office at its forcefulness. It sounded like the growl of a tigress that hadn't eaten for a week and food suddenly walked in front of her eyes.

'You alright, Raquel?' called over one of the male paralegals from his desk, who would have quite happily acquiesced to Raquel's demand even though his preference was for chocolate digestives; a minor detail in the circumstances, which he would have been prepared to forego.

With eyes still on the boss' butt as it disappeared into his room, Raquel gave a shudder at the obscene picture she had in her head, cleared her throat and said in a slightly higher pitched tone than normal 'Yes, thank you, Norman. I'm fine' And once again became the little demure receptionist as she returned to her typing.

Sadly for Raquel, she'd have had more chance, after the sex change op, of becoming the Pope.

Jeannie had the boss' double espresso waiting for him.

'Morning, boss. Nice weekend?'

'Fantastic, thanks, Jeannie' replied Gary enthusiastically as flashes of the pleasanter parts of the weekend went through his mind 'What about you?'

'Oh, not bad except there was a shooting around the corner from me. Some sort of gangland feud. You can't believe it could happen on your own doorstep, can you?'

'London's changing, Jeannie. In the good old days, the old gang bosses, like the Krays, kept those sorts of things away from the public; kept it amongst their own kind. Now the new breed of thugs don't care. They just start shooting in public places and screw the consequences. They think it makes them look big. Anyway, according to the papers this morning, there were about six murders around London this weekend and they're saying it's all related to the killing of John Pollock, our esteemed former client.'

'I know. I was shocked when I read about him. What an awful way to die! But they do say it comes to us all.'

'True, Jeannie but it makes me very...' he paused and a mournful expression appeared on his face '...very sad.'

'Why?' asked a mystified Jeannie.

'All the future fees we'll lose now that he gone!' chirped Gary returning his expression to its usual happy look.

'Gary Dean,' declared Jeannie in mock horror '...you...are... terrible!'

'I've been called worse, Jeannie! Trust me. Now, enough of this idle banter. What have you got for me?' he asked, glancing at the pile of papers she was carrying.

'Nothing urgent. Two drunk-driving and a GBH.'

'Just the usual then, eh? Keep my diary free will you, Jeanie? I have an interview arranged with Jake Vickers.'

'It's looking pretty light today but you're in Court tomorrow.'

'Thanks, sweetie.'

That was Gary's way of ending the meeting and certainly more polite than: 'Fuck off and let me get on with what I have to do' which he was not averse to saying to some people: Raquel would definitely qualify for that list.

Just before she closed the door behind her Jeannie threw one last quick glance at Gary only to see that he was already deep in thought about something. The something, of course, was 'the situation'.

'Better get this over and done with' was his overwhelming thought.

A deep sigh later, he stood up and put his coat on. He couldn't put Jake Vickers any longer.

Ninety Two

Jake was sitting on the loo when he heard the shuffling of boots outside in the corridor.

At least on Sunday, the Lord's Day of rest, an unspoken truce had broken out between him and the police: or at least there hadn't been any confrontation. They'd delivered the shit they called food and he'd attempted to pick at some of it. 'Might as well try to get used to it' he thought; this was going to be the level of cuisine he could expect for a long time to come.

There had been no name calling, no beatings, no banging on the door just as he was drifting off to sleep and in return, he hadn't attempted to kill, maim or bite off any of their extremities; that had been the extent of the suspension of hostilities. Until now: Monday fucking morning.

The shuffling was getting louder and was now accompanied by whispers. Jake's brain told him that whatever was going on outside was to do with him so he pulled up his trousers and moved over to sit on the edge of the bed, on high alert.

'What are the fuckers up to now?' he wondered. Assuming he was about to be on the receiving end of another kicking, Jake looked around for one of two things; something which could be used as a weapon, of which there was none or, something which he could use to protect his body. The pain was slowly easing but he must be getting soft in his old age; he was grateful for the respite the previous day. This morning, he found that he was able to move his left arm and both of his legs without searing pain shooting to every other part of his body.

The thin excuse of a mattress. It was the only thing he could use, he decided. He stood up slowly and carefully began to wrap it around his upper body. It wasn't much but it might reduce some of the impact from the steel toecaps which the police particularly favoured for situations like this.

There was a rap on the door.

'Jake Vickers, you're being moved to Wandsworth Prison where you'll be held on remand. There's two ways we can do this. If you resist in any way, we will restrain you. We're coming in now.'

Jake would have laughed at the euphemism if he could have done it without causing unbelievable pain. 'We will restrain you' or to put it another way: 'We WILL kick the shit out of you if you as much as look at us the wrong way.'

The key rattled in the door. When it swung open, Jake nearly burst out laughing. It looked like a scene from 'Star Wars'. There were six Darth Vader lookalikes standing there.

Jake wanted to call out 'Just for little old me?' but he didn't. He didn't want any trouble today.

'Turn around and place your hands behind you back. Do it now!' commanded the lead Darth, head to toe in riot gear.

Slowly, Jake dropped the mattress and turned his back to them. The pain in his right arm was bad but he wasn't going to let these bastards know, so he did as he was told.

There was disappointment among the Darths. They'd been looking forward to restraining him.

The sergeant who placed the cuffs on him had clocked the slower response of his right arm. Cuffing the left wrist first, he then had to use considerable force to cuff the right one.

If he'd hoped that Jake would kick off, he was wrong. It hurt like fucking hell but Jake was coming quietly. For now.

Once he'd been cuffed, the masks came off.

'Right you piece of shit, one wrong move from you and you will be very, very sorry and that's a promise' spat the leader.

'You're so fuckin' brave, you lot' thought Jake furiously 'Every one of you's tooled up with enough gear to stop a fuckin' elephant an' you wait until you've got the cuffs on me before you make your namby-pamby threats. No wonder I've been running rings around you for years. Me, the piece of shit? Yeah, right!'

Going up the stairs, one of the policemen accidentally tripped Jake up and he crashed onto the concrete stairs banging his head on the side of the wall on the way down. The pain came back with a vengeance. Jake quickly tried to mentally run through his bodily parts to find a bit that didn't hurt so that he could concentrate on that. He found it: the big toe of his left foot. He wriggled it and kept his mind focussed on that; it was how he used to do it as a kid. Keeping his mind completely concentrated on that one point, stopped messages getting through from the other parts which were screaming for attention. Nevertheless, it took his breath away. 'You clumsy bastard!' shouted the one who tripped him. 'Get the fuck up NOW before...'

'Enough!' cried out his boss. 'No more. And that's an order. I want the prisoner delivered with no further incidents. Is that clear?'

The rest of the team got the message.

All the way to Wandsworth, the wailing sirens of the police van and the accompanying convoy couldn't block out the charged atmosphere of hatred and pent-up frustration emanating from the six-man escort aimed at him. Six pairs of eyes stared intently at him throughout the short journey, willing him to try something.

'Go on, boys, I can take it! Keep it coming' thought Jake. It was like balm to his aching body.

'Don't forget to tip the driver, will you?' he goaded as they manhandled him out of the van into the dreary grey yard of the prison.

For a few moments, Jake inhaled slowly, deeply: it was good to suck in the fresh polluted London air into his lungs.

Forty minutes later, he was processed and looking forward to having a cosy little chat with his so-called gang and Mr Johnnie Parker; they were all being held on remand at Wandsworth.

Very convenient.

Ninety Three

Before he left the office, Gary buzzed Jeannie.

'Hi Gary. What can I do for you?' she enquired.

'I'm off to the nick to see Jake Vickers but is there anything I should be doing or anything that needs looked at before I go? I don't know how long I'm going to be, Jeannie.'

Jeannie consulted Gary's diary on screen.

'No, no, you're absolutely fine. There are a couple of things...but they can wait; as long as you have a look at them before the end of the week. Apart from that you're clear.'

'Thanks, Jeannie. Anything urgent just give me a bell, will you?'

'Sure, no probs. Good luck with Mr Vickers. Sounds like he's going to need it.'

'I don't think even Perry Mason could get him off this one, Jeannie!'

'If you can't do the time...'

'He will do time and a lot of it. The only question for me is how do I get the jury to look at a hard, nasty bastard like our lovely Jake and get them to feel sorry for him?'

'I'm sure you'll find a way' replied Jeannie laughing but meaning it.

'One day I won't, Jeannie but until then the show must go on.'

'Well, good luck anyway.'

'Thanks, Jeannie. See you later.'

As he walked through the office, Peter Ainswright waylaid him and asked if he could have a word about the case; he was representing nose-picking Dave.

'Can it wait, Peter? I'm off to see Jake Vickers now. Maybe we could pick up on it when I get back?'

'Sure. Or maybe we could arrange a case conference in the next couple of days?'

'Good idea. Speak to Jeannie and get her to co-ordinate everybody's diaries, will you?'

The truth was he should have thought of that but with everything that was going on with Jake; it had completely slipped his mind.

Ninety Four

The Monday morning rush hour in London seemed to be getting longer and longer.

'How long is a fucking rush hour supposed to last?' Gary asked himself exasperatedly, not for the first time, as he pushed into the familiar bumper to bumper queue when he drove out of the company car park.

Forty-five minutes later, for a journey which should have taken ten, he arrived at the Walworth Road nick. Except that the forty-five minutes turned into an hour as he drove around looking for a parking meter. Twice from his raised position in the Discovery, he saw one up ahead only for someone else to indicate and pull in just ahead of him. London.

Finally, he found a space and inserted enough coins to cover the maximum that was allowed, two hours, and boy was he going to need it. This was going to be one of the most difficult client meeting he'd had since finishing his training and walking out into the big bad world as a full qualified defender of justice; except in Gary's case, it would be as the staunch defender of some of the biggest crooks on the planet. Different strokes etc. Some of the doey-eyed idealists he'd studied with had become human rights lawyers: 'Good luck to them when the monthly mortgage payment is due', Gary used to think.

Strolling along in the morning sunshine, Gary's eyes and ears absorbed the atmosphere around him; it was something he couldn't turn off. No matter where he was; in Court or at a drinks party or just walking along the street, he just couldn't switch off from listening and observing people and all their attendant foibles.

There was an elderly couple walking ahead of him who looked like they'd been married in the year dot. The old guy was walking behind her like a beast of burden, dragging the trolley in one hand and a heavy shopping bag in the other while she sauntered along giving him an ear-bashing because he'd forgotten to pick up two tins of beans instead of the one he'd obviously picked up.

'... if I told you once...!'

She went on and on at the old geezer until in the end, it was on the tip of Gary's tongue to say to him: 'Go on, son, do her. I'll defend you free of charge. No jury in the land would convict you after they hear what a nit-picking old bag of misery she is. I could probably even get you a few quid out of the Criminal Compensation Board for what you've had to put up with over the years.'

The couple stopped at a bus stop and as Gary walked passed them, he glanced at the old man...and did a double take. The old geezer's hearing aid was hanging out of his ear; he couldn't hear a fucking thing!

'If only I could do that in Court sometimes with the old retirement home dodgers who sit up there and drone on and on when they're given the chance.'

It raised Gary's mood a few notches. 'Good on ya, son' thought Gary grinning from ear to ear.

As he walked past the rest of the queue at the bus stop, he caught 'the smell' and nearly gagged: the unmistakable odour of stale fast food had crept up his nasal passages. There's something about fast food joints that makes the smell stick to your clothes and for some people who ate there every day, a layer of 'smell' was added to their clothes each time they entered the place; his days at McDonalds came rushing back.

'Yuck! Wash your clothes, you dirty bastard' was all he could think as he held his breath until he got passed.

A couple of minutes later and he was standing at the bottom of the stairs to the police station.

'Think I need a quick drag before I face Mr Vickers'. He didn't really; he was just putting off the inevitable a bit longer.

After a couple of puffs, Gary looked at the lighted tip of the cigarette and decided he couldn't put it off any longer. It had to be faced.

Inhaling one long last lungful of smoke, he held it and then releasing it with a rush, threw the cigarette stub on the ground and stamped it out. There was something about the way he kept on and on squashing it; like he was crushing the life of the Jake Vickers' problem?

Ninety Five

The same desk sergeant was on duty as before when Gary walked in.

'This'll be fun' thought Gary as he remembered the cold shoulder treatment he got the first time he came in to see Jake.

'What can I do for you, Sir?' asked the sergeant in a tone which meant: 'What the fuck do you want, Sir?'

'I've come to see my client, Sergeant, Mr Vickers' replied Gary, keeping it on a formal footing.

'He's not here, Sir.'

'Pardon?'

'He's gone, Sir.'

For a few seconds, Gary couldn't speak. Was he missing something?

'You mean you've released him?' he asked, stunned.

'Oh, very droll, Sir! With a bit of luck, Mr Vickers will be unavailable for gainful employment long after I've retired...if there's any justice in this world' he added unpleasantly.

Gary decided to take back control of the conversation.

'Okay, sergeant, there's two ways we can play this now' said the real, no pussy-footing Gary Dean, excoriator of prosecution witnesses the length and breadth of the British legal system '...either you can tell me where my client is NOW or I WILL make a formal complaint about police obstruction. Which is it to be?'

The sergeant stood up to his full height and eyeballed Gary; they were pretty evenly matched. Gary didn't even blink. The sergeant got the message.

'They've taken him to Wandsworth' he said bluntly, dismissing Gary and returning his eyes to his paperwork.

'To Wandsworth?' repeated Gary. 'What? And no-one bothered to inform me?' asked Gary, the anger rising in him.

'Did no-one call you, Sir?' the sergeant asked looking up in mock surprise. 'Must have been an oversight. Tut, tut. I'll make a note and make sure it doesn't happen again...Sir.'

What Gary wouldn't have given to wipe the sick smirk of that bastard's face. He stood there for a full thirty seconds with scenario after scenario going through his head: everything from Gary paying Sham to do a job on the motherfucker and blowing him away to Kingdom Come to Gary himself flooring the prat with one well-aimed punch to his bulbous nose, spreading it across his face from one ear to the other. Instead he gave the sergeant one last scathing stare and got the satisfaction of seeing him flinch; only then did he walk away, in silence.

Ninety Six

Jake was escorted to his cell by two screws who Jake could tell were just bursting for him to put up some kind of resistance or give them a bit of lip. He could almost hear them pleading: 'Give us the excuse!' They so desperately wanted to give him a good kicking.

But not today; they'd have to wait their turn. They'd find their excuse soon enough or he'd give it to them.

No, today Jake wanted to find his way around the place, check out who was in charge, have that little chat he'd been looking forward to all over the weekend with Johnnie Parker; the one which helped take his mind off the fucking pain. That one. So, he didn't want to be banged up in his cell because this pair of nob-heads had done him over or put him on a charge or both.

He was burning with the fervour of a Grand Inquisitor of the Spanish Inquisition; desperate to get his hands on the guilty ones and burn the bastards.

Jake was in the remand section of the prison. He'd arrived during association, so all of those prisoners who hadn't volunteered for work were milling around.

Barely had he put his few possessions on the made-up bunk when a six foot three brick shithouse, huge snake's head tattoo popping out of the top of his tee-shirt on the neck and curling all the way down his massively-muscled left arm to a sting on his wrist, came striding through the door.

''You, Vickers?' he asked menacingly, narrowing his small beady eyes.

'Oh, fuck, 'ere we go' thought Jake resignedly.

'Yeah. An' you are?' asked Jake with equal menace.

'Charlie Baker' said the geezer with a grin that revealed half his front teeth missing, probably from a disagreement with a sledgehammer or some such weapon of mass destruction. 'Very pleased to make your acquaintance'. He held out his massive calloused hand to Jake. 'Anyone who helps rid the world of vermin has got to be one of the good guys. Right?'

Jake took the hand, which was like a weapon of mass destruction itself, and more than matched the firmness of the grip as he stared hard into those beady eyes. Jake had to make sure Mr Baker knew who was going to be top dog, at least in this cell.

'Eh yeah, right' replied Jake not knowing at first what he was talking about until the penny finally dropped. 'Yeah, right!' he agreed more heartily the second time.

'So who's in charge around 'ere?' asked Jake once the formal introductions were over.

'Ray Shap. He's looking forward to meetin' you and shakin' the 'and that pulled the trigger. He sent me over to come and get you.'

'Okay but first; is there a geezer here called Johnnie Parker?'

'Hmm. Dunno the name. How long's he been 'ere?'

'Came in a few days ago. He's the driver of the truck we tried to stick up on Friday an' found it full of those nasty little SO19 pieces of shit'. Jake spat in the stainless-steel washbasin on the wall.

'No. No' replied Charlie hesitantly, screwing up is beady eyes in concentration. 'Can't place 'im. What's he look like?'

'Short little runt, mousey hair, going bald, about fifty.'

'That covers half the prison population of Britain. Give us another clue, for fuck's sake!' said Charlie laughing at his own joke.

'Look, don't worry. I'll find 'im' Jake said, wanting to follow it up with: 'An' kick the shit out of 'im'. But he didn't. He'd find out what was what before doing anything.

Charlie stepped out of the cell first with Jake following, to be greeted by a round of spontaneous applause. Word had gotten around.

Jake stood for a moment taking in his new surroundings. From where he stood he could see four landings with balconies laid out in the shape of a huge quadrangle with cells leading off them. Guys were standing leaning over the balconies clapping and cat-whistling.

The screws were furious. Fucking furious. But there was nothing they could do. Not against so many. So, they had to bear it in silence. But

Jake knew that they'd make him pay but, for now, the stage was his and he was loving it.

He stood for a few moments before bowing deeply like a conductor whose orchestra had just given the performance of a lifetime. It hurt like fuck but he didn't half enjoy it.

The applause died down and Jake followed Charlie along the balcony. Everybody he walked passed greeted him with 'Well done, son!' or 'Good on ye!' or 'Nice one!' The few pats on the back and shoulders he received reminded him of how bruised and raw his body felt. But he didn't show it, he just smiled.

Jake knew his hero status would be short-lived but decided there and then that he'd milk it for all he could...for as long as he could.

He followed Charlie as he led the way down the stairway to the next floor and walked along the balcony to one of the open doors: association hadn't ended yet.

Standing around inside were four guys, three of them of similar appearance to Charlie. Jake later found out that those three all shared a prison and brain cell between them. The fourth member of the group was a small, dumpy guy of about sixty with a close- cropped beard which matched the salt and pepper hair and not a tattoo in sight.

So, this was Ray Shap: former accountant, whose staff, so the story went, cooked the books, liberated seven mil from the clients' accounts and poor old Ray was made the patsy. Yeah, right. The eyes gave it away; as cunning as a wolf with extrasensory perception. 'Cept, according to the grapevine, it was the perception part which let him down when he was making his getaway.

The story goes that the police only got hold of him because he didn't plug in his sat-nav; he knew the way to Heathrow. 'Course he did. Unfortunately for him, the queue on the M4 stretched all the way back to the Kew roundabout. As a result, he missed his flight and the police got their man. Had the perception been working that day instead of taking the day off, he would've plug the sat-nav in and it would've taken him a different route. He'd now be sitting in one of Buenos Aires' wonderful outdoor bars, sipping an expensive Argentina Malbec, Her Majesty would be saving on his board and lodgings and the police would be whistling Dixie. Perception; maybe it's not all it's cracked up to be.

'Nice to meet you' he said cautiously in his North London accent, extending his hand to Jake.

'Spurs?' was Jake's one word reply.

'Is there any other team worth supporting?' asked 'The Shap' as he was known, laughing.

For all his years of slapping people around, Jake knew that there were times when schmoozing was called for; this was one of those.

The rest of them lined up to shake his hand but none of them could match Jake's firmness of grip. The message went out: 'you want to mess with me, don't come alone 'cause I'll 'ave you'.

'I take it you're innocent, Jake?' said The Shap 'You don't mind me calling you Jake?'

Jake nodded his head in answer to both questions.

'You, me and the rest of the prison population!' exploded The Shap in gusts of laughter. 'Apart, that is, from the Born Agains who want to repent their crimes against society. Fuckin' repent? There'll be plenty of time for that in the next life, I'm way too busy in this one!'

The sycophants joined in with the boss. If he'd shit his pants, they probably would have too. Having money on the outside speaks in many tongues and languages. Very clearly.

'Is there anything you need? Anything I can do for you?' asked the North London accountant.

Jake was torn; inside, favours come, not with strings attached, but fucking great ropes that would hold the QE2 in berth and could take a long time to work off.

'Thanks. Nice of you to offer but I'm okay for now.'

'Anytime. Just let me or one of the boys know.'

'Sure. Just one thing: do any of you know a guy called Johnnie Parker?'

'Little guy, non-descript type, came in a few days ago?' said one of the tattoos.

'That sounds like 'im' said Jake.

'Yeah, he's on the third landing. Keepin' 'imself to 'imself at the moment. Hardly comes out of 'is cell.'

'Big mistake, Johnnie' thought Jake. 'You've got to make friends quickly when you're inside, people to cover your back. Otherwise you're fucked. Literally.'

'Would you like to have a word?' asked The Shap, his perception was working today.

'Yeah' was the monosyllabic reply of someone clearly not wanting to give too much away.

'Just one thing, Jake. I hear that he was the driver of the lorry you and your guys allegedly tried to turn over. Yeah?'

Jake nodded.

'It's none of my business but as he's in here, I assume he was in on it'. The Shap held up his hands to stop Jake saying anything. 'Don't answer that, Jake. Again, none of my business' he continued '…but if you're thinking that he blew the whistle on you, you're almost definitely wrong. If he was a stool, he'd be in solitary, not walking around with the rest of us. They'd be keeping him well away. That's all I want to say. Maybe stop you doing something you might regret.'

Jake looked in amazement at the man who had just fitted the pieces together better than Jake and he knew what all the pieces were! A clever man indeed.

Jake smiled and said 'Thanks for that.'

'Anytime' offered The Shap, returning the smile. 'Pete' he called over his shoulder to one of the tattooed brothers 'would you like to invite Mr Parker to pop in for a cup of tea or perhaps a small sherry?' They all guffawed at the boss' humour.

'Better you should see him here, Jake. If the screws see you taking him to yours, they'll be through the door of your cell faster than a bargain hunter on the first day of the Harrods' sale.'

'I like your humour' said Jake still smiling from the last quip.

''E's like this all the time!' chipped in Charlie chortling away with the rest of them.

'It keeps me sane' was the reply and the look on his face looked like he meant it.

Pete left to go on his little errand while the others filled Jake in on the 'who's who' of the screws and the other prisoners.

About five minutes later, a waif-like figure appeared in the open doorway and a white-faced Johnnie Parker entered helped by a nudge from Pete into the cell. He was already a broken man.

As soon as he saw Jake, his eyes flew wide with terror and he turned to flee; as if a weed like him could get past the human concrete block that was Pete.

'It weren't me, Mr Vickers! Honest!' Jake let him witter on for another thirty seconds before putting him out of his misery with the words: 'I know', looking over to The Shap, who nodded deliberately.

'Wh...at?' mumbled Johnnie, still thinking this was a trap and looking around for a way to bolt.

Jake repeated it slowly. 'I know it wasn't you, Johnnie. But I want to know who it was an' you're gonna tell me'. He left out the 'and if you don't...' part; wasn't necessary.

Johnnie looked bewildered. ''Ow would I know? I've been sitting in that fuckin' cell since I got 'ere trying to work that one out an' I can't.'

'Well, you can start by tellin' me who you told.'

'I didn't tell no-one. Honest, Mr Vickers. Not even the wife!' He started to reel off names on his fingers. 'Not Freddie who I've worked with for three years now an' is like a son to me, not the missus...oh, I've said that, sorry. None of the other drivers. No-one an' that's the truth. D'you think I'd risk welchin' on you, Mr Vickers? I've seen what you do to people who're late paying you. No fuckin' way! Maybe it was one of your guys?'

It was the wrong thing to say at the wrong time and Johnnie realised it as Jake, his inner fury spilling out, went for him but The Shap had already anticipated it and nodded to Charlie who politely put a restraining arm around Jake's shoulder and said 'Not yet, mate.'

'Then who the fuck was it?' said Jake to no-one in particular, shrugging off Charlie's arm. This not knowing was driving him mad.

'Johnnie, did anything out of the ordinary happen before the raid? Anything that might seem a bit iffy now as you look back at it?' enquired The Shap as gently as a counsellor in a therapy session.

'No, sir, nothin' I can think of' responded Johnnie as he went over the events prior to Friday morning. A silence fell over the cell as brains churned.

'Think, Johnnie' probed The Shap again '...nothing at all?'

'Well, they did swop my usual lorry over on the Wednesday and said it was due a service an' I'm not sure that it was due. The new one was the lorry I was drivin' with all those police in it. Christ! I had no idea they were there. You got to believe me, Mr Vickers!'

Jake said nothing, he just glared at Johnnie.

'Good. Well done, Johnnie' said The Shap interrupting the silence which ensued: he preferred to cajole the truth out of someone rather than use the Jake Vickers School method of beating it together with the shit of them, usually at the same time. However, if the Mr Vickers method was the only way, then so be it; it's just the other way made less in the way of mess.

When Johnnie realised that he wasn't for a kicking, he visibly relaxed. With the result that the body sent messages to the brain which probably passed the message on to the brain cells which in turn began to perform better.

''Ere, just a minute!' remembered Johnnie. 'The boss definitely seemed to be on edge the last few days; not very chatty like. Hmm, usually he'd pass the time of day with you but not...no, in fact, not for the past couple of weeks. Very abrupt, he was. I just put it down to the long hours he works and the stress.'

'What boss doesn't get stressed, eh, Johnnie?' offered The Shap, still trying to draw out more information.

'No, this guy had it really bad, especially last year. Rumour had it that the company was going to go down the pan and then suddenly... wham! Money was spent on updating the fleet, mind you it was looking a bit ropey an' he got a new car. Brand new Merc! A real beauty, it was' Johnnie lapsed into silence as his brain rummaged through the memories.

Jake was just about to lose patience when The Shap surreptitiously shook his head; he knew what was going on and didn't want Jake to interrupt.

'Yeah,' began Johnnie almost in a trance '...there were rumours back then that he wasn't gonna be able to pay the wages that month and the next thing we knew, we got a pay rise. There was all sorts of stuff flyin' around about some mystery investor who'd stepped in at the last minute. But we never found out who or even if it was true. Anyway, who cared as long as yer wage packet had the right amount in it at the end of the week, eh?'

He lapsed into silence again, lost in the memories. This time it was The Shap who intervened.

'Well done, Johnnie. I'm sure that's helped Jake a lot. Hasn't it, Jake?'

'Er, yeah. Cheers' was the bewildered reply from Jake.

'Pop in again sometime, Johnnie. It was nice to make your acquaintance. Boys make sure Johnnie finds his way back to his cell. It's not a very classy hotel here. They don't put room numbers on the doors.'

Johnnie hadn't a clue what he was on about but the rest of them laughed, so he joined in; scared not to.

If it had been up to Jake, he would have slung him out the door with a boot up his arse: he still had a lot to learn.

As Pete and Johnnie left the cell, The Shap turned to Jake and said: 'There you go, Jake. You've got quite a bit to work on. The boss was obviously in on it. Check him out. And there's this faceless investor. That could mean something or nothing but it's worth looking at and they swopped the lorries around before the raid. Why bother changing them? Why would they do that? Hmm?'

'Shap, thanks again for your help. I..' it stuck in Jake's craw but he had to say it '...I owe you one.'

The Shap smiled and replied 'My pleasure.'

And that's how it works inside. Jake left to make a phone call. Not long after, the bell rang to signal the end of association.

Ninety Seven

While Jake was having a break from his normal job, so was someone else: Dave Cosforth.

He and the missus were loving the new life style. They'd met up with a couple of couples from 'oop North' who were a good laugh and didn't ask too many questions. But fun costs money and Dave's hand was never out of his pocket.

'Oh, go on, Dave' Doris would say on a daily basis '...we're havin' such a lovely time.'

'It's a good job I've got a supplement to my pension' Dave thought to himself. 'I'm definitely goin' 'ome next week an' divvin' up what we've got on The Bus. This is the life for us!' For the first time in years, Dave was truly relaxed and happy.

Towards the end of their first week, they were introduced, through their new-found friends, to a couple, Jimmy and Annie, who'd owned a chain of minimarts somewhere North of Watford. They'd worked all the hours God had sent, building up the business and sold it for a tidy sum: now they were retired and enjoying the fruits of their labour. Their amazing villa was just five minutes from where Dave and Doris were staying. Detached with three en suite bedrooms, obligatory swimming pool and uninterrupted views of the sea. It was a dream.

But that dream had, overnight, become a nightmare.

Their only daughter back in England had just been diagnosed with cancer and together with two kids and a messy divorce in the offing, needed them back home yesterday…if not the day before.

The trouble was the market was flooded with properties of expats trying to sell up and move back home.

Dave and Doris were listening to all of this as their little group sat around the pool in the dream house, sipping cocktails before they headed off into town for dinner.

'We're gonna have to take a serious hit to sell it' Jimmy said to the group as he mixed another Mai Tai for Annie, who had begun to hit the bottle, or as Dave thought of it 'use the booze', to blot everything out.

'The estate agent told me today that they're getting ten new properties on the market every week and they're lucky if they sell one. Apparently, the number of people retiring here from the UK has dropped dramatically so they're really struggling and prices are in freefall.'

'Funny, we're thinkin'...' began Doris who was on her second large Malibu of the night.

'...of stayin' a bit longer than we'd planned' interrupted Dave in a loud voice while digging his elbow into Doris.

'No, that's not what I was going to say, Dave...' continued the tipsy one.

'Wasn't it, darlin'?' said Dave leaning over as if to kiss her on the cheek and whispering: 'Shut the fuck up!'

Doris got the message and looked at Dave pretending to be shocked. 'Not in public! Please, Dave!'

And everybody laughed.

'It must be the Spanish air.'

'I think that' offered Annie as she took her third Mai Tai from her husband 'Ooh, ta love! Yes, I think that' she repeated. 'Since we've been here we've been at it like bunny rabbits...!'

'Yes, alright, Annie. I'm sure no-one's interested in our nocturnal habits' offered Jimmy through slightly gritted teeth.

'But it's during the day as well' continued his wife who still hadn't got the message.

Dave looked at his wife and then at Annie and thought: 'I've heard booze numbs the senses but I didn't realise it made them fuckin' deaf as well.'

'I think it's the paella' continued one of the 'oop North' wives. 'All that fish: it makes you sexy!'

'We're convinced it's the sangria' laughed the other 'oop Northerner's missus.

'Well, whatever it is, we're makin' up for all those friggin' long hours we spent behind the counter in the shop, eh Jimmy?'

'Sure, Annie, sure' replied her husband wanting to close this conversation about their intimate life.

'So what'll you get for it, Jimmy?' asked one of the 'oop North' husbands.

'Thank you' thought Dave gleefully.

'We paid five hundred and fifty thousand euros for it but I reckon if we put it on the market for four hundred and twenty-five we'll be lucky to get three seventy.'

'An' you've just got yourself a sale' thought Dave bristling with excitement. He looked at Doris and gave her a slight shrug and a smile; she was too pissed to get it.

'I'll tell her later' decided Dave.

''Ere!' the other 'oop Northerner' husband called out looking at the flash watch on his wrist, 'We'd better get a move on otherwise we'll lose the table.'

'An' judging by the size of your stomach, pal' thought Dave '...you'll probably eat it!'

Doris and Annie were the first to finish their drinks, downed in a oner. All the girls fumbled in their handbags for some lippie; a girl couldn't go out without refreshing her lips. What would people think?

The men just looked at each other, eyes rolled heavenwards in that 'what are they like?' gesture.

Ninety Eight

Gary stormed into the office, still fuming at having his time wasted: it had taken as long to get back as it took to get to the fucking place.

'You're back early' called Jeannie from the other side of the office, bent over looking at something on one of the paralegal's computer screens. 'Mr Vickers kick off again?'

'Bastards!' yelled Gary, ignoring Jeannie and slamming the door of his office.

The whole office stopped what they were doing and looked over at the door which, despite their boss' best efforts, had managed to stay on its hinges; it just wasn't like Gary to be like this.

Jeannie walked quickly over to the closed door of his office, knocked and walked in without waiting for an answer.

'What's happened?' asked Jeannie in that patient voice which mothers use to ask their children why they're crying.

'Nothing. Nothing happened. That's the bloody problem' declared Gary still absolutely livid.

'So, tell me' replied Jeannie standing patiently, arms crossed, waiting for Gary to calm down.

'They've moved him to Wandsworth and didn't even have the common decency to let me know. Bastards!'

Jeannie had never seen Gary react so over the top before. Yes, it was annoying, inconvenient, but not much else. But then she didn't know that he'd psyched himself up for the meeting with Jake and had been as uptight as a virgin just before their first shag.

'D'you want me to phone over to Wandsworth and set up a visit?' said Jeannie calmly.

Gary looked at her and deflated; the realisation that he'd just acted like a spoilt kid, hit him.

'Thanks Jeannie and sorry. I'm very sorry' he said regaining his composure. 'It's the pettiness of it. If you'd seen the smirk on that sergeant's face.'

'Well, it's done with now. But can I suggest you say something to the rest of the office? They think you've gone past throwing your toys out of your pram and are half expecting to see you to throw your desk out of the window.'

Gary saw the funny side of what Jeannie had just said and laughed. 'My Conran desk? No chance of that, Jeannie. Cost me a bloody fortune. But you're right. I really let it get to me, didn't I?'

Jeannie didn't answer but put her head on one side, raised an eyebrow and pursed her lips; that answered his question without a single word being spoken.

Gary walked over to the door and stood in front of it for a second, adjusting his tie. Clearing his throat, he opened the door and announced:

'Excuse me everybody. I'd just like to apologise for my outburst a moment ago! A particularly stressful morning! So, sorry about that.'

The silence only lasted for a moment before a couple of voices called out in support. 'Don't worry! Happens to us all sometimes' and 'No problem, boss.'

Gary smiled with relief at their support and the smile developed into laughter and the others join in.

'Right! Enough of this frivolity, you lot! It's not what I pay you exorbitant amounts of money for.'

'If only!' quipped one of the paralegals.

'I 'eard that!' came back Gary and the tension was gone.

But in the back of his mind, Gary knew he still had to face Jake Vickers and then the tension would return with a vengeance.

Jeannie came out of his office and announced:

'I've spoken to Wandsworth and it can't be tomorrow. Apparently, it's his free visit tomorrow and he's already booked it. So, I've arranged Wednesday at eleven o'clock. Is that okay?'

'Terrific, Jeannie. Thanks.'

He walked back into his office and closed the door quietly behind him leaning his back against the inside of it. There was only one thing on his mind as the knots in his stomach multiplied and a thin film of sweat turned to droplets which slowly trickled down his forehead. Who had

Jake arranged to see so quickly? He didn't have any family to speak of, no steady girlfriend; not many women would go out with someone in Jake's line of business unless they were truly fucked up themselves and anyway, who was so important that they got ahead of his lawyer in the queue? More importantly: why?

Ninety Nine

There were a thousand questions bouncing around in Freddie's skull all day long on the following Monday morning as he sat in the cab of the lorry with his new driver, Bob.

The police had questioned him for hours on Friday but in the end let him go; they could see that he hadn't a clue about the heist.

'Didn't Mr Parker let anything slip about his arrangement?'

'Did he never talk about his money problems?'

'Did he seem out of sorts or nervous in any way in the run up to Friday?'

Freddie wanted to say 'Yes, he was more miserable than usual' and 'No, I had no idea that he was up to his neck in debt to a loan shark' and loads of other smart answers to their stupid questions but was it going to help Johnnie? No.

Was it going to make his or Johnnie's life easier? Again, a big fat 'No', in trumps. So, Freddie kept schtum and said enough to keep the police happy without giving anything away.

But the truth was, no-one, not even Mr Dean had mentioned anything. Yes, he had wondered what was going on when they switched the lorries but it wasn't his job to ask questions; probably why he got the job in the first place and he was that close to getting the deposit for his first mortgage.

The routine was back to what it was before Johnnie went crazy and tried to pay off his debts to his loan shark by putting both their lives in danger. Bob was alright but not like Johnnie; he missed Johnnie like stinko, even with all his moaning.

When he got home from the cop shop that night, Freddie went over everything that had happened. His initial reaction was that he wanted to kick the shit out of Johnnie. How could he do that to him? Do it to the both of them? But the more he thought about it, the more he could understand the pressure Johnnie must have been under from Mr Vickers, as he'd heard him referred to many times on the estate. The word was that

Mr Vickers wasn't your average understanding bank manager when it came to the matter of your account being overdue.

Then Saturday morning arrived and he walked into his local newsagents to pick up his paper, fully expecting to see pictures of the lorry ablaze at the Cobham Services but instead, on the front page of his red top was a picture of the scariest man in the world staring out at him under the banner headline: 'GANGLAND MURDER!' it screamed, followed by another smaller, but equally scary, one: 'ARE OUR STREETS SAFE ANYMORE?'

Freddie was fascinated by the lurid history of this guy who made his flesh crawl or at least used to. Unknown to Freddie and the rest of the public, most of it had been made up by journalists looking to get their piece on the front page; but there was a flavour of truth in it.

He decided there and then to call the boss, Mr Dean, on Monday morning and find out what the hell was going on.

One Hundred

Gary had just returned to his desk after apologising to the office when his mobile rang.

It was Freddie.

'Oh, shit! What's happened now? Yes, Freddie?' said Gary. This was not turning out to be a good day and it had only started.

'Mornin' Mr Dean. Busy weekend, eh?' began Freddie laughing nervously and not sure how to begin asking the questions that had kept him awake for most of the weekend.

'What can I do for you, Freddie?' asked Gary abruptly. He was in no mood for social chitchat especially with the hired help.

'Er, sorry Mr Dean, I just was wondering what was happening. Any special instructions? Things like that.'

Gary took a deep breath and let it out: no point in taking it out on the kid.

'No, Freddie, not really. Just keep an eye on Bob, making sure he keeps away when any clients are due. As you said, busy weekend so we'll just keep things ticking over and get ourselves back on track. Yes?'

The simple answer would have been 'Sure, boss' but Freddie felt that he was entitled to some sort of explanation.

'Is that it, boss? I mean what's gonna happen to Johnnie?'

'As far as I'm concerned, Freddie...' Gary paused for a second before continuing in a tone dripping with vitriol '...I hope they throw the fuckin' key away and let the bastard rot for all eternity in some rat-infested hole! Are you beginning to get an idea of how I feel about Mr Parker, Freddie?'

Freddie gulped. 'Got the message, boss.'

'Good, Freddie. Now shall we get on with the business of the day?' responded Gary clearly dismissing him.

'Sure, boss. Sorry to have troubled you' replied the young man, bowed by the nastiness in Gary's tone. The questions in Freddie's head would have to stay bouncing around there for now: that is, if they were ever going to be answered at all.

One Hundred and One

It was going to happen sooner or later but now was as good a time as any. Jake had just hung up the phone making the arrangements for his free visit the following day when he turned around and there was nose-picking Dave.

'Well, fuck me, if it isn't one of me merry men! Thanks for the back-up, pal. That was some struggle you lot put up, eh. Laid down yer pop guns as soon as the nice policeman asked you to' Jake growled. 'Ya load o' tossers!' he spat.

If it wasn't for the fact that every bone in Jake's body was screaming out in pain, he would have given Dave the pasting of his life and been up on his first charge: which wasn't bad considering he'd been there for nearly two hours already.

The rest of the guys in the queue for the phone and the others in the vicinity looked on in silence. Prison was no different to any other enclosed community; gossip and in-fighting were part its staple diet.

'Look, boss, don't start here, alright? 'Ow was we to know that the rozzers would be there? I mean, fuck sake, you was the one who pumped us full of Charlie. We was all off our tits an' 'ardly knew what day of the week it was. An' now we're all stuck in the same stinking, sinking boat'. Dave looked like he was finished but then continued, 'An' another thing, I can tell you: that fuckin' finger of blame that's pointin' at us should be pointin' back at the person who's doin' the blamin.'

Round one to nose-picking Dave.

Jake stared at Dave and Dave was waiting, waiting to dodge the flying fist. He'd worked with Jake long enough, knew his methods and expected the same treatment that he'd watched Jake dish out to others for years. But to Dave's surprise, he just walked away in silence; part of Jake knew that what Dave had said was true. When he'd come up with the idea of passing the Charlie around, he thought it would give them an edge but for whatever reason, it didn't. End of. Move on.

Jake's concern for the moment was finding the snitch and dealing with him or her. Dave and the rest of them could wait, they weren't going anywhere for now. He could pick his time.

One Hundred and Two

Jake and Gary both slept like babies that night; Gary was the one with colic.

Morning finally seeped through the expensive horizontal wooden shutters of the Dean residence at the same time as it crept through Jake's vertical metal ones; known to the rest of the population as bars.

Both broke their fast. Gary with organic free range eggs and bacon; Jake didn't think his eggs were free range.

Both had meetings that day. Gary's were going to be a pain in the derriere; Jake would be the one having the interesting one.

Both had diametrically opposed goals: Jake to find out who had set him up; Gary to avoid that happening.

It was going to be an interesting day.

During his restless night, Gary had worked out a simple plan to find out who Jake's visitor was.

So, when he arrived at the office, he called the prison and was put through to the central office.

'Hello, sorry to bother you, it's Gary Dean here, Jake Vickers' solicitor. My secretary's booked me in for a visit but she hasn't put it in the diary and I can't remember if it's today or tomorrow.'

Gary held his breath. 'Shut up now' he said to himself. 'Keep it simple.'

The prison officer looked up the register of visitors for that day.

'What did you say your name was?'

'Dean. Gary Dean.'

'No, it's not today. The name here is McTavish. James McTavish. Hold on...'

Gary could have hung up then once he'd gotten what he wanted but he played his part and waited.

'It's tomorrow you're booked in for 1100.'

'Thanks very much. Sorry to trouble you' and he hung up.

Gary made his next phone call to Pete Morris, the private detective. 'Who is this?' asked the voice at the other end of the phone. Pete Morris didn't presume anything. Just because a certain number came up, didn't always mean it was who you thought it was. As was the case when one of his male clients got hold of his missus' mobile and found the number of her lover. He rang it from her phone and was greeted with 'Hello gorgeous! 'Ave you told small dick that you're leavin' 'im yet?' The client dealt with it in his own way; suffice to say that lover boy was 'cut down to size'

'Hello, Pete. It's Gary Dean here. How are you?'

'Fine, Sir and how are you, yourself?'

'Good. Thank you, Pete. Good. Are you busy these days?'

'Never too busy for you Mr Dean. What is it you need done and when?'

'Slightly unusual one, Pete. I need you to follow a guy called...' he looked down at the name he'd scribbled on his pad '...James McTavish. Unusual because you'll find him visiting someone on remand at Wandsworth today and we need you to see where he goes, who he sees etc.'

Gary tried to sound casual; as if it was part of a job for a client.

'Today, Mr Dean?' Pete hadn't had a job for three days and he was going stir crazy but no need to let the client know that.

'Eh, yeah, Pete. Look, I'll tell the client that it's a rush job he'll have to pay double. He'll stand it. Would that be okay?'

'That's very decent of you, Mr Dean. Let me see now...' Pete shuffled a few papers around his desk for effect and then said '...that should be fine, Mr Dean. I'll re-arrange my schedule for the next couple of days. Fortunately, Mr McTavish is known to me. He's known as 'Jock' for obvious reasons. An extremely mean, pardon my French, Mr Dean, tight-arsed, nasty loan shark who works the South London estates. A bit like that Mr Vickers. Not someone you'd want to introduce to your mother.'

'Or your sister to marry?' enquired Gary, half laughing, trying to keep it light but suddenly his free-range eggs and bacon wanted to make a quick exit.

'Exactly, Sir, exactly; you got the drift. Listen, I'm sure you're very busy keeping the assets of innocent clients in divorce cases out of the clutches of their grasping other halves so I won't keep you but I'll be in touch.'

'Thanks, Pete. I knew I could rely on you.'

'Bye for now, Mr Dean.'

Gary made a dive for the loo.

As he sat there he thought about Jock McTavish. Another loan shark? Maybe he, Gary, was overacting. Maybe Jake just wanted his interests looked after while he was on remand.

'Remand? Huh! He'll be lucky if he gets life.'

'Or maybe...just maybe...' Gary knew that it could, and would, do his head in speculating about this visit. So, he decided to put it one side, like he did with any other case, and deal with it when he had the evidence in front of him: then he'd know which way to play it.

The knots vanished.

One Hundred and Three

Glaswegian ex-wrestler, Jock McTavish, six foot two in his socks, with his long grey-haired ponytail and D'Artagnan beard, had a penchant for dark suits and immaculate black Armani tee shirts which showed off his bodybuilder's physique to perfection. He had a reputation for using moves he'd learned in the ring on his customers to keep them in line. As his car pulled up near the gates, one of his boys rushed to open the door for him. Jock told them to wait; this wouldn't take long.

Before he got out of the car, he handed a few items over to his driver that might not get through the security scanner, the tools of his trade: knuckleduster, blade but no gun; the boys carried them. He couldn't be caught with one of them in his possession, not with his record.

He walked along silently mingling with the other visitors, trying not to draw attention to himself; he was not totally unknown at this establishment. As he went through security, he clocked at least two screws clocking him.

'Fuck 'em!' he thought. He was visiting this time, nothing else.

Jock could see that Jake was unsteady on his feet as he walked towards him and his face looked a fucking mess.

'Jakey, boy, what've you been up to?' asked the gravely-voiced Scot 'You been overchargin' again?' This was the in-joke amongst the local loan sharks.

'Don't make me laugh you ugly Scotch dick. It 'urts!'

'Sorry, son. Only tryin' to take your mind off this place for a wee while'. Jock looked around him. 'Still stinks, I see' he said, sniffing the fetid air of the place.

'Don't change, does it?' said Jake reflectively.

'Now then, son, I owe you one for the last time I was in here. You played your part and collected my dues and wouldn't take a penny for it which was very decent of you. So, what can I do for you in return?' A very straight to the point sort of guy, Mr McTavish; ask any of his customers.

'Thanks, Jock. Couple things. One is would you collect for me?'

Jock nodded. 'Consider it done.'

'Cheers. I'll get one of my guys to meet up with you and give you the lowdown.'

Again, the Scotsman nodded.

'And the other?'

'I've been stitched up, Jock. Some bastard's snitched on me an' the pigs were waitin' for me an' the boys when we made a move on the lorry. I want that bastard so bad I'd give me left bollock to 'ave five minutes in a room with 'im' he blurted out.

'Maybe you won't have to part with your precious dangly bits, son' said the Scotsman leaning closer to Jake and lowering his voice 'What exactly do you want me to do?'

'I 'aven't got much to go on but the boss of the firm must 'ave been in on it. Maybe you could find out what he knows'. The two men's eyes locked: 'find out' as in 'beat it out of him if necessary' was what passed between them.

'Understand. Anything else?'

'Yeah, but as we're talking I've just thought of another way to get to it' Jake wavered for a minute. 'Look, leave that bit with me for now, Jock. There's someone here who's better at that sort of thing than you an' me.'

He would ask The Shap.

'Don't worry, Jake. We'll find the bastard and string 'em up by their scrawny testicles.'

'Now that I would like to see!'

'I'll see what can be arranged'. The Scotsman was determined to make Jake laugh. He'd heard somewhere that it releases endorphins, which are supposed to be natural painkillers. From the state of Jake, he badly needed a whole lot of them released into his battered body and quickly. He pressed on: 'Hey, last time I was in here, they let some guy out to see a retrospective at the Serpentine. Maybe they'll let you out to view: 'Snitch dangling by his bollocks'.

'I told you not to make me laugh, you great caber-tossin' twat' said Jake holding on to his ribs to stop them hurting. 'You're doin' it deliberately, ain't you? You're enjoyin' watchin' me suffer!'

'As you get older, Jake' responded the Scotsman grinning, 'you'll find that it's the small pleasures that make life worth living.'

'Seriously, Jock, thanks for comin' an' if I can arrange anything for you out there…' he said jerking his thumb towards a world that he would not be seeing for many years '…while I'm in 'ere, just let me know.'

'As ever, the gentleman' replied the Scotsman bowing graciously from his side of the table. 'Take care of yourself in here, Jake, and I'll be back with any news as soon as.'

The visit ended and Jake returned to his cell, knowing that Jock would do his best to find the snitch.

As he'd been talking to Jock, he realised that The Shap's previous profession would lend itself perfectly to the other part of the search.

It would cost him but it would be worth it.

One Hundred and Four

Pete Morris was a meticulous keeper of records. Jock McTavish's arrival at Wandsworth was duly noted in the small notebook he'd picked up from the office before setting out. He kept a supply of them, using a fresh one for each job just in case the police or 'the other side' in a case he was involved in ever required it for forensic tests.

Wouldn't do if there were details of other delicate jobs in there, would it?

He hunkered down; this part of the job, the surveillance, was like an old comfortable cardigan to him. Most other people found this part of the job difficult; the sitting, waiting...and very often, waiting...and waiting. But for Pete, it was fine. He'd perfected a system where his brain could play all sorts of mental games while his eyes were constantly on the alert, scanning for movement, looking for something, anything, out of the ordinary. It had saved his bacon on more than a few occasions; adulterers, particularly the men, were not generally happy if they found out that they'd been sussed, according to Pete's colleagues. Pete wouldn't know; he'd never been rumbled.

''Ello, my old son' declared Pete as the distinctive figure of Jock McTavish emerged from the door of the prison. 'That didn't take long'. Pete reached for his camera sitting on the passenger seat and took half a dozen shots of the loan shark. 'So, where are we off to now, Mr McT, eh?' thought Pete sticking to his rule of referring to the people he shadowed by their formal title of 'Mister', 'Mrs' or whatever; wouldn't do to get on intimate terms with the mark.

Jock's preferred mode of transport was, unsurprisingly, a Range Rover Sport, silver in colour with wrap-around tinted windows. 'Must go with the territory' thought Pete impassively. 'Range Rover salesmen must rub their hands with glee when they see the McTavishs or Vickers of this world walk through their door. The sale's already made before they push the door open. The only question is: 'What colour and how many extras?'

Like all the gangsters he had ever come across, and Mr McTavish's driver was no exception, they all drive like bats out of Hell. Pete struggled to keep up with him as he wove in and out of traffic like a Formula One driver chasing the title.

'Take it easy, children' complained Pete as his eyes never left the other car. 'We all want to get there in one piece!'

Without any warning, the car mounted the pavement, stopped and the hazard lights began to flash.

'Damn!' swore Pete as he realised he couldn't stop without drawing attention to himself, a thing he would never do. Pete loved being invisible; it was a matter of pride that whenever he was called into court on a case he'd worked on, none of the people he'd followed ever recognised him. He could see it in their eyes as he entered the witness box, that 'Who the hell is he?' look.

He drove passed the Range Rover without as much as a glance at it. A hundred yards up the road he found a parking meter and pulled in. As luck would have it, there was another car parked behind him which gave him cover.

He picked up the camera and waited. Nothing happened. The car just sat there. Why pull up there just to talk? There were plenty of places they could have stopped which were legal.

'Maybe they're casing a joint' thought Pete. He began snapping pictures of the surrounding area.

A few minutes later, the Range Rover's hazards stopped flashing and it suddenly made a U-turn with a screech of tyres that would have done a Formula One driver proud.

'Or maybe he's related to one' thought Pete as he attempted his own version of it albeit without the fanfare of rubber tyres.

Mr McTavish spent the rest of that day working on his version of good customer service: leaving the punter with enough life in them to be able to go to work in order to make their next payment.

Pete also noted that Mr McTavish had either a limited vocabulary or that perhaps he had made up his very own catchphrase: 'Where's ma money?' in his very broad Glaswegian growl. Occasionally he would embellish it: 'Where ma fuckin' money?' Pete assumed he did this to relieve the boredom.

By seven o'clock that evening, Pete had had enough. Mr McTavish had settled down to an evening of relaxation in his local boozer. Mr McT had caught up earlier with the punters who thought they'd succeeded in dodging him that day; only to find him lying in wait for them as they arrived home for their tea. They'd gone off it by the time Mr McTavish had had a word.

Pete called Gary.

'Evening, Mr Dean. Caught up with our friend this morning and been with him ever since. Not a lot happened apart from one unexpected stop. Would you like me to send over what I've got?'

'If you could do that I'd be grateful, Pete' replied Gary who was sitting in his study preparing again for his meeting with Jake the following day.

'Give me ten minutes and they'll be with you.'

''Preciate it, Pete. Thanks.'

Gary sat in front of his computer waiting.

'Come on, come on!' Gary thought feverishly as he stared at the screen.

Ping!

Gary's fingers flew to the keyboard, opening the email and then the file attached: he pressed for the slideshow.

The first few pictures were of a stockily-built individual with a hardness in the eyes whom Gary assumed to be James McTavish.

The next picture took his breath away: a photo of the front gates to the James Irvine yard.

'Fuck! Fuck! Fuck!' uttered Gary under his breath as his heart rate rocketed.

The preparation for the meeting with Jake went by the wayside.

A new question started spinning around in his brain: 'What does this new development mean?'

It took Gary a full minute to recover.

'Right, Gary. Pull yourself together and detach yourself from the situation'. He waited as his brain shifted into a clinical, impartial mode of approach to the question.

'What can it mean?' he began.

He wrote down ideas as they surfaced in his brain.

'One, Jake's pride has been hurt and he wants McTavish to try again. Hmm'. Gary thought about this for a couple of minutes, tossing it this way and that before discarding it. What was in it for Jake apart from succeeding the second time? What would it prove? That a James Irvine lorry could be hijacked? No, it wasn't worth the trouble. And anyway, James Irvine himself had taken charge personally of a complete review of their security. By the time he was finished, a fucking flea couldn't stow away on one of their lorries without setting off alarms.

For the money? Jake wouldn't be splashing the cash for a long time to come. No, not the money.

'Next' he said out loud running his pen through that idea. The minutes passed. He leaned back in his chair with his elbows resting on the arms, twirling his thumbs.

'What's your game, Jake? Hmm. What're you up to? What are you looking for?'

That was the question he needed to ask. Once asked, it became obvious to the lawyer in Gary. 'Oh, shit! It's the snitch! He's looking for the snitch. The guy is completely obsessed. He won't rest until he finds out who did him over. And now he's goin' right back to the beginning where it all started: James Fucking Irvine. Fuck!' he swore again.

'So, what exactly are you hoping to find there, Jake?' Gary asked as if he were questioning a witness in court. There was only one answer: information. Information. Right.

So, who could tell Jake what he wants to know?

'Hmm, there's Freddie.'

Gary considered his young gatekeeper for a moment. 'I don't think he'll even appear on Jake's radar. He's only a kid and probably seen as being too far down the pecking order. I think he'll be looking further up the chain. Johnnie Parker? Hopefully, Jake's beaten the shit out of him to find that he doesn't know anything. Hope he gave him an extra boot in the nuts for me. The bastard! No, he won't find out anything from him. Who does that leave, apart from me...?'

That was when his second Damascus moment of the week arrived and hit him right between the eyeballs.

'James. James Irvine. It must be him that Jake's after. He's the boss. As far as Jake's concerned, he must be involved. He owns the bloody company, so SO19 would have dealt with him. And so...' Gary paused, allowing his brain to process that information, '...so, he thinks that James knows something and...he's set the McTavish guy on to him. Gotcha, ya bastard!'

Gary was feeling pretty pleased with himself at having worked out what Jake's intentions were until he remembered the kind of man that James Irvine was.

'McTavish would only have to say 'hello' to James and he'd spill his guts. Bollocks! Okay. So, what will I have to do to stop that happening?'

Again, Gary allowed various options to float through his formidable brain.

'If I tell James, he'll go to pieces and shit his pants...and not necessarily in that order. Not such a good idea. Alternatives? Leave him to the tender mercies of Mr McTavish? Oh, I don't think so.'

As he was ploughing through the options available, his mind took him back to when he first told James about the hijack.

'What about if the anonymous snitch was to make another phone call to Crimestoppers and tell them that something very nasty was about to happen to James?' Gary mulled that possibility over. 'Yeah, that might do it' he thought, warming to the idea.

'A threat has been made by criminal associates of the hijackers and James' life was in imminent danger. Better not use the word 'imminent' though; too intellectual for a snitch. That should get him police protection until the trial and keeps the McTavishs of this world away from him. But what happens after that, hmm? I'll have to deal with that when we come to it. But it should scare off the opposition for now.'

Satisfied that he'd found the best solution, Gary picked up the phone.

One Hundred and Five

The following morning, like ships passing in the night, the unmarked police car, blue lights blazing, whizzed passed a silver Range Rover Sport which had pulled in for them to pass. The fact that both cars were travelling in the same direction didn't register with the occupants of the Range Rover until the police car, by this time a hundred yards ahead of them, turned into the entrance to the James Irvine yard.

'What the fuck...?' stammered the passenger in the front seat in a strong Scottish accent. 'Keep goin'! Don't stop!' he commanded.

The car drove on and pulled onto the same meter that Pete Morris had observed them from the previous day.

'Of all the bastard luck. What'd they want?'

Jock McTavish sat there watching the gates in the passenger vanity mirror, waiting to see if there was any movement.

'They could be in there for hours yet. Let's go! We'll come back later for our wee chat with Mr Irvine.'

Without indicating, the driver pulled out to a cacophony of blaring car horns. It didn't even register with the occupants of the car; it was normal for them.

What they didn't know was that they'd missed their chance: twenty minutes earlier and it would have been a different story.

One Hundred and Six

The Inspector who had called James Irvine hadn't told him the real reason for his visit. He'd simply said they were making 'further inquiries'.

Gary was right though, when he was told, James collapsed into a chair.

'Oh, my God! What am I going to do?' groaned the crumpled bundle of nerves on the chair; all his years of dealing with the long distance lorry drivers of his fleet and the like and to date James Irvine still hadn't developed a backbone.

'There no need for you to worry, Sir. You'll have 24 hour police protection'. He didn't add 'until the trial is over'; there was no need to mention that at this stage. 'Just go about your daily routine and we'll do our best not to get in the way.'

Needless to say, Gary was stuck in his daily traffic jam when he received the frantic call he was waiting on from James.

'I wonder what this could be about?' thought Gary contemptuously when James' name appeared on the caller display screen of his mobile.

'Hallo? Is that you, James?'

'Yes, it bloody is, Gary! I've got the police here. They've had a tip off that friends of the hijackers have made threats against me. Me! What have I bloody done?' he complained.

'You've done nothing, James. But my professional advice to you would be to do as the police say and I'm sure you'll be alright. Remember, I deal with these sorts of people all the time; they can get quite nasty'. This was the tricky bit. Gary hesitated a moment and then continued: 'Listen, I could have a word with the ringleader of the gang if you like. He's my client.'

'He's what?' asked James in disbelief.

'He's been a client of mine for years, James. It puts me in a very awkward situation but I can't refuse to represent him, can I?'

James considered the offer to have a word but the complexity of the situation just sent his brain into a spin. 'No, don't bother, Gary, but thanks anyway. I'll just have to let the police deal with it.'

Gary had absolutely no intention of having a word with Jake; it would connect Gary to the company but there was no harm in letting James think that he would talk to Jake about it. Anyway, he'd soon find out that Gary was representing Jake Vickers; it would be splashed all over the papers.

'Just take it easy, James, and we'll get through this. Okay?'

A very resigned 'Okay' came back down the phone and the connection was broken.

'You could have said 'Thanks' for getting you the police protection' Gary said out loud as he took the phone from his ear and stared at it.

But then he remembered he'd done his good deed anonymously. So how could James thank him?

One Hundred and Seven

By the time Gary reached the office, despite the sunshine, his mood was descending into a deep, black hole; he was having his client meeting with Jake today.

His mood would've been much, much worse if he'd known that Jake had spoken to The Shap the previous evening and wheels had been set in motion which Gary definitely, definitely would not like.

Gary went through the motions of his daily routine but his mind was somewhere else and everyone he spoke to noticed it. Twice in the same meeting, a question was met with a blank stare. That just wasn't Gary: he was there before you finished your sentence but not today.

And to make matters worse, if he was asked once he was asked twenty times: 'Are you alright, Gary?'

He wanted to say 'Fuck off! Of course, I'm not all-pissing-right! Would you be with Jake Vickers sniffing around your ever so slightly dodgy business interests?' But he passed it off with a 'Sorry, I didn't sleep very well last night.'

Four trips to fag alley, as the non-smokers in the office referred to the place where their nicotine-addicted colleagues could have a drag without being scowled at, didn't really help. The time to leave for Wandsworth had arrived.

'Jeannie, call me if you need me, won't you?' he said as he packed his briefcase.

Jeannie noted a reluctance in his voice but let it pass. She knew something was going on but knew better than to ask.

''Course. Good luck.'

The traffic to Wandsworth Prison was bad but Gary didn't notice; he was on automatic pilot as his brain rummaged through, once more, what and how much he would tell Jake.

'Keep it simple; bare facts and let him figure things out for himself. The bastard would do that anyway' he concluded.

He went through security in a bit of a daze but as soon as he was shown into the room where he would be spending the next couple of hours with Jake, his resolve stiffened.

'It'll take more than you, Jakey boy' he thought.

As he sat there waiting for Jake to be escorted to the overheated, cramp, smelly interview room with the yellowed walls, he allowed his mind to drift for a minute and came up with a mad idea which tickled his fancy.

'If a visit to a place like this was put on the school curriculum and kids were told: 'This will be where you'll live if you get convicted of a crime and this is the shit you'll eat during that time', I'm sure it would reduce future membership of the criminal fraternity substantially in this country.'

He thought it through a little more and concluded: 'On second thoughts, I could lose a lot of business...so maybe I won't suggest it to the Home Secretary next time we're chatting over tea and crumpets.'

Gary was still grinning inanely at his nonsensical idea when Jake walked in.

'What's so funny?' asked Jake.

'I'll tell you sometime' replied Gary back to his old self; combative and in control. 'Here..' said Gary opening his briefcase and sliding a couple of packs of cigarettes across the table to Jake '...got these for you.'

In prison, packets of fags were like bundles of fifty pound notes; they always came in very handy.

'Thanks' said Jake who wasn't a smoker himself but knew the power they gave someone on the inside. 'So what've you got for me?'

Gary knew exactly what Jake meant but decided to stick to business first.

'Well, everything hinges on that minute between you chucking the young guy' he consulted his notes '...Freddie Johnson, out of the lorry and the dead policeman's sudden appearance at the driver's window.'

'Gary, I'm payin' a lot for your services an' we've got months to work on that one. What I meant was what 'ave you found out about that company?'

Gary opened his mouth to speak but Jake jumped in.

'...an' I mean the haulage company, James O'fuckin' Irvine.' The made-to-measure collar of Gary's expensive silk shirt suddenly felt as if it had been made for a man two sizes smaller but Gary managed not to run his finger around the rim of it.

'Ah, right! Gotcha. Well...' began Gary pulling more papers out of his briefcase '...I've looked at the latest company accounts registered at Companies' House and they seem in order: nothing out of the ordinary there. Do you want me to run through them with you? The profit and loss, I mean?'

Jake just sat; arms folded, and stared hard across the table at Gary.

'Are you thick or something, Gary?' he said finally.

'No, I don't think so, Jake' was Gary's measured reply. He was treading warily but at the same time, the more the pressure was piled on him, the calmer Gary became. Right now, his pulse which not thirty seconds ago was somewhere around the level of someone just about to do their first bungee jump was now back down to that of a sixteen-year-old virgin's: perfect.

'Then let me explain it in words of one syllable' said Jake leaning forward and propping his elbows on the table. 'I'm lookin' to find out who shopped me to the police. An' the profit and loss accounts ain't gonna help me, are they, Gary?' he finished, looking straight and hard into Gary eyes.

Even though he felt that Jake could see past his eyes into the thoughts swirling around in his brain, Gary's pulse didn't rise by a single beat. Once the pressure was on, he was your original Mr Cool.

Gary cleared his throat. 'I see where you're coming from, Jake. I'm... I'm not sure that I'm the right guy for that job. In fact, I'm not even sure how to go about it...but I'm happy to try for you. Any suggestions?'

If it wasn't for the fact that Gary had a hundred per cent success rate at representing Jake in the past, he'd have told him to 'sling 'is hook'. As it was, he had the other avenues to explore with Jock McTavish and The Shap; he decided to drop it with Gary for the present.

'Let me have a think about it an' I'll come back to you, Gary. So,' he continued, leaning back tentatively in his chair again 'let's talk about the oik I slung out of the cabin before I accidentally blew that nice policeman's brains all over the M25.'

Many of Gary's clients spoke in this detached, humorous way about their victims. It didn't upset Gary; as far as he was concerned, there was no need for them to have ended up that way in the first place. For instance, if they'd paid their loan on time, they wouldn't have ended up in hospital. If the cop had stayed in the service station where he should have stayed because his bullet proof vest wasn't functioning properly, he'd be out now looking for more clients for Gary instead of adding to the profits of some coffin maker. Stupid fucker.

'Precisely' replied the man with the toothpaste manufacturer's smile.

There were no other uncomfortable moments in the interview. From then on in, it was all business. Business being defined as: what could be thrown in the legal arguments pot to muddy its waters for the jury?

By the end of it, with travelling time, Gary clocked up just over three hours which Jake would be billed for.

Three grand…and the day had barely started.

One Hundred and Eight

That night during association, Jake spoke with The Shap.
'It'll cost you, son.'
'It'll be worth it.'
'I'll have a word with a guy I know who reads balance sheets like most of us read the sports section. A word of advice though, Jake; don't let this snitch thing get to you. It'll do your head in, especially when you're in here. By the way, I was thinking about it; how do you fancy the nickname Snitchfinder General?'

''Ow d'you come up with them, Shap?' said Jake holding his ribs again; it seemed that everyone was determined to make him laugh. 'I like it!' he added.

'Then, so be it. Among our little group that'll be your sobriquet.'
'My what?'
'Sorry, Jake; nickname' replied The Shap. 'Leave this with me. I'll make the call and he should be able to report back to me in a couple of days.'
'Thanks, Shap.'

Jake knew it was going to cost him twice; once for the guy who did the work and again for The Shap. Favours owed were beginning to build up.

If this guy failed, Jake knew he was running out of ways to flush out his nemesis.

After his conversation with The Shap, Jake stood watching a couple of guys playing table tennis; he used to play it regularly as a teenager at a local club. Watching the guys, he decided that when his body healed he would have a go at it; he was going to have plenty of time to practise if things went wrong at his trial. His daydream was interrupted when he was called to the phone.

It was Jock.

He didn't mess about.

'Sorry, Jake. That wee job you asked me to do is now under 24-hour pro'. Jake knew he meant 24-hour protection.

'When did that happen?' he asked suspiciously.

'They literally got to the gates ahead of us. So, that's gonna be a 'no go' for the present.'

'Appreciate you tryin', Jock. We'll speak soon' and they both hung up.

Jake went back to his cell, his paranoia growing by the minute.

'How the fuck did they know I'd sent Jock to sort that geezer out?'

He lay down on his bed and thought it through.

'The bastards must be bugging me' he thought, panic rising up in him. He stood up and stripped, half convinced that it must be in his clothing. He was sitting there, stark naked, checking the seams of his prison issue outfit when Charlie walked in.

'Jake, put some clothes on, would you? I wanna have pleasant dreams tonight, not fuckin' nightmares' he laughed.

'It ain't funny, Charlie. Somehow the police knew I was settin' someone on to the owner of that fuckin' transport company. Five minutes before they got there, the police turn up an' it looks like he's got 24-hour protection. So, how the fuck did they know? I wouldn't put it passed the bastards to sew a bug into my clothes. Hey, maybe they got this place bugged as well' he said looking around the room.

'Jake, chill' replied Charlie, when he heard the alarm in Jake's voice '...nobody's been in here. You'd 'smell' 'em if they 'ad been. So, you're okay here. 'Ave you found anything in your gear?' he asked pointing to the pile of clothes which Jake had discarded.

'No' he replied despondently. He was convinced they were bugging him; he just didn't know how.

Around three o'clock the next morning, Jake's eyes suddenly flew opened. As if from nowhere, a thought so powerful, forced him from deep sleep to wide-awake alertness.

'Did I say anything to The Shap or the boys about gettin' McTavish to visit James Irvine? Think, Jake, think.'

For the next twenty minutes Jake run through the conversations he'd had with The Shap and his cronies: had he mentioned it? His paranoia was beginning to see snitches everywhere. Could it have been The Shap ...or one of his guys?

Then he remembered that during association the previous night, when he was called to the telephone, he noticed a guy staring at him. He didn't take too much notice at the time but looking back at it: did it mean anything or, was he just one of those guys who're in awe of cop-killers? Was he just off his head on something or, was he watching Jake in the hope of seeing or hearing something which could help to get his own sentence reduced?

Jake didn't sleep the rest of the night; he spent the rest of it shuffling possibilities like a pack of playing cards.

As they sat eating breakfast, the bags under his eyes told The Shap that whatever Jake had been up to in bed, it hadn't been sleeping.

'So, what's happening, Jake?' The Shap asked casually.

Jake knew that he looked rough and tried to laugh it off.

'Missin' my foam memory mattress' he offered.

The Shap turned to his boys and said: 'Could you leave us for a minute, boys?'

Silently, the guys rose and moved to another table.

'It's this snitch thing, isn't it, Jake?' began The Shap.

Jake nodded.

'I'm telling you, son, if you don't stop it now, it'll eat away at you and you'll end up in the loony bin. Charlie tells me you were convinced that they'd bugged your clothes. Jake sometimes you have to accept that there are people out there cleverer than you...even cleverer than me...and that is hard to accept.'

That brought a smile to Jake's face.

'Surely not, Shap?'

'I know it's difficult to believe but if I'm as smart as I think I am, how come I'm not on a beach right now, surrounded by a bevy of beauties instead of being here with you load of shmucks?'

'Oh, I don't know...' began Jake.

'Seriously, Jake...you gotta let go sometimes. You think that maybe one of us ratted on you, don't you?' said The Shap softly.

Jake's head jerked up to find The Shap's eyes boring straight into his. Shocked again at the perceptiveness of the guy, Jake nodded.

'It's natural and good sometimes to be like that, Jake. But, believe me, you're wrong this time. I know these guys. None of them have spoken out of turn. Trust me.'

Jake looked at him. He considered himself a good judge of character; it was then that he realised that the snitch thing had gotten to him so badly that he wasn't thinking clearly.

'So how...' he started to ask but was interrupted by The Shap.

'You're doing it again, Jake. You're trying to work out the unworkoutable. Wait! Have patience. As my old babushka, God rest her soul, used to say: "It'll all come out in the wash". But Jake,' the Shap reached across and grabbed Jake's arm '...you have to wait for the wash cycle to finish. You got it?'

Jake smiled. 'You're right, Shap. I'll try.'

One Hundred and Nine

Three days. It took three days for The Shap's guy on the outside to come back.

The news was good and bad. First, according to Shap's contact, Michael, there had been a substantial injection of cash into the business the previous year: the bad news was that it came from an account in Liechtenstein. But the good news was that this guy knew someone who could penetrate their system: the bad news was it was gonna cost...a lot.

Without any hesitation, Jake said 'Do it' He was the kind of guy that once he started something he saw it through to the end...whatever that end and cost might turn out to be.

'It's gonna take a bit longer for this one, Jake' The Shap informed him. 'Maybe this could be the end of the wash cycle, eh?'

'Yeah, maybe' was Jake's cautious reply.

The wait could probably have driven him mad but Jake decided two things there and then. One, he would push any thought of snitches out of his mind whenever they tried to muscle into his brain. And two, he'd concentrate on his defence with his lawyer; he'd been playing with it until now.

Suddenly, Jake was sleeping like a baby, albeit, a baby with a murder charge, not a musical mobile, hanging over him.

One Hundred and Ten

One week seamlessly moved into two and it was time for Dave Cosforth to return home to divvy up the pot they'd built up over the last half dozen jobs: one last visit to The Bus.

'I still can't believe it, Dave' said Doris, sitting at the breakfast bar in her dressing gown, nursing a strong black coffee and the hangover from hell.

'What's that, Doris?' asked Dave who was tucking into his full English. While Dave had been showering, Doris had cooked breakfast and pebble-dashing the sink at the same time; she was pretty sure that none of it found its way into the frying pan but she couldn't be absolutely certain.

'That they've accepted our offer and we're gonna live in that palace of theirs. Who would 'ave thought that little Doris Mack from the Peckham estate would end up living in Spain in the lap of luxury' she mused, smiling at the thought, but only for a second; the effort of keeping her lips in the upward position for any length of time caused her too much pain. Doris looked over the breakfast bar at Dave as drunken thoughts crashed into one another in her head.

''Ere, Dave, you don't think you've overstretched yourself, do you? I mean, we 'ave 'ad a lot to drink on this holiday It wasn't a bit of that bravado or libido stuff or whatever it's called, was it? Can we really afford it?'

The look from Dave said it all: Doris had overstepped the mark again. If she'd been sober, the thought wouldn't have got passed her lips.

'Er...I mean...'

'Leave it, Doris!' said Dave in that tone which Doris knew meant there would be no further discussion on that particular subject. 'What's these little flecks in my egg? It tastes funny.'

'Em...I think I might 'ave burnt them a bit, Dave. Sorry.'

'You know I like my eggs underdone' Dave stopped, looking over at Doris closely 'Don't tell me you're still 'ungover?'

Doris adjusted her dressing gown and attempted to flick her hair back. She shouldn't have done that; the room began to spin.

'For fuck's sake, Doris, watch 'ow much you're drinking, will you?'

Luckily for Doris, Dave was sitting on the other side of the breakfast bar, far enough away not to get a whiff of the stale booze and vomit which might have given the game away. She'd started having a 'hair of the dog' midmorning, every morning, topping up with a couple or three at lunchtime before she got down to the serious business of throwing it down her neck in the evening with her new best friend, Annie: an' a right couple of lushes they were.

'So, 'ow long will you be gone, Dave?'

Doris knew the answer, Dave had told her a hundred times, but it was her way diverting Dave's attention away from what he might perceive as a problem; Dave didn't like problems. He liked things to run and be run, smoothly. As far as Doris was concerned, she was just 'aving a good time', after all, she was on her holidays. Some people sink slowly into alcoholism; Doris was already a fully paid-up member.

'I've told you Doris, I'll only be gone for four maybe five days to sort of the finance and get the house on with an estate agent. But before it's let, you'll 'ave to go back and pack up what you want to bring over; the rest will 'ave to go into storage.'

'I 'ave to pinch myself three or four times a day, Dave. I can't believe this is 'appenin'…an' so sudden like. It's a dream! Thanks, babe.'

Doris moved to lean across the bar to kiss Dave but then remembered that he might smell things he didn't want to smell on her breath, so she did a quick body swerve to scoop up his plate and carry it over to the sink. Unfortunately, she got a whiff of what she'd left there before and her shoulders heaved.

Dave saw it and asked anxiously: 'You alright, Doris?'

'I think I've been sitting in the sun too long, Dave. Maybe I should stay out of it for a couple of days' she said with her back to him.

'Not like the old days, Doris. You used to sit in it for hours. Must be old age!' he joked.

Doris turned so quickly she almost passed out but she managed to hold onto the sink and steady herself.

'I'm goin' for my shower now, Dave Cosforth an' when I come back, I'll show you who's gettin' old.'

Dave sat there in silence, his mouth hanging open in surprise and anticipation as he watched Doris flounce away. When she reached the stairs, she stopped momentarily on the first step and turned slowly, looking back at him with those 'I'm going to fuck you senseless' eyes and Dave's erection practically ripped through his shorts. By the time she was out of sight, Dave's breath was ragged. Doris could still do it for him...and how.

When she was out of sight, Doris continued mounting the stairs, but much slower, holding onto the banister for support. She reached the bedroom and began looking for her handbag which contained the tablets Annie had given her a couple of days earlier. She couldn't remember what they were called; she just knew they worked quickly and that was all that mattered.

By the time she'd brushed her teeth, had her shower and given her mouth a serious 'Listerineing', Doris was ready.

Dave didn't know what hit him; he nearly missed his plane.

One Hundred and Eleven

Since that night at the Library, Sham had been thinking things over and decided it was time to lay low for a while. In fact, he'd decided to take off and spend a couple of months travelling through Spain but he had one thing to do before he left.

Gary was sitting at his desk reading a particularly boring deportation brief; the client didn't stand a chance, when the phone in his bottom drawer rang.

'Hello?' he answered cautiously, especially with what was going on with Jake.

'How are you doin', Sir?' came the affable and unmistakable voice of Gary's favourite hitman.

'Fine, my boy. How are you?'

'Ah, Jesus, sure I'm grand meself. Look, Gary I'm going to take off for a couple of months but before I go I'd like to transfer most of my deposit to the usual place'. Gary had set up a Lichtenstein account for Sham; it would be easier to draw on from there when he was on the Continent.

'Usual commission?' asked Gary who only charged Sham ten per cent instead of the usual twenty by way of thank you for saving Harry.

'Sure, no problem.'

'Then I'll call you back in a couple of minutes with the next Bus stop and you can pick it up and bring it into the office.'

'Great. I'll wait to hear from you.'

Gary really liked Sham, which was more than he could say for his other clients but then again he didn't have to like them...as far as he was concerned, they were there to provide him with his birthright: large quantities of money.

By late afternoon, Sham had delivered a substantial parcel to Gary at the office and then went home to tell the parents that they could have the house to themselves for the next couple of months.

'...on yer own?' asked his mother anxiously.

'Ah, sure, leave the boy alone, Mary' pleaded his father as he turned to Sham and enquire in a quiet, serious tone, 'Would ye be lookin' for some company, son?'

It was mother and son's turn to turn to him; Sham with alarm written all over his face, his mother with a puzzled expression, wondering what Anthony was up to.

Sham considered the prospect of travelling with his father, whom he loved dearly, but...

'Wh...at?' stammered Sham.

His father wore a pained expression on his face, caused by the realisation that his only son did not desire his company...before breaking into a big cheesy grin.

'Gotcha, ya little gobshite! Did ye think your old man might cramp yer style, did ye? Let me tell ye, ye ungrateful seed of my body, between the two of us we'd have them queuing round the block. Sure, isn't that right, Mary Boyle?'

Like all Irishmen, he liked a joke but for Sham it was a joke too far.

'Ah sure now, da, ye know that I'd love to...'

'An' now you'll have to go to confession before ye go and confess that most heinous of sins; tellin' great big fibs to yer own father.'

The three of them screamed with laughter.

All the time, Sham was thinking:

'If I ever stepped inside a church again, which I will not be doin', an' told a priest what I'd been up to, he'd have a feckin' fit. In fact, the shock would probably totally kill him...an' that would be another one to add to me grand total.'

His father grabbed him around the shoulders and gave him a squeeze.

'Ye go an' enjoy yerself, son. But promise me when ye come back, ye'll knuckle down to gettin' yer degree. Deal?'

'Deal!' declared Sham returning the hug 'Thanks for understanding, da.'

Mary looked on, still concerned that her little lamb was going out into the big bad world on his own. If she'd known the kind of guys he'd already taken down in his short life, she would have known that he could look after himself and then some.

Sham went straight to his room and began work on his computer; booking his flight and plotting out his potential itinerate.

He didn't know it, but the luck of the Irish was with him that day.

One Hundred and Twelve

Fortunately for Dave Cosforth, of the soon to be disbanded 'Hand-Grenade Gang', the police were so busy dealing with the aftermath of the John Pollock murder and subsequent turf war that a piddly little unsuccessful, albeit armed, raid on a small jewellers shop was way down their list of urgent cases. The headlines in the London newspapers were what dictated their priorities: Dave and the boys were in the clear.

As the taxi dropped him off outside the house where he'd lived with Doris these past thirty-odd years, Dave felt strangely disconnected. He stood outside the two up, two down, red brick terraced house, looking both ways along the street, taking in all the familiar, comforting sights of this quiet suburb street. It wasn't one of those streets where people moved to briefly on their way up the property ladder. No, some of them had been occupied by the same family for over sixty years, passing down from generation to generation; the way it should be, in Dave's estimation.

As his senses lingered on everything which had made this place home for so long, Dave smiled as his eyes were drawn to next door's windows where the same yellowing nets had hung, unchanged, for years. That smile broke into a grin when the eyes found the peeling front door of No.34, a few doors away from his own.

Happy memories fought for attention.

Mr and Mrs Dixon who lived there had been going to paint that door every year for the past twenty-five years. 'Don't suppose they will now' thought Dave going all nostalgic. 'If they didn't do it when they were in their seventies, they sure as hell 'aint gonna do it now they're shufflin' along in their nineties. So, is this it?' he thought suddenly '...all those years wiped out as if they'd never 'appened?'

For a split second, Dave wavered; should they forget the pie in the sky dream and just come home?

Then it was gone as quickly as it had arrived and he pushed the key in the lock.

As soon as he was unpacked, he called Gary.

No preamble, just: 'When's the next Bus due?'

'Call you back.'

While he waited on the call back on his mobile, he used the house phone to call the boys.

'Dave' said Mikey, the cab driver 'Good to hear from you. How was Spain?'

'The best' replied Dave 'Boys alright? Everything okay here?'

'Bron's shoulder's doing fine, the boys are okay an' it's as quiet as a whorehouse the day before payday' chuckled Mikey.

'We need to have a meet. Tomorrow night okay for you?'

'You got something lined up already?' demanded Mikey incredulously. 'You sly old bastard!'

'We'll see' replied Dave vaguely, not giving anything away. No need to tell the boys what's happening until they arrived.

His mobile rang. ''Ave to go. I'll let you know if anybody can't make it. Otherwise, see you at seven.'

He picked it up and looked at the dial: 'Private Number' it said. He knew it would be Gary.

'Eleven tomorrow, okay?'

'Nothing sooner?'

'Sorry, a bit busy today.'

'That'll be fine. An' by the way, I won't be requirin' it anymore. At least not for the foreseeable.'

'Understand'. Gary knew that Dave and the gang were lucky to get away with the last job; if someone in the crowd had had the bottle to have a go, they could've been in trouble. He hung up and made a mental note to find a replacement for the gang on The Bus. 'Christ! Sham, now Dave, it's like they're all deserting a sinking ship...or should that be Bus?'

He had barely replaced the receiver when the phone rang again.

'Can you tell me when the next Bus is due, please?' It was Mr Huq.

'Back to business' thought Gary.

'I'll call you back.'

One Hundred and Thirteen

The following morning, Dave set off to rendezvous with The Bus; the boys had all confirmed that they were up for the meet that night.

As he closed the door, Mr Dixon walked past. A tall thin man with a jaunty little trilby perched on his shrunken head, trousers six inches shorter than his legs; he still walked upright but now with the aid of a walking stick.

'Off again, Dave?'

Dave placed the two large empty moulded plastic suitcases on the ground to pass a couple of minutes with the old gentleman; they wouldn't be so light when he returned from The Bus.

'Not yet, John' replied Dave kindly; him and Doris had kept an eye on the elderly couple for years. 'I'm just off to collect some stuff for Doris. You know what women are like' said Dave lowering his voice and leaning closer into the old man as if imparting a secret he didn't want anyone else to hear.

'My missus is the same' replied John, keeping his voice down to match Dave's '...why they need all that stuff, I'll never know. But that's women for you, I suppose, Dave. A mystery I'll never solve in my lifetime that's for sure!' he finished, lifting his hat to scratch at a sudden itch in his thinning thatch.

'How is Sissy?' asked Dave, referring to John's wife.

'Not so good, Dave. 'As her good and bad days' responded John nodding sadly.

'You know we're moving to Spain, don't you, John?' said Dave wanting to move away from the subject of Sissy's health; it was too painful to talk about.

John took a step back and looked Dave in disbelief.

'No! What d'you want to go an' do that for, Dave?'

'Women, John, you know what they're like' responded Dave putting the blame on Doris.

'You're too soft with her, y'know that, Dave? You should stick to my old dad's motto: 'You've gotta be mean to keep 'em keen, son!' he said, meaning it.

Dave laughed.

'An' I suppose you've been like that with Sissy?' asked Dave.

John looked around furtively and replied: 'Too right, mate. Too right.'

'You're 'aving' a laugh, John, 'aint you? She's got you wrapped round that!' Dave said waving around his little finger.

'But 'aint she lovely my Sissy, eh Dave? How could you be hard with a gorgeous little bundle of fun like her?' confessed John.

'You're right, John. You know if I wasn't with my Doris...' began Dave.

'Yeah? Well you keep your eyes off my missus, you young whippersnapper! I dunno...you youngsters these days!' he declared vehemently, not quite getting Dave's joke.

The truth was Sissy hardly ever left the house these days; she was doubled over with osteoporosis and the dementia meant she couldn't be left on her own.

'Betty with her now?' asked Dave. Betty was their eldest.

'Yeah, she's round most days now, Dave. She's a good kid.' The kid was nearly seventy.

'Listen, John, I've got to go now but I'll come in for a cuppa before I go.'

'You're welcome anytime, Dave, you know that. An' Sissy'll be pleased to see you, so will Betty.'

Dave set off on his last trip to The Bus.

One Hundred and Fourteen

As they each walked through the door that evening, the boys could sense that something wasn't right.

Dave had laid out four packages with four drinks in front of them on the coffee table.

'Pick one, any one. They're all the same. This is it boys, I'm off to the sunshine. That was our last job together and I, for one, would like to say 'Cheers!' and wish you boys all the best for the future.'

There was a stunned silence around the coffee table. No-one reached for their drink.

'That's it, Dave?' asked Mikey finally, deflated. 'No more?'

The others felt the same; it felt like they were attending the wake of a close friend.

Course it was nice to finally get their hands on the dough but there was still a lot of mileage in the gang yet...that's what they were all feeling. The last job was just a hiccup; the fact that Bron was still recovering from Manny's shenanigans was seen as an unfortunate part of the job. Nothing else.

But Dave's mind was made up.

'Sorry boys, I can see from the look on yer faces that you'd like to carry on. Well, do so with my blessing...' he said as he raised his glass to his lips, took a swig of the nectar coloured liquid and closed his eyes to savour the smoky, peaty taste trickling down his throat '...but without me' he finished as he opened his eyes.

It was the coup de grace: they knew he meant it.

'But Dave, we'd be like a blind man without his stick. You're the one who finds the jobs, cases the joints. You're what makes us complete. You hold us together; keep us from each other's throats. You're the boss, Dave' Markie said passionately, expressing what everyone else was thinking.

'I understand, boys, but you've got to understand: I'm not gettin' any younger an' I do not want to end up spendin' what time I've got left at

Her Majesty's pleasure. No, I've thought about it and the time to get out is now. Finito.'

Mikey slowly picked up his glass and grudgingly said: 'To Dave.'

Bron and Markie picked up their glasses and drained them in one. 'To Dave.'

The silence which followed lay heavy in the air and so less than twenty minutes later, three sorry looking figures exited the terraced house, each with their parcel tucked under their arm, closing the gate softly behind them as they left. With a perfunctory 'See you' to Mikey, Bron and Markie turned left towards where Markie's company car was parked up. Mikey turned right walking toward his cab with his head down. If he'd had lead shoes on instead of the latest Nikes, he couldn't have walked any slower.

'One more job an' I could've joined Dave in sunny ol' Spain. One more lousy, stinkin' job! Now what am I gonna do?' His depression deepened as another thought surfaced. 'An' the thought of drivin' muppets around London for the next ten years...I just can't do it.'

He walked to the rear of the cab and pressing the remote, opened the boot and chucked the parcel in, in disgust, like it was a pair of smelly old wellies instead of what for some people would be a lifetime's earnings.

Three very unhappy bunnies left Dave's burrow that night. But Dave had made up his mind. So, end of story...or not quite...yet.

One Hundred and Fifteen

Gary was in the middle of transferring the large deposit made the previous day by the highly profitable Mr Huq ('Boy! Am I glad I decided to have that conversation with him!') from his offshore account on the Channel Islands to his Liechtenstein account when a rap on the door made him jump.

He'd locked the door for obvious reasons.

'Who is it?' he called out.

'Gary, I've got Chief Superintendent Moore on the phone, he wants a word' the voice of Jeannie came through the door.

'Take his number, Jeannie, and tell him I'll call him back in ten minutes.'

'Will do.'

Gary carried on with the electronic transfer to the account, checking the balance on the account as he did it.

'Hm...m...mm! Look at that!'

Including this deposit, the account had just gone over the seven million mark.

'Here's to double figures...' he thought gleefully, '...if I can sort out our Mr Vickers. Irritating bastard!'

Pushing thoughts of Jake aside, Gary buzzed through and got the number from Jeannie for the Chief Superintendent.

'Any idea what he wants, Jeannie?'

'You know what that lot are like, Gary. They don't give anything away!'

Fifteen minutes later, Gary emerged from his office with a file tucked under his arm looking as if he was trying to remember something.

'Everything alright, Gary?' asked Jeannie looking up from her computer.

'Er...yeah, Jeannie. There a part of this file missing and I'm not sure if I've left it at home.'

'Which one is it?'

'Regina V Rafsanjani'

'What are you missing?'

'The psychiatric report.'

'I'll have a copy here. Give me five minutes and it'll be on your desk. So, what did that policeman want?'

Gary hesitated then said:

'Oh, the usual; make an appointment for me to attend an interview with Jake Vickers.'

'But he could've done that through me' replied Jeannie, irritated that Gary had been disturbed.

Gary laughed and said '...something about speaking to the organ grinder' as he turned and walked back into his office.

Jeannie looked at the retreating back of her boss, there was something about the way Gary had brushed off her enquiry that puzzled Jeannie but she didn't have the time to dwell on it as she printed off the report and went back to her own personal mountain of work.

One Hundred and Sixteen

A lot can happen in twenty-four hours. A week, so the saying goes, is a long time in politics. It had been six weeks since Jake's failed hijack and for some, what occurred during those weeks would change their world forever.

But for others, life was hustling along.

Sham was a dot dancing on the horizon; Dave and Doris had moved in and were enjoying their fabulous new Spanish home; John Pollock's successor had taken firm control of his new empire and things, much to the relief of the local constabulary, were beginning to settle down. The fact that Mr Huq had had to invest in another box on The Bus meant that the black economy was in full swing and the cash was rolling in for him and Mr Dean. Jack Clancy was throwing himself into his work and had taken delivery of fifty more mouths to feed from Eastern Europe and in return, the girls were providing him with sustenance for his own lonely table. His grieving took place behind closed doors, in private, for his little princess: no-one who worked for him had any idea of the inner despair he truly felt. But, for sure, Mr Pollock's demise and the manner of it, gave him more than a little solace.

However, flies have an unerring ability of finding their way into ointment.

There were two flies in this case: Bron and Markie and they were drawing attention to themselves, splashing the cash.

When Dave was there to keep a wary eye on them, it was a few beers down the pub after work. Now with him gone and megabucks burning holes in their designer suit pockets, it was spilling over into late night champagne and coke fuelled orgies in some of South London's finest.

You can take the boyos out of the Valleys...

Ironically, one of their preferred haunts was The Library which was back in full swing: like the rubbish and vomit from the previous night, the Mr Pollock incident had been cleaned up and forgotten.

But all sorts of people were beginning to notice the likely lads from the Valleys who were suddenly blessed with large wedges of readies. It's one thing to tip a waitress 'cause she's got nice tits; it's another to stuff a twenty down her bra every time she serves you a drink. All this was grist to the gossip mill of the South London underworld and the police informants who drifted through the ether of clubland like wisps of smoke that hung over the dance floors in the good old days of disco; ears were kept to the ground and eyes on those walking over it.

Later, much later, Bron would say to Markie over and over that they'd been '...stupid, stupid, stupid.'

But at the time it had seemed like fun, fun, fun. The police raided their flats simultaneously at 5am one rainy Tuesday morning.

The boys had fallen through their respective doors two hours earlier and were still in the deepest of alcohol/drug-induced sleeps; the young ladies lying beside them shook them out of it at the sound of splintering front doors and cries of 'Armed Police! Stay where you are. Do not move.'

It didn't take the police long to find their stashes; for a couple of career criminals, under the floorboards was hardly original. A week later, thanks to the detective work of one diligent young probationer, the front door of Bron's gran came off its hinges as she sat watching Countdown, sipping her tea and nibbling on her digestives; the gameshow never had the same appeal after that.

That's when the boys realised that they were in deep dodo. Up until then, they'd explained the money away with wins on the geegees; not the best or most original explanation and one which the CPS would have ripped to shreds in front of a jury but nevertheless it had held until then.

But once the hand grenades had been found tucked away at his gran's place, the game was up and the boys knew they were in for a long holiday at Her Majesty's expense and pleasure.

In their heads, the boys could hear the door being slammed and the key being turned and thrown away; they needed to get their hands on a 'Get Out of Jail' free card or at least one which would allow them to enjoy a bit of life before they collected their pensions.

It didn't help that the Chief Superintendent, with the able assistance of Sergeant Wallis, put the fear of God into them during the interview following the discovery of the grenades.

'Look,' the Chief Superintendent began in a fatherly tone 'we know you're just a couple of two-bit boyos from up the Valleys: you weren't the brains behind these jobs. We all know that'. Then, without warning, he went seamlessly off at a tangent, in a slow, meandering and extremely graphic way, about a recent incident in prison where one of the 'pretty boys' had had to have his arse sewn up after he'd been gang-raped in the showers.

By the time he'd finished, even Jim Wallis was feeling queasy.

The Chief Super just sat there quietly observing the boys: the slight green tinge on both of their faces was a pleasure to see. He knew they both were thinking the same thing: '...we're gonna end up some lifer's bitch' and those guys were well-known among inmates to be none too gentle in their lovemaking. So, the story of the guy with the sewn up arse made sense.

'Tell us who the others are and we'll see what we can do for you' was the offer on the table. That offer coupled with the fine film of sweat balanced on the older copper's upper lip told the boys that this was probably going to be his last big case and he wanted to go out on a high: nab the lot of 'em.

There it was: their only hope of keeping themselves intact was to give up the names of the other gang members.

Markie was the first to cave in. He asked for a loo break. The PC who escorted him told the Chief later that he'd heard Markie throwing up.

'Good. Then we know who to go after; the other one' he told Jim Wallis.

'How d'you make that one out, boss?' asked his perplexed sergeant.

'Easy. When the Markie boy threw up, he got rid of a lot of...' he paused, thinking about how to put it '...a lot of his anxiety about it. The other one's still got it bottled up. So, we'll just help him along by giving him an update on that guy's arse. Ideally, I'd like to show him a few photos; that would really get him talking...'

'They'd never allow it, would they, Sir?'

'Sadly, Jim, they would not. But can you see it? A lovely big blown up picture of that guy's ring...or what's left of it!'

Jim Wallis gagged.

'Enough, Sir! Too much information!'

'If that's the effect it's got on you, imagine what it'd do to him, Jim? Yeah, he's the one who'll give us the names. Trust me.'

It took nearly a week of long grinding interviews but finally the Chief's prediction came to pass when Bron Davies, late of the Hand-Grenade Gang, coughed. All that time on remand with nothing to think about but that poor guy's arse or what was left of it, had done the trick.

'Now didn't that work a treat?' asked a very smug superior officer of his sergeant when the interview was over.

'Amazing, Sir' replied Jim Wallis in admiration. 'You know, thinking about it, maybe if we could include a slideshow, like the one you suggested for the inmates of all the borstals in the UK, we could decimate the future criminal population of this country at a stroke.'

'Nice thought, Jim, but we could also be doing ourselves out of a job. So, we'll just let the buggers...if you'll pardon the pun...find out when they get there' said the Chief chuckling. 'Now then,' he continued 'let's get back to the station and see what we've got on these other two...'

Two hours later, Jim Wallis was sitting working on his computer when his extension rang.

'Sergeant Wallis speaking' he answered in his broad North of the border accent.

'Jim, it's Pete. 'Ave you managed to come up with anything on those two villains yet?'

'Yes, Sir. This Dave Cosforth character, the one identified as the leader of the gang used to be a regular customer. He's got form and a rap sheet as long as that scarf your auntie use to knitted you for Christmas...'

'How'd you know that my auntie knitted me a scarf?' asked his boss.

Jim Wallis stuttered 'Er...er...' He didn't know what to say.

'Only joking, Jim. Everybody's aunties knitted scarves for them. It's what they did during the war' and he laughed.

Jim cleared his throat. 'Right, Sir. Got it. Anyway...' Jim Wallis put on his reading glasses and consulted the file on the desk in front of him. 'Three counts of aggravated burglary, a bank job where a teller got shot, one of ABH...and that's just some of them. Been inside three times, but hasn't appeared on our radar for over ten years: apparently gone straight' he finished.

'Not according to our Mr Davies. It's gonna be a pleasure catching up on old times with Mr Cosforth' said the Chief with relish '...but we have to keep this out of the papers, Jim. If he's in Spain, like Davies says, and gets a whiff of it while he's sipping his Tequila Sunrise around his fancy swimming pool, he'll be off like a greyhound out of trap 4. Anything on the other muppet? What's his name?'

Jim Wallis was slightly perplexed at his superior officer's jocularity but decided to ignore it and consulted another file. 'Mikey Malone, Sir. Clean as a whistle. Not even a parking ticket but then again he's a black hack...and they tend to keep their noses clean; frightened of losing their licence. Also, we do give them a bit more leeway.'

'Not any fuckin' more!' said the Chief grimly. 'After what this lot have been up to, it'll be a wonder they don't have a lynch party waiting to greet them when we bring them in.'

Surprisingly, no word of the arrests slipped out.

One Hundred and Seventeen

Two days later Mikey Malone was 'invited' to an interview at the nick by ten armed police officers who kicked down the door of his three-bedroom semi at five o'clock in the morning in leafy Croydon: he accepted, gratefully as it turned out. Apparently, his good lady was none too pleased with '...that lazy bastard' and let him, the police and the rest of the street know it as they cuffed Mikey and frogmarched him out to the waiting squad car. She'd arranged to go to the bingo with her mates that night and now, she supposed, it would have to be cancelled.

'Cor, your missus goes for it once she's got the bit between her teeth, don't she?' remarked the PC sitting in the back seat with a relieved Mikey.

'You're jokin', aren't you, son? She ain't even warmed up yet. If I was you I'd warn the nick that she'll be on 'er way there soon. Give it a couple of hours. I know her; she'll be broodin' about it. She'll puff her way through a packet o' fags, then she'll come lookin' for me. An' that's when it'll all kick off. Trust me. You'd better hope that you're off duty when she gets there.'

The PC, John Marshall, had no idea how lucky he was that he was in the car with Mikey and not back at the house.

The officers who remained there were harangued and subjected to language they didn't even hear in the locker room: she was the original South London Harpy.

It took the police all of two hours to find Mikey's stash in the attic.

Meanwhile at the station, Mikey had been whisked through reception and was sitting in front of Chief Superintendent Moore and Sergeant Wallis by six thirty.

The day had begun and it was going to be a long one.

The Chief went straight for the jugular.

'Your former colleagues, Mr Morgan and Mr Davies' he began, looking at his watch '...will just be sitting down to their breakfast in the dining room of their five-star accommodation in Wandsworth. They've been very co-operative over the last week or so and we hope you will be too. So, tell us then, Mr Malone, how can you help us?' he finished and sat back.

The shock was etched in every line of Mikey's face. He had been so close...so close. Now retirement was just a dream; and a bad one at that.

'Oh, bollocks!' thought Mikey. 'The wife's gonna kill me.'

The three of them sat in the interview room with only two of the occupants comfortable with the silence which followed.

'I'm on overtime' Jim Wallis mused to himself. 'Take your time Mikey lad. No rush!'

'Well ...' began Mikey hesitantly.

'Yes?' enquired The Chief Superintendent gently like a parent waiting for a child to explain why they'd done this naughty thing.

But the fact was he already knew everything there was to know about the gang's exploits. Once Bron had started there was no stopping him; every single gruesome, grimy little detail of their escapade poured out of his mouth. But the Chief wanted to see how far or how much Mikey was prepared to admit.

Suddenly Mikey's face scrunched up and he blurted: 'No comment' and that was it.

For the next two hours, they tried but the answer was always the same: 'No comment', even to 'Do you reside at 37 Fredericks Close, Croydon?'

No fucking comment.

Fine. They had all they needed anyway. Even though he was only the bag man, as an accomplice and accessory, he'd still go down for a very satisfyingly long time.

The Top Brass were all for letting the PR people have a field day with the Nationals: announce a Press Conference, leak a few titbits to their pet reporters etc. They bloody well needed some good press after the last few weeks of murder and mayhem in the Capital.

But the Chief Superintendent managed to persuade the AC to hold fire.

'Three more days, Sir, and we'll have the whole bloody lot of them behind bars' the Chief had pleaded with the Assistant Commissioner.

At the 'bloody' the AC's left eyebrow rose a fraction; he wasn't used to subordinates using that kind of language in his office.

'Three days, you say?' he enquired, knowing what he did of the country of 'manana'.

'Yes, Sir. Our lawyers have spoken with the Courts over there and they reckon we'll be on a plane back to the UK within forty-eight hours. The Spanish police are more than happy to get shot of them straight away these days. Apparently, they've got enough home grown ones to keep them going without our lot adding to their statistics' replied the Chief Superintendent.

Instinctively he realised that they were at the point where, from years of interviewing suspects, it could go either way. He knew he had to keep schtum and not move a muscle.

The AC picked up a piece of pink plasticine from his tray and began squeezing it. 'So that's how he gets rid of his stress...an' I thought it was lapdancers!' mused the Chief.

'Hmm' the AC muttered as his eyes flickered between the plasticine which he was now rolling into a ball and the Chief's face. Finally, letting out a sigh he said:

'Very well. I'll give you seventy-two hours, no more. We desperately need some positive press, Chief Superintendent, and this is manna from heaven for us. But a picture of...' and here he run his hand through the air, across an imaginary headline and exploded: "Leader of the Notorious Hand-Grenade Gang Caught!" and pictures of him being led through Customs in handcuffs, taken from his palatial hideaway in the Costa del Crime, would make an even better front page for us in the Nationals! Which reminds me; I must make a note to get our Press people to release the address in Spain to our friendly reporters so that they can include some tasty photos of the house bought with his ill-gotten gains! Yes, I can see it now! Do it, Chief Superintendent. Make it happen. It would certainly be a fitting end to a glittering career.'

At the end of his boss' outburst, the Chief managed to keep his facial expression from changing, but only just. Not a single muscle moved: unlike his thoughts, which for the most part, could not possibly be repeated in polite society. But a few of his less slanderous thoughts were sprinkled with gems of alliteration such as 'pen-pushin' prat!' and 'useless underperformer!'

The Chief Superintendent shook the AC's hand, thanked him profusely and promised him a 'good collar' before making his way to the gents' and retching up his guts. He still didn't feel any better when he came out.

'No wonder I didn't get beyond Chief Superintendent. I couldn't be one of that lot. What a load of tossers! No wonder...' he stopped in his tracks and looked up and down the corridor as another thought began to surface. 'Hmm, maybe best not to think about that here. Never mind, I'll be away from it all soon! But it'll be a pleasure to sort out Mr Cosforth before I go.'

One Hundred and Eighteen

So, the lid was kept on it until all the extradition papers had been signed and agreed and Chief Superintendent Moore together with his sergeant were seated on a plane bound for sunny Spain with a bunch of end of season tourists for a meeting with their opposite numbers of the Spanish Guardia Civil and a certain Mr Cosforth; the latter meeting they were both definitely looking forward to.

They were met off the plane by a polite English-speaking Inspector who arranged a swift, smooth exit for them ahead of the rabble who no doubt would be throwing up on the streets of Marbella later that evening. After all, what's the point of a holiday in Spain without waking up with a stinking hangover?

The Chief and Sergeant Wallis had chosen to wear short-sleeved Hawaiian shirts, slacks and straw fedoras so as to blend in and not draw attention to themselves. Problem was, two older men travelling together to Spain; either they were dirty old men on the pull or a couple of gays. Whichever, they were noticed and one or two snide comments made by some of the younger bucks on the plane who, judging by the way they were chucking their duty-free down their necks might be aiming to start their throwing-up cycle before they'd left the airport.

Santy, as the Inspector informed them he was known as, short for Santiago, Santiago Rodriguez, was coming up to his twentieth year in the Force and had worked everything from Narcotics to Robbery. As the conversation evolved on the journey into central Marbella to the small, quiet, mid-range hotel which had been arranged for them at taxpayers' expense, they found a lot of common ground: crooks were the same the world over.

Unpacking took all of five minutes while the Inspector kindly dealt with the checking in and then they were on their way to Police Headquarters; no point in hanging around.

Throughout the ten-minute drive to the station or as the locals called it, comisaria de policia, Santy pointed out the local places of interest; a couple of them were for tourists, the others were of 'professional interest'.

On arrival at Headquarters, the formalities were swiftly dispensed with and arrangements made to arrest Dave Cosforth the following morning, local time 6am.

An hour and a half later, they were standing outside on the steps of Police Headquarters with the rest of the day to themselves.

'Two o'clock, Jim,' said the Chief looking at his watch which he'd put forward one hour on the plane 'we've got loads of time. The car isn't picking us up from the hotel until 4am to bring us back here. Fancy an all-nighter?' asked his boss as he donned his sunglasses.

'Are you serious, Sir? Staying up all night?' asked the sergeant, unable to keep the surprise from his voice. With no visible sign from his boss that he was 'just kidding', he added 'Not for me, Sir.'

'Shame' replied the Chief. 'I thought you might fancy getting some practice in for when we retire, Jim.'

Little did the Chief know that on his nights off, Jim Wallis was tucked up in bed by nine o'clock with a good book; lights out by ten.

'I'll definitely pass on that one, Sir, but don't let me stop you. For myself, I prefer to do my collars with a clear head. But for the rest of the day, I'm easy, Sir' replied his sergeant as he felt the powerful rays of the sun beating down. Jim Wallis sighed, enjoying the sensation of the sun's rays warming his pallid skin. He reached for his own shades.

'Can we drop the formalities while we're here, Jim? Pete will be fine.'

'Er...sure, Si...sorry...Pete. I'll tell you one thing I do not want to do and that's sample the local food and wine. I've got a dodgy stomach at the best of times and I don't want to be askin' Mr Cosforth where his ensuite is in the middle of reading him his rights' asserted the dour Scotsman.

'I understand, Jim. So, you don't necessarily fancy a pint of Sangria with a paella then, eh?' said Pete smiling at his cruel suggestion.

The Scotsman made a heaving motion.

'Exactly...Pete. Just the thought of it...'

'Right, so we'll pass on that. How do you fancy one of those tours of the city on an open-topped bus? Every time I go up to central London you see them packed with tourists: I reckon they must be interesting.'

'Sounds good to me. I did one, years ago, in Nice and you really get to find out about a place and its history in the space of a couple of hours.'

For the next two hours, they sat on the top deck of a tour bus taking in all the landmarks the city had to offer.

'Ah, some interesting sights, eh, Jim?' Pete remarked; and wasn't only referring to the places of interest. Some young ladies, on their way to the beach already dressed...or, in some of cases, not, for an afternoon's sunbathing, waved up to the two old men, who reminded them of their grandfathers, observing them from the top of the tour bus as it slowly drove passed.

'Cor, I can't wait to retire to somewhere like this, Jim! Sun, sea, sangria and knockers so big that it would take Isambard Kingdom Brunel to come up with a cantilever system to stop their owners from toppling over!' laughed the Chief as the eye-popping sight of nubile young lasses waving nearly pushed his sunglasses off his nose.

'I don't think I'll see much of that where I'm retiring to' answered Jim Wallis with a hint of regret.

'And where's that going to be?' asked Pete curiously.

'The Isle of Bute. My sister and I are planning on taking over a wee bed and breakfast place. No, I don't think we'll be seeing such magnificent ...' he gulped at the sight of the same young ladies' bottoms wiggling off towards the beach 'specimens...sorry I meant sights...sorry what I really meant...'

'I think I get the gist' laughed Pete as he watched regret/lust/passion all intermingling and fighting for control of his sergeant's face. 'Priceless!' he thought wickedly.

'Whoa! I think I need a drink!' said Jim removing his straw hat to wipe the sweat trickling down his brow into his eyes.

'The tour's nearly over, Jim. We could go and have a beer or something' remarked Pete.

'I think I might need the 'or something'' said Jim with one last rueful glance behind at the disappearing rears/specimens/sights.

'Not while we're on duty, Jim! I can just see the headlines now: 'Police caught with pants down on the job.'

'Not even a wee quickie?' pleaded Jim Wallis.

'Sadly, Jim, no fucking chance. The AC would have my guts for garters' guffawed Pete Moore.

'Aw, well' thought Jim 'maybe when we get back I could pay Cynthia a visit and she could sort me out.'

Cynthia being a young lady Jim had met while he was pounding the beat in Soho many years before; they still kept in touch. He'd let her off with a minor indiscretion and in return, she had 'obliged' him from time to time. To Jim, it was a small, slightly illegal perk of the job. Nothing more...but that's how it always starts.

They wandered around admiring some more of the 'sights' until they found an English pub serving passable beer.

Sitting outside watching and listening to the world go by, it was difficult to turn off their copper's antennae; as a policeman, you're always on the lookout for villains or things that don't quite seem right.

'We've been sitting here for...' Pete looked at his watch '...forty minutes, Jim. How many languages d'you think we've heard? Hm?'

'I don't know, Sir, sorry Pete,' Jim corrected himself, 'maybe a dozen?' he guessed.

'Well, I recognised eighteen. Eighteen! Can you believe that? And that doesn't include Spanish! And, there were two that I wasn't sure of; I find it difficult to distinguish between some of the smaller Asian dialects.'

'That's amazing, Pete. How d'you do it?' asked Jim.

'Well, I did my degree in languages. Ever since I was a kid I could hear the flow of language; sort of catch inflections and things like guttural sounds and I'd be able to put them all together and come up with the language.'

'The only thing I was good at in school was 'times tables'. But that's because the teacher we had in Glasgow, Miss Heefey, I'll never forget her name, hammered, and I do mean hammered, it into us. To this day when someone says "what's twelve nines?", the answer comes straight into my mind '108''

'Okay then, what're...eight elevens?' asked Pete in a rush of words.

'Eighty-eight.'

'Eight nines?' demanded Pete.

'Seventy-two.'

'Seven nines?'

'Sixty-three. I don't have to think about it; it just comes out.'

'That's amazing in its self, Jim. I panic when I have to do my expenses every month. I'm terrified of getting it wrong' revealed his Chief Superintendent.

They both lapsed into a companionable silence, each of them savouring the intimacy of the situation where two people, who have worked in close proximity, sometimes for years, suddenly find themselves brought together in unexpected circumstances and discover things about each other that they never knew.

Unconsciously, the two men leaned closer into each other, their bodies touching, not in an intimate way, more in a comforting 'pilgrims on the same journey' sort of way; nevertheless, they still looked like a couple of old queens.

A couple of pints later, they decided to take a stroll and admire the last of the returning sun worshippers making their way to their hotels to rest up before the evening festivities began.

'An' just think of it, Jim; we're being paid for this' said Pete as his irises dilated to take in one young lady's particularly massive bouncing boobies.

'It's one of the few times you could twist my arm to work overtime!' rejoined Jim with a look of serenity on his face that Pete had never seen before.

As the returning bronzed bodies began to thin out, the two men decided to look for a restaurant and have an early night.

'I'll get us an alarm call for 3am when we get back to the hotel, if that's okay with you, Jim?' enquired Pete.

'Perfect. Then we don't need to rush and we can be downstairs waiting for the driver when he arrives.'

In the end, they plumped for an Argentinian steakhouse where they both had well-done steak with chips washed down with another couple of beers.

Pete was up for a night cap at the hotel bar before they turned in, but Jim, who regretted not bringing his Ovaltine with him, declined but '...don't let me stop you, Pete.'

Pete rounded off the night with just a couple of snifters of brandy, known locally as 103; it left the lining of his throat intact, so, not as bad as some others he'd tried on earlier jaunts.

Regretfully, he decided to call it a day despite the fact that he was just beginning to warm up: he couldn't have his sergeant thinking that he was a serious piss-artist. A Chief Superintendent of the Metropolitan Police? Perish the thought!

Both of them had very similar 'interesting' dreams that night relating to their earlier sightseeing adventure.

One Hundred and Nineteen

Showered and dressed, Pete and Jim met in the foyer at 3.40am as some of the late-night revellers were just returning, a little the worse for wear.

'In the good old days...' began Pete.

'Don't, I know what yer gonna say!' said Jim intervening as they both ogled a particularly voluptuous young lady snogging the face off her bronzed, tattooed '...lucky bastard!' as she dragged him toward the lift.

'I'll give you 10/1 she doesn't make it to her room...!'

'I know, I know' repeated Jim frustratedly. He had just thought the exact same thing.

'Chief Superintendent Moore?' enquired a uniformed policeman in heavily accented English, interrupting some very rude thoughts.

'Si...yes' replied Pete with just a hint of regret as he dragged his eyes away from the perfectly formed rear of Miss Voluptuous entering the lift.

'Please to come with me.'

'Excuse me, senor, but how did you know it was me?' asked Pete.

'I enquired at the desk, Sir. Besides, you don't get too many tourists dressed in formal suits and ties and sober at four o'clock in the morning here in Marbella. By now, most of our English male tourists are exposing themselves to the young ladies or are 'bladdered', I believe is how you express it in England.'

The 'bladdered' came out like 'blathered' but the meaning was clear.

Pete and Jim took this in, in silence.

'Doesn't have a very high opinion of us, does he?' said the look that passed between them.

The local constabulary made them welcome at the briefing. Breakfast of polystyrene cups of steaming hot coffee and doughnuts were provided, making it almost feel like home.

Six marked Policia cars drove in convoy to the quiet, plush neighbourhood where Dave Cosforth had chosen to pitch his tent, on the very large assumption that he'd be spending the rest of his days there.

Not ten minutes from the centre of Marbella and only five minutes from the famous Puerto Banus, the marina complex popular with celebs, it couldn't have been further from Dave's humble abode in sunny South London if it'd tried.

'I have a confession to make, Pete; this is my favourite part of the job' said Jim in hushed tones as they were driven in the lead car.

'I know what you mean, Jim. I can't wait to see the look on his ugly mug' responded Pete rubbing his hands with glee.

Their Spanish counterparts just smiled. Policemen were no different the world over.

As they drove passed the property, Jim Wallis let out a whistle.

'Would you look at that!' he said in amazement. 'And they say crime doesn't pay!'

'They say a lot of things, Jim. Don't take too much notice' his superior shot back, annoyed.

A couple of the younger Guardia climbed over the low wall of the property, found the switch to open the electronic gates and suddenly the night air and the driveway was filled with the sound of sirens and uniforms with guns drawn.

'Come to papa!' declared Chief Superintendent Moore as he and Sergeant Wallis marched up to the front door.

One Hundred and Twenty

When it came to it, 'The Knock' went amazingly smoothly.

Dave and Doris had both jumped up at the sound of the sirens.

'Sounds like they're in the bloody house' complained Doris still half-sozzled from her regular nightly binge earlier on.

'They are in the bloody house!' declared Dave sitting upright and shaking his head to clear it. 'Fuckin' Spanish police! Probably nickin' some poor sod for not paying their parkin' fine. Well, they've got the wrong bloody 'ouse this time.'

A week earlier, Dave had heard from one of the expats that the police were hot on collecting parking fines in Marbella; especially early in the morning.

'Aaaah! What a bleedin' pain!' he yelled as he pushed back the covers.

'Tell 'em to shut that bleedin' noise off will you, Dave? Me head's splittin'.'

Dave slipped his silk dressing gown over his new Egyptian cotton PJs. Since his arrival several months earlier, Dave had grown into his new role of wealthy retired expat and had enjoyed splashing a bit of the cash on himself in a discreet way, of course: nothing too flash to draw attention. Apart, that is, for one big splash: a little runaround Merc 350cls. But he was always careful to park it legally. No point in drawing attention to yourself unnecessarily, he thought.

Whoever it was banging on that door was gonna get a volley.

'What's their fuckin' problem?' he thought as he legged it down the marble staircase.

He pulled back the bolts and flung the door open, ready to give whoever the prats were a mouthful only to be confronted by a couple of toothy smiles from some very unSpanish-looking geezers. Those grins started Dave's guts churning.

'Ah, Mr Cosforth, I presume?' announced the first suit. 'I am Chief Superintendent Moore and this is Sergeant Jim Wallis of the Metropolitan Police' he continued as both of them flashed their warrant cards. 'I have a warrant for your arrest in connection with a number of robberies carried out in the Metropolitan area. Read him his rights, will you, Jim?'

'With pleasure, Sir' Jim cleared his throat and began: 'You do not have to say anything. However, it may harm your defence if you do not mention when questioned, something which you later rely on in court. Anything you do say may be given in evidence. Do you have anything to say?'

'You got the wrong guy, guv' said Dave deadpan.

'Did you get that, Jim? The gentleman said: "You got the wrong guy, guv". Lovely, I like it! Never heard anything like it before in my life. The judge'll split his sides laughing. Now if that's all you've got to say...' he turned to his sergeant and with real satisfaction said '...cuff 'im, Jim.'

A very dishevelled, disoriented Doris suddenly appeared behind Dave.

'Who is it Dave?' Doris saw the handcuffs in Jim's hand. ''Ere what d'you fink you're doin'? Get off 'im!' she screamed.

The scuffle that ensued ended with the Spanish police politely but firmly taking hold of Doris while their English colleagues accompanied Dave upstairs to put on some clothes before escorting him to the lead car and sitting either side of him on the back seat.

'How'd you find me?' asked Dave, numb as a bum that'd been sitting on the seat of a plane for five hours.

'You'll find out soon enough, my son' answered a very smug Chief Superintendent.

The journey to the airport was completed in silence...apart from screaming sirens.

One Hundred and Twenty One

'I wouldn't admit it, but it'd be great if there's a loads of photographers waiting for us when we get to Gatwick' Chief Superintendent Moore thought as they waited to board the plane. 'I need to get in the 'upstairs' good books after that last mess.'

The journey went without a hitch and they touched down a little after 9am.

It was only when they'd gotten through Customs and reached the end of the Nothing to Declare zone that all hell broke loose as the automatic doors on to the concourse slid open.

'There they are!' shouted one of the paparazzi and the cameras began flashing.

Dave Cosforth turned his head away and asked if he could have a jacket over his head. The Chief agreed and led him through the hustling, bustling photographers trying to stick their camera lens up his jacket.

'Enough, gentlemen!' said the Chief Superintendent fiercely but at the same time not trying too hard to stop them. This was his moment of glory and he wanted it to last.

The pictures that appeared in the nationals later showed two policemen with the suspect's head covered by a designer, possibly Armani, according to some of the red tops, jacket. The only visible parts of him in the photos were his arms attached to a couple of smug plainclothes policemen who posed like a couple of professionals, turning this way and that as the photographers called out to them.

By the time their escort, with sirens blaring, of course, had delivered them to Walworth Road station, the custody sergeant had the paperwork already prepared and shortly afterwards Dave found himself back in a cell after an absence of ten years.

'Still smells the same' he, like Jake, noted despondently. 'How am I gonna get the fuck out of this?'

Gary was unavailable when Dave was allowed to make his one phone call but one of the partners with a small 'p', Bill Flint, attended the initial interviews before Dave appeared at a special hearing and was remanded to Wandsworth.

'At least,' mused Gary when he heard about his client's new postal address 'they're all banged up in the same place.'

Wandsworth: interesting place and even more interesting things about to happen.

One Hundred and Twenty Two

Jake's wounds had all but healed, apart from an occasional twinge in the gonads, except now he was wound up tighter than Robin of Sherwood's bow at full stretch. For weeks he'd been waiting for news from Liechtenstein. What the fuck was holding this guy up? And it didn't help that every time he asked The Shap, the reply was always the same: 'Patience, my boy, patience. You're gonna have a long time to think about this, twenty years, maybe more, so a few more days or weeks ain't gonna make much difference'

And so he waited. Maybe not as patiently as The Shap would have liked, but he waited nevertheless.

Until one Thursday night, fifteen minutes before the end of association. There was a rap on Jake's door. 'Yeah?' he called out from his bunk; he was getting ready to turn in.

'Mr Shapiro would like to have a word, Jake' said Pete, one of The Shap's brick-shithouse messengers, poking his head around the door.

His boys always referred to The Shap as 'Mr Shapiro'. Jake was never quite sure why. Were they on the promise of some wedge from the stash which The Shap had undoubtedly salted away somewhere safe, when they got out? Or was it his brainpower that they respected or maybe needed? Whichever, it was "Mr Shapiro".

'What about?' asked Jake who was dog-tired.

'Dunno, Jake, but it sounded urgent.'

The hairs on the back of Jake's neck stood on end. Could it be what he'd been waiting for? Word from Liechtenstein? Suddenly energised, Jake swung off his bunk 'Let's go' he said and began racing along the corridors toward The Shap's place.

Two minutes later they were walking through the door of the cell.

'You wanted to see me?' asked Jake as he entered, slightly breathless.

'I have news' was the monotone reply accompanied by one raised eyebrow: a sign which Jake had come to recognise in The Shap as disapproval.

'Yeah?' said Jake. 'Well, go on. Put me out of my misery, for fuck's sake, Shap!'

'You might not like it, Jake' was not the reply that Jake had been expecting. It took Jake by surprise. How could he not 'like' it? It could give him a clue to or even the name of the snitch that put him in here.

'Come on Shap. Don't fuck about, tell me!' he demanded.

The Shap gave a slight incline of his head to let his boys know that he wanted to be left alone with Jake.

When the door was closed behind them, The Shap said to Jake:

'Sit down, son.'

Jake just stood there.

'I said...sit down, Jake' repeated The Shap, but this time more forcefully.

Jake flopped down frustratedly on the edge of the bunk while The Shap leaned against the opposite wall.

'I'm really sorry, Jake' began The Shap with what seemed like genuine regret.

Half a dozen scenarios raced through Jake's head.

'Oh, fuck! He couldn't find out. I've wasted the money. I've driven myself barmy thinking, dreaming about this and now it's come to nothing.'

But out loud he said: 'Just tell me, Shap. Please!' He almost said: 'For Christ's sake' but decided it could be disrespectful given The Shap's persuasion.

'Michael had more trouble getting this information than he thought but a deal's a deal' Jake took this to mean that it cost more than Michael had expected but the price wouldn't change: like Jake should care.

The Shap took a deep breath. 'There's no easy way to tell you, Jake. This Liechtenstein account is in the name of...' he paused '...Gary Dean.'

When there was no reaction from Jake, The Shap asked:

'Isn't that the name of your brief, Jake, Gary Dean? Was it him who stitched you up?'

Jake felt like he was going to pass out. He struggled for breath.

Thought after thought zoomed through Jake's mind like a line of cars that had been waiting ages for the lights to change to green and then all rush through before they went to red again. 'Gary Dean?' he thought incredulously 'Can't be!'

Shap took the three steps from the wall to the bunk and patted Jake's back gently like people do for babies who are choking on something.

'You okay?' he asked, concerned.

'I...I...the bastard!' screamed Jake coming out of it and giving vent to his rage. 'I'll put a contract out on him! I'll fuckin' 'ave 'im! I'll rip the bastard's throat out with my bare hands!' A threat Jake could easily have carried out.

His rage filled the cell. He was shaking violently, uncontrollably. Both fists clenched, his face contorted; at that point, Shap thought Jake could easily have punched a hole in the cell wall...and kept on going.

'Jake slow down' ordered The Shap.

'Slow fuckin' down?' roared Jake, disbelieve and feral rage fighting for control of his facial features.

The door opened and Pete put his head around the door.

'Everything alright, Mr Shapiro?'

Shap waved his hand in a dismissive gesture 'We're okay' he said.

Pete stayed peering into the cell a moment longer before Jake threw him a look: Pete got the message and quietly closed the door.

'What the hell is going on, Shap? My own brief?' said Jake in total disbelief.

The bell to end association brought Jake back with a jolt. He had five minutes left to ask what he needed to know before returning to his cell and for what would be a long sleepless night ahead.

'Look, how kosher is this Michael? I mean, how reliable is his information? Could he have made a mistake? I mean, my own fuckin' lawyer, for Christ's sake, Shap?'

'To my knowledge, Michael has never got it wrong; it's what he does. Look, sleep on this, Jake. This information could be a powerful weapon. Don't waste it on a knee jerk reaction. Sure, you want to kick the shit out of this guy, I understand that. But could there be a better way to do it? A way that would give you the instant gratification you want but, at the same time, make his pain last longer? Longer and more painful, hm? Now there's a thought. Think about it, Jake. Don't rush into things.'

'I dunno, Shap. But...thanks. At least I think I mean thanks. Jesus, my own brief!' Jake was numb with shock.

He stood up and wobbled precariously, The Shap grabbed his arm.

'Steady, Jake! I know it's a shock and a lot to take in. Look, we'll talk more about it in the morning. Goodnight and for what it's worth, Jake, I'm truly, truly sorry.'

The Shap shepherded him to the door of the cell.

'We'll speak in the morning, Jake.'

Jake stumbled back to his cell knowing that for the next eight hours, while everyone else in the nick would be getting some sort of sleep, his brain would be performing Olympic mental gymnastics; trying to find answers to the myriad questions bouncing around inside his skull...and knowing that most of them would probably stay unanswered.

One Hundred and Twenty Three

And he wasn't the only one having a sleepless night. But then, this wasn't Gary's first one.

Over the last few days, he'd taken to checking out the bottom of, at least one bottle of wine in the belief that it would blot out his problem and give him a decent night's sleep: wrong on both counts. Around two o'clock each morning, the booze wore off and the first thing to leap into his consciousness was Jake; Mr Jake fuckin' Vickers. The rest of the night was spent tossing and turning and no matter what he did to get him out of his head, Jake came sneaking back in, one way or another. This particular night, he decided to get up.

Two guys, two sleepless nights, two people hell-bent on destroying the other and what you have is a recipe for catastrophe...with fireworks.

Gary, sitting at his well-appointed desk slugging generous measures of good malt whisky, tap, tap, tapping away with his pencil, attempting to rein in his emotions unsuccessfully, while working out the best way to eradicate 'his problem'.

Jake trying, with limited success, to blot out the buzzsaw of Charlie Baker's snores above his head as he decided on a way to destroy his nemesis.

As the truth of The Shap's findings sank in, a two-year-old child could have knocked Jake over, he was so totally gutted. His own brief? What was the world coming to when you couldn't even trust your own bent solicitor? What next? Straight policemen? Never! How could anybody to do an honest day's skulduggery?

The more Jake thought about it, the calmer and more detached he became. Was it finally knowing who the bastard was that had shopped him that allowed him to think straight for the first time in weeks? For sure, he was already beginning to feel the tension slowly fade in his body. His neck muscles, so taut since arriving at Wandsworth, were beginning to loosen up; he could even turn his head from left to right without having to turn his whole upper torso simultaneously.

As the night hours slowly wore on, Jake turned into the mental doppelganger of his nemesis, Gary; able to subdue the emotion attached to the situation and let his brain take over, looking for the perfect solution. Or, was it being away from the pressures of running his empire that gave him the space to consider his options instead of using his fists as an instant solution to a problem?

The Shap was right: this was one of those situations where you have to make it last. Yeah, stick yer boot in, be able to feel and enjoy the other guy's pain but...make sure it hangs around a long time. Work it so that when they think they're over it, you pick at it slowly, like a sore, and open up the pain for them all over again.

By the end of his long sleep-deprived night, Jake had come up with three different scenarios. The first and definitely his favourite, he ruled out: too quick and too final.

Nonetheless, he entertained the thought (or did it entertain him?) for a while. He closed his eyes and imagined the scene playing out:

Gary arrives for their next meeting. In the interview room, while Gary is distracted pulling papers out of his attaché case, Jake bends down and surreptitiously wedges a tiny slither of wood under the door he'd slipped into his sock as he left his cell for the meeting: warders only frisk you on the way back in, not on the way out.

Gary tosses a couple of packs of fags across the table to Jake. Jake plays along, asks how the family is, had Gary found out anymore about James Irvine? Maybe there'd be a few laughs with his mate, Gary. Gary, the bent solicitor: Gary, the charger of exorbitant fees; Gary who'd gotten rich defending people like Jake...and all the time siphoning everything he could into his secret Liechtenstein account. Gary...the snitch.

All the time the image of what was happening was crystal clear...but he couldn't hear it. He watched his and Gary's mouths working but there was no sound; as if someone had turned down the volume.

Then, the scene changes: Jake says something; the soft expression on his face as if he was whispering sweet nothings to a lover. Gary frowns, appearing not to have heard it correctly. Jake, looking very calm, repeats it, but louder this time. Gary goes white. In his mind's eye, Jake can almost see the sweat dripping off Gary's shaking palms. Gary says something, throwing his hands up, maybe protesting his innocence. But Jake can see everything now in Gary's eyes; the guilt...the terror.

Suddenly, Jake's across the table, his massive callused hands around Gary's throat, his grip so tight that Gary can't get any air into his lungs. Jake had done this so many times before for real that he had no problem imagining how it would end. He also knew he had enough time to do the job before the warders could break the door down.

All too quickly, the scene finishes with Jake being pulled off Gary but by then it was too late. The warders drag him away but not before Jake gobs on the lifeless body whose tongue is protruding horribly out of a mouth that had gasped its last breath of air, the face contorted into a frown which seemed to say: 'What have I done?'

Jake opened his eyes stopping the scene. There was no point in continuing. He knew the ending; he'd get the shit kicked out of him... but he probably wouldn't feel it because he'd be on such a high.

'And let's face it,' thought Jake grinning in the dark 'it 'aint gonna increase my sentence by much. Policemen: people can be funny about - they either like 'em or 'ate em - but lawyers? Ha! Who the fuck actually likes lawyers?'

At this thought, he chuckled so loudly that he nearly woke Charlie up. He put his hand over his mouth listening for Charlie to fall back into his regular pattern of snoring again; it sounded like someone massacring a rainforest with a chain saw.

By 4.30am, the penny had dropped for Jake as to why Gary had been so interested in his, Jake's, interest about what James Irvine lorries carried. By 5am, everything else had dropped into place and a plan formed in Jake's head to extricate a truly delicious revenge.

For the last hour, he slept like a baby.

The not knowing was over.

One Hundred and Twenty Four

At the same time as Jake was having a not-so-quiet chuckle to himself, Gary was also feeling quite pleased with himself: he'd found his own very simple solution.

Oddly enough, his scenario included cigarettes too...but with a twist. When he gave Jake the packs of cigarettes at their next meeting, they'd be laced with a fast-acting poison.

'Shame Sham wasn't here. He'd have given me a discount. Still, with the people I know I should be able to find someone to arrange it for me. And who's ever gonna think that a lawyer would kill his own client? Hmm, not bad' he thought relieved.

Unfortunately, that idea didn't last long: he remembered that Jake didn't smoke and only used the fags for currency.

'Bollocks! That would have been so easy' he thought frustratedly. 'Never mind, plenty more ideas where that one came from.'

But he struggled. Short of arranging for someone on the inside to do a job on Jake, he couldn't work out how to eliminate this little problem.

A sleepy voice came through the door; it was Nicki.

'Gary, are you there? Would you like a coffee?'

Gary opened the top drawer of the desk and quickly hid the whisky tumbler.

'Come in, darling' he called out trying to sound nonchalant.

Nicki opened the door tentatively.

'Are you alright?' she asked in a small voice.

'What?' asked Gary, surprised by the question but then realised that she'd missed him when she woke up and he wasn't there.

'Oh, just one of those cases that gets to you, darling: nothing to worry about. It'll all be over soon.'

'It's not like you to let a case get to you, Gary' she said frowning.

Gary wanted to scream at her: 'And it's not every day you get some bastard trying to wreck everything you've ever worked for!' but just in time he caught himself and replied quite calmly:

'I know, Nicki, but when the murder of a policeman's involved, it's complicated and emotions run high. The public don't like to see the upholders of the law getting the chop because they think: "If the police can't protect themselves what chance have we got of them protecting us?"'

'Hm, I see what you mean; it does make one feel a bit vulnerable' replied Nicki reflectively.

'And we've had a few nasty calls at the office. There are members of the public who go to great lengths to find out who's representing a police killer and then bombard them with abusive calls. It's the frontline staff who get most of it and then we get the letters; some are just downright abusive, others threatening, and unsurprisingly, the police are not overly concerned about stopping it. But hey-ho! The show must go on' said Gary breaking into a grin that he didn't really feel. 'So, how about that cup of coffee?'

What Gary told Nicki was the truth; it's just that it hadn't started yet. But it was just a question of time.

Showered and dressed forty-five minutes later, Gary left early for the office; the cleaners were still there when he arrived.

He had a visit booked in for Jake for the following day and wanted to spend a bit of time at the office while it was quiet to see if he could come up with something...anything, in fact. He was getting desperate.

'Maybe it'll all blow over once they've thrown the book at him' was one of his more hopeful thoughts.

But somewhere in Gary's gut, a worm of doubt was wriggling its toes.

One Hundred and Twenty Five

'You look rough' was The Shap's opening shot as Jake placed his breakfast tray on the table and sat down opposite him.

'Cheers and Good Morning to you too!' replied Jake beaming at his mentor.

'There is an expression' The Shap began hesitantly as if trying to remember '...something about cream and cats that is reminiscent of the look on your face right now.'

Pete, the brick shithouse, who was wiping up the juice of his beans and runny egg with a thin slice of white bread looked up and said:

'What'd ya say, boss?' the creases on his face intersecting like a London tube map.

'My dear Pete,' began The Shap 'your colleague, Mr Vickers, unless I'm very much mistaken, is feeling much better this morning. Would that be a fair statement, Jake?'

'It would' replied Jake continuing to beam.

'And would it have something to do with what we discussed last night?'

'It might' said Jake beginning to laugh.

'And after a sleepless night, judging by those rather large bags under your eyes, have you reached a satisfactory and satisfying conclusion?'

'I have' replied the Cheshire cat with finality.

Now brick shithouses are generally good for one thing and one thing only: their ability to knock down walls when required. Otherwise, it's best not to involve them in any kind of cerebral pursuits.

So, considering his brick shithouse status, Pete very wisely butted out of the rest of the discussion and left them to it as he joined a couple of other brick shithouses to discuss the tits on Page 3.

'Pray tell' requested The Shap folding his arms across his chest patiently like a professor whose star pupil had just revealed they had found the answer to the very fucking question he's spent the majority of his life working on.

So, Jake told him.

'Delicious!' offered The Shap when Jake finished outlining his plan.
'So, you approve?'
'Can't wait!' was The Shap's enthusiastic reply.

One Hundred and Twenty Six

Gary's hand-holding services seemed to be more in demand than ever, lately.

So, it came as no surprise to Gary at all that a few days earlier, Bill Flint, one of the Partners with a small 'p', had received a phone call from one of The Bus' erstwhile tenants, Dave Cosforth, informing him that the police had, amongst other things, violated his human rights by extraditing him from Spain's sunny shores for crimes that he had not committed nor indeed knew anything about…of course.

It had come as no surprise because pictures of Dave being led out of the passenger exit at Gatwick Airport handcuffed between Chief Superintendent Moore and his smiling colleague were plastered across every daily with vitriolic headlines.

'Hand-Grenade Gangster finally tracked down to Costa del Crime!' Gary yawned at that one. 'Not very original' he thought.

But he liked the Standard's banner headline: 'Grandson stuffs grenades in Granny's drawers!' accompanied by a picture of the grenades recovered from Bron's granny's house. That made him smile.

The following day, Gary had dropped everything and spent it by Dave's side as he answered 'No comment' to any and all questions thrown at him in his interview.

But there was no doubt about it; the police had Dave by the short hairs.

During the interview, the Scottish sergeant, Wallis, enjoyed goading Dave.

'You know Mr Cosforth, I personally interviewed the manager of the Lloyd bank after you and your gang did it over...'

'Excuse me, sergeant, at this time, nothing has been proven, so could we say 'allegedly', please? Thank you' requested Gary.

Dave appreciated Gary's intervention and smiled his thanks.

'Certainly, Sir...' replied the policeman through gritted teeth '... 'allegedly did it over' and the manager, who has been retired on medical grounds due to this incident, was completely baffled as to how you and your accomplices knew everything about the layout of his office; where everything was placed...that sort of thing.'

The sergeant produced an evidence bag.

'I'm showing the suspect a mini video camera retrieved from his lock-up. Of course, it never occurred to the bank manager that the window cleaner would be videoing him from the extending washing pole while the windows were being washed.'

Dave looked at Gary who shook his head.

'No comment.'

'There's no need for you to comment, Mr Cosforth. We found the equipment in your lock-up with recordings of every job you did. Handy, those extending poles, eh, Sir?' goaded the policeman.

'No comment' replied Dave but they could see he was rattled.

'Why didn't I get rid of that fuckin' lock-up?' Dave thought to himself as he saw a very long stretch inside looming closer with each piece of evidence the police revealed.

Later, when Dave was alone with Gary, the first words out of his irate client's mouth were: 'How could they be so fuckin' stupid? Flashin' their dough around like that? Leave them alone for two minutes and that's what they get up to. A couple of fuckin' morons...that's what they are.'

Gary thought it best not to mention at that point that in some of the later editions, there were photos of Dave's 'ill-gotten' villa with 'Olympic-size swimming pool'. One of the photographers had even managed a humdinger of a photo of Doris swaying towards the camera with a cocktail in one hand and a hammer in the other.

Gary would definitely object to that one appearing in the prosecution's bundle.

Did Dave think putting a few miles between him and his crimes made it okay to flash the cash?

Well, since he'd been remanded to Wandsworth, Dave would have plenty of time to discuss that with the boys before they all came up for trial. In the meantime, Dave might come up with a plausible alibi for his sudden riches. But Gary doubted it.

One Hundred and Twenty Seven

The following day, Gary was up with the lark and at his desk before anyone else had arrived at the office. He'd loads of paperwork to get through for Dave but it lay there untouched on his desk as thoughts of Jake and what the fuck to do about him came flooding back. What the fuck was he going to do? A knock at his door put that on hold.

'Yeah?' he called out, annoyed that his train of thought had been interrupted.

Jeannie came sweeping in.

'Morning!' she announced gaily. 'I thought I heard someone in here. Jesus, Gary, what happened? Did you forget to go home last night?'

Gary laughed. An honest laugh. Jeannie had broken the black spell of his mood.

'No, Jeannie, I had to start work early today to make sure I had enough money in the bank to pay your wages this month with all the overtime you're working.'

'Let me stop you there' laughed Jeannie holding up the palm of her hand towards Gary. 'You haven't. But I'll accept a post-dated cheque!'

For one brief moment, Jake Vickers was forgotten about.

'Coffee?' asked Jeannie still enjoying a bit of repartee with the boss before the madness of the day began.

'Can I afford it, I ask myself?' enquired Gary.

'Probably not but I'll treat you. D'you want me to run through today's diary with you now?'

'Later, Jeannie, if you don't mind. I've got a couple of things to sort out.'

'A couple of things being Jake Vickers and what to do about him' thought Gary descending into the blackness again.

One hour later, Gary's internal phone rang.

'Yes?'

'Good news, Gary' It was Jeannie's chirpy voice.

'Go on' replied Gary in a non-committal voice.

'Jake Vickers has phoned to cancel your meeting. You've got some free catch-up time.'

'Oh, fantastic, Jeannie! Thanks.' said Gary with enthusiasm he seriously did not feel and hung up the phone.

Normally, a client cancelling a meeting at such short notice was good news; they were still billed for it and it gave you time to catch up with other cases.

Not this time. Not with this client. No, the feeling Gary had about this one wasn't good.

And he was right. The 'Who chased who' had been reversed; the mouse was now chasing the cat.

Game on.

One Hundred and Twenty Eight

No reason given. Gary asked Jeannie twice and the second time got a funny look in reply.

'As I said, Gary,' repeated Jeannie '...he just said to cancel the visit. He didn't give any reason. Is something wrong? I thought you'd be pleased.'

'I am, Jeannie. No, no, I am. It's just unusual, as you know, for a client on remand to cancel.'

Still she was giving him that 'there's more to this than you're telling me' look so he said:

'I'll ask him next time I see him. But thanks, eh?'

He knew there was a reason and a bloody good one at that. Who gives up the chance to have a break from the boredom of prison life and a couple of packets of fags that was precious currency in any nick? No, there was a good reason and Gary had to work out what it was.

The truth was Gary had been replaced by a different visitor: Jock McTavish.

And at that moment, Mr McTavish had just walked into the visiting area of Wandsworth Prison and was scanning the tables for Jake. Jake saw him first and waved.

'How ye doin', son? Prison food obviously agrees with ye, Jake. Yer lookin' grand!'

'An' you can fuck off as well, ya great big lump of Scotch shit!'

'My, my! I'm not used to such refined company. What a welcome!' retorted the Scotsman hugging Jake and laughing at the same time.

'Brought ye these' said Jock pulling two packs of cigarettes out of his pocket.

'Seriously, Jock, thanks for coming. An' the gift is much appreciated.'

'Yer lucky I could fit ye intae ma busy work schedule at such short notice. Whit can I dae fur ye, son?'

Jake's expression changed. The banter was over.

'Y'know I appreciate what you've done for me so far, Jock. But I've got one more favour I need from you.'

'Go on, I'm listening' replied the Scotsman following Jake's lead and getting down to business.

'I found out who the snitch is' announced Jake.

The Scotsman was all ears.

'Who is it? D'ye want me to make them disappear? Or, maybe hurt them a wee bit?' asked his fellow moneylender excitedly.

'Oh, nothin' like that. No, I've got plans for him. I've got it all worked out, Jock.'

'So tell me; where dae I come in then, eh?' demanded the Scotsman, his appetite whetted.

Jake told him while the Scotsman wrote down what was needed.

When Jake finished, the Scotsman replied 'Is that aw? Dae ye no' need me tae dae anythin' else? Ur ye absolutely sure? Nothin' else?' the disappointment clear in his voice.

'Just do it like that, Jock, an' everythin' else will fall into place. Trust me.'

The Scotsman scratched his head in total amazement. 'Yur fuckin' havin' a laugh, Jakey boy. Yur brief? Whit's this world coming tae when yer own brief shops ye tae the police?'

'Disgusting, innit just?'

The bell rung to end the visit and the two men stood up, hugged and the Scotsman walked away while Jake stood there watching his retreating back.

'Welcome to my world, Mr Dean!' thought Jake gleefully.

'Come on, Vickers! Get a move on. We ain't got all day' called out one of the screws.

Normally, Jake would have given him a look that would have withered fresh flowers but to the screw's surprise, he replied: 'Yes, Sir! Sorry, Sir!' and under his breath with his back turned to the room he said excitedly: 'Three fuckin' bags full, Sir! I cannot fuckin' wait.'

One Hundred and Twenty Nine

By the time he reached the Range Rover, Jock had already made two phone calls putting out feelers to track down the individual Jake had asked him to contact.

One of the stooges opened the front passenger door for him while the other gunned up the engine.

'Where to, boss?' asked the driver.

'Before we go, I want ye tae speak tae yur contacts and find out where a guy called Freddie Collins lives. He works for that mob 'James Irvine', ye know the haulier company the police beat us tae the other day. There's a hundred notes in it fur the one that finds it first.'

The boys needed no further incentive, the three of them sat for fifteen minutes calling in favours mingled with a few threats. As they drove off Jock's mobile rung.

Jock said 'Hullo' and then listened.

'Hod on a wee minute. Jimmy,' he said turning to the minder in the back seat '...have ye got a pen? Take this doon.'

Speaking again into the mobile he said 'Go ahead. Aye...' and he repeat 'Flat 27, Doverdale Court, St James' Road...hod on a minute.'

Turning to Jimmy he said 'Ur ye gettin' this?'

'Sure, boss, no problem.' Back to the mobile '...right, St James' Road. Whit? Oh, Battersea. Right.'

To Jimmy he said 'Huv ye got all a' that?'

'Yeah, boss. 27 Doverdale Court, St James' Road, Battersea.'

'Thanks fur that, Benny, I owe ye one. Oh, by the way, dae ye happen tae huv the postcode fur ma satnav?' Jock held the phone well away from his ear while Benny let rip at the other end of the phone.

'Aw, hod on tae yer knickers, Benny! I was only kiddin'!' Jock said. He was a big kidder. 'Next time I see ye, I shall put ma hand in ma pocket an' buy you a snifter of Scotland's finest. Cheers, Benny. Aw the best!'

Jock pulled his wallet out of his jacket pocket and pulled out two fifties. He passed it from one hand to the other and said 'Cheers, Jock. Thanks for your help. Get yerself a wee drink wi' that!'

While Jock was laughing at his own joke, Jimmy's mobile rung.

'Hello?' Silence. 'Ah, fuck off!' he screamed and closed his phone.

'Whit wis that?' asked Jock. 'Wan o' those companies tryin' to sell ye somethin'?'

'No' replied Jimmy huffily.

'It wis somebody with that wee gobshite's address, wisn't it?' said Jock nearly wetting himself with laughing.

The silence from the back of the car answered him.

'Aye, son, ye've got tae get up early to get money oot o' ma wallet!' continued Jock.

'Don't we fuckin' know it' whispered Jimmy under his breath.

'Whit did ye say?' asked Jock who had the hearing of a bat that hadn't eaten for two days.

'Nothin', boss. Nothin'.'

One Hundred and Thirty

'Hello, Jeannie.'

'Yes, Gary?'

'I'm going to close my eyes for half an hour. I haven't been sleeping well the past couple of days. Hold all calls, will you?'

'Sure. Do you want me to wake you?'

'Would you? What time is it?' he said glancing at the digital clock he kept on his desk: the one he used to record the length of client meeting for billing purposes. 'It's eleven o'clock. Would you call me at, say, eleven forty-five?'

'Sure. No probs. Sleep tight.'

Gary relaxed. He knew that Jeannie would bring him a strong black coffee to get him started again at 11.45 precisely. That's why he paid her so much. It's what he needed in his PA: total reliability.

For the first couple of minutes, Jake kept pushing his way into Gary's thoughts.

'I need to forget you for now, if you don't mind' thought Gary desperately 'What can I do?'

And then he heard muffled laughter from the outer office: a couple of the paralegals were having a laugh. That laughter reminded him of the day out he'd had in Brighton with Nicki and Harry.

He spent the next few minutes reliving that memory: the lunch, the stroll along the Lanes, the drive to Rottingdean admiring the views out to sea and before he knew it, he was off into the deepest sleep he'd had for nearly a fortnight.

At 11.45 precisely, Jeannie tapped on Gary's door: no response. She opened the door and closed it quietly behind her. For a moment, she just stood there with the cup and saucer in her hand looking at the angelic expression on her boss' face.

'The sleep of the innocent' thought Jeannie, although somewhere in the back of her mind she was not quite so sure that was the case.

'Gary' she called out: no reaction. Finally, she put the cup down and shook him gently by the shoulder.

'Huh? Wh...at? Oh, Jeannie, thanks, thanks. God, I was in a deep one. Oooh! Aaaah!' he let out as he stretched the stiffness out of his body. 'I needed that.'

A couple of sips of the strong black brew which Jeannie had made to perfection and he was sitting up shuffling his papers. 'Right, let's get on with it. Thanks again Jeannie.'

'That's what you pay me that miniscule amount every month for' joked Jeannie. She knew something was going on, Gary had never had to sleep during the day before like that, but her job was to keep the boss happy. So, she did that by pandering to his every need. Well, almost.

After that, Gary's day seemed to slip by with Jake barely intruding.

By five o'clock, Gary was looking forward to spending some time with Nicki and Harry and getting things back to normal.

'After all, Jake's just another client. Nothing else. You're getting things all out of proportion' he told himself 'He knows nothing. Now get on with making the Dean family fortune.'

One Hundred and Thirty One

The drive home was the usual snarl-up but it didn't bother Gary tonight. That sleep earlier had put things back in perspective.

'You have a great imagination, Gary Dean, that why you came up with the idea of The Bus and how you manage to get clients off scot-free from things they should go down for, for years. But this time you let your imagination run too far and too fast. But it's over now. So, let's enjoy this evening' he thought contently.

Frank Sinatra came on the radio singing 'Strangers in the Night' and Gary joined in; he was no Michael Buble.

By the time he reached the front door, he was back to the old Gary: footloose and carefree. He opened the door and tossed his briefcase and coat carelessly on to the chair.

'Hi babydoll!' he cried out to Nicki wherever she was. Judging by the delicious smells emanating from the kitchen, she was well on her way with the supper preparations.

'Hi, Gary!' responded Nicki, wiping her hands on her apron as she came through to the hall from the kitchen. 'How was your day?'

'Excellent, thanks, darling. What's on the menu tonight?'

'Well,' began Nicki 'there's salmon en croute accompanied with crunchy runner beans, ratatouille and new potatoes. And for sweet...'

'I know what I want for dessert...' Gary said with a glint in his eye which Nicki recognised.

'Well, I'm not sure that's on the menu tonight!' replied Nicki, teasing.

'It bloody well better be!' replied Gary in need of his conjugals.

'Hmm, we are frisky tonight' responded Nicki who now had the same glint in her own eye.

'Mum...Dad, please! Way too much information!' yelled Harry as he strode down the stairs into the hallway.

'Oh, shut up you old prude!' declared his father.

'Can we talk about something else? I'm just about to eat my supper and the thought of my own mother and father doing it. Yuk!'

'All I can say is if we hadn't, you young rascal, you wouldn't be here now. But it's thanks to your lovely mother and...'

'Enough!' said Harry with finality 'I will not be able to eat anything tonight if you carry on.'

'Alright, alright! Stop teasing the boy, Gary' said Nicki joining in the banter.

'Shame, and just when I was beginning to enjoy it' said Gary laughing and tussling Harry's hair. 'How are you, son? Had a good day?'

'Yeah, dad, not bad. And you?'

'Good, good. Managed to sort out a few things that were messing with my head. So yeah, a good day' said Gary with a sigh.

Both Nicki and Harry exchanged glances. They could see the change: he looked so much more relaxed that he had over the past few weeks.

'Cool, dad, I'm pleased. Now...what did you say was for supper, mum? I could eat a rhinoceros...'

'Harry Dean!' cried Nicki, pretending to be shocked 'We did not bring you up to repeat such coarse...!'

Before she could finish Gary and Harry both yelled together'...from the toes upwards!'

'Honestly, you two! You really are the limit.'

But they all went off to the dining room to share their meal and evening together like the old times. The evening culminating in Gary getting his just desserts...as previously requested.

One Hundred and Thirty Two

The council block where Freddie Collins lived with his parents was considered quite posh: people put their rubbish in the bins instead of all over the stairs.

So, it came as a surprise to Freddie when he left the flat the following morning for work that the lights in the corridor on the fifteenth floor where they lived, were all out.

With a 'Tsk' and thinking nothing of it, Freddie groped his way along the wall to the lift.

When he pressed to call the lift, the doors opened and for a second the light blinded him but then he saw the figure of a tall man standing inside.

'Come in Freddie, son. Come on in!' he heard in a broad Scottish voice.

In the couple of seconds it took for his eyes to adjust, his brain went from nought to sixty.

'I don't know any big guys with Scottish accents. So, who the fuck is this guy and how does he know my name?'

Freddie went to make a run for it, but was too late as four strong hands grabbed him and roughly shoved him inside. Jock released the hold button and the lift descended with Freddie and the three strangers. 'Okay, Freddie, just to let ye know, son,' began the Scotsman, whom Freddie took to be the leader 'I'm a close associate of Jake Vickers. Dae ye remember him? He's the one that blew the cop's head off his shoulders in that wee accident at the Cobham Services the other week. An' I understand he gave yerself a wee bit of a kickin'? Well, let me tell ye, he's the big softie in our partnership. So, this is the situation: Mr Vickers would like ye to do him a favour. An' he asked me tae ask ye! D'ye think ye're up for that, Freddie?'

Freddie hadn't a fucking clue what the favour was but whatever it was, it seemed rude to refuse...especially big bruisers like these three. So, Freddie nodded.

'Good son, that'll make life easier, if you catch ma drift. Okay. A couple of questions first. Dae ye take yur orders from a Mr Dean?'

Freddie took a massive gulp. His fear did not go unnoticed.

'Trust me, son. Ye don't want to get on the wrang side a' me. So, let's be friends and answer the fuckin' question. Okay?'

'Okay' replied Freddie and nodded his head in response to the question.

'Very good. Now that wisna hard, wis it?' replied Jock encouragingly.

'And when dae ye knock off tonight?' he continued.

'Half past eight.'

'Is that when ye get back tae the yard?'

'Yeah.'

'I think ye meant "Yes, Sir", didn't ye, Freddie?'

Jock always liked to remind people who they were talking to.

'Yes, sir!' replied Freddie with alacrity. He knew the consequences with guys like Jock and he had just gotten over Jake's handiwork.

'Good, son. Ye're a fast learner.'

'Now where's yur last stop and what time's it at?'

'The Cobham Services at seven thirty…' a pause and then a narrowing of the eyes from Jock provoked a '…Sir.'

'Goo...od!' said the Scotsman stretching out the 'oo!' of good. Now here's what I want ye tae dae. Or, should I say Mr Vickers would like ye tae dae.'

Freddie took the piece of paper Jock gave him, and read it for a full minute before nodding. By then the lift had arrived at the ground floor and the two minders escorted Freddie to the back seat of the Range Rover parked outside.

One Hundred and Thirty Three

Gary was sitting at the breakfast table, full of the joys of spring, summer and all the other seasons rolled into one: life was good.

His mobile buzzed. Unusual at that time of the morning; maybe a client who'd been nicked coming home from a club with a skinful needed his hand-holding services.

It was Freddie. What did he want?

'Hello?'

'Mr Dean, it's Freddie. Listen, I gotta to see you' Freddie spoke fast as if he was in a panic...which he was. 'There's trouble brewing, Mr Dean. Big trouble' he read from Jock's note. 'You'll 'ave to meet me at The Bus'. Jock, who was sitting in the front passenger seat listening, turned around quickly and threw him a look, he'd gone off script, but Freddie raised his hand as if to say 'bear with me'.

'What? What is it Freddie?' said Gary, his voice and pulse rising in tandem.

'I can't say anything, not here, Mr Dean, but we've got to meet an' talk...an' it 'as to be at The Bus. Our last stop tonight is at seven thirty at the Cobham Services. I'll make sure Bob goes for his break then. But you 'ave got to meet me there.'

Gary's brain was racing. What the fuck was going on? Just when things were starting to get back to normal. 'Are you sure this can't wait, Freddie? I mean, couldn't you come and see me at the office?'

''Course I can't come to your office, Mr Dean! That's one of your rules that I never come to your office. An' you know I can't say what it's about, Mr Dean but I'll tell you tonight.'

There was a long silence before Gary said resignedly, 'Sorry, Freddie, forgot my own rules for a second. Okay. Seven thirty it is. This'd better be important, Freddie.'

'Honest, Mr Dean, it is.'

Gary hung up.

It was going to be one helluva day.

When Freddie disconnected, Jock said 'What was that all about? Was that some kind of code?' Then the anger took hold of Jock and his voice started rising. 'Were ye warnin' him, ye wee bastard? 'Cause if ye were, yer dead meat. Believe me.'

Freddie could hardly speak; his throat seized up with nerves, choking off his air supply. He was finding it difficult to breathe.

'Please, please!' he begged hoarsely. 'That's the code for the lorry. It's...it's his code. That what he calls it in case anybody's listening.'

'It better be, son, or else yoo're in big trouble' Jock's vowels got rounder the angrier he got.

On the back seat, Freddie began to cry. Unfortunately for him, Big Jock McTavish had seen the tears, heard the pleas and was bored with the videos. 'Ye're wasting yer breath and yer waterworks, son. I've seen it all; kids, auld women, pregnant women and their husbands cryin' and it don't mean a fuckin' thing tae me or the rest of the world. So blaw yer nose and shut the fuck up, will ye? There a good wee boy!'

Turning to his driver, Frankie, he said: 'Drive us tae the yard an' drop him aff. We don't want him being late fur 'is shift.'

Looking in the front passenger seat vanity mirror at the pathetic, shivering specimen in the back seat, he tried to placate Freddie: 'Sit back and relax, son, and don't say yer uncle Jock wasn't good tae ye, givin' ye a lift to work.'

Jock then addressed the other occupant on the back seat 'Jimmy, get word to our friend that everything is set up for seven thirty at the Cobham Services tonight. He'll like the irony o' that!' and Jock guffawed at his own joke.

One Hundred and Thirty Four

It was probably the worst drive into the office he'd ever experienced. Gary nearly got out of the car twice to other drivers he was convinced had deliberately cut him up: instead, the air in the car was a deep shade of indigo.

He had three Court attendances that morning, one of them in front of that old fart, Farquar, when it was on the tip of his tongue, several times during the hearing, to tell him to shove his wig where his boyfriend had undoubtedly paid a visit the night before. Fortunately, for decency's sake, he somehow managed to resist. He lost all three cases.

The rest of the day was taking up with interminable, boring meetings and conference calls about existing cases. Gary wanted to tell them all to fuck off but professional courtesy, nothing else, stopped him.

There was only one thing occupying one of the best legal brains in the UK: this meeting with Freddie at The Bus and this so called 'Big Trouble'?

One Hundred and Thirty Five

'Our friend', got the message from a screw that Jimmy 'knew', as in, Jimmy supplied the gear for the screw's distribution network inside Wandsworth. Even after paying Jock his cut, it was still a nice little earner for Jimmy. And the screw's daughter managed to keep her pony at stables near Hyde Park Corner...among other things. Oh, and the inmates were very glad of the arrangement too.

Once he'd got the time and place, Jake waited in line to make the call. Lucky for him, it was a Freephone number so he didn't have to waste any of his precious phonecard minutes on it.

He was brief and concise as to the what, the where and the when and then disconnected. He knew they'd act on it; birds in the hand like that don't come often. And Jake had worked out that this bird was the Thanksgiving and Christmas turkey rolled into one.

He, for one, was looking forward to it being well and truly stuffed.

One Hundred and Thirty Six

Within an hour of the call being received, senior figures from all over the south London boroughs were converging on Walworth Road station for a conference. Inspector Morrison of SO19 also attended.

Chief Superintendent Moore had been put in charge of the operation due to his familiarity and experience of the recent stakeout at those Services as well as his personal acquaintance with a number of the participants. His experience from the earlier fiasco would be invaluable in not letting this one get out of hand.

At least, that was the theory.

'Gentlemen...and lady!' he barked to silence the hum of the room, acknowledging the Deputy Assistant Commissioner, Jan Banks with a nod. She'd been brought into the loop on a non-operational role; simply to oversee the proceedings.

'I would bet you didn't expect to be doing a re-run of Cobham Services again so soon' he continued.

Some of the audience gave a half-hearted laugh.

'Before we start, can we have a minute's silence to remember our colleague, Bunny Hare.'

One generous minute later, the Chief cleared his throat to signal that they would be resuming.

'Right, we do not want what happened to Bunny to happen to any of you lot...even if I do owe you money. So, be careful! Very fuckin' careful!'

The Chief remembered the presence of the DAC and said: 'Sorry, ma'am.'

The DAC acknowledged the apology with a dismissive wave: she'd heard worse and certainly used worse herself in the days when she used to get her hands dirty.

The important thing was that his attempt to ease the tension in the room had worked; shoulders loosened and necks were cracked but the room, to a man, maintained their focus.

'Gentlemen, we have received information that an alleged kingpin of London crime, someone who's apparently worked below our radar for years, is meeting a consignment of...' the Chief looked at the notes he'd received from Crimestoppers '...goods resulting from a number of robberies of late in the London area.'

'Three things.' he continued 'Firstly, I know the suspect, I've faced him in Court many times. A bit of a surprise...but nevertheless,' he said very forcibly, '...if this tip-off is correct, we could solve several serious crimes that have been committed on our watch in one stroke. And I, for one, would welcome it.'

There was a general murmur of agreement.

'Secondly, it involves the James Irvine Company. Most of you will recall that that's the company whose lorry was involved when we nicked Mr Vickers, who, at this present time I am very pleased to say, resides at Her Majesty's pleasure in Wandsworth and may he do so for a very long, 'scuse me, ma'am,' this time he apologised before he said it '... fuckin' time!'

A cheer went up around the room.

This time the DAC caught The Chief Superintendent's eye. There was no mistaking what the pursing of her lipstickless lips meant: 'Get on with it.'

'Finally,' he continued when the room had subsided, 'SO19 are involved because we haven't been told how many of them there'll be and whether they'll be carrying or not. So, we're taking no chances' he paused '...any questions?'

'The name of the suspect, Sir?' asked a PC.

'Gary Dean, member of the legal profession and representative of some of the worst scum of London...including the aforementioned Jake Vickers, by the way.'

Comments of 'Why are we not surprised that he's lawyer?' and '...let's make sure he joins his client' flew around the room.

'Settle down. Settle down. Okay, I want everyone back here and ready to go at...' he glanced at his watch '...four o'clock. The meet's due take place at seven thirty and I want everyone well in place before then. No fuck-ups this time, gentlemen, I want a nice clean collar.'

Don't you just love theory?

One Hundred and Thirty Seven

For the umpteenth time, Gary checked the time to find that, at last, the hands on his Rolex had creeped up to five o'clock.

'Thank Christ' he thought, relieved to be able to get away from the stifling atmosphere of the office and sort out this problem, whatever it was.

Gary slammed his case notes shut, stood up and announced 'Okay, folks that'll do us for today. We've got a bit of time on this one. This is one client who's not going to be going anywhere fast.'

In the room, smiles intermingled with puzzled expressions on the faces of those present.

Yes, the client was Jake Vickers who was certainly not going anywhere for a very long time. So, funny...ish. But the quizzical looks lingered because Gary was never a clock watcher. He was a great believer in sticking at it until a job was done. One of his greatest strengths was his ability to squeeze the living daylights out of the minutiae of every piece of evidence until there was nothing left of it but motes of dust floating in the air; leaving the police with no chance of being able to use it unless they'd developed a system of sticking particles of dust back together again. Not an easy thing to do.

At the beginning of big cases like this, Gary was like a dog with a selection of juicy bones; meetings like these could last well into the late evening. Hence, the collective confusion: there was still a mountain of evidence to get through.

Gary was first to the door of the conference room.

'Goodnight all! See you in the morning.'

Jaws did drop but Gary was not there to see them, he was racing to his office to collect his coat and briefcase.

He'd just stepped out of the office and was locking his door when he heard the phone in the bottom drawer of his desk ring.

'Bugger! Do I or don't I?' he thought 'There's no chance of whoever it is getting anywhere near The Bus today.'

With a sigh, he thought 'business is business' and turning the key, rushed to open the drawer. 'Funny…' he thought as he looked at the display panel of the phone '…number withheld. Who could it be?'

'Hello?' he answered, suspicion dripping off each syllable.

'It's me' the voice announced.

Gary froze. He knew the voice; knew it only too well. It could only mean one thing; things were just about to get worse.

'It's gonna be double the usual fee' stated the voice.

'Double?' queried Gary, thinking he'd misheard. The fee was already exorbitant.

'Trust me' the voice said.

'Call me back in five' said Gary and the connection was broken.

Gary dialled a number in Liechtenstein and transferred the amount requested by the owner of the voice to an account held in the same branch as Gary's.

Gary had never questioned the owner of the voice's information: it was always solid and worth every penny…so far. So, when he said double, Gary's hesitation was only momentary.

He hung up the phone and mentally commanded it to ring again.

'Ring you bastard. Ring!'

But the owner of the voice was busy confirming receipt of payment into his own account before calling again.

When it finally rung, Gary had it in his hand before the first ring had finished.

'Yes?'

The voice made two statements: 'It's a trap' followed by 'They'll be waiting for you tonight' and hung up leaving Gary with a dial tone in his ear.

Gary flopped into his chair.

'A trap?' he repeated to himself in disbelief. Most people would probably give up at that point then and hand themselves into the police. Not Gary Dean.

He stood up, removed his coat, pressed the 'Do Not Disturb' button on his internal phone, locked his door and walked back again to his desk.

By the time he sat down, he'd ditched the fear and panic.

'What to do?' he thought as he began tapping the pencil he'd unconsciously picked up.

He dismissed the 'who shopped me?' scenario. It would take up too much of his limited thinking time and he'd find out eventually anyway.

'If I don't show and do a runner, they'll put out an APB on me.'

Option one dismissed.

The next one didn't appeal much either.

'If they catch me anywhere near The Bus and they discover what's on it, I am well and truly fuckin' sunk. I'll either spend the next forty years in solitary or Nicki will look stunning in black.'

Gary knew the sort of people he dealt with. With them, you fuck up; you fuck off...permanently.

Option two gone.

Fortunately, Gary Dean had an enormous talent for thinking outside of boxes and prison cells. Hence, the idea of The Bus, together with a bunch of grateful criminals who, collectively, should have been serving prison sentences running into hundreds of years instead of being at liberty to roam the streets of London and ply their various nefarious trades.

'So, what's left?' thought the man who knew there was an answer to every problem so long as you left your mind open to the universe. 'It's there...but what the bloody hell is it?'

As he sat listening to the clicking of his pencil, he heard another noise... it was coming from the outer office.

'What's that?' he thought curiously.

It was that laughter...again. The carefree sound of people who'd put their worries on hold temporarily. It reminded Gary of something which in turn made him think of something else. And then, Mr Gary Dean, lawyer to the criminally-inclined, came up with the solution. A solution so bold and simple that a lesser man would never have considered it; could not even have contemplated it. But, could he really pull it off?

Another five minutes of sifting through the ramifications and his mind was made up.

'Not perfect but in the circumstances and all things considered, definitely my best option.'

He took out his mobile, scrolled through his contacts and chose a number, rang it and waited. It answered on the second ring.

A nervous voice answered.

'Hello?'

'I need you to do something for me.'

And suddenly everything changed.

One Hundred and Thirty Eight

Oh, the bloody rush hour traffic was busy. In London, all roads seemed to lead to the M25 and they were all jammed with commuters desperate to get home.

'Never mind,' thought Gary 'more thinking time' He called Nicki to tell her he'd be late so '...don't wait up.'

If only she knew.

There were a couple of incidents but unlike earlier in the day, Gary just let them float over his troubled head.

He checked the time on the dash: 6.47

'Less than 40 minutes before the whole world turns upside down. Funny how things pan out' mused Gary the pragmatist. 'One minute you're running your own successful practice, topping up your pension fund on the side for your early retirement and the next...hmm.'

The thought didn't trouble him. Gary Dean was a fighter, a real fighter; dirty if need be, but at the end of the day, he dealt with whatever the situation was as it presented itself and got on with it.

'What will be, will be' he concluded.

Waiting for the lights on the junction of East Street to change, he looked out of the window and saw a young panhandler, no more than twenty-five, making a beeline for the car. It was happening more and more in London... and they were getting younger. They'd take one look at the Maserati and think 'Got to be worth a punt. Whoever's driving that ''as got to 'ave a few quid.'

'Evenin' boss' the young, scruffy homeless guy said to Gary giving him his most engaging smile. 'Any chance?' he asked rattling his paper cup of coins in Gary's direction.

Gary reached over to the container where he kept his spare change and then an idea came to him.

''How d'you fancy makin' a hundred quid?' Gary asked.

'Sorry, boss, I'm not that way inclined' replied the young man almost apologetically. He'd lost everything for the sake of the drugs that blotted out the bad things that had happened to him in his childhood but he'd not stooped to selling his body...yet.

'No, you prat, I don't mean that. I mean earn it legitimately' said Gary, mildly amused that if he was 'one of them' that this kid thought he was of an age where he'd have to pay for it. Cheek! 'What do I 'ave to do?' enquired the homeless guy suspiciously.

'Not a lot. Jump in and I'll tell you on the way.'

He didn't need a second invitation; he was opening the passenger door before you could say: 'Spare any change?'

'Okay,' said Gary as the car moved off 'what's your name?'

'Er, John' replied the young guy hesitantly. He wasn't going to give his real name to this stranger...just in case. He'd heard all kinds of stories about the DSS people trying to reduce your benefit because you made a few quid begging. 'Although,' he thought 'I don't suppose many of them drive Maseratis. But you can never be too careful.'

'Yeah, whatever' said Gary, keeping his eyes on the road but making it clear that he didn't for one minute believe that was his name.

'Here's what I want you to do...'

In less than two minutes Gary had told him.

'What? That's all? Nothin' else?' asked the guy who'd learned to be suspicious of gift horses and men in Maseratis.

Another idea came to Gary. There was nothing like being boxed into a corner for Gary Dean to come out fighting and thinking.

The next time they stopped Gary scribbled an address on a piece of paper and handed it to John.

'And if you deliver what I give you to that address, tell them that Gary sent you and that they've got to give you another hundred quid. What d'you think?'

'If you're for real, gov, I think I've died an' gone to the big crack 'ouse in the sky!'

'Hopefully, not for a long time yet, John' And as an afterthought he added: 'For either of us.'

As the clock on the dash showed twenty past seven, the car pulled into the Services.

'Do me a favour will you, John? Just slide down nice and low on the seat.'

Before driving into the lorry park, Gary drove onto the garage forecourt and filled up; they were great cars but they were gas guzzlers.

One Hundred and Thirty Nine

The car was clocked by a number of police teams who were doted around the perimeter in unmarked cars. The Chief Superintendent and Sergeant Wallis, on top of the roof as before, were scanning the lorry park using night binoculars when the sighting was reported.

'Legal Eagle' the code name they had devised for Gary '...has landed on his perch.'

'Everybody to your places and stay there. No-one moves in until I say so' announced the Chief over the walkie-talkie.

Unseen by the watchers, Gary stopped in the shadow of the very trees where Jake Vickers had nearly escaped. Thirty seconds earlier, he'd passed the scorch marks on the road where the lorry had collided with the police cordon. The area had minimal lighting, so at that time of night nothing of the inferno could be seen and anyway; it really wasn't a part of the Services where people would be out walking.

No-one, that is, except a homeless guy with the made-up name of John trying to earn an easy hundred quid: a guy who'd been told where to find a certain lorry with a certain name on the side. Gary kept the engine running as John slipped out to find the lorry.

'What's he doing?' the voice of Chief Superintendent Moore came over the mike, clearly getting agitated. 'Anyone see him?'

'Negative, Sir' reported all of the unmarked cars. It hadn't occurred to anyone that Gary would stop before entering the parking area.

'This is all we fuckin' need, Jim' he said to Sergeant Wallis.

'We just have to wait, Sir. We can't go in yet. At the moment, he's just another member of the public. He hasn't committed any crime.'

'I know, Jim. I know. It's just memories of the last time, you know' replied the Chief as a worm of failure wriggled down his backbone.

Jim Wallis hesitantly put his hand on his boss' shoulder, an uncommon action on his part; he wasn't a touchy-feely sort of guy but since Spain, an unspoken bond of sort of friendship had formed between the two of them.

'Thanks, Jim' said the Chief, feeling reassured that he wasn't alone.

'We'll get there, Sir.'

'Let's hope so, Jim.'

Five minutes later, John reappeared at the passenger door.

'Did you get it?' asked Gary as he got in. Gary could feel the adrenalin beginning to pump through his body.

'Yeah. And I told him what you told me to tell him.'

'Good. Well, give it to me and here's your hundred quid.'

John handed it to Gary and his eyes lit up as he checked the five twenties. How easy was that?

'Okay, what we're going to do now is drive up to the public parking area and when we get out, I'll give you the keys to this car. I want you to deliver them to the address I gave to you. Got it? When you deliver them, as I said before, just say Gary told you that you were to be given a hundred pounds for your trouble and tell them where the car's parked. Have you got that? And whatever you do, do not even think of trying to nick this motor because I will have your fuckin' bollocks removed with a blunt blade. Do I make myself clear? Have you got that?'

'Sure, boss. No problem. Couldn't afford the petrol anyway' replied John trying to laugh it off nervously.

'Then my friend, we have a deal! Let go.'

Gary chose a space near a clump of trees in the public parking area that shaded the passenger side door. The police might or might not see John getting out but he hadn't done anything, had he? John would be alright, Gary decided.

Gary cut the engine and turned the internal light switch off so that when he opened the door it wouldn't light up the interior. He handed the keys to John.

'Press that button when we get out to lock the car and...spend the money wisely, son.'

Suddenly, Gary was on his own walking towards the lorry park and the craziest stunt he would ever pull in his entire life.

One Hundred and Forty

'Hindsight is a truly wonderful device' thought Chief Superintendent Moore wistfully.

Looking back on the events which unfolded that evening, it was pointed out to him that his team had all been concentrating on the mark, Gary. No-one had been watching the lorry. But then again, why would they? Gary was their man.

Which is why they hadn't see John approaching the lorry.

Freddie heard the footsteps approaching.

'Is 'at you, Mr Dean?' he called out.

'No, but he sent me. Are you Freddie?'

In the darkness Freddie nodded then realised that the guy couldn't really see him so he said 'Yeah.'

'He told me to collect the keys from you and to tell you to get in the cab and wait for 'im.'

'How do I know you 'aint up to no good?' asked Freddie suspiciously.

'He said you might say somethin' like that, so I was told to tell you to "Wait on The Bus". Does that make sense?'

'Yeah' replied Freddie, relieved. 'Here take these.'

He handed over the keys and climbed into the cab to wait for...he realised then that he didn't know what he was waiting for.

He settled back and stared out into the night. Ahead of him, through the smattering of scattered cars and vans, he could see the Services building, all lit up. For a minute or so he was absorbed, watching the matchstick-like figures to-ing and fro-ing inside. It looked to Freddie like the people on the first floor were walking on air and should be falling on the heads of the people down below. Suddenly, in his imagination, it happened. He could see the people on the first floor losing their balance and falling on to the heads of the people below. He laughed at that.

'You are such a tit, Freddie' he said out loud and laughed again.

In the cafeteria, he watched the few customers that were around at that time of night, queuing up at the till to pay for their trays of food. All in all, a scene that he'd watched many times before.

A movement at the top of his vision level caught his eye. It was a sudden, urgent sort of movement against the dark clouds floating above the bright lights of the building. He assumed it was a bird perched on top of the building waiting to swoop for its supper; something he'd watched with amazement many times.

However, when it moved again, he could see that it was too big for a bird. It was a man...or woman, dressed in dark clothing. It didn't click at first what he was watching until he saw that there were others in similar dark clothing moving around. Only then did it dawn on him.

'Not again' he pleaded despairingly. 'Please, not again!'

But as he watched, some of them began moving away from the front of the building. Suddenly he caught a flash; it looked like...a camera...no... it was the light of the building reflecting off glass. Binoculars! Someone was using binoculars and the light had caught them when the person using them had moved them to look at something else!

'Oh shit! It's a replay of a few weeks ago. The police are here and we've got enough knocked off stuff in this truck to put us away for years.'

His hand instinctively reached for the door handle when the driver's door suddenly flew opened. It was Mr Dean.

'Mr Dean, oh God, Mr Dean, the police are here. We've gotta get out of here. Quick!'

The panic in Freddie's voice served only to increase Gary's composure. Although his adrenalin was pumping the blood around his body and brain like a storm drain at full flow, he was in complete control. His thoughts were as clear as a cloudless blue sky...and just as sharp.

'That's precisely what I intend to do, Freddie! Fancy a trip to...' he said as he placed a purchase he'd made earlier on the floor.

One Hundred and Forty One

'He's just entered the cab of the lorry, Sir. What should we do? Do you want us to go in?'

The voice belonged to Inspector Morrison of SO19.

'Jim,' said the Chief to his sergeant 'I think we should wait. It's too early. There could be others arriving any minute. What d'you think? Do we go in now? Or should we wait to see who else is coming to the party?'

'It's your call, Sir. Maybe you're right: we should wait. Then we can nab 'em all at once.'

'Negative' the Chief announced into the mike 'We'll wait to see who else is coming. It'd be a shame to break it up before the party got started. So, everyone hold your positions' he commanded.

'...the seaside!' said Gary in the cab to Freddie.

Without waiting for an answer, Gary turned the key in the ignition; the key which Gary had instructed Freddie to have ready when he called him from the office. The same key which John had picked up from Freddie not five minutes earlier.

'It's time to do it!' yelled Gary as the engine roared into life.

The Chief jumped at the noise 'What's that?' he said furrowing his brow, trying to place the sound.

'Jesus Christ, the lorry's moving' shouted Jim Wallis whose binoculars were trained on the vehicle.

'What?' screamed Chief Superintendent Moore as he wrenched the binoculars out of his sergeant's hands 'Let me see that.'

He could hear agitated voices over the radio.

'Do you want us to move in, over?'

He opened his mouth to speak and stopped.

'Wait a minute, there's something not right here, Jim. He still hasn't committed any crime, has he? If we go in now, we've got nothing.'

The sergeant nodded reluctantly.

'Legal Eagle is heading for the exit. What do you want us to do, Sir?'

Anyone listening could hear the strain in the 'Sir'. Replace the 'Sir' with 'for fuck's sake!' and that would've been closer to what the voice was trying to get across.

'Maybe they're taking the lorry to a meet somewhere else?' said the Chief hesitantly.

'Hmm...don't know. I don't think you have a choice, Sir. I think you need to move in and stop him getting away right now.'

The sergeant had realised something which he was not quite sure his superior was aware of; every second they delayed they came closer to losing control of the situation. Here in the lorry park at least they were in control. Elsewhere, who knows?

But still his boss hesitated.

Finally, he said into his wrist mike 'Those of you who are not yet in cars...get moving. I want everyone following that lorry...but keep your distance. I do not want Legal Eagle to know we're there. I want two at the front and the rest of you will be shadowing from behind. No blue lights. Not yet. Now move out! Just keep him in sight and see where he's going.'

For a few seconds longer, Jim Wallis kept the night binoculars trained on the lorry as it slowed down to take the bend into the exit slip road where Jake had abandoned the juggernaut that had caused such mayhem.

Two unmarked vehicles were already tucked in behind the truck. Surely it would have been better to block off the exit? Stop this before things started to get out of control?

'I hope the boss knows what he's doing' thought the sergeant as he dashed for the stairs.

As they rushed down the stairs to the waiting car, the Chief called up to his sergeant who was following him 'Jim, get on the blower and get a chopper down here. I think we're gonna need it!'

'You wouldn't have needed it if you'd stopped things a few minutes ago, guv' thought Jim Wallis. 'What were you thinking about? It would've been all over by now.'

Within minutes of the call being received, a police air support helicopter took off from Battersea heliport and ten minutes later joined the chase.

One Hundred and Forty Two

'Where's he goin'?' asked the Chief 'That's what I want to know.'

'It could be anywhere' was Jim Wallis' reply. 'We're on the M25 goin' towards Dartford with a million turn offs before and after it. But why is he driving? I'm gettin' a bad feeling about this, guv.'

'Yeah, yeah alright, Jim. That hindsight malarkey's a marvellous thing, you know' said the Chief getting irritated.

Suddenly, the lorry snaked across into the middle lane three or four times. In and out. In and out.

Half a dozen cars that were bombing along at 80-90 mph in adjacent lanes had to swerve to avoid it. Hands were held on horns long after they'd gone passed the truck.

Inside the cab, Gary was laughing.

'You are so funny, Freddie' he chuckled.

'What's so funny about asking if you're qualified to drive an HGV, Mr Dean?' asked Freddie who was trying not to show that he was shitting himself.

Driving a weapon of mass destruction like that and swerving in and out of other lanes for a bit of fun smacked of someone who'd lost the plot, at least, a little bit, to Freddie's mind. To take his mind off the situation or to concentrate Gary's, he wasn't sure which, Freddie asked 'What are your plans, Mr Dean?'

'D'you know what, Freddie, just for tonight, will you call me Gary? Please?'

'Okay, so what are your plans, Gary?'

'Now that would be telling, Freddie. But one thing I can tell you is that you are gonna be okay. Not only okay but you'll get a big fat bonus this month 'cause I'm not sure you'll be acting as gatekeeper for me much longer. But one thing I will guarantee; you will be alright' Gary laughed again, almost maniacally.

'Thanks for that, Mr Dean.'

'Gary.'

'Sorry...Gary' Freddie corrected himself and decided that he might as well relax because he was there and there wasn't a lot he could do about it and anyway the boss had promised he'd be okay and that he'd be getting a lovely big bonus. So, everything was cool. Wasn't it?

In the meantime, Freddie wasn't the only one with loose bowels. After Gary's lane violations, there was a funny smell in all three pursuit cars. It had become apparent that a very large dollop of you-know-what was about to hit the fan and land in the Chief's lap. But no-one bothered to mention it...yet.

'What the fuck's he doing?' yelled the Chief as the lorry snaked across into the adjoining lane to the sound of blaring car horns.

'Sir...don't you think we should stop this now?' Jim Wallis offered quietly.

Before he could answer, the radio squawked.

'Chief Superintendent Moore, this is Deputy Assistant Commissioner Banks. I've just heard a report from the air support team that the lorry you're following is swerving across lanes on the motorway. Is this correct? Over.'

'Oh, fuck' thought the man in charge '...this is where I get it.'

'Chief Superintendent Moore here, ma'am...that report is correct.'

'Then what are you thinking about, Chief Superintendent? We can't have members of the public's lives being put in danger! You need to take immediate action. Do I make myself clear?'

'Very clear, ma'am! Over and out.'

He picked up the radio in the car and announced 'Attention all vehicles in pursuit of Legal Eagle, we do not have time to call in marked cars to bring him to a halt so we'll have to do it ourselves. So, hit the lights. I repeat...hit the lights!'

Turning to his own driver he said 'And that includes us, son. So, move it!'

Gary heard the sirens first then looked in his side view mirror to see three cars in different lanes, their blue lights flashing and sirens blaring, racing to catch up with him. Ahead he saw two other unmarked cars with their blue lights flashing, beginning to slow down: they were going to box him in...or try to. They seemed to forget that he was driving one motherfucker of a truck. He could crush all of them as easily as an empty fag packet.

'Good job we're nearly there, Freddie!' he exclaimed.

'Where, Gary?'

'Watch' was the reply.

The hill they were driving down at that point was very, very steep, the road signs overhead whizzing passed before they could even read them but Gary wasn't worried, he done this journey a thousand times. He could almost do it with his eyes closed although probably not a good idea in a forty-foot truck.

The speedometer showed sixty but as they freewheeled downhill, it was probably more like seventy or eighty. With forty-odd tons of wrecking machine, the police pulled back; they weren't going to try anything for now, they'd hold fire until they could stop him safely.

'Fine' thought Gary. 'Perfect timing.'

By the time they reached the bottom of the hill he saw that the three cars at the rear were closing in again: they were going to make another attempt.

'Too late, my lovelies' cried Gary suddenly, frightening the shit out of Freddie again 'Just too late!'

What he was talking about became clear to Freddie as the filter lane for Croydon and Brighton appeared.

'Watch this, Freddie' said Gary who was bouncing up and down on the driver's seat; he really was getting off on the whole thing.

Gary watched the two cars in front intently.

'Get a move on. Come on!' he called out.

'Come on what?' asked Freddie completely confused.

'I want the two in front to get past the turn off then I only have to deal with these prats at the back.'

Freddie sat back in silence. He still didn't have a clue what Gary was going on about.

There were two filter lanes at the junction. Gary sailed past the first. It looked like he was driving on towards Dartford until, at the last possible moment; he veered off onto the outer chevrons of the second filter lane. He resisted the temptation to indicate.

The swerve was so violent that a couple of wheels lifted on the driver's side.

For one brief moment Freddie held his breath: it was touch and go as to whether the lorry would go over but it only heightened the buzz for Gary.

'This is better than Formula One' he declared. Freddie could see that glazed, slightly mad, look in Gary's eyes; the sort he saw in a lot of his pals when they went out clubbing together and they'd taken "something".

Because of the suddenness of his actions, the pursuit cars in the two outside lanes could only look on in frustration; there wasn't enough space or time to reach the slip road without serious risk to the other road users. They sailed past the slip road, much to the frustration of their Chief Superintendent.

'Yeah!' shouted Gary punching the air 'Even better. Only three of them to deal with now.'

Freddie looked in his side view mirror to see the three blue lights in close pursuit.

'Now then...' said Gary deep in concentration, '...let's see if we can get rid of anybody else.'

Freddie looked at the speedo and decided to keep schtum, a word from him at that point could have caused Gary to lose his concentration and at that speed, a split second's loss of concentration in a huge artic like that, could be disastrous.

The decision to keep quiet didn't last long. They were driving along the middle of the chevrons when suddenly the barrier was only meters ahead of them.

'Ga..r..r...r..y!' he yelled, instinctively arching his back as he waited for the impact.

'Don't worry, Freddie. I know what I'm doing but they don't. Let's see what they do, eh?'

To the left: the slip road to Croydon. To the right: Brighton. But which way was he going? In the end, the Chief's car sat in the middle of the chevrons on Gary's tail while the other two took a lane each. Croydon lost.

Gary saw the faces of the two plainclothes policemen as they sailed past. He waved to them.

'Bye, boys! Enjoy Croydon! Me and your pals are off to see the bright lights of Brighton.'

As he came around the next steep bend, one lane closed before it joined the M23 to Brighton. Once on the road he straddled the two lanes so that they couldn't overtake.

All the time, Gary's eyes flitted between the road ahead and the two cars in pursuit. If it looked like they were going to try to overtake, he would start snaking; that kept them where they belonged; at the rear...where he could see them.

One Hundred and Forty Three

The helicopter, in the meantime, was providing commentary from the sky on the situation.

The pilot called in the latest twist, alerting headquarters and DAC Banks of the temporary loss of the three pursuit vehicles.

'What a bloody mess!' the DAC bawled for all and sundry in the control room to hear: she was past caring about the protocol of the situation.

'Chief Superintendent Moore, can you please tell me what's happening on the ground?' she demanded.

'Not good, ma'am' observed the Chief. 'He's in front and blocking us every time we try to pass. I think we should fall back and wait to see what develops...unless you have any suggestions, ma'am?'

The DAC looked around the room at the people present; none of them could look her in the eye but they all had sneaky little grins and smirks spread across their ugly mugs. All of them.

'I know what you're thinking' she thought as she scanned those faces '...and believe me I'd like to say it to him loud and clear! But I bloody well can't.'

Instead she turned back to the console and said:

'We've already put a call through to Sussex police for assistance but they have their own major incident they're dealing with, so I'm afraid you're on your own.'

Jim Wallis looked at his Chief Superintendent when the DAC uttered those words: '...their own major incident.'

'Jesus Christ, Pete, what were you thinking about back there in the car park? This could all have been over by now and the bastard nicked' he thought.

'I think it's fair to say I've made a complete fuck-up on this one, Jim' Pete Moore announced.

'It's not over yet, Sir.'

'Not until the fat lady sings, I believe is the expression, Jim' replied the Chief '...and in this case, I think the fat lady has DAC insignia on her shoulders.'

The silence was palpable in the car.

You might think certain things about your superior officers but you did not voice them in front of the lower ranks.

Two became four again after the other two cars, which they'd lost at Junction 7, put their respective size elevens to the floor and came tearing down the M23 to join the chase.

One Hundred and Forty Four

All the time, Gary kept one eye ahead watching for late commuters making their way back to the seaside town, calculating their speed and when it would be safe to overtake. The other eye dealt with the riffraff who insisted on following him.

'They must be bursting to know where we're going' thought Gary 'But they'll just have to bloody well wait. Thank God it wasn't the weekend otherwise traffic would've been at a standstill' thought the lawyer-turned-HGV-driver.

The exit to and from Gatwick passed like a blur as they raced on towards their final destination '...wherever that is' thought Freddie seeing as Gary wasn't saying.

'I hope your mum didn't have your tea waiting for you, Freddie. It'll be gettin' cold by now!' joked Gary.

Freddie looked at his watch: 8.15pm.

'Any idea how long it's gonna be?' he asked.

''Bout another twenty minutes. Then, Freddie, all will be revealed or is that exposed?' Gary roared with laughter at his own private joke; the punchline known only to him.

'I don't suppose there's any point in asking what you mean?'

'You're right, Freddie! None at all. Just be patient.'

They flew past the stone pillars, known as 'Pylons' which were there to welcome one and all to Brighton since 1928.

'I'm not so sure they'd be extending a welcome to yours truly if they knew what I had in mind. Hmm, now we come to the tricky bit' thought Gary. 'Gettin' through Brighton and all those fuckin' traffic lights is not gonna be easy. But then; did I ever think it was gonna be? God, people dream about doing things like this and here I am actually doing it! I might as well enjoy it!' he thought light-heartedly as he performed a quick snakelike movement to remind the police behind who was in charge. He hadn't felt this free for years.

He slowed right down to manoeuvre the Mill Road roundabout intending to go straight across. As he pulled onto the roundabout he saw it: a marked police BMW blocking the entry to London Road. He continued going around the roundabout with the lead car on his tail and the three others close behind.

'Shit!' yelled Gary 'What the fuck do I do now?'

Ten minutes earlier, Sussex police had called it in to say that they could spare one car and that they would position it to block off the main road into suburban Brighton. That would mean that the only choice he'd have was to go back on to the motorway thereby reducing the danger to the public.

Sergeant Wallis, in the car behind, was whooping, prematurely really, for an officer with his experience.

'We've got him now, Sir!' he announced with glee to his superior.

'You should know by now boys,' said 'Legal Eagle' thinking out loud as his brain cells pinged off one another '...try to box Gary Dean in and he'll come out fighting.'

In the five seconds that it took to negotiate the roundabout again, Gary knew what he had to do.

He came around again to the point where he'd first spotted the police car except this time, completely unexpected by those following, he put his foot down as he came off the final bend. He hit the police car with such a crunching impact that it attached itself to the front of the truck for twenty yards before finally being discarded by the side of the road; a heap of crumpled, useless metal, petrol spilling everywhere.

'Damn! Better get onto the local Fire Service, Jim, and get them down to clear up this mess' was all the Chief could say despondently.

Gary put his foot down, determined not to be caught out like that again. 'Bastards!' he screamed over the roar of the engine.

'Alright, Freddie?' asked Gary cheerfully as his Mr Nasty persona reverted back to Mr Nice.

Freddie sat in numb silence at his side, white with fear.

'Sure, Mr Dean' he finally managed to mumble.

'It's Gary tonight, Freddie. Remember?'

'Yeah' replied Freddie robotically.

'You sure you're alright?'

'Yeah, Gary.'

Gary let it rest there. He knew Freddie was still recovering from his encounter with Mr Vickers and probably didn't need to be involved in another life-threatening situation like this so quickly. 'But hey-ho, Life is one motherfuckin' bitch and you really do have to grab her by the balls and get on with it!' thought Gary. 'Just look what's happening to mine.'

Two minutes later the next obstacle appeared in Gary's destructive path in the shape of traffic lights; the lights at the junction of London Road and Preston Drove...they were at red...and they weren't changing. Gary slowed down to fifty miles an hour but he clearly had no intentions of stopping.

Out of the corner of his eye, to the left, he saw a Renault Clio belting down the steep hill to do a right turn...right into the path of the lorry. By the time the driver realised that the fucking great truck on the main road was not gonna be stopping, he hit the brakes so hard that they locked and he skidded into the path of the oncoming lorry.

Gary could see the blood draining from the face of the young guy driving it, abject terror in his eyes.

'Shouldn't be driving so fast, you idiot!' Gary yelled, unheard by the other driver.

'I'm a gonner!' thought the eighteen-year-old driver who'd passed his test not two weeks earlier and, true to form, believed that after you've passed your test you can drive like a Formula One schmuck on suburban roads and get away with it.

Wrong.

But lucky for him, some of his ancestors must have come over on the boat from the Emerald Isles because he bounced off the near side fender: he didn't even sustain a scratch. His ten-year-old car wasn't quite so lucky but then it was French...not Irish.

'That's not bad' thought Gary 'Two write-offs already. I wonder how many more before we get to where we're going?'

The answer was none but Gary didn't know that.

The Chief Superintendent had asked the DAC to 'have a word' with Sussex Constabulary and put in a request for a couple of bikes to clear the traffic up ahead when he realised that the lorry was stopping for no-one and nothing. The local constabulary had kindly obliged.

So, Gary had a free run all the way to the roundabout at Brighton's famous pier, still all lit up and looking as good as ever. But he didn't have time to admire the magnificent example of Victorian craftsmanship that it was; he was too intent on getting the job finished. And he was close. Very close.

Within minutes of turning left along Marine Parade with his entourage, which, by then, had grown to six with the end of the Sussex Constabulary's own major incident, Gary caught sight of the landmark he'd been looking for: Roedean School.

'You'll be pleased to know that we're two minutes away from our final destination, Freddie.'

There was no response: Freddie was either in a catatonic state or so fucked off at his luck that he no longer cared whether he lived or died. Either way, for him, it was simply a question of how deep the shit was that he was in. He was regularly, as the Geordies say 'plodging in the clarts'; at the moment, it felt as if it was creeping up his chin. Soon, he'd be eating it...not a welcome prospect.

Finally, Gary slowed down; he'd seen the small side road leading to the two flimsy wire gates which Harry, his son, had pointed out what seemed like a lifetime ago.

Gary turned into the narrow lane.

The radio conversation in the six squad cars behind went ballistic.

'Where's he going?' asked a demented Chief Superintendent Moore 'We're in the middle of no-fucking-where' he declared.

'Chief Superintendent Moore! May I remind you that you are on an open channel?' the DAC squawked across the airwaves.

'Sorry, ma'am. Just expressing myself in the vernacular.'

'So I understand, Chief Superintendent, but please don't.'

'For tuppence, I'd wring your scrawny neck, you fuckin' old cow! Why don't you get a proper job?' thought the furious Chief Superintendent.

'Okay, does anyone know where we are? No smart comments, please.'

One of the local team replied:

'Sir, Sergeant Billy Hunter here. From what I remember, it's a small boat repair yard. They've been working on the place for months, Sir.'

'Thanks for that, Sergeant. Anyone got any ideas as to why he's here? Over.'

Silence.

'Thank you for that, gentlemen' the Chief added sarcastically 'Sergeant Hunter, could he be meeting a boat here? I mean, do you get smugglers landing stuff along this part of the coastline? Over.'

'No, Sir. If they were going to land drugs or contraband, they wouldn't be thinking of doing it here. Too busy.'

'Thanks again, Sergeant.'

He turned to Jim Wallis 'What's he up to, Jim?' The Chief made a decision. He'd allowed this to go on long enough. 'Er, Jim, can you hand me that megaphone, please?'

The Chief Superintendent got out of the car and flicked the switch of the megaphone to the 'on' position.

'This is the police. Get out of your vehicle and lie face down on the ground with your hands behind your head.'

The other officers tumbled out of their squad cars: this was it...the end. There was no place else to go. But why here? Was he trying to make a point? Was he drawing the heat/attention from someone/somewhere else? The team had gathered from the radio chatter that he was indeed a high-flying London lawyer. So, what did someone in his position think he was doing driving a juggernaut around the place in such a dangerous manner? But then again, nothing surprised these guys: they'd seen it all...and more.

It just didn't make sense.

Until, that is, Gary heard Superintendent Moore's voice floating on the high wind of the storm that was blowing. It was the official tone in his voice which brought him back to the here and now, to the situation he was in, to...the final nail of realisation in The Bus' coffin. That's when it all made sense.

A very calm Gary Dean turned to Freddie and put the poor sod out of his misery, saying:

'Okay, Freddie. End of the road! I just need you to do one more thing for me and then I want you to walk back to the police and tell them I kidnapped you or forced you to come with me. Whatever you think they'll believe.'

He told Freddie what he wanted.

'But Mr Dean...' began Freddie.

Gary looked in the side view mirror and could see the police in their high visibility jackets edging slowly down the rough track towards the lorry.

There was one small street light in the side road giving off a pathetic, feeble glow and there were dark clouds above, so nothing for the light to bounce off. With such poor visibility, the police could probably have crept up on the lorry but 'God Bless the British bobby's adherence to the rules' thought Gary 'You could see them coming a mile off in dense impenetrable fog in those jackets!'

'Freddie, I don't have time to argue, son, the police are on their way down the hill.'

Freddie glanced in the mirror on his side; Gary was right...two more minutes and they'd be there.

'You sure, Mr Dean?'

'You've forgotten, Freddie; it's Gary tonight.'

'Sorry, Gary...'

'Now fuck off you little twat and do as I say or you won't get that bonus I promised you!'

Freddie didn't need telling again. He swung the door open, jumped down and moved quickly to the back of the lorry.

That stopped the police in their tracks for a few precious moments. Even with the meagre lighting they could see some kind of movement.

Maybe they were going to surrender after all.

'Course they were.

Chief Superintendent Moore switched the megaphone setting to 'on' again.

'Lie face down on the ground with your hands behind your head. Now!' he commanded.

Instead of lying down, Freddie turned suddenly as he reached the rear of the lorry and deftly opened the back doors, letting them swing wide.

'What was that?' asked the Chief squinting to see what was going on. He heard two bangs; it was the doors hitting the side of the lorry, but with the sound of the waves crashing against the sea wall, he wasn't exactly sure where the noise had come from.

'Don't know, Sir' replied Jim Wallis squinting himself to try to make out what the darkened figure was doing. In the cab, Gary, who'd been watching in his side view mirror, saw the doors swing open; that was his cue.

He quickly opened the driver's door and picked up the purchase he'd made earlier.

The police were busy concentrating on Freddie; just what Gary wanted.

When he reached the open doors at the back of the lorry, he unscrewed the cap of the container he'd purchased earlier and splashed its contents inside.

One Hundred and Forty Five

As was their ritual for the last ten years, retired couple, Gertrude and Siegfried were walking Dolly, their Daschund, along Telscombe Cliffs.

Once Dolly has done her 'duty', they would all turn back and make for home where the Horlicks and sugar were already in the cups waiting for the hot milk to be poured. Half-read books lay by their respective sides of the bed. Within half an hour of reading, the Horlicks would work its magic; time for lights out.

Tonight, the air was bracing and the waves were crashing noisily onto the rocks below, the sky above heavy with dark cloud.

'Looks like it's going to come down any minute, darling' offered Siegfried.

'You could be right, darling' replied Gertrude. They very seldom addressed each other by their first names, which they didn't like.

'You're getting good at getting the conundrum' said Siegfried, referring to one of their great pleasures, Countdown.

'Not bad' replied Gertrude modestly 'And what about you getting that nine-letter word...'

She stopped mid-sentence, she'd just spotted...something that looked out of place.

'What's that?' she cried as Dolly started yapping: she knew something wasn't right too.

They both squinted, looking towards the object which was about half a mile away.

'Goodness me!' exclaimed Siegfried 'It looks like...like...a lorry. But what's it doing there?'

They knew the man who owned the small pier which the lorry appeared to be stopped on.

'Surely John's not having a delivery at this hour of the day?' asked Gertrude.

'And look! There are other lights there...behind it' said Siegfried excitedly, pointing to the area behind the lorry. 'Can you see them? Cars, I think. Are those blue lights flashing? What is going on?'

From that distance, the outline of the lorry was clearly lit up against the blackness of the sky by several bands of lights wrapped around its trailer.

Seconds later, the scene erupted.

'What in God's name...' cried Siegfried over the noise of the waves as the two of them stood rooted to the spot when the sky suddenly lit up.

One Hundred and Forty Six

Gary had turned his purchase upside down and shaken it, making sure that it was empty before tossing it into the interior of the lorry. He pulled out his gold Dunhill lighter, lit it, and threw it into the back of the trailer.

There was a 'whoosh' before the flames spread along the rivulets of petrol deep into the recesses in the lorry where the liquid had seeped. The fire took quickly.

It wasn't only Gertrude and Siegfried who were dumbstruck. A hundred yards away, the police were in complete disarray; nobody had a clue what was going on and that included Freddie.

But Gary wasn't finished yet.

He rushed back to the cabin and revved up the idling engine, releasing the air brakes which gave a great belch of hissing like a giant cobra about to pounce on its victim. Suddenly the juggernaut jumped forward, racing towards the wire gates.

Gertrude and Siegfried stood speechless, totally unaware of Dolly's persisting yapping as the long dark bulk of the juggernaut, flames belching out of its rear, raced towards the wire gates.

As always, Chief Superintendent Moore did not disappoint. His stock phrase for situations like this flew out of his mouth just before his jaw dropped.

'What the fuck...?'

Jim Wallis and the others all joined in the jaw-dropping exercise.

The gates sheared off the gateposts, disintegrating into a twisted mass of pulverised scrap as sparks flew from the metal-on-metal contact.

Gary kept his foot on the accelerator: this was it.

In front of him lay the small pier, 150 feet in length.

'I hope this flimsy fuckin' jetty holds' thought Gary gritting his teeth.

The front wheels of the juggernaut hit the first wooden struts of the jetty, giving Gary a serious jolt and almost causing him to lose control.

'Sh...i...t!' he screamed at the Universe 'That fuckin' hurt!'

But the lorry was gaining momentum; the only thing the police could do was watch when they realised there was more to come.

The sea beckoned as the rev counter lurched dangerously into the red zone. The engine screeched in protest as it took exception to Gary's immaculately polished loafer pressing the pedal hard to the floor...and the flames were greedily attaching themselves to everything and anything in their way. By now, the trailer roof was beginning to catch the flames.

Suddenly, the lorry jack-knifed; one of the struts had snapped and the two front wheels were jammed in the hole where the strut had been.

'Come on!' bellowed Gary 'We're so close! Come on!'

The police heard the bang and saw that the juggernaut wasn't moving.

'Quick!' shouted Jim Wallis. 'Move it!' as the team raced towards the stranded lorry, brushing past Freddie in their rush to get to their quarry.

Gary saw them tentative step onto the wooden jetty which was beginning to make nasty creaking, groaning sounds as it swayed under the weight of the lorry.

But they didn't hesitate for long and Gary could see the first couple of yellow jackets move to within twenty feet of lorry.

'I didn't come this far to be stopped now, you bastards' Gary screamed and stomped on the accelerator with all his might, standing up out of the seat for extra leverage.

The jetty rocked precariously at the vibrations caused by the forty tonner's efforts to free itself.

The policemen froze.

'Get back! Get back! That's an order!' screamed Chief Superintendent Moore to the officers closest to the lorry: they didn't need a second telling.

The whining of rubber against wood was deafening as smoke began to billow from the tyres and mingle with the flames now gushing from the roof.

The stench of burning rubber was overpowering. After what seemed like an eternity, the front wheels found purchase and suddenly the wide-open sea was rushing towards Gary.

'Ye...ee...ssss!' Gary yelled as the juggernaut sailed into the night sky, a blazing mass, before doing a belly flop into the deep waters of the high tide.

The sea churned and bubbled as it sucked the juggernaut slowly to its floor, forty feet down.

Just as suddenly, it was all over and the only sound that could be heard was the crashing of waves.

'Well, that was different' said Siegfried to Gertrude as they turned back.

'I suppose.' sighed Gertrude nonchalantly. 'I'm looking forward to a nice hot drink.'

'I should cocoa-cocoa' replied Siegfried, laughing as they shuffled their way along the path. Nothing interfered with their routine.

Down at the dock, the police just stood around dumbfounded.

'I did what I could' said the voice with the Lichtenstein account.

'Sorry, Sir' said Jim Wallis '...did you say something?'

'No, Jim, just thinking out loud' replied his boss.

THE END

Printed in Poland
by Amazon Fulfillment
Poland Sp. z o.o., Wrocław